DUPLICITY

DUPLICITY

Ingrid Thoft

G. P. PUTNAM'S SONS
NEW YORK

G. P. Putnam's Sons
Publishers Since 1838
An imprint of Penguin Random House LLC
375 Hudson Street
New York, New York 10014

ISBN 9780399171192

Printed in the United States of America
1   3   5   7   9   10   8   6   4   2

BOOK DESIGN BY AMANDA DEWEY

In loving memory of Fina's fairy godmother,

HELEN BRANN

DUPLICITY

ONE

"He just boarded a flight to Boston."

Fina Ludlow swore under her breath and pulled the comforter up to her chin with her free hand. The ringing phone had awoken her. "Did he check any bags?" she asked.

"Four big ones," the PI in Miami said. "Looks like he's planning to stay awhile."

"Thanks for the update, Bobby."

Fina placed the phone on her bedside table and weighed her options. She could curl up in a ball or kick off the covers and get the job done.

Choosing option B, Fina walked into the bathroom and turned on the shower. Standing under the hot water, she could think of just one thing:

How the hell would she get the job done?

How the hell was she going to get rid of her miscreant brother?

"Did you break up with Ceci or did she break up with you?" Fina asked her father.

Carl Ludlow sat next to her in a matching wingback chair, his ankles crossed, exposing a black silk sock with tiny plum-colored dots.

"I'm not going to answer that."

"Come on, Dad." She grinned. "Humor me." The situation was like a car crash: Though it made her queasy, she couldn't look away from her father's romantic past.

"Leave it alone, Fina." He rose and walked over to the fireplace before circumnavigating the room. Fina watched as he gazed out the French doors to the expansive yard, perused the titles on the bookshelves, and studied an abstract painting that anchored the wall opposite the fireplace before returning to his seat.

"Why so antsy?" she asked. "Nervous about seeing your first love?"

Carl grimaced.

"You don't want to talk about it? How about Rand?" She consulted her watch. "I heard he left Miami this morning. How can you let him come back?"

"I don't want to discuss this, Fina. Your brother is coming back, and you just need to deal with it."

Before she could respond, Ceci Renard came into the room. "I'm sorry I've kept you waiting."

In her early sixties, Ceci was the picture of understated wealth, the kind of woman featured in pharmaceutical ads for the worried well. Her hair was chin length, shiny, and a variegated blond that can only be achieved at great expense in an upscale salon. She wore black trousers and a light blue silk blouse under a gray cashmere sweater.

Carl and Fina stood, and Ceci and Carl embraced stiffly. "Carl, I can't thank you enough for coming."

"Of course. Happy to be of assistance."

"And this must be Josefina?" Ceci extended her hand. "I haven't seen you since you were a little girl."

"All grown up, and please, call me Fina."

Ceci gestured for them to sit down as she took a few steps closer to the fire. She stretched her hands toward its warmth. "Hard to believe it's spring and there are flowers blooming somewhere."

"That's New England in March," Carl commented.

"Elaine and the rest of the family?" Ceci asked. "They're well?"

At the mention of her mother, Fina's back tightened. Not too long ago, she'd dropped a bombshell on Elaine, and their already strained relationship would put the Cold War to shame.

"Everyone's great," Carl said. Fina could detect a note of impatience in his voice. Her father wasn't much for small talk.

Ceci took a seat on the sofa facing them and crossed her ankles. "I wish I could say the same for the Renards. We have a situation, and I need help."

"Of course," Carl said, shifting forward in his seat. Her father was a problem solver at heart—he liked to get stuff done. "My assistant said that you sent a retainer, so anything you say to me is protected by privilege."

Ceci glanced at Fina, a question on her face.

"She's covered by attorney-client privilege," Carl assured her. "Just think of Fina as an extension of me."

Fina fought not to roll her eyes.

Ceci pushed a strand of hair behind one ear. "I'm very concerned about my daughter Chloe. She's recently become involved with a church, and I think they are having undue influence on her."

"In what way?" Carl asked.

"She's drifting away from our family, and her judgment has been compromised."

"Is she in danger?" Carl asked.

"No, but I'm worried—I'm actually starting to feel panicked, truth be told." Ceci looked away. "I'm not sure how to best describe the situation."

"Why don't you start at the beginning," Fina suggested. "How old is Chloe?"

"Thirty."

Fina and Carl exchanged a glance.

"I know she's not a child anymore, but this isn't like her, and there's a great deal at risk." Ceci's gaze drifted to the family photos on the mantel. She focused on one of a young woman in cap and gown, her hands clasping a diploma.

There was rustling in the hallway, and Ceci looked toward the door. "I've been so rude. I didn't even offer you coffee or tea." She pushed herself out of the deep couch.

"We're fine," Carl said. "Your housekeeper already made the offer."

"Oh, good." Ceci settled back into the cushions.

"So this church," Fina prompted.

"It's called Covenant Rising Church, and it's based in Framingham. It's a born-again evangelical organization."

"And you're not evangelical?" Fina asked.

"No. I was raised as a Methodist and my husband, Victor, was raised Catholic. He's from France. I didn't like Covenant Rising's theology from the outset," she continued, "but I tried to be supportive. I worried that if I were critical, Chloe would resent it and that would only strengthen her commitment to the church."

"What's your relationship with your daughter like?" Fina asked.

Ceci met her gaze. "We've always been close, but she's become distant as her involvement with the church has grown."

"Has something changed recently?" Carl asked. "What's happened that's made you so worried?"

Ceci adjusted the delicate gold watch on her wrist. "My husband and I created trusts for Chloe and her older sister, Veronique, which pay out money to them at various milestones. We've also deeded property to them. I recently learned that Chloe is in the process of turning over a significant holding to Covenant Rising."

"Ahh," Carl said, nodding. "But she's thirty . . ."

Ceci shook her head. "I know what you're going to say, Carl. That she's an adult, and she can do what she wants with her money, but if she were thinking straight, she wouldn't give away this property. Chloe went through a very difficult breakup about a year ago, and I think that is influencing some of her choices."

"In what way?" Fina asked.

"I think she's been having a quarter-life crisis. The man she thought would become her husband and the father of her children was not, in fact, 'the one.' She was at sea trying to figure out what was next, and a friend introduced her to the church. They've given Chloe free rein to develop an arts therapy outreach program, which has been a dream of hers."

"But just to be clear, you don't have control over the property, correct?" Carl asked.

"That's correct."

They were quiet for a moment, contemplating the limits of Ceci's influence.

"And there's no point in calling the cops," Carl commented, "because there's nothing illegal going on."

She nodded. "Lest you think I haven't tried to deal with this on my own, I was in touch with the church leadership, but no one will speak with me or at least tell me anything substantive."

"They're stonewalling you?" Fina asked.

"Yes." Ceci was literally wringing her hands as she recounted her experience. "Even though no crime has been committed, they are, in essence, stealing from Chloe."

Fina looked at her father. That was a bit of a stretch.

"I found some articles on the Internet," Ceci said, moving to a small desk in the corner of the room and picking up a file folder. She shuffled through the papers before handing a small sheaf to Carl. "I want to sue them for alienation. I know it's a difficult prospect, but there have been other cases."

He scanned the papers, and Ceci returned to the couch.

"This sort of case is very difficult to win, Ceci."

"I know, but I'm desperate. It's not just about the money and the bequest. I feel like I'm losing my daughter, Carl. We've always been so close, and now there's a wall between us that I can't seem to breach."

"She doesn't live with the group, does she?" Fina asked. Carl passed the printouts to her.

"No, and she has a job unrelated to Covenant Rising. Believe me, I would hire an extraction expert if that would help, but it's not like that." Ceci rubbed her temple as if massaging away a headache. "It seems like she's not making her own decisions anymore: The lead pastor is. He's only in it for the money and the power, but Chloe doesn't see it that way. I know you think I'm overreacting, but I'm telling you this is a dangerous situation."

"Nobody joins a cult," Fina murmured. Her father looked at her. "Nobody signs up thinking they're joining a cult," she clarified. "They only figure it out when it's too late."

"Exactly," Ceci said. "I don't want it to be too late."

"A lawsuit becomes very public, very quickly," Carl cautioned. "Are you and Victor prepared for that?"

Ceci swallowed. "Victor spends most of his time in Paris."

Carl considered that for a moment. "But the world is a small place these days, Cee. He won't be immune to publicity and gossip, even on another continent."

"I'm not happy about the possibility, but if that's what it takes to get Chloe away from this organization, that's what we need to do."

Carl massaged his knuckles. "Maybe there's a chink in the armor we can use," he said, "and a suit won't even be necessary."

"I can do some digging," Fina offered.

"And I'll research our legal options."

"Does Chloe know how you feel about the church and her bequest?" Fina asked.

"We've had numerous discussions about my objections to both the church and the property transfer, but she won't budge. There's no point in continuing to have the same dead-end conversation. I've let her know that I'm hiring some people to perform due diligence, and my hope is something will come up that will change her mind."

"And that's okay with her? Due diligence?"

"She didn't object. We've always impressed upon our children the need to take care of their assets," Ceci said. "Obviously, Chloe didn't learn that lesson. That's the thing about my daughter: She's extraordinarily trusting, which is both an asset and a liability."

"But she won't be surprised if I contact her?" Fina asked.

"No. I've told her to expect a call," Ceci said. "I would just ask that you not discuss the possibility of a lawsuit. Not yet, at least."

"I'm sure Fina can navigate the situation," Carl said.

"Of course," Fina said. She appreciated the vote of confidence, but worried that Carl was making a promise she would have to keep.

"Can you start right away? The bequest is already in motion."

"I'll get right on it," Fina said, while her father nodded.

Ceci exhaled loudly. "You don't know what a relief this is. I'm at my wit's end."

"You should have called me sooner," Carl said.

"I know. It didn't occur to me, until I saw one of your ads." Ceci dipped her head sheepishly. Fina wasn't sure if she was embarrassed on her own behalf or on behalf of Carl. He starred in his own TV ads that aired with alarming frequency, touting the benefits of Ludlow and Associates, the family's personal injury law firm. The TV ads were cheesy and seemingly ubiquitous, but obviously effective.

Carl smiled. "I know that my ads aren't your style, Cee, but they get the job done."

Ceci smiled briefly, and they sat for a moment in awkward silence.

Fina spoke, hoping to break the weird spell between the former flames. "Depending upon how cooperative Chloe is, I may need more information from you."

"Of course. Just let me know." Ceci stood, and Fina and Carl followed her to the door of the living room.

"That's a beautiful painting," Fina said, pointing to a large canvas. It depicted a man and woman sitting in a crowded restaurant, the man leaning toward the woman as if to whisper in her ear. She looked distracted, her hand reaching toward the candle on the table.

"That's one of Chloe's," Ceci said with a wide smile.

"She painted that?" Fina took a step forward to examine it more closely. "I'm no expert, but it's beautiful."

"She's very talented," Ceci said.

Fina offered Ceci her card, and they shook hands. Her father and Ceci reenacted the fumbling embrace that had kicked off the meeting.

Back on the street, Fina and Carl stood next to their cars. "Remind me," she said, "when did you guys stop dating?"

"A long time ago. Around college." He clicked his keys, and his car started remotely.

"Huh."

"What's that supposed to mean?"

"It just seems like it was more recent than that. Usually after forty years, people loosen up a little."

"We're from a different generation." Carl opened his door. "I want you to give this your full attention."

"Okay."

"Top priority."

"Yeah, I get it, Dad."

"Good. I expect results." He ducked into the car.

"You always do. Dad! Wait! We never finished our Rand conversation."

"It'll have to wait, Fina. I'm late for a meeting," Carl said.

"This is bullshit! What the hell is going on?"

"We will discuss it later," he said before slamming his door. He took off in the direction of Harvard Square.

"Dammit," she exclaimed, watching him drive away. Fina climbed into her car and turned the key in the ignition.

She didn't know exactly what Rand's return portended, but one thing was sure: It was nothing good.

Fina pulled into the parking lot of her niece's school and scrolled through her e-mail. Haley was due out of her after-school activities at any moment.

It had been nearly a year since her brother Rand's wife, Melanie, had been murdered, and since then things with their daughter, Haley, had been touch and go. Fina's brother Scotty and his wife, Patty, had become her de facto parents. Haley was adjusting to their household and to her role as an older sister to their three young sons, but Fina didn't underestimate how difficult such a change could be.

Haley emerged from the school five minutes later and scanned the parking lot. When she started back toward the front door, Fina called her cell phone.

"Don't go back inside," she told Haley. "I'm here to pick you up."

"Why are you picking me up? I thought it was going to be Aunt Patty."

"Since when do I need a reason to see my favorite niece?" Fina watched Haley start back into the lot.

"Your only niece. I don't see your car."

"Walk to your right."

Haley did a slow turn and started walking in her direction. "Why don't you ever drive something fancy?" Haley asked. It was odd watching her lips move as she approached, but only hearing the words through the phone.

"Because of my job. I don't want to be conspicuous. I need to blend in."

Haley ended the call and slipped her phone into her pocket before reaching for the car door.

"Hey. What's shakin' bacon?" Fina asked, leaning over to give her a kiss once she got inside.

Haley rolled her eyes and reached for her seat belt. "Nothing."

"What do you want to do?"

The girl shrugged and stared out the window. "Whatever."

"We could get something to eat. We could go shopping." Fina felt the shopping offer truly demonstrated how much she loved Haley. She didn't like shopping, but was willing to brave the hordes at the mall if Haley wanted to.

"Let's just go home."

"You don't want a frappe or some pizza or something?"

Haley looked at her. "I kind of have a headache. I think I'd rather go home and take a nap."

"Okay. Whatever you want."

Fina's attempts at small talk were unsuccessful, and the car ride was awkward.

"Thanks, Aunt Fina," Haley said when they pulled up in front of the house. "Sorry I'm a party pooper."

"It's okay, sweetie."

Haley reached for the door handle.

"Is everything okay?" Fina asked. "Within reason?" She didn't know if Haley was aware of her father's return and if that was the reason for her demeanor.

"It's fine."

"You know, if you ever need to talk, I'm here for you. So are Aunt Patty and Uncle Scotty."

"Yes, and I have a shrink, too," Haley replied impatiently. "I'm fine. I wish you guys would stop bugging me."

She pushed open the car door and slammed it behind her.

Fina watched her enter the house and wondered if she should follow her in and report the failed outing to her sister-in-law. That would probably annoy Haley even more, so she pulled away from the curb instead and made a mental note to mention it to Patty.

How did parents figure out when to push their children and when to back off? If you were too involved, you could alienate your kid, but if you weren't involved enough, they might drift off for lack of solid ballast.

Did Haley really want to be left alone or was that her way of asking them to come closer?

TWO

The next morning, Fina was starting to delve into Chloe Renard's background when her phone rang. The number on the display gave her pause.

"Good morning, Detective," she said.

"Morning. How are you?"

"Good. How are you?"

Cristian Menendez was a detective on the Major Crimes squad of the Boston Police Department. He and Fina had been friends and colleagues of sorts for more than ten years. They'd also slept together on a number of occasions. Cristian had recently expressed a desire to start dating like a normal couple, and since then, their friendship had moved into an awkward phase that called to mind junior high.

"I'm good. Are you free for dinner on Monday?" he asked.

"Yeah, I think so. Unless something comes up."

"Of course."

That would be one of the advantages of dating a cop—his line of work was equally unpredictable. Cristian wouldn't have a hissy fit if she had to cancel at the last minute. One of the disadvantages, however, was that he had sworn to uphold the law. Fina upheld it when it suited her, and she worried that was a difference they couldn't reconcile.

"So, is this an actual date?" Fina asked.

"As opposed to?"

"Just a friendly dinner, like we usually have."

Cristian sighed. "Let's just go to dinner, Fina. I promise I won't bring napkin samples for our wedding reception."

"Oh barf. That's not happening under any circumstances."

They made a plan to meet at Toscano, an Italian eatery on Charles Street, and Fina got back to her research.

Chloe Renard was the poster child for a savvy social media presence. Her Facebook page and Instagram account had privacy settings that barred strangers from viewing them, and the only pictures Fina found on the Web were those of her looking resplendent in striking gowns at charity balls. She worked as an art therapist and was mentioned in a couple of articles related to the field. There was also a brief write-up about some of her paintings that had been shown at a local gallery.

The Covenant Rising website was slick—lots of smiling people representing a rainbow of skin tones. Fina surfed the site, which featured their service projects, their various ministries, and a significant dose of their theology. She read about Pastor Greg Gatchell, his wife, Gabby, and their two children, Faith and Charity. All this virtuousness was making Fina hungry, so she grabbed a Hostess cupcake and a diet soda from the kitchen and returned to the couch.

Neither the couch nor the condo was technically hers. Carl had purchased the condo for his mother and, shortly after her death, Fina had moved in and claimed it as her own. Nanny wouldn't mind—she and Fina had been close—and Fina found it oddly comforting being surrounded by her grandmother's belongings. She hadn't made any real changes to the place, with the exception of a better TV and the removal of any family photos that included Rand. She had what she needed: privacy and a great view.

Fina nibbled a bit of white frosting from beneath her nail and clicked through the links providing background on the Gatchells. Originally from Ohio, they had attended a Christian university, where Greg had earned a master of arts in ministry. It wasn't clear how they ended up in Boston, but what started as weekly Bible study in the Gatchells' cramped living room had grown into the largest evangelical church in the state. That wasn't saying much, given Massachusetts's liberal leanings, but it suggested that the church had staying power. Fina found photos showing the Gatchells doing various good deeds, looking wholesome and energetic. They had a house in Wellesley that they'd purchased for $1.7 million ten months earlier, and their eldest daughter was a student at a Christian day school.

Another link brought up a selection of Pastor Greg's sermons. After watching for about twenty minutes, Fina felt quite sure that she was not a "godly" woman. She didn't believe in Satan, wasn't interested in deferring to a husband, and didn't spend time worrying about what came after death. Raised Protestant, Fina's religious upbringing consisted of attending church on Christmas Eve and Easter. She didn't begrudge anyone their right to worship whatever god they wanted, but she didn't think religion should demand the subjugation or mistreatment of one's fellow man or woman. And the faith thing—that always got her.

She fired off an e-mail to her financial investigator, Hal Boyd. He did more-detailed searches on her behalf that tended to stray from the bounds of legality, and Fina instructed him to take a look at the church and the Gatchells.

They were living large, and Fina had to wonder: Did the pastor and his wife have an independent source of income, or was their lovely home due to the generosity of their followers?

With a deep exhalation, he thrust the weights up, away from his chest. His arms shook, and the dumbbells swayed slightly. He grimaced and started counting to ten, but only made it to six before dropping the weights to the floor with a slam.

Greg Gatchell peeled his sweaty back off the bench and swiveled to the side, planting his feet on the floor. Sweat trickled down his face and over his lip as he chugged from a bottle of water. Resting his elbows on his knees, he struggled to take deep breaths.

He hoisted himself off the bench and plucked his iPod from the docking station near the door, turning down the Christian rock that had motivated him throughout the workout. Catching his reflection in the mirror, Greg took stock.

Not bad. Not great, but not bad. He was carrying a few extra pounds here and there, but there were hints of muscle definition. Every week, Greg stood before his growing congregation and preached to them. If he wanted to move them—to inspire them—he had to convince them that his path was righteous and fruitful. Looking good was one way to do that. It was also doctor's orders: His most recent checkup had revealed rising cholesterol, and his blood pressure was creeping up. He looked forward to the afterlife and meeting his Heavenly Father, but not just yet.

Greg was lifting his damp shirt from his stomach to assess his midriff when the door opened, and Gabby popped her head into the home gym.

"Stop checking yourself out," she said, leaning against the door frame, her face forming a wary smile.

"Just assessing my progress."

"You look good."

Gabby ran her hand over one of the weight machines before taking a seat on a bench. The home gym may have seemed like an extravagance to some, but the couple had decided it was a reasonable investment. Both of them needed to project a certain image, and as the church's influence grew, they felt less comfortable exercising at the neighborhood YMCA.

"You need something?" Greg asked.

"Elder Ben called. He's concerned about the Raffertys. Their son was suspended again."

Greg sighed. "That kid."

"You going to go over there?"

"I suppose I need to. Give Jane Rafferty a call later, after I've had a chance to stop by. See if she wants to pray with you."

"I'll do it after Prayer Group."

Greg looked puzzled. "I thought Sue was leading that?"

"She has a conflict. I'm just filling in for her." She stared at him. "Is that okay?" Her voice was tinged with sarcasm.

He blinked. "Of course it's okay. It's Christ's work."

Gabby left, pulling the door closed behind her. Greg looked in the mirror and flexed his biceps.

His flock needed a strong shepherd to lead them.

Fina gazed up at the brick-covered brownstone in Back Bay. It was four stories high with bay windows and a miniature balcony around the roofline, sized for small children rather than adults. She'd called ahead, and Chloe Renard had agreed to speak with her.

"It's Fina Ludlow," she said into the box in the lobby. Chloe buzzed her up, and she climbed the wide, carpeted stairs to the second floor. The young woman who greeted her at the door had her mother's expensive hair color and glowing skin.

"Please come in," Chloe said, stepping back into a sun-filled living room.

"Thanks for seeing me," Fina said, extending her hand and entering the room.

Chloe's home was a compact version of her mother's; it was welcoming and well-appointed, but smaller. A couch and two matching chairs were placed in front of a modest fireplace, and a dining room set was tucked into the area under the windows. Fina could see a modest but modern kitchen off to one side and a hallway leading in the other direction. It wasn't a large or fancy space, but she was willing to bet it cost well over a million dollars.

"Your home is lovely," Fina said, sitting on the couch. She reached behind her to unearth one of the many pillows nesting there. Fina liked pillows as much as the next person, but when did half a dozen throw pillows become standard? Wasn't room to sit the point of the couch in the first place?

"Thanks. Can I get you something to drink?" Chloe asked. "I was just brewing some tea."

"Tea would be lovely. This is such a great location," Fina commented while her hostess puttered in the kitchen. She didn't want to get to the meat of their conversation until Chloe had taken a seat. "Maybe I should move to Back Bay."

"Where do you live?" Chloe asked.

"Down on the waterfront, near the aquarium."

"Do you have a view?"

"A very nice one. I see the harbor and the goings-on at Logan."

Chloe came into the living room with a tray holding a full tea set. The pot was silver, its surface dotted with an exaggerated pattern of flowers and leaves. The cups matched, as did the cream and sugar containers. A plate of scones completed the tableau.

"That doesn't look like Pottery Barn to me," Fina said, gesturing toward the tea set.

Chloe smiled. "It's from France—rococo. It belonged to my great-aunt on my father's side."

She poured the beverage using graceful motions and offered the plate of scones to Fina.

"So my mother has sent you," Chloe said after taking her first sip.

"Yes. She and my father are old flames."

Chloe broke off a piece of scone. "She didn't tell me that."

"Really? Well, it was a long time ago," Fina said, downplaying the relationship.

She picked up her silver teacup and drank. The brew was strong and malty. Fina tended to like her maltiness in malted milk balls and ice cream malts, but you couldn't be a good PI if you weren't willing to embrace other people's preferences.

"It's Assam tea," Chloe explained, noticing the expression on Fina's face. "From India."

"I'll admit, I'm not much of a tea drinker."

"We grew up drinking it all the time; my mother is a real tea snob." Chloe smoothed her hair. "Speaking of my mother . . ."

"Yes. She's asked me to conduct some due diligence on your proposed real estate deal with the Covenant Rising Church."

Chloe sighed. "I think it's a waste of money, but if it will make her happy."

"She's just looking out for you."

"I suppose."

"I love your painting in your mom's house, the one of the couple in the restaurant. Is that also one of yours?" Fina gestured toward a canvas propped against the wall.

"Yes." Chloe studied the painting. "I'm trying to decide if I should hang it."

"Why wouldn't you?"

"I don't know. It seems boastful."

"People hang their diplomas," Fina noted, "and your painting is much more interesting." Smaller than the canvas at Ceci's, it depicted a young man sitting in a garden, a sketchbook open on his lap. "You're really talented. Do you paint full-time?"

"No. It's hard to make a living as an artist, not that I need the money," she said, acknowledging the obvious, "but my parents have always insisted we work."

"What do you do for work exactly?" Fina already knew the answer from the research she'd done, but it was always interesting to hear people describe their jobs.

"I'm an art therapist at some area hospitals and nursing homes."

Fina chewed a piece of scone. "Do you enjoy it?"

Chloe tilted her head in thought. She had a button nose and hazel eyes. Her ears were rather large, but her thick hair provided a blind of sorts. "I do. I'd rather paint full-time, but it's good for now."

"So tell me about Covenant Rising."

"I'm sure my mother has given you an earful."

"I'd like to hear your thoughts. When did you join the church?"

"A year ago. A friend of mine was a member, but she's since moved away. We met at one of the nursing homes. She was volunteering, and she invited me to attend a couple of events at Covenant Rising. They're incredibly welcoming and do so much for the community. It's a wonderful group of people."

"That all sounds great, but it sounds like a lot of churches. Why not attend the church you went to as a child?"

Chloe shook her head. "We didn't go to church. My mom was raised Methodist, and my dad's a lapsed Catholic."

"And Covenant Rising seemed like a good fit? Even with their evangelical beliefs?"

"I wasn't sure at first, but they gave me the chance to start an arts therapy outreach program, and it was an amazing opportunity. I couldn't pass it up."

"How does the program work?" Fina asked.

"We've partnered with a couple of shelters, and we provide art therapy to women and children and in one case, veterans. I got to design the whole program, and any time I've needed supplies, the church has come through. I feel like I'm making an impact in a way that wouldn't be possible without the resources and network of Covenant Rising."

Chloe picked up the teapot and refilled her cup. She stilled it over

Fina's cup, waiting for a nod. "If there's a need in the community," she continued, "the church works to fill it. They step in when people are in crisis. You can't imagine how many people lose their homes because they miss one mortgage or rent payment," Chloe said, pouring the liquid in an arc into Fina's cup. "One month overdue, and families are out on the street. CRC stops that sort of thing from happening."

"It sounds like the church is a lifesaver."

Chloe gazed at Fina, trying to determine if she was being sarcastic. "It is a lifesaver."

Fina wanted to ask her more about the tenets of the church, but decided to hold off. She suspected that Chloe would only get defensive and clam up.

"What's the bequest you have in mind?" Fina asked.

"It's a large piece of land in Vermont and the buildings on it. There's a main house, a barn, and a few outbuildings."

No wonder Ceci was worried. "That's a large gift to give after only a year, particularly given that their theology is so different from the way you were raised. I know that the art therapy program is extremely important to you, but enough so that you can ignore the church's doctrine?"

Chloe shook her head. "My mother is too focused on the theology. I don't agree with every aspect of the church, but at least they actually do things for other people. That's what's important to me. And since when do worshippers have to believe in everything their church espouses? How many Catholics don't use birth control?"

Fina smiled. "But Catholics are usually born into the faith."

"I suppose, but faith is complicated and highly personal."

"Your mom mentioned the pastor," Fina said, deciding to head down a different path.

Chloe frowned. "Pastor Greg. She's made it very clear she doesn't like him."

"Why do you think that is?" Fina asked.

"She thinks he's sexist and bossy and that people idolize him, in the true sense of the word."

"Do they?"

Chloe shook her head. "He's a leader, and sometimes leaders have to take unpopular stands. With the exception of the Quakers, every religion has spiritual leaders, other than God, I mean."

"Sure, but those leaders are supposed to be middlemen, right? Not objects of worship."

"It's not like that. Pastor Greg knows so much about scripture and applies it to everyday life. You should hear him speak. He's inspiring."

"I'd love to hear him speak."

Chloe's face lit up. "Join me at services. You'll see that my mother's fears are unfounded. Covenant Rising is about love and service and living the scripture." She placed her teacup on the tray and rested her long fingers in her lap. "My mom just can't accept that I've chosen a different path. She can't accept that I'm my own person."

"I know something about that," Fina said. "My brothers are lawyers, and I was supposed to be one, too."

"What happened?" Chloe asked.

"I flunked out of law school. I didn't really apply myself," she confessed.

"But you still work for your father, right? That must make him happy."

Fina smiled dubiously. "It's hard to know what makes him happy, but I can promise you he would be happier if I'd graduated and passed the bar. What does your father think about the church?"

"I'm sure he doesn't approve, but he's in Paris so it doesn't really matter what he thinks. The family company is based there, and he and my sister are, too."

Neither Ceci nor Chloe had been explicit about the state of Ceci's marriage, but the long-distance nature of it suggested that perhaps it wasn't a strong union.

Chloe sat back in her chair. "I'm glad my mom hired you. Come with me to church, and I'll introduce you to people. You can see for yourself how special it is."

Fina grinned. "Are you trying to convert me, Chloe?"

"Maybe," she said with a hint of a smile. "At the very least, you can help me reassure my mom that I know what I'm doing, and that what I'm doing is a good thing."

Fina didn't respond.

Chloe's willingness to fling open the doors of Covenant Rising could be seen as a good thing: Obviously, she didn't feel the organization had anything to hide. Or it could mean that the church's secrets were well hidden, and she'd been dazzled by the smoke and mirrors.

Fina wouldn't know which was true until she went to church.

Lord have mercy.

Christa Jackson glanced at her watch.

Damn.

Ten more minutes.

She was a terrible mother. Her daughter McKenna struggled with the words on the page, tripping and stumbling, trying to skip over them in the hope that her mom wouldn't notice.

"Usually," Christa finally said, tracing the word with her finger.

"Usually," her daughter repeated, the word sounding like a distant relative to Christa's version.

They made slow progress, and Christa could barely suppress her sigh of relief when the kitchen timer started ringing.

McKenna hopped off the couch and ran into the other room where her sisters were watching TV. The other girls had already finished their homework and were transfixed by a home decorating show on HGTV.

Christa got up from the table and studied them from the doorway. They were slumped on the couch—a foot here, an arm there, a splayed ponytail in between. She was always amazed by the fluidity of boundaries that separated them. One minute they'd be on top of one another like puppies, and the next, they'd be clawing at one another like kittens.

"Fifteen more minutes, girls, then it's time for brushing and reading."

Her middle child, Nicole, liked to read on her own, but McKenna and Tamara still liked to curl up next to her, one under each arm, for a story or a chapter before bed. It was Christa's favorite part of the day; she only wished that after turning off their lights she could go to her room and read a book or spend some quality time with Paul. Instead, she had to fold laundry, pick up wayward shoes, and pack lunches. Paul was no help since he was always at class or studying at the dining room table. She didn't blame him for not pitching in more. He was just as tired as she was, and the night-school MBA would benefit the whole family, but still. Christa couldn't help but feel that every moment of her day was spent supporting and furthering other people, while she stayed in the same place.

In the kitchen, she glanced through the notices she'd pulled from the girls' backpacks. Did she and her brother do this much stuff when they were younger? School chorus, soccer, gymnastics, Brownies. Sometimes she worried that her children would grow up with a host of specialized skills, but not know the first thing about moving through the world as functioning human beings. Who cares if you're a competitive chess player—at the age of six, no less!—if you're sleep deprived and a ball of stress? She tried to limit their activities, but was embarrassed to admit how much pressure she felt from the other parents. Christa already sensed she was at a disadvantage—with no college education and an eldest child who'd clearly been born before

Christa was out of her teens. She knew she had more sense than a lot of her peers, but she still felt like an outsider.

She poured herself a cup of coffee and made room for it on the dining room table amid the file folders and paperwork crowding the surface. She needed to prep for the meeting with McKenna's classroom teacher, Mrs. Bay. She was well aware that her daughter required extra attention and took the teacher away from the other children, but it wasn't McKenna's fault. She shouldn't be punished because her brain didn't work the same as the other kids, but Christa knew that if a classmate was taking teaching time away from Nicole or Tamara, she'd be annoyed and advocate on their behalf. You do the best you can for your kid, but Christa could have done without Mrs. Bay's impatience and the edge that seemed to creep into the phone messages she left with increasing frequency.

Peeking out from beneath the pile of papers was the corner of a glossy brochure. Christa hesitated for a moment, her hand hovering, but then gave in and tugged on the paper. There was a slight wrinkle across the bottom, which irked her for a moment before shame flooded in. It was just a piece of paper, after all. The pictures showed a bucolic setting, but it was the implied promises that made her reach for it again and again.

Everything would be better—easier—there. It was the portal to a better life, and she would do just about anything to step through it.

THREE

Fina paced her brother Scotty's office to the sound of the pinball machine's incessant dinging. The lights flashed, and Fina watched the digital scoreboard climb.

"I'm heading for a new high score," Scotty announced, jamming the buttons that activated the flippers.

"Doesn't that thing have a volume button?" Normally, the noise wouldn't bother her, but Fina was on edge in anticipation of her conversation with her brothers.

"It's not as much fun with the sound turned down," Scotty said. "It's Saturday. Things are a little looser around here."

"Hey." Their brother Matthew walked into the room and plopped down on the sofa. Single, handsome, and rich, there were a lot of women in Boston who'd like to keep company with Matthew. He had a dimple on his cheek that made him seem boyish when he smiled and dashing when he didn't. If he weren't her brother, Fina would have difficulty resisting his charms, but he was her brother, and therefore she had no trouble at all.

"Why'd I get the bill for your security sweep?" he asked Fina.

Matthew was taking the lead on a recent high-profile case she had investigated, a lawsuit against New England University for sports-related brain injuries. The publicity associated with the case—and the real or imagined challenge to college athletics—had brought out the crazies, and Fina had received some colorful hate mail.

"Because it's your case," she said, grabbing Scotty's hands. "But my name is in the paper, so everybody sends their complaints to me."

"Hey!" Scotty objected.

Fina glared at him. "We have things to discuss."

"Since when are you afraid of a little controversy?" Matthew asked.

Scotty abandoned the game and took a seat. Fina sat down next to Matthew, tucking her feet underneath her on the sofa. "I'm not, and I'm not afraid of the death threats, but it's inconvenient. I needed help weeding out the whackadoodles from the ones who seemed more action-oriented." She brushed a stray hair away from her face. "What's the date on the bill, though? The last review was a month ago, and I called off the extra measures."

Matthew shrugged. "I don't know. I'll have to ask Sue." The assistants at Ludlow and Associates were the keepers of all information.

"It *would* be bad if you got hurt," Scotty said.

"Gee, thanks," Fina said. "That sounded really heartfelt."

"It'd be great for the case, though," Matthew added.

Fina swatted at him.

Her brothers were all high-flying attorneys, although Rand had been exiled to Miami due to his bad behavior. Scotty and Matthew were the true heirs apparent, and although she'd flunked out of law school, Fina's job as the firm's primary investigator suited her to a T.

Scotty leaned forward and rested his elbows on his knees. "So what do we need to talk about?"

Fina glanced at her brothers. "Rand is back."

Scotty sunk back in the leather club chair. "Since when?"

"Since Thursday."

"How'd you find out?" Matthew asked.

"I have my sources, and Dad confirmed it."

"Dad knows?" Scotty asked.

"Not only does he know, he's completely on board."

Scotty shook his head. "We've got to do something."

"I did do something, remember? But apparently, it wasn't enough."

The Ludlows had agreed that turning Rand over to the police and forcing Haley into the public eye was a bad idea. But while Carl seemed content to keep him around, Fina couldn't stand it. Since the knowledge that Rand had sexually abused his daughter didn't prove compelling enough for Carl to banish his son from the family, Fina scrounged up more damning information. The threat of exposure had prompted Carl to send him to Florida. She didn't know why the dirt was no longer keeping him away.

"Can't you just do more of what you did?" Scotty asked.

"I don't think it's going to work that way," Fina said. "I'll have a conversation with Dad, but something has changed. I'll tell you what hasn't changed, our brother is still a perverted creep."

"This is bad, Fina," Scotty said. "Haley's not doing so great, and if Rand shows up on our doorstep that will undo the progress she's made since he left."

"I know." She looked at Matthew. "Why are you so quiet?"

He smoothed his hands down the front of his pants. "Well, it's early days, but I've started seeing someone."

"What does that have to do with Rand?" Scotty asked.

Matthew's gaze ping-ponged between his siblings. "She has a kid. A young daughter."

"And you don't want Rand around her," Fina said.

"I don't want him around either of them."

Fina was relieved that Matthew was taking the Rand situation seriously, but also a little annoyed that it took another child to awaken his protective spirit. Why hadn't everyone in the family been more outraged when Haley's abuse came to light?

"So what's the plan?" Scotty asked.

"Why are you looking at me?"

He shrugged.

"If we're going to put an end to this," Fina said, "we need to be a united front."

"What do you have in mind?" Matthew asked.

"No idea."

"We're not going to be able to do anything," Scotty noted, "if Dad isn't on our side."

"Can someone explain to me why Dad insists on defending him?" Fina asked.

"Rand is his kid," Scotty said. "Dad's just being protective like any parent would."

"That feeble argument aside, we need to figure out how to get rid of him."

Scotty swallowed. "When you say 'get rid of him,' do you mean . . ."

"Oh, I'd consider killing him if I thought I could get away with it," Fina said. "But I'd be the number one suspect, and contrary to what we see on TV, prison isn't actually a wonderful bonding experience where you spend all your time making cosmetics from food products."

"Unless he's convicted of something—if he could even be arrested—he's always going to be a problem," Matthew said.

"Which would suggest that using the criminal justice system is the best bet," Fina said.

Scotty raised his hand. "Hold on. We need to think very carefully about this."

"That's what we're doing," she said.

"The fallout would be huge."

"What are you suggesting, Scotty?" Fina asked. "Doing nothing?"

"Absolutely not, but this doesn't just affect you, Fina."

"That's my whole point. Rand leaves a path of destruction in his wake, and we need to do something about it."

"And when you go to the police? What happens to the firm?" he asked.

"Nothing happens to the firm, except that the sociopath pedophile is no longer an employee."

"What do you think?" Scotty asked Matthew.

Matthew ran his hand over his face. "We're assuming that it's our choice, that we'll always be in control of the information. What if it gets out some other way? What if people find out we've been protecting a pedophile?"

"Exactly!" Fina exclaimed. "We can't leave him on a long leash, not only because of what he might do, but because of how that might look."

"What do you mean 'if it gets out some other way'?" Scotty asked. "Who else knows?"

"I don't have anyone in mind," Matthew said, "but you know that secrets tend to get out. It's just how things go."

"That's why we need to control this," Fina said. "That's why going to the cops may not be the worst idea."

"And what about the kids?" Scotty's face darkened. "My kids are going to have to go to school and hear all kinds of gossip. You want to do that to them, Fina?"

"It's not going to be good for Haley if her father gets arrested," Matthew added.

"If you have a better idea, Scotty, I'm all ears," she said, rising from the couch.

"Where are you going?" Scotty asked. "We still don't know what we're doing."

"But the best legal minds are on it." She rolled her eyes. "I'm sure you two will figure out something."

"Keep in touch," Matthew said as Fina neared the door.

"I will. I'm going to church in the morning, but you should be able to reach me after that."

Her brothers exchanged a look.

"Why are you going to church?" Matthew asked.

"To pray on it," Fina replied, relishing the bewilderment on her brothers' faces. "Because someone's paying me to, dumbnuts. You think I'd go for free?"

Scotty exhaled. "Don't scare us like that."

"You deserve it," Fina said, and left.

"I think you should come to church with me," Fina said to Milloy on Sunday morning. They were sitting at her dining room table, the newspaper scattered across the top.

"I like church," he said before putting a forkful of omelet into his mouth.

Milloy Danielson was Fina's best friend, massage therapist, and occasional investigative operative. They had met during freshman orientation week at college and bonded over their shared dislike of trust exercises and lame parlor games. In the years since, they'd always had each other's back, and occasionally, when the mood struck, more than that.

Although he'd slept over the night before, it had been a chaste evening dominated by take-out and the Bruins game.

"It's an evangelical born-again church. I don't know how they feel about your kind," Fina said, referring to his mixed Chinese American heritage.

Milloy shook his head. "We're not going to find out today. I've got appointments."

"The captains of industry need a good rubdown?" she asked, grinning.

"You make it sound so dirty," Milloy said.

Fina smiled. "Thanks for breakfast."

She didn't cook and was the beneficiary of Milloy's culinary know-how. In addition to her junk food necessities, her regular grocery delivery included ingredients that Milloy requested; she had no need for chicken breasts, fresh produce, or whole grains.

"You're welcome. I'm assuming the churchgoing is for a case?"

"Yes. An old flame of Carl's has hired me to vet the church. Her daughter is a member and wants to give them all her money."

"How old's the daughter?"

"Thirty. She can do whatever she wants, but her mom thinks the place is more cult than house of worship. I'm going to check it out." Fina popped a bite of buttered toast into her mouth.

"Hard to believe a born-again church would have enough members to survive in Boston."

"I think that's why they survive: a pocket of conservatism in a bastion of liberalism. I've watched a couple of sermons, and I think the pastor likes being the underdog."

"Us against them?" Milloy asked.

"Something like that." Fina pulled the Sunday Style section from the stack. "Do you still consider yourself a Catholic?"

"Sure." He proceeded to crack various joints, which produced horrible sounds but a lovely flexing of his muscles.

"Even though you aren't practicing?" she asked.

"I was raised in the Church. I don't agree with all the teachings, but I still identify with it."

Fina chewed thoughtfully. "I don't get that. If you don't agree with them, why do you still feel a connection?"

Milloy rested his forearms on the table and grinned. "Really? You don't get the concept of disagreeing with something, but strongly identifying with it nonetheless? Seriously, Ludlow?"

Fina sat back in her chair and smiled. "Oh, right. Those people."

"Yes. Those people. You can't ever get away from where and what you came from. Even if it's not part of your DNA, it seeps into you."

"I get that, but that's not true for my client's daughter. She wasn't raised in this tradition. In fact, the church's ideology is contrary to how she was raised."

Milloy shrugged. "Maybe that's the point."

Fina considered that. "Maybe, but I'm not sure what she gets out of it."

"I wish I could go with you," Milloy said, stacking their dishes and bringing them into the kitchen with Fina in his wake. "I imagine the eye rolling on your part is going to be epic."

"No, no. I'm going to behave myself. I'm a guest, and I don't want to offend anyone."

"Maybe you'll learn something."

"I already have. I learned from my research on Friday that I'm not a godly woman."

"Fina," Milloy said, smacking her butt as she sauntered out of the kitchen. "I could have told you that."

Covenant Rising was located a couple of miles off Route 9 in Framingham. It occupied a parcel of land bordered by a nondescript low-rise office complex and undeveloped woods. Tucked into the trees, the structure was brick and fronted by three sets of glass double doors. Fina couldn't decide if it looked more like a state park welcome center or a medical office. The large parking lot was full, and young men in orange traffic vests were directing cars onto a grassy area nearby.

Fina stepped out of the car and smoothed down her skirt. Since the visit was work related, she'd tamped down her desire to rebel and had chosen a fairly conservative getup. Her skirt was topped with a V-neck sweater and scarf, worn with black tights and low heels. She wore her long brown hair loose, and her minimal makeup consisted of tinted moisturizer, mascara, and lip gloss. She wanted to look harmless and virtuous.

Chloe met her at the front door.

"I'm so glad you're here," she said, leading Fina through the lobby. The space was high ceilinged and open. There were chairs and couches against the walls, with coffee and tea service situated on a console table. "I know that my mom is paying you, but it doesn't matter what brings you through the door."

Fina smiled. That sounded like rehab-speak.

"Would you like coffee or tea?" Chloe asked.

"I'm good, thanks. Are you going to get some?"

Chloe leaned toward her and lowered her voice. "I can't drink tea made from a tea bag and definitely not from a paper cup."

"Ah. Now who's the tea snob?"

Chloe laughed and moved in the direction of the parish hall.

A young man in jeans and a button-down shirt handed them printed programs. The room was large with vaulted ceilings and stained glass windows behind the altar, which was on a raised area. There were three sections of pews made from a warm-colored wood, separated by two aisles. Off to the side, a seven-person rock band played enthusiastically. Potted plants framed the pulpit, and on the walls, ten painted canvases were devoted to the Ten Commandments. Each featured a commandment written in large script with an abstract depiction of the order. "Thou shall not kill" showcased dark swirls and fearful eyes. It was weird and creepy.

They took a seat in a pew halfway down the left-hand aisle. A few congregants greeted Chloe and she, in turn, introduced them to Fina. Everyone was friendly and jovial. Most of the people looked to be in their thirties and forties, many with young children, although there was a handful of twentysomethings and retirees. Everyone was dressed neatly but casually, and Fina felt overdressed.

There was a frisson of excitement in the air when a woman and two children came down one of the aisles and sat in the first pew.

"That's Pastor Greg's wife and kids," Chloe told her.

Gabby Gatchell looked to be in her mid-thirties. A petite woman with dark blond hair spilling down her back in big, loose curls, her face was just shy of being too made-up. There was no hint of her pregnancies in her flat stomach and toned legs, both of which were on display in a fitted dress with modest long sleeves and a scooped neck. The whole package reminded Fina of a porn version of a teacher: appropriate, pretty, and modest, with hints of a smoking body that would be revealed during detention.

The band kicked it into high gear and started playing a raucous number. The worshippers stood and clapped with the beat as the lead singer vocalized about salvation and eternity.

After a couple of minutes, a man in jeans, T-shirt, and an expensive-looking leather jacket came down the aisle and ascended to the stage. The jacket was deep brown and shone under the lights. Coupled with his sleek headphone mike, the outfit looked more "sober rock star" than religious leader.

"That's Pastor Greg," Chloe told her once the music had ended, and the crowd had returned to their seats.

Pastor Greg was cute enough, with a round face and wavy brown hair. He was of average height and had a sturdy build. Fina thought she could see a battle of the bulge in his future.

He beamed at the congregation. "Welcome and bless you. Seeing your faces, ready to worship and exalt Jesus Christ, makes me a very happy man." His eyes panned the room. "Today is a most sacred and beautiful day!"

*Amen*s rang out throughout the parish.

"I want to talk to you today about temptation," Pastor Greg said, his smile evaporating. "I know every single one of you struggles with it. We all wrestle with sin on a daily basis. That's the way Satan wants it." He walked from one side of the stage to the other. "He wants to wear you down, to tire you out. He wants you to cut corners and take shortcuts 'cause that's what makes him happy. That's what fuels him: your sin. It gives him strength, which spreads and infects every part of our lives."

Pastor Greg stopped moving and faced the audience for a moment before looking down and smiling, as if he were in on a big joke that the worshippers didn't yet know. He looked up at them. "Now, I see some of you out there, and I know what you're thinking. You're thinking, 'But Pastor Greg, I don't really sin. I'm a good guy. I don't cheat on my wife or drink too much.' Or you gals think, 'I follow my husband and set a good example for my children. I'm righteous and godly and always choose the way of the Lord. I honor Jesus's sacrifice by living a holy and pure life.'" The audience chuckled nervously.

"And that may be true of most of you—although we know there are sinners amongst us who are not following the word of God, who are not obeying their Heavenly Father—but I'm not talking about you today. I'm talking about the little sins, the trespasses, and you know what?" He leaned forward, his hands clasped together as if in prayer. "Those sins make Satan just as happy as the big sins do. You see, Satan wants to lull you into thinking that some sins are small and don't matter, that God isn't watching and taking notes, but God is watching, and he didn't sacrifice his only son so you could take the easy way out. He loves you. He loves you no matter what, and you need to honor him by fighting temptation and saying no to sin."

His voice grew louder, and he began pacing. "Did you gossip about your neighbor? That's a sin. Did you ding someone's car at the mall and not leave a note? That's a sin. Did you lie to your wife about how many beers you had at the game with the guys? Or to your husband about how much that new purse cost? Did you tell Mom and Dad you brushed your teeth when you didn't? Those are sins. When you sin and hide it, you're not protecting God, you're promoting Satan, and you have to ask yourself, whose team am I on? Who am I playing for every moment of my earthly life: God or Satan?"

Is there a third option? Fina wondered, looking around at the rapt faces. Chloe was nodding along to Pastor Greg's words, and the room was sprinkled with *amens* and other murmurs of agreement. Fina strained to keep her face a mask so as to impede her gag reflex.

Fina had always had difficulty with the concept of sin. Who defined it and how? She knew the evangelicals would claim that Jesus did in the Bible, but that claim seemed dubious. Her personal philosophy was to try not to hurt people, unless they deserved it, which brought her back to that definition problem and a whole lot of gray area.

"We all know that goodness in our hearts is the best way to follow the Lord's path, but goodness alone isn't enough. We live in a materialistic world, a world where good intentions are not enough."

Here it comes, Fina thought.

"You need to give to the mission. You need to give to the fight. You need to give everything you can, and then, you need to give more. Does it hurt? Yes. Does it require sacrifice? Yes. But you will never regret serving and supporting the work of the Lord. You will only regret it if you don't."

Pastor Greg continued on for another ten minutes, and then the band played as the elders came up the aisles, passing brass bowls down the pews. When they walked the bowls back to the pulpit, they were overflowing with cash. An elder was welcomed to the stage, and he spoke for a few minutes about upcoming prayer groups and service events. There was another song, a few more prayers, and then Pastor Greg left the stage to fetch Gabby and the girls. The foursome held hands as they came up the aisle, beaming.

Outside the sanctuary, a crowd congregated around a table laden with refreshments, and a long line formed on the other side of the lobby.

"I want to introduce you to Pastor Greg and Gabby," Chloe said, stepping to the end of the line.

"Great," Fina said, taking a spot next to her. They chatted about the sermon as they waited, reaching the front of the line ten minutes later.

Chloe and Pastor Greg shook hands and exchanged blessings.

"Pastor Greg, I want to introduce you to my friend Fina Ludlow," she told him.

Fina extended her hand. "It's nice to meet you, Pastor. Thank you for welcoming me this morning."

"I am so glad you're here," he said, looking into her eyes and grasping her hand. "God loves you."

Fina offered a wide smile. "I know, and I couldn't be more pleased. He loves you, too!"

"Amen to that," Greg replied.

"Fina is helping with the land bequest," Chloe said.

"Uh-huh," Fina agreed, glancing at Chloe. "I'd love to talk with you about it, Pastor."

"Of course. Just call the office and set something up," Greg said, squeezing her hand once more before releasing it.

Next, Gabby and Chloe embraced. One of the children—Fina didn't know if it was Mercy, Faith, Charity, or Chastity—held on to Gabby's waist, twisting her mother's dress in her grip.

Introductions were made, and Gabby tried to pry her young daughter off of her. "We're so glad you're here," Gabby said to Fina, shaking her hand.

"Thank you. That's so kind." *And so hard to believe*, Fina thought. They didn't even know her, but if they did, they'd probably be less enthusiastic.

The long line behind them discouraged small talk, so Chloe and Fina moved toward the front door.

"Chloe," Fina said. "I'm not sure I'd characterize my involvement as 'helping with the land bequest.'"

"I know." Chloe smiled ruefully and shrugged. "I know my mom wants to stop it, but I want a chance to change your mind about the church."

"I should warn you, my mind isn't easily changed."

"I'm not worried," Chloe said, brushing aside the topic. "Can you stay for a little while? I'd like to introduce you to some more people."

"Of course."

After an hour spent meeting lots of earnest congregants and eating delicious baked goods, Fina and Chloe took their leave.

"Thanks for letting me join you today," Fina said as they stood next to Chloe's car.

"It was my pleasure. I hope it was useful."

"It was. Can you suggest some people I can speak with to get more information, particularly financial information?"

Chloe considered the question for a moment. "Pastor Greg, obviously, and probably someone from the leadership committee: Lucas Chellew or Nadine Quaynor might be helpful."

"If you could send me their contact info, that would be great."

"Of course."

Fina started to extend her hand, but Chloe reached over and hugged her instead. Her hair smelled like strawberries.

"I'll talk to you soon," Chloe said, pulling open her car door.

Fina walked in the direction of the grassy parking area.

"Fina!"

She turned back toward Chloe.

"You may not agree with our beliefs, but I hope that doesn't taint your impression of the church. I know my mom wants to protect me, but I'm an adult. I can make my own decisions."

Fina shook her head. "I won't let a difference of opinion cloud my judgment. I promise."

Chloe smiled. "Thanks."

Fina got into the car and pulled out of her makeshift parking space.

She didn't agree with what she'd heard that morning, but neither was she a fan of parents imposing their will on their adult children.

Fina couldn't understand the appeal of the church, but maybe she never would.

She wasn't exactly a "joiner."

During the drive home, Fina couldn't help but ruminate about her family situation. Like a barnacle on a rock, her mind kept attaching itself to the fact of Rand's return.

As she inched through the E-Z Pass lane on the Pike, Fina forced herself to take a step back. She needed to assess the situation as she would for a client. The ability to see gray areas and still make tough choices while practicing empathy made Fina good at her job, and perhaps that was what was missing in this scenario. It wasn't unusual for Fina to feel a connection with a client or someone with whom her path crossed in the course of an investigation, but she never let that cloud her judgment or inform her investigative choices. Fina was so invested, so desperate to fix the Rand situation, that she had let her emotional involvement cloud her judgment.

She needed to stop thinking like an aunt and start thinking like a PI. If a client showed up at her door and asked her to do a background check on a prospective employee or boyfriend, she'd get to work. Whatever information she uncovered would be shared with her client with the understanding that information could be wielded like a weapon. Weapons served as deterrents, tools of punishment, and means of revenge, their form dependent upon who was wielding them. Fina needed to build an arsenal.

She knew that Rand had gotten into trouble long before he started abusing Haley, but she didn't know all the details of his past sins. Those sins might just provide the leverage that Fina needed.

Starting now, Fina was her own client.

FOUR

Fina kicked off the next day by working the phones. Her efforts netted unsatisfying results, including voice mail messages for Lucas Chellew and Nadine Quaynor. Chloe had given her the basics on her fellow members, but she needed more info. She inputted their names into one of the pay search services. Neither had criminal records, and both had a couple of non-moving violations. Lucas owned a house in Dedham with his wife, Heather. Nadine owned a home in Dorchester, but despite being married to an Evan Quaynor, only her name was on the deed. They'd both attended college, and Nadine was employed by Williams & Lewiston, one of the largest accounting firms in the state. Lucas had worked for Macy's for the past decade. If they had any skeletons, they were buried deep.

Next, she put in a call to Pastor Greg's office. The pastor was a very busy man, or perhaps he was just too busy for Fina. Despite his enthusiastic greeting after the service, she doubted he wanted to speak with her about Chloe's land bequest. When it became clear Fina wouldn't be deterred, his secretary agreed to fit her in a bit later in the day between a food pantry project and an elders' meeting. It was like getting an audience with the pope.

Fina was hopeful that her meeting with Hal Boyd, her financial wizard, would be more fruitful. Hal was an expert at ferreting out financial secrets and wasn't overly concerned with pesky notions like whether or not something was legal.

"What did you find out about Covenant Rising Church?" she asked him. They were meeting in Central Square at a diner a couple of streets off Mass Ave. It was midmorning, and Hal was sipping coffee while Fina nursed a mug of hot chocolate. "I hope it's something good, and when I say good, I mean bad."

Hal sighed and sagged in the booth. The motion made his beach ball–like stomach inflate slightly. "You're going to be disappointed. It's not a slam dunk."

"Oh well, lay it on me."

"The church is a 501(c)(3), as most churches are."

"Meaning they're tax-exempt," Fina said.

"Basically. They're exempt from federal taxes and usually state taxes."

"What about property taxes?" Fina asked.

"It depends on the usage of the property." He sipped his coffee. "They can't be taxed for their physical church building, but if they have other holdings that aren't used for church purposes, those are supposed to be taxed."

She raised an eyebrow. "Supposed to? They get to deduct their housing, right?"

"Generally they can take a housing deduction on income tax, but not necessarily on their self-employment taxes. The tax code related to the clergy is very complicated."

"All tax code is complicated. A housing deduction doesn't seem unreasonable, given most clergy are underpaid and overworked."

"Sure, but you have the rare instances where people abuse it. Think of Jim and Tammy Faye Bakker in the mid-eighties. Covenant Rising has the Gatchells' primary residence on the books—"

"The one in Wellesley," Fina interrupted.

Hal nodded. "But there's also a house on Cape Cod and a condo in New Hampshire."

Fina chuckled. "Is it near a ski resort by any chance?"

"Ten minutes from Loon Mountain."

"That's convenient." She sipped her cocoa. "They must be spreading the good word on the slopes."

"They also have a van and a few luxury cars listed as part of the church fleet, and I found evidence of trips to Florida and the Bahamas." A waitress stopped at the table to refill Hal's coffee.

"Could the trips be legitimate?"

"Maybe, but I didn't find trips to places like Detroit or Omaha, no offense to those places."

"Lots of people fudge stuff when it comes to work travel," Fina said, "not that I'm condoning it."

"Sure, but it's a red flag when so many of an organization's expenses are geared toward leisure and luxury." Hal rotated his coffee cup on the table. "When you donate money to charity, most of it should go to the cause, not to overhead. If you donate to the church, why is your money paying the mortgage on a condo near the slopes or for a trip to the beach?"

"Why, indeed?" Fina used her spoon to scrape tiny pillows of whipped cream off the surface of her hot chocolate.

"I'm sure it's pitched as being necessary to the pastor's spiritual well-being," Hal said, "if the congregants even know about it."

"They might not?"

Hal shrugged. "Why would they, unless they have access to the church's financial reports or my resources? I can't imagine the pastor publicizes his getaways."

"Probably not. So, what if I told you I wanted to sign over a big piece of land and some buildings to Covenant Rising?" Fina asked. "What would be your response?"

"Don't do it, or at least not until I get a lot more information about their financial standing."

"And there's the rub. I'm guessing the church won't be eager to share any information."

"And I would wonder why that is," Hal said. "Frankly, there are so many needy places that are forthcoming in their bookkeeping. Why not give to one of them?"

"Because you really believe in the mission? Because making the donation wins the donor favor in the community?" Fina mused.

"Okay, but then you need to think about why you're really making the donation. To help others or yourself?"

"Most giving isn't completely altruistic, Hal."

"Of course not, but you should ask yourself some tough questions before parting with your assets."

"Good point." Fina reached into her bag and pulled out some cash for the bill. "Thanks. Let me know if anything else turns up."

"Will do, Fina." His gaze lingered on her face for a moment. "It's nice to see you in one piece." Hal and Fina had worked together for a number of years, and he had witnessed the numerous physical injuries she endured in the course of her work.

"It's nice to be in one piece, but don't expect it to last." She smiled and scooched out of the booth.

Hal shook his head.

Poor Hal. He was one of the few people genuinely concerned with her safety—truly a thankless job.

A few hours later, Fina arrived at Covenant Rising Church full of questions, but with little hope of getting answers. The church's food pantry was located at the opposite side of the building from the administrative offices, in a room lined with wire storage shelves packed with nonperishable food items like pasta, canned soup, and chili. There was a small refrigerator/freezer section with glass doors, like one you might find in a grocery store. Milk, eggs, yogurt, and cheese were on display, and the freezer held chicken nuggets, fish sticks, pancakes, and cans of orange juice concentrate. Three women stood at a table packing boxes and chatting. The location of the meeting seemed a bit heavy-handed to Fina: Look at us, we feed the hungry!

She stood off to the side and checked her e-mail, waiting for the pastor.

Fina was beginning to feel the familiar tug of impatience when he strode into the room. He nodded at her, but then went over to the women at the table and greeted them warmly. Fina watched as they exchanged a few words, and he managed to touch each of them before heading in her direction. The physical contact wasn't inappropriate—a hand on a shoulder or arm—but it struck Fina as contrived and practiced. The women ate it up.

"Fina! Good to see you," he said. He extended one hand and patted her shoulder with the other, not realizing she was immune to his charms.

"You, too, Pastor Greg."

"Let's take a seat." He gestured toward a corner of the room that was full of broken-down boxes and recycling bins. They claimed a couple of folding chairs, and Greg leaned forward, his elbows resting on his knees. "What can I do for you?"

Fina fought the urge to lean back. This wasn't Europe; she didn't like people in her personal space.

"I'd love to hear about the church's plans for Chloe Renard's Vermont property," she said.

"Right, right. Are you a lawyer?"

"I work for a lawyer."

He sat back and eyed her. "Did Chloe hire you?"

"Her family did." Fina smiled. "I'm sure you can understand her family's desire to make sure that Chloe isn't taking this big step without having all the necessary information."

"Of course, I don't want Chloe to do anything she isn't comfortable with, but I'm not sure what could possibly be wrong with her donating to the church. Look at the work we do." He raised his hands toward the ladies who were still packing away, chatting and laughing like happy minions.

"It's wonderful, but you hear the most awful stories these days."

Greg frowned and straightened up in his seat. "Not about CRC, you don't."

"Of course not, but surely, you don't frown upon being cautious. 'Therefore be careful how you walk, not as unwise men but as wise,' Ephesians 5:15," Fina said helpfully.

He gave her a pitying look. "'It is better to trust in the Lord than to put confidence in man,' Psalm 118:8."

"We could do this all day, Pastor Greg," Fina said, hoping he wouldn't want to, because actually she couldn't. The only other quote in her ecclesiastical bag of tricks was "Love is patient, love is kind," and that was really off topic.

"Fina, I want nothing more than to reassure the Renards that Chloe's bequest is the right thing to do. I'd be happy to meet with them if that would help."

"And tell them what? The same thing you're telling me?"

"Impress upon them what a wonderful gift Chloe is providing and what a tremendous example she's setting for the rest of the congregation."

Fina clasped her hands in her lap and sighed. "Yeah, it's the lack of specifics that I find troubling, and I don't think a blanket reassurance is going to make her family feel any better."

Pastor Greg held open his hands. "I don't know what more I can do."

"I do. You can open the church's books to the Renards' financial adviser."

He frowned. "You can't really expect me to share that information with someone we don't know."

"And yet, you're expecting the Renards to do the same; trust people with whom they have no relationship."

"Chloe has a relationship with us," he protested.

"And she has a relationship with her family's financial adviser. In fact, I think she's known him longer than she's known you and her fellow congregants."

Greg took a deep breath and placed his hands on his knees. "I think we should both take some time and pray on this."

Fina was quiet for a moment—hoping she looked more contemplative than annoyed—and nodded. "Of course."

"Will we see you at services on Sunday?" he asked, as they walked toward the front door.

She turned and offered her hand. "I suppose that depends on what I hear from the Lord, but I'll be sure to keep you in the loop."

"Well, I sure hope we do."

On the road, Fina contemplated the paradox of Pastor Greg that seemed to encompass religion in general: Why was it that the man had all the answers and no answers at the same time?

"I have an idea," Fina said, dropping into a plush wing chair next to Scotty. He was in a hotel bar not far from the office.

"Possibly the scariest sentence I'll hear all year," he said, grinning.

Fina shook her head. "So dramatic. Why are you hiding out here?" She looked around at the other patrons, most of whom seemed to have kicked off happy hour with mixed drinks, their jackets abandoned against their chairs, the outside portion of their days complete.

"I'm between a meeting and a client dinner. Didn't make sense to head back to the office. So what's your big idea?"

Fina squeezed the arms of her chair. "I'm the client. I'm going to hire myself."

He looked at her. "I don't know what that means."

"It means that I'm going to treat the Rand situation as if I were a client, and I'm going to investigate him."

"But we already know what he's done."

"Sexually abusing his daughter?" Fina clarified, and Scotty winced. Fina was repulsed by the reality of Rand's crimes, but it irritated her that her brothers wouldn't call it what it was. Until people started saying it out loud, incest would remain a shameful secret.

"We know *some* of what he's done," she continued, catching a waitress's eye and ordering a diet soda. "Where there's smoke, there's fire."

"To what end?"

"I'm going to amass a case against him, and then I'm going to bring it to Dad, and he'll have to act."

"He doesn't have to do anything, Fina." He stirred the lemon wedge in his club soda with a slim straw.

"You didn't let me finish. If he doesn't act, I'll find someone who will."

"But couldn't you do that now?" Scotty asked.

"In theory, but I would never do that to Haley. She's not the first person he's hurt, Scotty, right? If I can make a compelling case about his irredeemable qualities, someone is going to want to punish him. Hopefully, it will be Dad."

Scotty sipped his drink. "That sounds like a dangerous game to me."

"Okay," she said, feeling irritation rise in her chest. "What's your solution?"

"You know I don't have one."

"And I haven't heard one from Matthew. As soon as you have a better idea, I'm all ears, but in the meantime, I'm kicking off an investigation."

"Don't you have a real case at the moment?"

"Yes, but I can multitask."

He shook his head. "As long as Dad doesn't find out."

"About my multitasking or Rand?"

"Either."

"Nobody can know about the Rand stuff. We can tell Matthew, but it stops there. I don't even want you to tell Patty."

"I don't want to tell her," he said, raising his eyebrows.

"Good, but I do need your help."

"Okay."

"Remember that incident when Rand was in college?"

Her brother snorted. "Which one?"

"The one where a young woman accused him of date rape."

Scotty glanced around the room. "How do you know about that?"

"Seriously? Eavesdropping on Mom and Dad was a full-time job growing up."

"It was an alleged rape."

"Yeah, yeah. Stop being a lawyer. I assume you know the identity of the 'alleged' victim?"

Scotty nodded.

"I need the name."

His face pinched in discomfort.

"Scotty," Fina said, leaning across the table and covering his hand with her own. "Either you're in or you're out. You gotta make up your mind."

"I'm in. I'm in. I just wish being in didn't require me to get involved."

"That's the definition of being out, knucklehead." She sat back. "How can you be so ruthless on behalf of your clients and so wishy-washy the rest of the time?"

"It's different when it's family, and I'm acting as a brother, not a lawyer."

"Exactly! That's what dawned on me; you can't act like a brother in this instance. You have to act like a lawyer. If a client wanted to go after Rand and he wasn't your brother, you wouldn't think twice about giving me the information."

Scotty considered that for a moment. "Her name was Lindsay Kaufman. I don't know what her name is now, whether she changed it or not, but she shouldn't be that hard to find. She's from Duxbury, and her dad worked in finance."

"Thank you." Fina leaned over and kissed him on the cheek. "Talk to you later."

Investigators, whether private or members of law enforcement, were often jaded and cynical, believing the worst of everyone. But it was also true that you would never find a group of people more excited to unearth or stumble upon a shred of information or the mere hint of a clue. Fina felt the faint thrum of hope when she left with that name.

FIVE

Given Carl's edict to deal with the Chloe Renard situation tout de suite, Fina decided to make a detour to the office and update him. Dealing with her father always reminded her of dealing with her niece and nephews when they were toddlers: Try to anticipate any possible obstacles and frustrations before they become big issues and have a bottle within reach.

Fina went to her father's office and, finding it empty, took a seat on the couch. She was scrolling through her e-mails when her father's assistant, Shari, walked in.

The attractive blonde glared at her.

"I'm not going to steal anything," Fina said. The women shared a mutual lack of trust and respect.

"Your father doesn't like it when people wait in his office."

"I'm not 'people.' Trust me. He'll let me know if my behavior displeases him."

Fina heard him outside the office a few minutes later. Carl came in, closed the door behind him, and dropped into his chair.

"You have an update?"

"Of sorts." She stood in front of his desk. "I'm not making much progress speaking directly to the holy rollers."

"Did you really think you would?"

"I thought they might make some attempt at transparency, but it's not going to happen. I have my financial guy on the case, but even if he finds something, I'm not sure it will do the trick."

"Why not?"

"Chloe is really enamored of the church and the pastor in particular. Even if we present her with evidence of wrongdoing, I'm not convinced it will change her mind."

Carl glanced down at some folders on his desk. "You just need to find some damning evidence."

Fina opened her eyes wide. "So that's how it works!"

"Do you think Ceci is overreacting?" he asked, ignoring her sass.

"No. I'm not sure I'd characterize them as a cult, but I think her concerns are well founded. I think Pastor Greg is slippery, and there may be some dirt to dig up."

Carl held up a hand. "I don't want to hear specifics."

"I didn't say I would do anything illegal."

He raised an eyebrow. "Sit down for a minute."

Fina's muscles tightened. She didn't want to sit, but she suspected she needed to save her objections for whatever was next.

"There's going to be a family dinner," Carl said once she was seated. "And I expect you to be there."

Fina looked at him and waited. She could guess what was coming, but she wanted him to say it.

"Rand will be there," he said, and held her gaze.

She sighed. "Then I won't be."

"That's your choice, but the rest of the family will be there."

"You've spoken to Scotty and Matthew about this?"

"I sent them an e-mail."

"You shouldn't assume you have their support, Dad."

"Why not?"

"Because they're just as unhappy as I am about Rand's return."

Carl shrugged. "They haven't told me that."

Fina didn't know if her brothers had chickened out or not yet had the opportunity, but she didn't like being out on a limb by herself.

"And it's not like your brother is thrilled to see you," Carl added. "It's no easy task convincing him to back off you."

Fina shook her head. "Are you even listening to yourself? You have to get your son to stop harassing your daughter; you don't see a problem with that?"

"The only problem is that two of my adult children keep acting like children."

"What happened to the file I gave you and Rand last fall?" she asked, tapping her nails against the armrests. "I thought we agreed that the information would stay between us if Rand made himself scarce."

"He did make himself scarce, but that wasn't enough for you, was it? You still had to interfere."

"His girlfriend had young children, Dad." Fina had made a call to the woman on deck in Miami and warned her about Rand's proclivities. That call had set the current situation in motion, but she'd had no choice. Standing by while a child was abused was not an option.

"Which is why it's better that he come back. I can keep an eye on him here."

Fina stared at her father. "I disagree."

Carl reached into a drawer and tossed a file onto the desk. He nudged it toward her with his fingertip.

She opened it, scanned the contents, and put it back down on the desk. "What is this?" She glowered at him. "Tit for tat?"

Carl glanced at her before picking up his phone and fiddling with the screen. "I like to think of it as mutually assured destruction."

She tapped the file. "That isn't proof of anything."

"It's enough to get you a hearing in front of the state licensing board."

"And I have enough to get you and Rand brought in front of the bar."

Carl spread his arms wide. "And then we all lose."

"Welcoming him back into the family is winning? How are you going to look Haley in the eye, bringing her abuser back to the dinner table?"

Carl dropped his phone onto the desk and leaned forward, his jaw clenched. "He will not touch her."

"Damn right he won't, but he shouldn't be looking at her or speaking to her. He shouldn't be anywhere near her."

"That's not realistic, Josefina. I don't think you appreciate how complicated this situation is."

Fina shook her head. "Oh please."

"You have this fantasy that I can somehow get rid of your brother and there will be no fallout. No consequences for the rest of us."

"Those consequences pale compared to the ones being visited on Haley now that Rand's back."

Carl stared at her. "You're being naïve."

"So are you, Dad. You're underestimating the damage that Rand's mere presence will unleash."

Carl sat back. "You have another problem. Your mother is still very upset with you."

Fina rested her forehead against her fingertips. The pulse in her temple was throbbing at a rapid pace. "Because I told her the truth that her son is a pedophile, which I might add, she doesn't even believe, so why is she so upset? But, back to your plans to blackmail me."

"I told you not to threaten me."

Fina got up and walked to the door, pausing with her hand on the knob. "What happens when the secret gets out and people learn that you protected a molester?"

Carl puffed up his chest. "You need to give your strategy some serious thought."

"*I'm* not going to tell anyone, but do you really believe Haley was the first and the last? Maybe you can contain this within the family, Dad, but unless Rand can contain himself, it's just a matter of time until this blows up."

"Just focus on the case. Let me worry about your brother."

"But you're *not* worrying about him."

He shook his head.

"Why do you insist on defending him?" she asked. "And don't tell me it's because he's your kid."

"That's exactly the reason why."

Fina shook her head. "I don't buy it. You can't be that blind or that forgiving."

"I don't expect you to understand, not until you're a parent yourself."

Fina exhaled through her nose, like a bull waiting to charge. In her experience, playing the "you're not" card—be it you're not a parent, gay, female, or any number of variations—was a means to short-circuit conversations, not deepen them.

"I'm not a parent, but I'm an aunt, and sometimes I feel like I'm the only one looking out for Haley."

Carl shook his head and started dialing.

Fina wasn't surprised that appealing to Carl's better nature had failed, but her brothers were right: They'd never neutralize Rand if Carl was in his corner.

Were the paternal bonds really that unbreakable, or was there a way to make Carl see Rand for who he was?

Fina arrived early at Toscano, where she was meeting Cristian, so she ordered a beer and ruminated about her new investigation. She was filled with anticipation to get started and track down Lindsay

Kaufman, but she also felt a sense of dread. Digging into Rand's past was not going to be pretty.

Fina had already downed half of her beer when Cristian came through the door.

"You started without me?" he asked.

"I was thinking about family stuff. I needed to take the edge off."

"Ah." He ordered a beer, and they both studied the menu. When the waiter returned with his drink, Fina started to order, but Cristian stilled her with his hand. "Actually, we'd like a few minutes," he told the young man.

"Is that okay?" he asked Fina when they were alone.

"Sure."

They sipped their beers and sat quietly for a moment. Fina fiddled with the coaster, and Cristian shifted in his seat.

"So how was your day?" he finally asked.

Fina took a big gulp and put the bottle down on the table. "How about we just pretend we're having dinner same as we always have."

He shook his head. "But it's not the same."

"That's not what you said on the phone. You can't have it both ways, Cristian."

He studied the other patrons, and Fina could tell from the look on his face that he was annoyed.

She drained her beer and nodded to the waiter for another. "Let's start over, shall we? My day was fine."

"What are you working on?" Cristian asked after a moment, signaling his willingness to move on.

"Have you heard of Covenant Rising Church? They're in Framingham."

He tipped his head side to side. "Sounds familiar. Is that one of those born-again places?"

"Indeed it is. I'm working on something related to them."

He grinned and took a chug of beer.

"What? Just say it," Fina implored.

"Just that I would pay good money to see you at church."

"Someone's already paying me good money, but thanks for the offer. The client is an old girlfriend of Carl's."

"Really? There was someone before Elaine?"

"Yes, and she seems lovely, which begs the question: What was he thinking?"

"You wouldn't be here if he made a different choice," Cristian reminded her.

"I suppose. What are you working on, Detective?"

Cristian gave her the broad strokes of a murder investigation. It was nice to talk about work with someone who could relate. Cops and private investigators worked for different masters, but they were both trying to uncover the truth, or some version of it.

"My presence has been requested at a family dinner," Fina told him once her second beer had taken hold. "Rand and Elaine are both going to be there."

"Rand's back?" Cristian was one of the few people outside the family who knew the true nature of Rand's crimes.

"Yup."

"If Haley were willing to testify against him . . ." he trailed off.

"Not going to happen, Cristian."

"Well, I'm sorry. No wonder you needed that beer. What are you going to do about it?"

"I'm working on it. You know that whole 'He ain't heavy, he's my brother' thing?" Fina asked.

"Yeah?"

"Utter and complete bullshit."

The disturbance registered in Fina's body before her brain made sense of it. She froze on the threshold and tried to slow her breathing even as her heart raced. Her condo was generally a mess, but the sight that greeted her when she got home was definitely the work of an intruder.

Couch cushions were strewn across the living room, and the drawers of Nanny's sideboard yawned open, table linens tumbling out. Shards from the glass side table glinted underfoot, and magazines and files had been tossed in the air and then had floated back down to paper the floor.

Fina pulled out her gun and gently put down her bag. She crept through the condo, checking each room, making sure that whoever had redecorated had left the premises.

Satisfied that she was alone, Fina slipped the dead bolt into place, returned a couple of cushions to the couch, and flopped down on them. She put down the gun and wiped her sleeve across the thin sheen of sweat that had emerged on her face.

Everyone assumed that if you were brave it meant you weren't scared, but the two emotions weren't mutually exclusive. Fina knew how to use a gun and how to handle herself in a dangerous situation, but that didn't mean she wanted to be *in* a dangerous situation. She hated the idea of someone violating her personal space as much as the next person. What set her apart was that her fear quickly morphed into anger. She was pissed.

When the racing had subsided—in her mind and her heart—Fina retrieved her bag by the door and pulled out her phone. She held it in her hand for a moment, contemplating her options. Most people would call the cops, but calling them was an invitation into her business and that wasn't necessarily a good thing, depending upon who was responsible for the burglary. If she called Cristian, he'd want her to report it, which would open that same can of worms. Scotty would freak out, and Carl wouldn't care as long as it didn't have a negative impact on his bottom line. She wanted to ask the concierge if he'd seen anything suspicious, but she didn't want word to get out about the break-in. Some of Fina's neighbors were already convinced she was bad for the neighborhood; she didn't want to give them any more ammunition. Surely other people didn't have these sorts of dilemmas.

Tucking the gun into the back of her waistband, she moved into the kitchen. Dishes and glasses were smashed on the floor, and pots and pans littered the counters. She didn't even know the proper home for the kitchen items, having spent so little time there. The thieves had been considerate enough to leave some of her items in the fridge, including a cold diet soda. The hiss of the carbonation was a reassuring sound, and she took a long drink before returning to the couch.

Milloy answered on the second ring.

"I have a question for you," Fina said.

"Shoot."

"Do you happen to know where I keep the drainy thing, you know, the thing you put spaghetti in?"

There was a long pause.

"The colander?" he asked.

"Yes! That thing."

"It's in the lower cabinet to the left of the stove."

"I knew you would have the answer."

"You could have just looked, genius."

"Which brings us to the problem: I *couldn't* have just looked. Everything that was once in the cabinets is now out of the cabinets."

"What happened?"

"Someone broke in and rearranged everything."

"Do you want me to come over?"

"No, I'm good. I'll just shove stuff back in."

Milloy sighed. "I'm coming over."

"You don't have to. I'm good."

"I'm not worried about you. I'm worried about how I'm going to find that drainy thing the next time I need it."

"So selfish, Milloy. You only care about yourself."

"I'll be there in half an hour."

Fina looked around Nanny's living room and felt weary. Not be-cause the place had been trashed, but because the suspect list was long: She had a knack for pissing people off. Fina was certain that the break-in was targeted and intended to send a specific message.

But it was hard to decode the message when there were so many possible senders.

Fina spent the next morning quizzing Stanley, the head concierge, and reviewing the security footage in an effort to identify her unwel-come visitor from the night before. She swore him to secrecy with the help of a generous tip. The tape offered a fuzzy image of a man in a Red Sox cap, which described half the men in Boston. Stanley hadn't gotten any other reports of an intruder or disturbance in the building, confirming her suspicion that the attack was indeed targeted.

Next, she contacted Dennis Kozlowski, a PI who had been in charge of the security sweeps related to the NEU lawsuit. He promised to comb through the collection of hate mail and see if any one missive jumped out at him. Fina also made a halfhearted attempt to review her older case files for a potential perpetrator, but it was fruitless. She couldn't differentiate between the people she had annoyed and those willing to do something about it.

Tired of waiting for a callback from Lucas Chellew or Nadine Quaynor, she tried their office numbers. She got a recording asking her to leave a message for Lucas, and the woman who answered the phone at the accounting firm where Nadine worked said she was out for the day. Feeling antsy and dissatisfied, Fina decided to drop in at Ludlow and Associates. Generally, she liked the freedom of working on her own, but politically, it made sense to occasionally remind peo-ple of her existence.

Scotty was in court, but she found Matthew with his feet propped on top of his desk, the soles of his handmade leather shoes barely showing wear.

"I need to talk to you," she told him.

"You better make it quick. I've got trial prep in about two minutes."

"Damn."

"Why? What's up?"

"Someone trashed my condo last night," Fina said, sinking into the chair in front of his desk, "and I'm frustrated by my case. I wanted to hear about your new paramour. You know, a success story, to boost my spirits."

"Who trashed your condo?"

"No idea, which is exacerbating my frustration, as you can imagine."

He leaned forward, dropping his feet to the floor. "How did your condo get trashed in a secure building?"

"Some resident probably let the guy in. You'd be surprised how lackadaisical people are about security; anything not to be rude and offend a potential criminal."

"Spoken from experience, I'm guessing."

"Indeed."

"Do you want to come stay with me?" her brother asked.

"Nah, but thanks for the offer. I want to stick around in case he makes a return visit."

"That sounds like a terrific idea." He stood and grabbed his coat from a hanger on the back of the door.

"I'm full of them."

"Any of them have to do with Rand?"

"Yes, actually."

"Tell me later." Matthew leaned over and gave her a kiss on the cheek before heading out the door.

Fina was left sitting in his office. Her brothers claimed to be on board, yet she couldn't help but feel she was on her own.

SIX

Fina was meeting Ceci and Chloe at the Isabella Stewart Gardner Museum to give them an update and used the drive over to contemplate her strategy. Ceci had insisted Chloe be part of the discussion, despite Fina's misgivings. Generally, clients wanted to hear the results of an investigation in private, but Ceci seemed to think that hearing the report directly from Fina would have a greater impact on her daughter.

Fina had hoped to have concrete information to support a recommendation regarding Chloe's donation, but instead, all she had to offer was suspicions, suppositions, and a bad feeling in her gut. Why should Chloe pay that concoction any mind?

The Café G was an airy space with two walls of windows. Streamlined red chairs flanked the tables, and red light-shades hung overhead. The overall feel was contemporary and spare, a sharp contrast to the rest of the museum.

Fina arrived first and perused the menu.

Mother and daughter arrived within moments of each other and greeted each other warmly.

"I hope we didn't keep you waiting, Fina," Ceci said, unfolding her napkin onto her lap.

"Nope. How are you two?"

"I'm well," Ceci said, and looked to her daughter.

"I'm good," Chloe said. "Busy with work and church. The usual stuff."

At the mention of the church, Ceci's shoulders tightened in her boucle jacket. Conversations about the church were doomed if Ceci had a physical reaction to the mere mention of Covenant Rising.

"What do you recommend?" Fina asked, scanning her menu. "I haven't been here in ages."

They debated the relative benefits of quiche versus chicken salad and steered clear of any serious conversation until they'd ordered.

"I wanted Chloe to join us," Ceci said, "so she could hear the update directly from you, Fina."

"I understand," Fina said, looking at Chloe. She sat primly, her hands folded on her lap. "I can give you an overview of the investigation."

Ceci nodded.

"Obviously, I spoke with Chloe, and I joined her for a service at Covenant Rising. Pastor Greg and I met yesterday, and I had my financial expert dig into the church's finances. I haven't been able to connect with Lucas and Nadine yet, the two committee members you suggested I contact."

"But you've had a chance to see what the church is all about," Chloe said.

Fina shook her head. "Not really. Pastor Greg wouldn't tell me much about the church's finances."

Ceci looked at her daughter, but before Chloe could speak, the waitress arrived with their drinks.

"This is exactly what concerns me, Chloe," Ceci said a moment later, shaking a packet of sweetener before pouring it into her iced tea.

"I'm not quite finished," Fina said.

"Of course. I'm sorry to interrupt."

"The church is protective of itself," Chloe interjected. "And rightly so. We're always being misrepresented and misunderstood." Fina stared at her, indicating that the "no interrupting" rule applied to her, too, and Chloe sat back as if to cede the floor.

"The church has every right to protect itself," Fina continued, "and given that it's a 501(3)(c), it's not legally obligated to disclose financial information. That said, I'm troubled by the secrecy that the organization perpetuates. When people aren't forthcoming, others assume they have something to hide, whether or not that's a fair assumption."

"It's *not* fair," Chloe said.

"The other issue that raises a red flag," Fina continued, "are the church's assets."

"Such as?" Ceci asked, accepting a plate of chicken salad from the waitress.

"The Gatchells' home in Wellesley. Of course, they have to live somewhere," Fina said in an effort to preempt Chloe's objection. "But there's also a ski condo in New Hampshire and a house on Cape Cod. There are luxury cars and trips to tropical locations."

"All of which is related to church business," Chloe insisted.

"Maybe," Fina said, digging her fork into her quiche, "but my financial adviser thinks the spending could be part of a pattern. It may not be illegal, but it may be ethically questionable."

"Pastor Greg is completely devoted to the church," Chloe said. "He and Gabby built it from the ground up. They work all the time, and never turn down anyone in need. And they've been incredibly supportive of the art therapy program."

"I understand that," Fina said, "but I'd like to know what percentage of church donations supports the good works of the church and what percentage supports their lifestyle. Those are reasonable questions that Pastor Greg won't answer."

They were silent for a moment. Chloe busied herself spooning up some polenta. Ceci watched her daughter over her iced tea.

"It sounds as if you don't think the bequest is a good idea," Ceci said after setting down her glass.

"No. Not at this time," Fina said. "And I really am saying that with your best interests at heart, Chloe. I know that you love the church, and it is a welcoming community, but there will be plenty of time to make a generous gift once you have more information."

"But there isn't time," Chloe insisted. "Pastor Greg has plans for a retreat center, and the land in Vermont is critical to moving forward."

"But don't you see, Chloe?" Ceci asked. "He's creating a sense of urgency so you won't ask questions. Surely a few months' deliberation won't derail the plans. If he really cared about you, he wouldn't rush you."

"He does care about me, Mom," Chloe said, her voice rising. "But he cares about the church and the community just as much. I don't want to be the reason that people don't get the support they need. *I* don't need a huge spread in Vermont, for goodness' sake."

Fina loathed Pastor Greg at that moment and the way he used shame and guilt to manipulate others. Her father did it all the time, but he was a personal injury lawyer; it was practically in his job description.

Ceci gave Fina a pleading look.

"Perhaps if your mother had a better understanding of what draws you to the church, you two could find some common ground," Fina said. "The theology of Covenant Rising seems at odds with your family's values."

"I've already explained it to her." Chloe didn't look thirty in that instant; she looked more like a sulky adolescent.

"Well, how about you explain it to me," Fina said. "Humor me."

Chloe straightened up. "First of all, there's no perfect belief system, but I feel like I matter at CRC—like my participation matters."

"You don't feel that at work?" Ceci asked. "Or in our family?"

"Does my participation matter in our family?" Chloe asked.

"Of course it does!"

"Really? Is that why Dad and Veronique are in charge of the

company, and you and I are supposed to keep busy with art and charity?"

Ceci looked perplexed. "But Chloe, you love art, and charity is what you're choosing to do at the church."

"I have a role at the church. I belong, and I love the other members. Mom, they came through for me during a very difficult time."

"I know, sweetheart, but don't you think that what was right for you then may not be right for you now? You were at a low point after the breakup."

"So you think I should leave now that they helped me? Just use them?"

"That's not what I mean, Chloe."

"The members of CRC are wonderful, and they care about people regardless of their circumstances." She glared at her mother. "It doesn't matter to them how much money you make or where you went to school."

It may not matter to the other members, but Fina was certain it mattered to Pastor Greg.

"Chloe," Ceci implored.

"This conversation is a waste of time," Chloe said, crumpling her napkin into a ball.

They sat for a moment, an awkward silence cloaking the table.

"I'm not sure what more I can do," Fina said.

"Could you please talk to Nadine?" Chloe asked. "I'm sure she could put your mind at ease."

"I'd love to talk with her if I can get ahold of her." Fina doubted that Nadine would add anything of value. She probably toed the company line.

"I know she's been sick. That may be why you've had trouble connecting with her."

"I'll reach out to her again," Fina promised.

Ceci chewed a bite of chicken and studied a framed sketch on the wall. Fina knew that changing Chloe's mind would take a miracle of biblical proportions. She suspected that Ceci knew that, too.

They left discussion of the church behind, and after a few minutes of stilted conversation, hit a rhythm. Both Ceci and Chloe were knowledgeable art lovers who put Fina—with her meager "intro to art history" knowledge—to shame.

Ceci had to run to a meeting, but once they'd finished eating, Chloe insisted that Fina join her for a brief lap of the museum. Fina thought the building was spectacular, and the art it contained impressive, but the setup always brought to mind a flea market in an Italian piazza. Everywhere you looked there was another item that was fighting its neighbor for space.

They finished up in the Dutch room, in front of the empty frames in which the stolen Rembrandts had once resided.

"It's so horrible," Chloe said, studying the blankness. "Stealing from everybody so that a privileged few can benefit."

"I couldn't agree more," Fina said, studying the young woman for a trace of irony.

There was none to be found.

Fina returned to Ludlow and Associates and spent the rest of the day reviewing files for another case. Carl wanted her to spend every free moment on Covenant Rising, but that wasn't realistic; other people didn't abide by Fina's schedule, and there was always paperwork that required her attention.

She called it quits around dinnertime, and since Nadine lived in Dorchester—closer than Lucas's Dedham address—Fina decided to pay her a visit. Much could be gleaned by catching an interviewee off guard in her own environment.

Nadine's house was a modestly sized Victorian with a front porch and a window in the pitch of the roof. There was a small yard and a freestanding single-car garage at the end of the paved driveway. Like most of the houses on the street, the paint was in good shape and the yard tidy. It was a solidly middle-class neighborhood, and the pride of its residents was evident.

The Toyota Camry sitting in Nadine's driveway buoyed Fina's hopes that she was home. A light glowed on the first floor, but when Fina rang the bell, there was no response. She cupped her hands against the front window and stared into an empty living room. Fina started back down the front steps, but something made her stop. She returned to the window and studied the scene more carefully. Beyond the living room, the kitchen was visible. There were café curtains in the window over the counter, and a tall plastic trash can was off to the side. Fina scanned the doorway and drew her breath in sharply when she computed what she'd seen the first time she looked. There was a shoe peeking out from the door frame, and inside that shoe, what appeared to be a foot.

Fina banged on the front door, calling out Nadine's name. Running around to the back of the house, she tried to open the door into the kitchen. Through the window, she could see a woman lying on the floor, motionless.

Fina pulled out her phone and dialed 911. The eerily calm voice on the other end asked for specifics and instructed her to stay on the line until the cops and ambulance arrived. She trotted back down the steps and searched for something with which to break the glass in the door. At the edge of the yard, Fina found a rock roughly the size of a softball. As she pulled back her arm to throw it, a shout stopped her.

"Don't throw that!" a man yelled from the neighbor's yard. "There's a key!"

He jogged over and knelt down by a basement window well. He pulled out a small key box from its depths and tossed it to Fina. She shoved the key into the lock and threw open the door.

In the kitchen, the neighbor dropped to the floor and felt the unresponsive woman's neck for a pulse. After a moment, he touched his palm to her face.

"Is this Nadine?" Fina asked, crouching down next to him.

"It's Nadine," he said, sitting back on his knees, his expression pained.

Fina felt sure that Nadine Quaynor was dead. There was no rise or fall to her chest; her body was shrouded in stillness.

"Ronnie McCaffrey," the man said, offering his hand. In his early sixties, he had a ruddy face and snow-white hair. He was wearing jeans and a Patriots sweatshirt.

"I'm Fina Ludlow." She studied Nadine's face. "She's dead, I'm guessing."

"No pulse and cool to the touch. Goddamnit."

"Are you a firefighter or a cop?" Fina asked. His levelheaded response suggested some experience with the deceased.

"Boston Fire Department, retired. If you were a desperate family member, I'd go through the motions, but I don't think that's necessary." Sirens could be heard in the distance.

"You're right. It isn't."

"Are you a friend of Nadine's?" Ronnie asked.

"Not exactly."

Fina caught sight of flashing blue and red lights on the wall. She went to the front door and ushered the first responders inside.

Firefighters, EMTs, and a couple of cops crowded into the small space.

"DOA," Ronnie told the man who seemed to be in charge. The EMTs got down on the floor to conduct an assessment, and Fina wandered into the living room. The firefighters tromped back out of the house, while the medics continued their work, and one of the cops came over to Fina.

"What's your name, ma'am?" He pulled out a small notebook and pen from an inner pocket of his jacket.

"Fina Ludlow."

"Is this your house?"

"No, it's hers." She gestured toward the kitchen.

"And she is?"

"Nadine Quaynor."

"What's your relationship to her?"

"We don't have one. I've never met her before."

He cocked his head. "But you found her?"

"Yes. I stopped by to speak with her, and I saw her foot through the window. I called you guys right away."

"How'd you get in the house?"

"I knew where the spare key was," Ronnie said, joining them. Radios crackled in the background.

"Did you hear me yelling?" Fina asked him.

He nodded. "And I heard the call on the scanner."

That explained his prompt appearance. It wasn't unusual for retired cops and firefighters to listen to the emergency frequency from the comfort of their living rooms. It was a way to hear the language they'd spoken all their lives, a language spoken in few places.

"I checked her out," Ronnie said to the cop, gesturing at Nadine, "but it was obvious she was gone."

One of the EMTs tidied his bag of gear while the other filled out a form on a clipboard.

Ronnie walked over to the doorway. "You put a call in to the ME?" he asked the one filling out the form.

"Taken care of, Chief."

He gazed down at Nadine, shaking his head. He sighed loudly.

"Why are you here exactly?" the cop asked Fina, his voice laced with impatience. "You said you didn't know the victim."

"I'm a private investigator." Fina showed him her license. "I wanted to ask her some questions related to a case."

Ronnie raised an eyebrow in Fina's direction, but didn't say any-thing.

She took a step toward Nadine's body. Nothing looked off except for the lack of color and movement. "It doesn't look like there's any trauma."

"She'd been sick recently," Ronnie said.

Fina remembered Chloe's comment from lunch. "Sick with what?"

He shrugged. "Don't know exactly, but I didn't think it was serious."

The cop was fishing through a purse sitting on the counter. He took out a wallet and examined Nadine's driver's license. "She was thirty-two."

"Young," Ronnie said. "I hate seeing the young ones." The EMTs nodded in agreement.

"Any idea about next of kin?" the cop asked.

"She's married—separated, actually. Her husband's living in Natick," Ronnie said. "She also has family in Waltham."

"Do you still need me here?" Fina asked.

"You have some place you need to be?" the cop wondered.

Fina swallowed the urge to make a flippant response. As a rule, sassing cops was a bad idea. "I feel like I'm intruding. I didn't know the victim, and I don't think I can be helpful."

"I need your contact information," he said. "Then you're free to go."

Fina gave him her card and headed for the front door. Ronnie followed.

"Sorry to meet you under these circumstances," he said.

"Me, too. Thanks for rushing over. Your neighbors must sleep eas-ier knowing that you're nearby."

"I do what I can."

Fina felt badly for Nadine and her family—that her life was cut short and theirs would be derailed—but she didn't feel the deep sad-ness that occurs when someone you know has died.

For Fina, Nadine's demise was just a big pain in the ass.

· · ·

Something about seeing a dead body made Fina crave human connection, but she also needed to break the news to Chloe. She left her a voice mail asking to meet and contemplated dropping in at Risa Paquette's house. Risa was a family friend who had become a confidante of Fina's in recent months. A close friend of Rand's late wife, Risa was picking up the slack with Haley, and Fina had supported Risa during a recent family situation when her biological aunt came calling for her kidney.

Fina checked the time. She worried that she'd be interrupting the domestic Bermuda Triangle of dinner, homework, and TV-watching at Risa's, so she turned her car in the direction of 56 Wellspring Street in Newton.

The living room of Frank and Peg Gillis's modest ranch house was illuminated, and with no kids at home, Fina was confident her drop-in would be a welcome diversion, not a distraction. Frank had been the lead investigator at Ludlow and Associates and taught Fina everything she knew—everything that wasn't illegal or unethical. These days, Frank and his wife, Peg, served as Fina's surrogate parents when Carl and Elaine didn't measure up, which was always.

"Hi, sweetie," Frank said when she rang the bell and poked her head in the door.

"Hi. Where's Peg?"

"Book group." He was sitting in his favorite recliner, a book on his lap. He glanced at his watch. "They're probably discussing genocide over a nice cobbler."

"I'd skip the genocide and go straight for the cobbler," Fina said, taking a seat on the sofa.

"You and me both. Do you want something to eat? There are some leftovers in the fridge."

"I'll take a look."

Fina made herself a meatloaf sandwich on white bread with mayonnaise. She knew there were no chips in the house; Frank had had some heart scares, and certain foods were verboten. She grabbed a diet soda and took her meal back to the living room.

"How are you?" she asked him. "Taking care of yourself?"

"Always," he said, smiling.

"No tree removal? Driveway paving? That sort of thing?" Frank liked to do manual labor despite his doctor's admonitions.

"You know, you tease me, but wait until you can't do things you used to do all the time."

"Believe me, I get it," Fina said, taking a bite of her sandwich. "I can't do things I used to do in my twenties. I can't fight the way I used to, or at least, I don't recover as quickly."

Frank stared at her. "I'm not talking about hand-to-hand combat, sweet pea. I'm talking about household chores."

"No one but you considers tree removal a household chore."

He waved her away. "It's frustrating when your abilities decline."

Fina wiped mayonnaise from the corner of her mouth. "Indeed, but it beats the alternative. I just left the scene of the sudden death of a thirty-two-year-old woman."

He winced. "Foul play?"

"It didn't look that way," Fina said, pulling off a morsel of sandwich. "But still—thirty-two?"

"That's a tragedy," Frank said.

She nodded. "Did you ever work on any cases related to churches or religious organizations when you were at the firm?"

He narrowed his eyes in thought. "A couple. Churches are tough. They've got lots of legal protection and lots of passionate people. Is that what you're working on?"

"It's coming to an end, but your description is spot-on. It has not been a satisfying experience."

They sat quietly for a moment, Fina eating contentedly.

"Everything else okay?" Frank asked.

"Yeah. It's fine. There's some family stuff going on."

He nodded. "Anything I can do to help?"

"Nah. I'm good. I always feel better after seeing you."

"The feeling's mutual, sweetie."

Frank turned on the local news, and they watched the top stories. Fina decided to hang around until Peg got home from book club.

She knew there'd be talk of human atrocities, but Peg was worth it.

Fina was speeding through the E-Z Pass lane when her phone rang. It was Chloe returning her call.

"Are you at home?" Fina asked.

"Yes."

"Do you mind if I stop by?"

"Sure. Is everything okay? I didn't expect to hear from you so soon."

Fina never knew if it was better to break bad news over the phone, thereby putting the recipient out of their misery, or waiting to share it in person. Given her vivid imagination, not knowing was always worse to Fina, but not everybody shared her preference.

"Yeah," she lied to Chloe. "I'll be there soon."

Fina snagged a resident parking space on the street, and Chloe buzzed her into the building. She was standing in her open doorway on the second floor, dressed in a cashmere sweat suit. Her hair was pulled into a messy knot at the back of her head.

"What's going on?" Chloe asked once they'd taken seats in the living room.

Fina took a deep breath. "There's no good way to say this. I stopped by Nadine's house a couple of hours ago. I'm sorry, Chloe, but she's dead."

Chloe was still, the only movement the blood leeching out of her face. "What?"

"I know it sounds unbelievable, but I saw her myself."

"I don't understand. Was she in an accident?"

Fina recounted the events of the evening. Chloe's eyes widened in disbelief, and she hugged herself.

"Can I get you a glass of water or some tea?" Fina asked.

"I don't know," Chloe said, at a loss.

Fina went into the kitchen and began opening various cabinets in search of a glass. "Do you have anything stronger than water?" she asked.

"Look in the cabinet next to the fridge."

Fina found two glasses and a well-stocked bar. She pulled out a bottle of tequila and a bottle of scotch and brought them over to the coffee table.

"What's your preference?" she asked.

Chloe pointed to the scotch. Fina poured her a shot and then put some tequila in the other glass. She downed it in one gulp. Chloe sipped her drink delicately.

"This is horrible," Chloe said. "It's not like we were best friends, but still."

"I know. That's why I wanted to tell you in person."

"I don't understand what happened."

Fina placed her empty glass on the coffee table. "There may be an autopsy. You mentioned she'd been sick. The medical examiner will confer with her doctor, and they'll decide."

"Her death must be related."

"Probably," Fina said. "If they can explain her death, then there's no need to do an autopsy. Most families don't want one performed unless it's absolutely necessary."

Chloe finished her drink and shook her head when Fina made a move to pour her another.

"Is there anyone you want me to call? Someone to keep you company? Your mom?"

Chloe blinked back tears. "No. I think I just want to be alone."

"Okay." Fina rose from the couch and took the empty glasses into the kitchen, where she placed them in the sink. "Call me if you need anything."

"Thanks, Fina."

In her car, Fina allowed herself to contemplate the potential upside of Nadine's death. She felt crummy for thinking that way, but maybe it would put the brakes on Chloe's bequest, at least temporarily. In her experience, a sudden death either arrested progress or prompted swift action.

Time would tell.

SEVEN

The next morning, Pastor Greg bent his head when he heard a noise at the back of the sanctuary. The footsteps coming down the aisle alerted him to the identity of the distraction. A congregant would take a seat in the last pew and wait patiently for him to finish his worship. Only Gabby would interrupt him in prayer.

She dropped down onto her knees next to him and clasped her hands in front of her.

"I've been looking for you," she told him.

"And you found me."

"We need to talk."

He looked at his wife. "I'll be done shortly."

Gabby rolled her eyes and pushed herself to a standing position. She sat down in the first pew and pulled her phone out of her pocket.

Greg closed his eyes and added his wife to the list of souls who needed attention. The addition extended his worship by a few minutes, but that seemed appropriate.

"What is it?" he asked, joining her in the pew. She turned her phone facedown in her lap.

"Betty just told me the news about Nadine Quaynor," Gabby said. "I can't believe it."

Greg took a deep breath. "God moves in a mysterious way."

"I'll say."

"We should both be available for those who need our support."

"Of course." She turned her body in the pew to face him. "What happened? Betty said she was found dead in her house."

"That's what I was told," he said. "Didn't she miss some events because she was under the weather?"

Gabby nodded.

"I'm assuming it's related to that," he said.

His wife sighed. "She was so young."

"Makes you thankful for what you've got."

"What's the plan for the funeral?"

"I need to meet with her family. You should come with me."

"Great." She held out her hand and examined her manicure. "I'm sure that will be a hoot."

"'Blessed is the man who remains steadfast under trial,'" Greg said, taking her hand and squeezing it.

She made a sour face. "That doesn't make it any easier."

"If it were easy, it wouldn't be so fulfilling."

She shrugged. "I don't know. I think it'd be very fulfilling if everyone would just do what we wanted."

Greg grinned. "Come on, Gab. You like the challenge."

"Pastor," Betty called from the back of the sanctuary. "You have a call."

"See you later." He gave his wife a peck on the cheek and walked up the aisle.

Nadine's death was sad news, but crises were really just opportunities to lead.

Adversity was Pastor Greg's time to shine.

. . .

"Pitney wants to talk to you," Cristian told Fina. She'd just finished a run on the treadmill and was bent over, staring inside the refrigerator, contemplating her next move.

"What did I do now?" The phone was moistened by the sweat on her cheek.

Lieutenant Marcy Pitney was Cristian's boss, and she and Fina had a difficult relationship. They were both strong, hardheaded women who thought they knew best.

"You found Nadine Quaynor. Dead."

"I would have preferred to have found her alive." Fina stood up straight. "Wait. How do you know about Nadine?" The Major Crimes unit only took on cases that were high profile and politically sensitive.

"We're taking the lead on the case, and I saw your name on the report."

"Why are you guys taking the lead?"

"Because we're not convinced it was natural causes."

Fina pushed the fridge door closed. "Huh."

"You don't sound surprised."

"I'm not easily surprised, you know that."

"What did you think when you found her?"

"I wondered why a thirty-two-year-old would drop dead with no signs of trauma." Fina walked into the living room and plopped down on the sofa. "What's the cause of death?"

"TBD." Cristian paused. "This is not good, you know."

"That Nadine died under suspicious circumstances? I agree."

"That you're involved in the case. Pitney is going to have apoplexy."

"Excuse me, I knew Nadine first. I'd been trying to talk to her for days. But you don't need to worry. This has nothing to do with me."

"You're going to need to come in and tell us about it anyway."

Fina groaned. "Can't we just do it over the phone or during one of our dates? Nothing says romance like an unexplained death."

"So now you're eager to call it a date? That warms the heart."

"I'd rather not deal with Pitney."

"Too bad. She can't wait to see you."

"Ugh. That woman is so demanding."

"She's in court, but you should be here when she gets back later this morning."

"Great. My day is shaping up to be a real corker. I'm scheduled to visit the tenth circle of hell tonight."

"That's gotta involve the Ludlows," Cristian said.

"Yup. A family dinner, including Rand."

"Promise me there won't be any gunfire."

"Well, that limits me," Fina said, "but it doesn't rule out all my options. So yes, I promise."

"See ya." Cristian hung up.

Fina wasn't shocked that Nadine's death was under scrutiny, but it introduced a whole new element into her investigation of the church. Bad publicity and scandals were never good, but if anyone could find the silver lining of a suspicious death, it was Pastor Greg.

Kentucky Rose, Mother's Rest, Praying Hands, Going Home. Christa's stomach flip-flopped as she walked the perimeter of the room and read the small placards by each casket. She and Paul had wills, but she wondered if she needed to be more specific with her wishes. A simple pine box would do the job. She certainly didn't want her kids to spend money on something that was going to be dropped in the ground only to decompose.

Christa examined an option that resembled Cinderella's carriage, the corners of her mouth turning down in distaste. Her cousin Nadine was such a control freak; it was hard to believe that, even at her young age, she hadn't sorted out her funeral arrangements.

Voices floated in from the hallway. The funeral home was in a large old mansion in Dorchester. Dated-looking floral upholstery and the generous entrance hall made the place seem frozen from an earlier decade. Did people need to feel like they were going back in time to deal with this particular present?

The conversation sounded tense, and Christa strained her neck to look toward the hallway. Evan, Nadine's estranged husband, and Mr. Murphey, the funeral director, were standing close to each other. Evan's motions were animated and jerky while Mr. Murphey stood still, his hands clasped before him. Christa wondered if she should intervene, but surely the director knew how to deal with an agitated client.

A room next to the casket display held rows of gold bamboo chairs with cream-colored seats. Christa looked around to make sure she wasn't disturbing anyone—dead or living—and took a seat. Her phone dinged with a new e-mail, and she was silencing it when Evan plopped down in the seat next to her.

"What's going on?" Christa asked.

Evan smoothed his hand over the cowlick in his sandy-blond hair. The pointy collar of his shirt was folded in on itself, suggesting that he'd dressed in a hurry without looking in a mirror.

"She's not here," he said in a hushed voice, sucking in his cheeks and blinking rapidly.

"I'm sure she'll get here soon. We can still make arrangements."

Evan shook his head. "They don't know when she's coming."

"What do you mean?"

"She's still at the medical examiner's office."

"And why don't they know when she's coming?" she asked evenly. A tide of impatience was rising in her. Christa fought the urge to shake him and insist he get to the point.

"Because they won't release the body yet. They're doing more tests."

"What kind of tests?" Christa had volunteered to help Evan, to spare her aunt and uncle the misery, but she was starting to regret the offer.

He threw his hands up. "I don't know!"

"Why don't I speak with the funeral director and see if I can get more information." She reached into her bag and pulled out a bottle of water. "Have some."

Evan took a swig. "He won't be able to tell you anything."

"But he can tell me who to contact at the medical examiner's office, and we can still make whatever decisions we need to."

"Maybe we should come back later."

Christa put her hand on his. "This isn't going to get any easier, Evan. Do you really want to come back here a second time?"

His leg started bouncing. "No," he said, barely above a whisper.

"Why don't you take a look around while I find Mr. Murphey?"

He nodded, and they returned to the room with the caskets. Evan stood staring at them.

Christa left in search of Mr. Murphey and a coherent explanation for the absence of her cousin's body.

Christ.

Why was she always in charge of finding people's lost stuff?

Fina decided to swing by the Ludlow and Associates office on the way to the police station and update Carl. He was finishing up a meeting, so she found an empty conference room and got to work on some administrative drudgery. Generating invoices and writing reports was tedious, but she was conscientious when it came to record keeping and billing. Frank had taught her that there was no good time to do administrative housekeeping, but it was essential to running a successful business.

Not long after she sat down, she got the uneasy feeling she was being watched. Fina looked up to find Rand standing on the other side of the glass, observing her like she was a trapped animal. He strolled in and took a seat across from her.

"I was hoping to see you before the big family dinner," he said. If ever there were a wolf in sheep's clothing, it was Rand. He had thick, wavy hair like the other Ludlow men and looked like a younger version of Carl. His full lips and straight teeth—appealing to some women—struck Fina as more threatening than enticing.

"I can't imagine why," she said, reaching into her bag. Her brother flinched. "What's the matter, Rand? Afraid I'm going to shoot you?"

"You have threatened before."

"Good point. What do you want?"

He placed one hand on the tabletop and tapped his pointer finger on the surface. His nails were manicured, and his suit was impeccable. "I want to make sure we aren't going to have any problems."

"I don't see why we would, as long as you keep your dick away from underage girls."

Rand reached across the table and grabbed her wrist. "That's exactly what I'm talking about," he whispered. "Your goddamn filthy mouth."

"Says the pedophile," Fina said before bashing his hand down on the table.

"Fuck!" He released his grip and rubbed his hand. "I swear to God, Fina—"

The conference room door slammed shut, and the siblings jumped. Carl stood there, glowering.

"Stop making a goddamn spectacle, both of you." He strode to the table and leaned over, pressing his hands onto the smooth surface. "I don't want you to talk to each other. Don't even make eye contact. Do you understand?"

Fina and Rand glared at each other.

"Do you understand?" He enunciated every word.

"If those same rules apply to Haley and other girls," Fina said, "then yes, Father, I understand." She could feel a drop of sweat rolling down her back.

"She's calling the shots now?" Rand whined.

"Shut up, Rand," Carl said. He looked at Fina. "Yes, those rules apply to Haley and others."

"Okeydoke," Fina said. She gathered her things and stood. "I think dinner is going to be a resounding success. Good work, you two."

Rand sneered at her. "Unbelievable."

"Go away, Fina," Carl said.

"With pleasure."

She left the conference room and found the nearest ladies' room so she could lock herself in a stall and fume.

Fina tended to get her way, and if she didn't, she decided that getting her way didn't really matter. But that wasn't true in this case: It did matter. If there was nothing she could do to fix it, Rand would roam free.

She splashed cold water on her face, reapplied her lip gloss, and readied herself to face her father again.

She found him standing behind his desk, a file folder in one hand.

"What now?" Carl asked, taking a seat. He often complained about Fina's lack of manners, but really, did he expect her to develop them spontaneously?

Fina dropped into a chair across from him. "One of the church members who Chloe suggested I speak with turned up dead yesterday under suspicious circumstances. I found her body."

Carl's eyes widened. "You really know how to pick 'em."

"You brought me into this, remember?"

"How'd she die?"

"She was thirty-two years old, and according to my police contacts, she didn't die from natural causes."

He rocked back in his chair. "So what are you thinking?"

Fina rubbed her shoe against the chair leg to stop an itch. "I'm thinking that a member of the Covenant Rising leadership committee died under suspicious circumstances. Her death may not have anything to do with the church, but it's an opportunity to dig around some more and maybe postpone Chloe's donation."

Carl was quiet for a moment.

"But it may be a hard sell," Fina added, "convincing Ceci to keep footing the bill."

"Don't worry about Ceci. You'll get paid."

"Meaning?"

"Meaning keep investigating. Let her know you're still on the case. I'll take care of the money."

"You're offering our services pro bono?" Carl never waived his fee, not unless there was an angle he was working. "What's in it for you?" Fina asked.

"Who says there has to be something in it for me?"

Fina stared at him. "Is this some kind of a psychotic break? Should I call for help?"

"No. You should get back to work."

"All righty then. I'll get back to work."

Fina waited for the elevator and contemplated her father's lax attitude about his fee. Was it the identity of the client? Was he doing it for Ceci? And if so, why? Or was there some other explanation for his generosity?

A charitable Carl was like an endangered species in the wild: rumored to exist, but rarely seen.

Fina was on her way to the police station when Cristian called and asked her to meet them at the emergency room at Mass General instead. They were tied up there on another case.

The ER was divided according to the level of care required, shunting patients with different needs into different areas. Lacerated knees requiring stitches and tweens with skateboarding injuries were jettisoned off far from the gunshot wounds and serious car accidents.

Fina followed the painted red line on the floor to the critical area, where she showed her ID to a cop and was ushered into an empty exam room. She could hear wailing a few doors away, which made her marvel at the people who work in ERs. Bearing witness to such anguish must be exhausting and soul crushing. Her inclination would be to shut up the ill and infirm at any cost, but nobody wanted a caregiver who smothered the patients.

Fina was sitting in the room's only chair when the curtain parted ten minutes later, and Lieutenant Pitney appeared.

If a stranger were to guess Pitney's occupation, Fina was quite sure that "cop" wouldn't even make the list. Her short stature, unruly curly hair, and the jarring color palette of her clothing suggested children's birthday performer more than accomplished investigator.

"Thanks for meeting here," Pitney said. "We've got someone down the hall."

"Not a cop, I hope."

"No, a perp."

"Is he going to make it?"

"Too soon to tell."

"How can I be of service, Lieutenant?" Fina asked.

Pitney snickered. "That's you, Fina. Nothing but helpful."

Fina and the lieutenant had spent their careers jousting with each other, and with each case they started anew; trading and withholding information, revealing and evading.

Pitney took a seat on a wheeled stool. "Tell me about Nadine Quaynor."

"There isn't much to tell, and I'm not just giving you the runaround."

"Uh-huh."

"I never met her. I've been trying to talk with her since Monday." Fina described her case without mentioning any names and shared her impressions of Covenant Rising.

"So it's a cult?" the lieutenant asked.

"*Cult* is a bit extreme. I think they have undue influence over some of their congregants, but that's true of many organizations."

Cristian ducked into the exam room and nodded at Fina.

"How's our guy?" Pitney asked.

"Hanging on."

She looked back to Fina. "What else do you know about Nadine?"

"Nothing. I wasn't investigating her."

"But you're done with the church case?" Pitney rose and pushed the stool under a counter.

"Ahh, well."

Pitney folded her arms over her large bosom and glared at her.

"I thought you said you were done," Cristian remarked.

"I thought I was, but it looks like Nadine's death may have a bearing on my case."

"What does that mean?" Pitney glared at her.

"It means that I'm going to be doing some investigating, but before you start—" Fina held up her hand. "I know. Stay out of your way, but tell you everything. Our usual inequitable arrangement."

"Nobody said life was fair, Fina."

"You're telling me."

Pitney pulled the curtain aside and left, while Cristian lingered in the exam room. He tugged the curtain closed and extended a hand to Fina. "When's our next date?" he asked, pulling her to her feet.

"I don't know. When would you like it to be?"

He grasped her face with his hands and kissed her. "I think it should be soon."

Fina placed her hands on his waist. "That's going to be tough, given our respective caseloads." She leaned in to kiss him again, but was interrupted by a ruckus in the hallway.

Cristian stepped out to see what was going on. Two cops were struggling with a tall, skinny man who was twisting and contorting, trying to elude their grasp. Cristian jogged over to assist and after a few moments, they pinned the man to the floor.

"Let's continue our conversation when there isn't a tweaker vying for your attention," Fina said, sidestepping the excitement.

"Sounds good," Cristian said, his knee pressing down on the man's back.

As she made her way to the exit, Fina noticed that the waiting room was full of patients of every age and race. Some of the occupants looked homeless, while others wore expensive outerwear.

Sickness and calamity were equal opportunity afflictions.

EIGHT

Back home, Fina had a snack of leftover fried rice and a handful of Nutter Butter cookies. Appropriately fueled, she grabbed her computer and started plugging in names. She needed to know more about the people in Nadine's universe.

Evan Quaynor brought up one measly result: He was listed as the coauthor on a paper about the city's primary ship channel and the Massport Marine Terminal. She skimmed the article, which focused on the proposed plan to deepen the shipping channels, thereby improving ship safety. The Quaynor who seemed to have the larger Web presence was Nadine herself, whose activities with Covenant Rising were well documented. There were photos of her manning a table at a clothing drive and serving meals to the needy on Thanksgiving.

Nadine's neighbor Ronnie McCaffrey netted more hits, most of them related to his tenure in the Boston Fire Department. A battalion chief at the time of his retirement, Ronnie was quoted at the scenes of various incidents, including a few fires, a tractor-trailer rollover on Route 128, and a skirmish with wild turkeys, who were becoming increasingly bold in residential neighborhoods. There was not a whiff of controversy to be found. Someone had posted a picture on Facebook from his retirement party that showed Ronnie standing with his wife, two daughters, two sons-in-law, and a few small children. Everyone was smiling, and his wife had a large corsage pinned to the front of her dress.

Fina got up from the couch and wandered over to the window. She watched the airplane traffic at Logan. Nanny had loved to sit in the same spot with a high-power telescope—a gift from Carl—and watch the flights landing and taking off. Her grandmother wasn't interested in traveling, but she loved the idea of all those planes and all those people, coming and going.

At her computer, Fina launched a search for Lindsay Kaufman, Rand's alleged victim, and a few results popped up. The first was a high school track-and-field coach in Spirit Lake, Iowa. The next was an obituary for a ninety-three-year-old, but the third was a woman named Lindsay Kaufman Shaunnesy, a real estate agent in Back Bay. According to her bio, Lindsay was originally from Duxbury and had attended BU, just like Fina and her brothers. Fina grabbed the photo off her Web page and sent it to Scotty for confirmation. Man, she loved the Internet.

She placed her computer on the coffee table and snuggled into the couch and was rudely awakened an hour later by her phone. It was a telemarketer desperate to sell her a new roof, which was particularly irksome.

"I live in a high-rise," she told the man.

"So you don't need a new roof?"

"I don't have a roof."

"Why don't we check back with you in a few months in case you change your mind," the man suggested.

"I'm not going to miraculously get a roof in a few months," Fina started to explain, then hit the cancel button. Enough of that non-sense.

She took a quick shower, got dressed, and dialed Milloy.

"I have a favor to ask." The phone was tucked under her chin and she was struggling to pull on her shoes.

"Ask away."

"Will you come with me to my family dinner?"

"Tonight?"

"I know it's last-minute. I should have asked you sooner, but I was pretending it wasn't really happening."

"Good strategy."

"You can bust my chops all you want, but please, come with me."

"I can't," Milloy said. "I have a client."

"You can't reschedule?" Fina leaned against the front door, exhausted by the prospect of the night ahead.

"I can't cancel a client because you didn't plan ahead. I'm sympathetic, believe me, but this is business."

"I know. It's just . . . I'm dreading it. You're such a good buffer."

"If Rand is here to stay, you're going to have to figure out how to be in the same room with him."

"How?"

"Beats the hell out of me. Hang in there. Call me later and let me know how it goes."

"Thanks, Milloy."

For a fleeting moment she considered inviting Cristian. He was trained in crowd control and knew how to manage unstable individuals, but she quickly dismissed the idea. Carl wasn't a fan of law enforcement, and Fina didn't want to subject Cristian to a big dose of Elaine. Also, her family would read too much into it if she brought a man other than Milloy over for dinner.

She was on her own.

Ryan, her eldest nephew, opened the door of Scotty and Patty's house and gave Fina a big hug.

So far, so good.

She followed him to the great room, where the kitchen spilled into the family room and informal eating area. Her other nephews, Teddy and Chandler, were setting the table, and their mom, Patty, stood near the stove in conversation with Fina's mother, Elaine.

"Aunt Fina's here," Ryan announced before flopping down onto the couch.

"Hi there," Patty said, giving her a hug.

"Hey," Fina said. She looked at her mother. They were barely on speaking terms since Fina had told her about Rand's abuse of Haley. Elaine didn't believe her, and her denial made Fina's blood boil. "Mom," she said in greeting.

Neither mother nor daughter made a motion to touch, so Fina walked around the large counter and took a seat on a barstool on the other side. Patty gave her a searching look, but Fina shrugged slightly. If Patty thought Fina was going to extend an olive branch to Elaine, she was deluded.

"Where are the guys?" Fina asked.

"In Scotty's office," Patty said.

It always annoyed Fina that the female Ludlows congregated in the kitchen, and the male Ludlows huddled in a home office or living room. Who were they? English gentry at the dawn of the First World War?

Fina slid off the stool and headed out of the room.

"They're discussing work, Fina," her mother said.

"Okay."

"I don't think it concerns you."

Fina stopped and turned toward her mother. "You do realize I work with them, right?"

Elaine sniffed, but didn't respond.

If Elaine had her way, Fina would be married with three children, living in an enormous house in Chestnut Hill. Fina had accepted that her mother's plan for her and her own plans bore no resemblance to each other, but it was her mother's unwillingness to accept reality that was so frustrating. Whether it was Rand's deviance or the fact that Fina drew a paycheck from Ludlow and Associates, Elaine ignored how the world actually was in favor of how she thought it should be.

In his office, Scotty sat behind his curved desk, which was cluttered with papers and files. There were LEGOs on the coffee table by the couch where her father and Rand were sitting. Matthew was leaning against the built-in bookcase. The TV mounted on the wall was tuned to the Bruins game, which they watched intently.

"Hey, sis," Scotty said.

"Hey. What's going on?"

"Just watching the game."

Fina took in the scene. "Right. Mom thinks you're all in here hard at work."

There was no response, their eyes glued to the screen.

"Where's Haley?" Fina asked Scotty, avoiding making eye contact with Rand.

"In her room."

She lingered a few minutes, but it was like watching cavemen study cave paintings—deathly boring, punctuated by grunts.

Fina ventured upstairs to Haley's closed bedroom door. Getting no response from her knock, she opened it slowly and peeked around the door. Her niece was on her bed, earbuds firmly planted.

"Haley!" Fina said, motioning her arms to try to get her attention.

The girl started and popped the tiny speakers from her ears.

"Hi, Aunt Fina."

Fina sat down on the bed next to her. "How's it going?"

Haley shrugged.

"I talked to your dad today," Fina said, brushing hair away from the girl's eyes.

"About me?"

"Kind of. Pap was there, and your dad has been warned to keep his distance from you."

The girl was silent.

"How are you feeling about this?" Fina asked.

Haley reached up and pulled on a strand of blond hair. "I don't know."

Fina knew that ambivalence toward one's abuser was common. The insidious part of abuse was the perfect storm of emotions in which victims were trapped: guilt, love, shame, disgust. No wonder bad choices and self-destructive tendencies were victims' MOs.

"You know what?" Fina said. "Let's get out of here."

Haley's face twisted in a question mark. "What do you mean?"

"I just got the most intense craving for a lobster roll from Kelly's."

The girl glanced toward the door. "Aunt Patty's making dinner."

Fina shrugged. "She'll understand."

"Seriously?"

"Seriously."

Haley hopped off the bed and rummaged through a pile of clothes on the floor before pulling out a fuzzy fleece jacket.

She followed Fina down the stairs, and they'd almost made their escape when Matthew wandered into the front hall. He gave Fina a questioning look.

"We've got to go," she said. "Tell Patty we'll be back in a bit." She gave him a kiss on the cheek.

In the car, Haley turned the radio up and for a moment, Fina saw something unfamiliar on her niece's face.

It was delight.

"What can you tell me about Nadine Quaynor's cause of death?" Fina asked Cristian the next morning. They were meeting in a coffee shop in Cambridge, not far from his son Matteo's preschool.

He sipped his coffee and carefully placed the cup down on the table. "She was poisoned. That's all I can tell you."

"With what?"

"That's all I've got."

"You must have more than that," Fina said, cutting off a corner of omelet. Cristian had ordered for her when she arrived late. The omelet, mixed fruit, and wheat toast weren't terrible, but they weren't a large, gooey cinnamon bun, either. Fina unwrapped a pat of butter and spread it over the toast.

"It's already buttered, you know," Cristian said.

"Barely," Fina said.

He took a bite of toast. "I don't have anything else to give you yet."

"'Yet,' which means you have something," Fina clarified. "You just won't tell me."

Cristian was silent.

"Fine," she said. "I'm not sure why we had to meet only for you to shut me out."

"Because I wanted to see you," he said. "That's what people do when they're dating."

"Right."

Cristian put down his fork. "You know we're dating, right?"

"I know, but you make it sound so serious and exclusive."

"That's something we need to talk about."

Fina shook her head. "Not now. Seriously, I can't have a relation-ship/feelings conversation first thing in the morning."

Cristian put his napkin on the table. "You're sending me mixed signals, Fina."

"That's because I'm mixed up! I think you're underestimating how complicated this will get." She spread the butter more evenly over her toast. "In the past, Cristian, if you didn't give me information, I was annoyed with you and got it someplace else. Now what am I supposed to do? Not be annoyed and not get it someplace else?"

"That's an option."

"I can understand the not being annoyed part, but the other part is asking me to not do my job."

"But what you're doing is probably illegal anyway," he argued.

"You don't know that for sure." She prodded at a piece of apple that was browning in a shallow dish. "But that's the issue: If I'm your girl-friend, suddenly you have a problem with how I do my job."

"I always have a problem with how you do your job."

"Right, but as my friend, you just have to deal with it. I get the feeling that as my boyfriend, you think you'd get a vote."

He looked at her. Cristian was extremely handsome, with caramel-colored skin and thick brown hair. Fina found it distracting when she was trying to make a point.

"Won't I?" he asked.

Her eyes widened. "Ah no. And not just because you're a cop. Boy-friends don't get a vote just because."

"No wonder you're a loner. Do you have any concept of com-promise?"

"I've got an idea: Why don't you stop being a cop, and I'll keep doing my job the way I see fit."

Cristian reached into his jacket and pulled out his wallet.

"Doesn't seem right, does it, when the shoe's on the other foot?" Fina said.

"Except that what I do is legal." He picked out a twenty and put it on the table.

"It's not that black-and-white to me, Cristian."

"Clearly." He pushed back his chair with a scraping sound. "I've got to go."

Fina frowned. "Don't leave mad."

"I don't know what to tell you, Fina. We'll talk later."

She opened her mouth to speak, but didn't know what to say. Fina wasn't going to apologize for her point of view, but she didn't like arguing with him, either. "Fine. We'll continue this later. I think I'm free next year."

"Bye," Cristian said, grabbing his coat from the back of his chair.

"Bye."

What was so great about compromise? The people who heralded it were usually just explaining why they'd settled for something they didn't want.

What was the upside of that?

Fina picked up an angry voice mail from Carl regarding her and Haley's absence from the family dinner. Since he didn't pose any questions in his rant, Fina decided he didn't require a callback. She deleted the message and put the issue aside for the time being.

Next, she put in a call to Stacy D'Ambruzzi, her contact at the medical examiner's office. They arranged to meet in the Common near the Boylston Street T station.

She found Stacy thirty minutes later on a bench under a large oak tree. Fina sat down and handed her a cup of coffee.

"Why are we meeting outside?" Fina asked, sipping her hot chocolate. "It's cold."

"There have been some leaks to the media recently," Stacy said. "I didn't think it was smart to be seen with you too close to the office or anyplace I might bump into my colleagues."

"Fair enough. How have you been?"

Stacy nodded. "I'm good. Really good, actually."

Fina examined her friend's beaming face. "Do tell."

"I met someone." Stacy was extremely pretty, though not in a traditional way. Her hair was cut exceedingly short, her skin littered with tattoos. Stud earrings climbed her lobes. She had a beautiful complexion and bright blue eyes.

"That's fantastic. Tell me about her."

Stacy waxed rhapsodic about the new love in her life, and Fina watched her. Even if her description had been inaudible, it would have been obvious that Stacy was in love. The color in her cheeks, her wide smile and broad gestures said it all.

"But you didn't call me for an update on my love life," Stacy said after a few minutes.

"Alas, I didn't, but I'm happy to hear things are going so well."

"What can I do for you?" A few years earlier, the Ludlows had helped extricate Stacy's brother from a legal scrape, and she was eternally grateful. Fina had made it clear that they were always available to help, and in turn, Stacy had provided good intel on a number of occasions.

"Nadine Quaynor. I know she died from poison, but I'd love to get more details."

Stacy grinned. "Menendez not being cooperative?"

"Not really."

"As always, you didn't hear this from me, and you can't be spreading it around. If it gets traced back to me, I'll be in big trouble."

"Understood."

An older Asian man took a seat on the bench across from them and pulled a plastic bag out of his rolling cart. He sprinkled some kind of seed on the wide, paved pathway, and a flock of pigeons magically appeared.

"Why do people feed these birds?" Fina asked. "They're dirty, and they shit all over everything."

"Not a nature lover?" Stacy asked.

"Just choosy about the nature I love. They are literally the bottom-feeders of the bird world. Anyhoo, we were talking about Nadine."

"It looks like antifreeze poisoning."

Fina slowly rotated her cup in an effort to distribute the chocolate more evenly. "That seems to be an increasingly popular murder weapon these days. Why is that?"

"It's a combination of things: It's easy to purchase; it tastes good so victims don't notice; you can administer it over time so it looks like the victim is eventually succumbing to an illness, or all at once. Either way, the death appears natural, unless you know what to test for."

"And you guys knew what to test for?"

"Nadine was young, and except for her recent illness, she was very healthy. Young people in good health generally don't just keel over."

"Any idea how it was administered to her?" Fina asked.

"There's no way to tell through an autopsy, but Gatorade or a sports drink would do the job, even coffee." Stacy held up her cup. "If you like your cup of joe on the sweet side, you'd be none the wiser."

Fina sipped her hot chocolate, hoping that Rand never caught wind of the murderous virtues of antifreeze.

"Manufacturers are starting to use additives that make it taste nasty," Stacy said, "but that's mostly for the protection of children and pets, not potential murder victims."

"Has her body been released yet?"

"Yeah. The funeral home got it this morning."

The old man tired of the feeding frenzy he'd created and ambled down the walk. A smattering of pigeons remained in his wake, pecking at the pavement.

"That's all I've got," Stacy said. "I'm not sure it's helpful."

Fina shrugged. "It's information, which is good. Unfortunately, it doesn't narrow the suspect field much. I'm looking for somebody who had access to antifreeze—which is everybody—and somebody who had access to Nadine, which is everybody who had access to Nadine."

Stacy smiled. "Sorry. I wish I could tell you it was Mrs. Peacock in the lounge with the revolver."

"You and me both."

They walked out of the park and hugged at the corner.

"How's your brother doing?" Fina asked.

"Staying out of trouble, thank God."

"Well, if that ever changes, give me a call."

"Thanks, Fina. I'll let you know if I hear anything new on the case."

Poisoning someone with antifreeze didn't require special access or a special set of skills, but it did require something possessed by few people: slow-burning rage, cold calculation, and no qualms about taking a life.

Fina arrived at the Renard home and was ushered into the same room in which the case had started just one week earlier.

A small fire danced in the fireplace, and Fina stood, rubbing her hands together in its warmth.

"I'm sorry to keep you waiting yet again," Ceci said when she entered the room five minutes later.

"It's a lovely place to wait," Fina said.

Ceci was dressed in her usual style of rich casual, a style that can only be achieved with thousands of dollars. She wore gray pants with a silk blouse and a zippered knit cardigan cut on the bias.

"Iris is bringing tea," she said, beckoning Fina to the sofa.

"Have you spoken with Chloe recently? The past day or so?" Fina asked.

"No." A look of concern crossed Ceci's face. "Why? Has something happened?"

"The woman she asked me to contact, Nadine—she died."

Ceci looked alarmed. "What happened?"

A maid tapped on the door and brought in a tray with a silver tea service. When she left, Ceci busied herself pouring two cups and offering a plate of mini pastries to Fina.

"I found her," Fina said. "I stopped by her house not long after our lunch at the Gardner, and she was dead."

"I'm surprised Chloe didn't tell me."

"She's probably still processing it. She seemed shocked when I told her."

"You said you found her at her house. What happened?"

Fina slowly stirred sugar into her tea. "According to the cops, she was poisoned."

Ceci put down her cup and stared at Fina. "I don't understand."

"It's not clear yet if it was accidental or malicious, but Nadine didn't die of natural causes."

Ceci's hand moved to her mouth, as if to keep a response from spilling out.

"Obviously, the police are working on the case," Fina said, "and if you're amenable, I think that I should dig around a bit."

Ceci's brow creased. "Are you suggesting her death has something to do with the church?"

"I'd like to know what happened, and maybe I'll find something that will have an impact on Chloe's donation."

"I don't like the idea of using this woman's death for my own purposes," Ceci said, running her hand down the armrest of the couch.

Fina took a deep breath. "There's something going on here, Ceci, and it's in Chloe's best interest to know what that is. Hopefully, Nadine's death has nothing to do with the church, and we'll be left with our original problem."

Ceci looked out the window. The grass that had recently been revealed by the melting snow was yellow and flat. "Fine. How much more do you need for your retainer?" She glanced around as if looking for her purse.

"Don't worry about that. I spoke to my father, and he said it's taken care of."

"Fina, I can't accept charity from your family. Clearly, I don't need it." She swept her arm around the room.

"You two will have to work that out," Fina said. "You should be flattered; my father rarely gives things to people." Or at least not without there being strings attached.

"Carl always seemed very generous to me."

Fina grinned. "Well, I suspect we see different sides of him. I'll be in touch when I have an update."

"How is your mother?" Ceci asked at the front door. She stood before a large painting showing a threatening sky dominated by storm clouds. It seemed like an appropriate backdrop for the question.

"She's fine. I didn't realize you two knew each other."

"Not well, but we bump into each other on occasion." Ceci fiddled with her thick wedding band.

"She's the way she always is," Fina said ruefully. "She's Elaine."

"Well, she hasn't had an easy time of it," Ceci said.

Fina looked at her.

"Your sister-in-law's death, and of course, your sister's."

Fina had had an older sister who died before Fina was born. Josie—Josephine, for whom she was named—had been a toddler when she was struck by a lethal strain of strep. It was a crucial piece of the Ludlow history, but as is too often the case in families, rarely discussed.

"I suppose. Thanks for the tea."

"Thank you for your help, Fina. I'm going to call Chloe right now."

In the car, Fina pondered her mother's history. Sometimes she wondered if her sister's death had changed her mother, but she tried not to dwell on the idea. After all, what was the point? Whether Elaine had been mother of the year before Josie's death or always the current iteration, it made no difference.

She was the only mother Fina had.

NINE

Christa moved her foot over the pedal to rewind the audio. She stared at the blank wall in front of her and listened to the foreign accent.

"The nucleus was hydrodelineated and hydrodissected with balanced salt solution on a 26 gauge cannula, and the phacoemulsifier was used to phacoemulsify the nucleus using a bimanual technique..."

Phacoemulsify. That's what it was. *Phacoemulsify* always tripped her up, which was ridiculous since she'd heard it countless times. She finished the section and pulled the headphones off. Even though they were expensive, they still made her ears feel sore and hot if she wore them for long stretches.

Christa stood up and raised her arms over her head, reaching for the ceiling. The doorbell chimed. She reached for her toes, and it rang again.

"One sec," she called, padding to the front door and peering into the peephole. A man and a woman stood on the front step. They didn't look threatening, nor did they look like Jehovah's Witnesses.

"Who is it?"

"Boston Police Department, ma'am," the woman answered. "I'm happy to pass you my badge."

Christa unlocked and opened the door. The woman offered her badge, which Christa took, not really knowing what to look for. She'd heard you could call the precinct and ask for verification of the badge number, but she didn't have time for that. She'd take her chances that they weren't a pair of serial killers.

"What can I do for you?"

"Are you Christa Jackson?" the man asked.

"Yes."

"We'd like to speak with you about your cousin, Nadine Quaynor."

"What about her?"

"I'm Detective Menendez, and this is Lieutenant Pitney," he said. "Can we come in? It's better we discuss this inside."

Christa's stomach flip-flopped. "Sure. Come on in."

The cops followed her into the family room, which was crowded with too much oversized furniture. Christa tossed a pair of hot-pink pom-poms off the couch and pushed a large stuffed walrus out of the way with her foot. "I was just getting some coffee. Do you want a cup?" The offer was less gracious than it seemed; Christa was desperate to get some caffeine in her system.

"If it isn't any trouble," Cristian said.

"Yes, thanks," Pitney added.

Christa filled three cups at the coffeemaker and put them on a tray with milk and sugar. She rooted around in the pantry until she found an Entenmann's crumb coffee cake, which she cut into slices and plated. In the family room, she took a seat in the recliner while they doctored their drinks.

"We're very sorry about your cousin's death. Please accept our condolences," Pitney said after taking a sip of coffee. Her hair was curly and copper-colored, and her nails were painted a deep red, like the cherry you find under a robe of chocolate.

"Thank you. I still can't believe it."

Cristian took out a small recording device and held it up to her. "Do you mind if we record this?"

Christa hesitated. "No, that's fine."

He turned on the digital recorder, stated the date, time, and names of those present. He asked Christa to confirm that she agreed to the recording, which she did.

No one spoke for a minute.

"Were you and your cousin close?" Pitney asked.

"Have you released her body?" Christa asked in reply.

The cops exchanged glances. "Yes," Cristian said. "The funeral home should have it."

"Good. Her husband was upset when we went to make the funeral arrangements, and she wasn't there."

He nodded. "Someone should have contacted you from the ME's office."

"Yeah, well, someone didn't."

"Our apologies," Pitney said. "I know this is hard, but we have to ask questions in order to determine exactly what happened to Nadine."

"What do you mean?" Christa asked.

"Have you spoken with Evan today?" Pitney took a bite of the coffee cake, crumbs spilling down her front and settling on her bosom.

"No."

"We believe that your cousin didn't die from natural causes," Cristian said, watching her.

Christa looked at him. He was extremely handsome, like an actor who might play a cop on TV. "What are you talking about?"

"Her death was unnatural," Pitney said.

Christa put down her coffee cup and uncrossed her legs.

"What are you saying?"

"We believe someone poisoned her," the lieutenant continued.

"What? Somebody must have made a mistake," Christa said, sitting back in the recliner, like an important matter had just been settled.

"There's no mistake," Pitney said. "That's why we wanted to ask you some questions."

"How was she poisoned?" Christa asked.

Cristian started to explain, but she only caught certain words. Her mind didn't so much drift as fail to compute, like he was speaking a foreign language that was completely unfamiliar to her ear.

"Do you know of anyone who wanted to hurt Nadine?" he asked.

"No, of course not."

"Was she afraid of anyone or have a conflict of some sort?" Pitney asked, picking up the thread.

"Not enough to kill her. She was a churchgoing accountant for Christ's sake."

"Unfortunately, anyone can become a victim under the right cir- cumstances," Pitney said.

Christa shook her head. "I can't imagine what those circumstances might be."

"So were you and your cousin close?" Pitney asked again.

"Yes. We grew up together."

"What sort of things did you do together?" Cristian asked.

"Lots of family gatherings, and sometimes she would come to my daughters' events. We were both very busy, though."

"But you got along?"

Christa looked askance at him. "Yes. Why would you think other- wise?"

"We'd heard that you'd had a bit of a falling-out."

"Who told you that?"

"That's not important," Pitney said.

Christa smirked. "Let me guess: my aunt. She always blows things out of proportion."

"So you and Nadine didn't have a falling-out?" Cristian looked at her.

"We're cousins. We've known each other since we were little girls. Occasionally, we argued."

"About?"

She held up her hands. "I don't know. It was probably something related to parenting. Ever since she married Evan and became a stepmother, Nadine thought she knew best about all things child-related. I've got three kids of my own. I do know a thing or two."

Cristian nodded. "It's irritating when other people tell you how to parent."

"And God forbid she take any advice from me." The detectives exchanged a look, and Christa backpedaled. "But it was all good. Nadine and I were good." She picked at something crusty on the armrest with her fingernail.

Cristian reached for his coffee and brought it to his lips.

"We understand that she and her husband were separated," Pitney ventured.

"Uh-huh."

"Do you think they were going to get a divorce?"

"You'd have to ask Evan that."

Pitney broke off a piece of coffee cake. "We did. We're interested in your opinion."

"I know Evan was hopeful they'd get back together, but he wanted Nadine to leave the church, or at the very least, be less involved. I don't think that was going to happen."

"You're referring to Covenant Rising?"

"Yes."

"You thought she would choose the church over Evan and her stepdaughter?" Cristian asked.

"She already had, but she didn't talk to me about her marriage."

"I never understand when people choose an organization over family," Pitney mused.

"If the organization promises you eternal life, and you believe in that hooey, I bet you'd find it pretty compelling," Christa said.

"I suppose."

"Obviously, you don't like the church," Cristian said. He'd hardly touched his coffee cake, and Christa saw Pitney eyeing it.

"I don't share their particular beliefs, and I think the pastor is sleazy."

"Pastor Greg?" Cristian asked.

"Yes, Pastor Greg and his perky wife, Gabby."

"Why sleazy, exactly?" Pitney chimed in.

"He's fake, like a used-car salesman, and he's always asking for money."

"That's true of most churches," the lieutenant said.

"But it's different if the church has been around forever. This place is younger than a couple of my kids. It seems more like a business than a nonprofit."

Pitney put down her coffee mug and placed her hands on her knees. "Is there anything else you can think of that might be relevant?"

"Have you talked to her colleagues? There was one guy in her department she really disliked."

"We're looking into her work situation," Pitney said, starting to stand.

"You never said what kind of poison," Christa commented.

The lieutenant lowered herself back to the couch. "Antifreeze."

"How do you poison someone with antifreeze?"

"You put it in their drink." Pitney gestured to her cup. "Coffee, for instance."

Christa swallowed.

"Do you have any?" Menendez asked. "Antifreeze," he added when Christa looked confused.

"I have no idea. My husband would know."

"Do you mind if we take a look around?" he asked.

Christa rose from her chair. "I do mind. I've got nothing to hide, but I'm not comfortable having you snoop around my home."

Pitney stood. "Suit yourself. I think you should let us look, but we can come back."

Cristian started gathering the plates and cups.

"You can leave those, Detective," Christa said.

"You sure?" He gave her a wide smile, which showed off his straight, white teeth.

"I'm sure."

At the front door, they each handed Christa a card.

"We'll be in touch," Pitney said.

Christa closed the door behind them and stood for a moment with their cards in her hand.

She probably should have just let them look, but it wasn't her job to make their jobs easier.

Fina needed to speak with Chloe to alert her to her new task and possibly glean more information. She called her, and they agreed to meet at the nursing home in Cambridge where Chloe was spending the day.

Hidden Forest was a rehab and nursing facility near Fresh Pond. Given that the facility was neither hidden nor in a forest, Fina thought the developers must have had an odd sense of humor. Located just off the parkway, it was a four-story building with two wings and a large circular drive in front. Fina found a visitor parking spot and entered through the glass double doors. The man behind the reception desk was having a heated exchange with a woman who Fina assumed was a resident.

"Mrs. Markey, you have to leave that plant where it is!"

The older woman was grasping a potted fern and starting down the hallway with it.

"They told me I could take it," the elderly woman replied, her expression a mixture of ignorance and defiance.

"Who told you?"

"The nurses."

Fina glanced between the two of them. The man exhaled in frustration. "Can I help you?"

"I'm here to see Chloe Renard."

"She's in the art room." The phone rang on the desk. "Down that hallway to the right," he said, dismissing her.

Mrs. Markey tucked the plant under her arm and went in the direction that the receptionist had indicated. Fina trailed behind her and peeked in when the elderly woman ducked into a room a few doors down. A TV was blaring, and another old woman sat in a chair, staring at it.

"Mary! Look what I brought you," Mrs. Markey declared.

How sweet. Hidden Forest had its own Robin Hood.

Fina found Chloe in an activities room at the end of the hall. There was an upright piano and a sitting area on one side of the room. The other side was filled with folding tables, each with two chairs. Another table held stacks of art supplies. Chloe stood, sorting through a pile of paper.

Fina leaned against one of the tables. "Hi."

"Hi. That was fast."

"I have a lead foot. It's a genetic condition."

Chloe glanced at a large wall clock. "Good, because I don't have much time before my painting class begins."

"I'll be quick. How are you?"

"I'm okay."

Fina smiled. "Care to elaborate?"

"Obviously, I'm upset, but it's not like Nadine was my best friend.

It doesn't seem right to be *too* upset. I don't want to be an emotional vampire. You know, one of those people who makes someone else's tragedy all about them."

"Sure, but even if you weren't close, it's disturbing when someone you know and like dies."

Chloe nodded. "It is. I still can't believe it."

"It may take a while to sink in."

"My mother just left a message checking in with me."

"She was very concerned when I told her about Nadine," Fina said.

Chloe handed her a box of watercolor tubes. "Do you mind?"

"Not at all." Fina began to distribute a few tubes to each seat. "How much do you know about the cause of Nadine's death?"

"Just what you've told me."

Chloe followed behind Fina, doling out paper and brushes.

"Well, it appears that Nadine's death wasn't from natural causes."

"What do you mean?"

"The medical examiner thinks she was poisoned, and the police are investigating."

Chloe stopped what she was doing and dropped into a chair. She closed her eyes.

"I'm going to look into her death, too," Fina said.

"Why?"

"You don't want me to?"

Chloe looked at her. "Obviously, whoever hurt Nadine should be caught, but are you only investigating so you can sully the church?"

Fina shook her head. "No. I'm investigating because that's what I do, Chloe, and getting the facts might put your mind at ease. If the church is involved, you should know that, and if the church isn't involved, then that's wonderful news."

Chloe stood and resumed her task, dropping the materials down on the tables with a succession of loud thumps. "The church isn't involved."

"I don't mean that the church was involved in a conspiracy to kill," Fina clarified. "I'm talking about making sure that Nadine's death has no connection to the church, even tangentially."

"I know what you mean," Chloe said. "I would never be involved with an organization that had something to do with someone's death."

Fina sighed. "I just said that I don't think the church is involved, but don't you want to know if a *member* of the church is?"

Chloe squeezed her fists by her side. "People do all kinds of terrible things that have nothing to do with their affiliations."

"Agreed, but that's information that should be acquired and evaluated, not ignored."

A pair of elderly women tottered into the room and exchanged pleasantries with Chloe. Fina smiled at them as they claimed spaces at a table.

"My class is about to start."

"Okay. Can you give me the names and contact info for the other members of the church's leadership committee, in addition to Nadine and Lucas Chellew?"

"How can they help?"

"I don't know, but I think it's worth speaking to them."

Chloe pulled out her phone and tapped the screen. "I have the contact lists for the various church committees in my e-mail. I'm sending it to you right now."

Fina pulled out her phone and waited impatiently for her e-mail to sync. She would not have done well in the era of smoke signals or the pony express.

"Got it. Anyone you suggest I start with?"

"Maybe Mary Boudreau or Donna Anderson. Kyle Roady isn't in the church anymore. I think he moved, so he won't be able to help."

"Great. I'll get on it." She started for the door.

"Fina," Chloe called to her. "Of course I want to know what happened to Nadine. I'm just . . ."

"Conflicted," Fina offered. "Don't worry. I get it."

Fina didn't know what she would uncover about Nadine's death and the church's possible involvement, but she knew that even if Ceci had pulled the plug on the investigation, she would keep digging.

The more people tried to warn her off, the more intrigued she became.

Given how much time people spent working, it was an obvious next step to see where Nadine Quaynor worked. In the modern age, people took it for granted that they spent hours each day toiling beside relative strangers, with whom the only points of intersection were an interest in fruit flies or health benefits or, in the case of Nadine, accounting principles. That didn't mean that people didn't genuinely like their coworkers, but Fina was always struck by how much personal satisfaction rode on the fragile web of a shared workplace.

Williams & Lewiston had a stellar reputation in the field of accounting, and Nadine's employment there suggested she was good at her job.

Oftentimes when visiting a more formal work environment, Fina dressed up to fit in, but she also occasionally found it useful to stand out and create a small ripple in a more conservative setting. She always looked put-together—there was no payoff to looking homeless—but her jeans and hoop earrings made her harder to ignore. Buttoned-up receptionists were usually anxious to move her along, which is how she came to be seated across from Monica Zafira, Nadine's boss.

Monica was a black woman in her forties with cropped hair, wearing a smartly tailored suit. A thin gold chain boasting a monogrammed charm the size of a quarter hung around her neck. It was her only jewelry except for a watch with a rectangular face. Her nails were short but shiny, as if they'd been given attention but weren't meant to draw attention.

"What can I do for you, Ms. Ludlow?" Monica asked, returning Fina's PI license.

"Call me Fina. I'm investigating the death of Nadine Quaynor."

Monica nodded. "In addition to the police?"

"Yes, but I'm coordinating with them."

"I'm surprised Nadine's family has hired a private investigator. I only met her parents once, but they didn't seem like the type."

"What type did they seem like?" Fina unscrewed the top of the water bottle that Monica had given her. She didn't correct the woman's assumption that Nadine's parents were footing the bill.

"Like I said, I don't know them, but I had the sense that they tended to roll with things."

"That's certainly not the impression I've gotten of Nadine," Fina said. "It would seem the apple fell far from the tree."

"My sense was that they were quite different," Monica said. "Nadine was as you would expect an accountant to be: organized and detail-oriented."

"Was Nadine having any trouble that you knew of?"

Monica shook her head. "No, and I would know about anything going on in the office. I keep a close eye on my team."

Fina didn't doubt it and thought Monica's office space reflected her no-nonsense approach. There were no personal touches, but a couple of framed paintings provided some warmth. A rich berry-colored pashmina rested on the back of her chair, suggesting that she too got cold in her office, like every woman Fina had ever met. Monica was human, but Fina didn't think she tolerated a lot of bullshit.

"Was Nadine a good employee?"

"She was excellent. Extremely thorough and conscientious. That's not to say that she was infallible, but I was very pleased with her performance."

"And when she was fallible? What did that look like?"

Monica tapped the floor with her toe so that her chair rotated slightly. "Occasionally, I had to coach her about the best way to effect change with her colleagues."

"She didn't play well with others?"

Monica took a moment before speaking. "Nadine was an asset to any team she joined, but sometimes she rubbed people the wrong way. She didn't always couch her concerns in the most productive terms."

"But she was amenable to your coaching?"

"She was. I think she had a very bright future at the firm. It's extremely sad."

Fina nodded. "It is. She was young and hadn't been married long. Did you ever meet her husband?"

Monica thought for a moment. "Just once at a company picnic. He seemed like a nice man, and her stepdaughter was cute."

"I've been told that Nadine was unwell in the months leading up to her death. Did that affect her work performance?"

"She took a couple of sick days, but nothing out of the ordinary." Monica folded her hands on her desk. "She was the kind of employee who would meet her deadlines even if she took time off. I never worried about her productivity."

"So you can't think of anyone at work who would want to harm her?"

"I really can't, and I would tell you if I could."

Fina smiled and rose from her seat. "I'm quite sure you would. You seem like someone who doesn't brook a lot of bull."

Monica smiled. "I like to get the job done."

"You and me both. Thanks for speaking with me."

"Of course. Let me know if you need anything else."

On the way out of Williams & Lewiston, Fina stopped in the ladies' room and loitered by the elevator in an effort to gather any dirt. She chatted with a few people, but none of them had much to say about Nadine.

You might die of boredom at the accounting firm, but Fina thought that was as dangerous as it got.

TEN

Conducting a death investigation required tact and sensitivity, particularly when the family of the deceased weren't the ones who'd hired you. When Fina approached grieving family members for interviews, she usually got one of two responses: either disgust that she was asking, or a warm welcome. An interview with Fina gave family members an opportunity to discuss their loved one in depth, something they were often eager to do, which is why you often saw distraught loved ones doing TV interviews. Talking about the deceased kept them alive.

Nadine's parents seemed to fall into the first category, and Fina left them a message. She was able to get Nadine's estranged husband on the phone, however, and set an appointment for later that afternoon.

With time on her hands, Fina checked in with Scotty, who confirmed that the real estate agent she'd found online bore a strong resemblance to the Lindsay Kaufman he remembered from college. He couldn't guarantee they were one and the same, but Fina could live with a likely ID.

S. Mullins Real Estate was a small firm that specialized in high-end listings in Boston, Brookline, and Cambridge. Fina knew it was dicey showing up unannounced—agents were often out showing properties—but she didn't want to schedule an appointment, for fear it was a nonstarter. If she used her own name, Lindsay probably wouldn't meet with her, and arranging a get-together under false pretenses would probably backfire once the woman cottoned to Fina's subterfuge.

The office was located in the basement storefront of a brownstone straddling Back Bay and the South End. The space offered a small reception area furnished with a love seat and a matching chair in a tonal paisley pattern, anchored by a dark wood coffee table festooned with home decorating magazines. A receptionist's desk faced the area and acted as a sentry to the six desks behind it.

"May I help you?" the young man behind the desk asked. He was wearing an earpiece and held up a finger when Fina began to talk. Apparently, he wasn't speaking to her. Fina gazed at the occupants of the desks, but none looked like her target.

"Uh-huh. Uh-huh. One moment, and I'll transfer your call." His fingers scattered across the touch pad of a sophisticated-looking phone, and then he smiled at Fina.

"Can I help you?" he asked.

"Yes. I'm here to see Lindsay. Is she in?"

He whirled around in his chair. "She was just here a minute ago. Let me go find her." The phone rang as he walked toward the back of the room, and Fina watched him depress a button on his earpiece to pick up the call. Four of the desks were unoccupied, but a man and a woman were planted behind two of the others. The woman was wearing bright red lipstick that made her lips practically pop off her face.

The receptionist returned to his post a moment later, followed by Lindsay Kaufman Shaunnesy. She extended her hand and introduced herself, which Fina did in kind, but omitted her last name.

"What can I do for you today?" Lindsay asked, leading Fina to her desk, where they each took a seat. Lindsay had blond hair cut into a pixie, a style that Fina always considered during the humid summer months. Tortoiseshell glasses framed her blue eyes, which were edged with liner.

Fina drew her chair closer to the desk. "It's actually a delicate matter."

"Okay." Lindsay looked confused, but kept smiling.

"It's not really related to real estate."

"What is it related to?"

"It's related to my brother Rand Ludlow."

Lindsay's smile melted from her face. "There's a conference room," she said stiffly, pushing back from her desk.

Fina followed her to a subterranean space that was windowless and cold compared to the outer office. Lindsay closed the door, but remained standing.

"I'm sorry to just show up like this," Fina said.

Lindsay shook her head and glared at her.

"Listen. Whatever you said my brother did in college, I believe you."

"What are you talking about?" Lindsay asked.

"I'm not here to question you or defend my brother. I'm here because I believe you, and I need more information."

She looked at Fina and then dropped into a chair. "Why do you need more information?"

Fina sat down across from her. "I'm trying to stop him from hurting more women."

"Good luck. It didn't matter twenty-five years ago. Why would it matter now?"

"It does matter."

Lindsay picked at a cuticle on her hand.

"I gather things weren't handled well when you were in college," Fina continued, "but—"

"Handled well?" Lindsay leaned across the table. "Are you kidding? I was treated like a liar. I was shamed and humiliated. Even my parents told me to forget what happened and move on."

"Your parents didn't believe you?"

"Believing me had nothing to do with it. They weren't going to take on your family. I was the one who was tainted, not your brother."

"I'm sorry."

"You should be. Your family . . ." Lindsay stilled one shaking hand with the other. "You just covered for him."

Fina was silent. She had no response to an accusation she now knew to be true.

"And nothing has changed," Lindsay continued. "Have you picked up a newspaper recently? They're never punished. They just explain it all away."

Fina didn't have to ask who "they" were. She knew. They were men who abused women and children. Husbands, professional athletes, fathers, doctors, priests. Women had made a lot of progress over the years, but they were still treated as less than.

"I know, but I'm trying to stop my brother, Lindsay. I'm trying."

"Again, so what? You want a prize for doing the right thing?"

"No, of course not, and I have no right to ask you for anything, but I can't stop him on my own. I need your help."

"There's nothing I can do."

"You can tell me if there were other victims at school. You can tell me their names."

"So you can show up unannounced at their workplaces and dredge up the past? And the statute of limitations ran out a long time ago. What's the point?"

Fina took a deep breath. "I'm trying to build a case against my brother."

"A legal case?"

"I don't know yet." Fina didn't want to make a promise she couldn't keep, and she wasn't sure whether her father or the DA would be the recipient of her findings. She was walking a very fine line: One step in the wrong direction might destroy the rest of the Ludlows, the very people she was working so hard to protect.

"I know it's too little, too late, but I'm here now, and I believe you."
Lindsay got up and left the room.

Fina waited, contemplating whether the meeting was over. She knew getting Lindsay to tell her about the attack was a long shot, but she also knew that an attentive listener was what most victims wanted. Being heard didn't make up for trauma by any stretch of the imagination, but it was a step in the right direction.

Five minutes later Lindsay returned with a drink and took her seat. Her face was blotchy, and her lipstick had faded.

"You can't take notes or record this," she said, sipping from a mug emblazoned with the BOSTON STRONG logo. "And I'm going to deny that we had this conversation."

"I understand." Fina pulled herself closer to the table. "Start at the beginning."

Fina's conversation with Lindsay left her drained, craving some kind of release, but there was more work to be done. So instead of calling Cristian or Milloy, she made the drive to Evan Quaynor's apartment.

A new-construction mid-rise between the Pike and Route 9 in Natick, its location was ideal for commuting, but it was so characterless it could have been in Dallas or Raleigh or Tacoma. Fina parked in the visitor parking lot and circumvented the large fenced-in pool area. She called Evan's unit from the touch pad in the lobby and was immediately buzzed in.

The man who opened the door of number 413 was close to Fina's age, but looked tired, his eyelids droopy.

"Evan?"

He nodded.

"Fina Ludlow." She offered him her ID. "I'm so sorry about Nadine."

Evan motioned her in. "Thanks."

Fina stepped directly into the kitchen, which flowed into the living room. A little girl was sitting at the granite breakfast bar with what looked like the remains of dinner. There was a lone chicken nugget and a few baby carrots on a plate. A half-filled glass of milk was next to it.

"I'm sorry," Fina said. "I didn't realize you were eating."

"Molly was just finishing. Let me get her settled, and then we can talk. Why don't you sit?"

Fina moved into the living room and took a seat on the couch.

"You finished, Mol?" Evan asked the girl, who looked to be about five.

She nodded, and he put the plate and glass in the sink. "You want to watch some TV in the bedroom?"

"Yes!" She jumped off her stool and hopscotched into the other room.

"Give me a minute," Evan said to Fina, following the child.

Fina sized up the place. It looked like a high-end corporate unit with nice finishes and few personal touches. Fina would bet money that the unit came furnished; all the furniture was dark wood with metal accents, and the prints on the wall were bland, but perfectly sized for the space. There were pillar candles on a side table that had never seen a match and abstract sculptures vaguely resembling elephants. Fina could see a bedroom through one doorway and a bathroom through another.

She poked a finger at the papers on the large, round coffee table. There was a stack of coloring books, a *Boston Globe*, and some folders with labels like "cruise port" and "shipping terminal."

A rousing sound track started up in the next room. Fina leaned back on the couch and pretended to be admiring the neutral, coma-inducing color palette.

"Want some wine?" Evan asked Fina.

"Sure."

"Is red okay?"

"Works for me."

He uncorked a bottle and brought it over with two glasses. "What kind of a name is Fina?"

"It's short for Josefina."

Evan took a seat on the other end of the couch. "Sounds Spanish."

"Nah. I was named after someone named Josephine." Someone of her own generation, which was weird and kind of creepy, hence the reason that Fina stuck with her nickname. Nobody needed to be reminded of their dead namesake on a regular basis.

"I've already talked to the cops. Are you working with them?" Evan asked. "I didn't completely follow what you said on the phone."

"Not with them exactly. I was hired to do some background on Covenant Rising Church, and I tried to connect with Nadine during the course of that investigation. My client has asked me to continue gathering information."

"What kind of information?" He took a long drink.

"Financial mostly. It's related to a possible bequest to the church."

Evan shook his head. "I don't know what it is about that guy that makes everyone want to give him their money."

"Are you talking about Pastor Greg?"

"Yeah. Those church people fall all over themselves to hand over their cash."

"So you're not a fan of Covenant Rising?"

"No. I am definitely not a fan."

"Was that the reason you and Nadine split up?"

Evan kneaded his neck with one hand. "I still don't get what my wife has to do with your client."

Fina took a sip and put her glass down on the coffee table. "It may not have anything to do with the church, but as you can imagine, a suspicious death has made my client skittish. She doesn't want to make a donation until she's sure that the church isn't going to be embroiled in some kind of scandal," Fina said, treating the truth like saltwater taffy.

"You think someone in the church did this to Nadine?"

"I have no idea, but if they did, don't you want them to be punished?"

Evan held his wineglass by the stem and tipped it back and forth. "Of course. As far as I'm concerned, they should be punished even if they had nothing to do with Nadine's death."

"Because they caused problems in your marriage?" Fina ventured once more.

"Because they convinced my wife that her future was with them, not with me and Molly."

"That's a serious allegation."

Evan held up his free hand. "Look where we are. Molly and I didn't move out because we wanted a change of scene." He leaned toward Fina and lowered his voice. "The whole thing was seriously fucked up."

"Was Nadine involved in the church before you got married?"

"Yes, but not to the extent that she is now." He swallowed. "The extent she was."

"So it wasn't a problem initially?"

"No. I was raised in the Methodist church, and I admired her religious commitment, but it got to be too much."

"In what way?"

"Every free moment was spent doing church activities, and she wanted Molly to join the youth group and go on trips with them."

"Is Molly's mom in the picture?" Fina asked.

Evan shook his head. "She lives in California. She wasn't really cut out for motherhood, and she only sees Molly a couple of times a year."

"But you didn't want Molly to get more involved in the church?"

"No. They treat women like second-class citizens. I didn't want her thinking that was okay."

"Daddy!" Molly hollered from the bedroom. "It stopped working!"

"I'm coming." Evan left and came back a minute later, the peppy music from the next room indicating that the problem had been solved.

"Why do you think Nadine bought into the 'women as second-class citizens' thing?" Fina asked. "It doesn't really jibe with what I've learned about her."

"I don't think she really did, but she was willing to overlook it. Nadine liked order. She liked clarity, and the church was a part of her life where she didn't have to be in charge, but someone else was. Have you met her parents?"

"Not yet."

"They're nice people, but parenting was a loose concept to them. Nadine kind of raised herself. I think she liked having a strict doctrine that had clear rules and expectations."

"So when she started pulling Molly into stuff, that's when the problems started?"

The expression that spread across Evan's face resembled a sneer, a facial manifestation of bitterness. "It was that and the money. Nadine did pretty well, largely because she's made a lot of smart investments, and she kept giving them money. As far as I was concerned, our first priority was Molly, particularly her education. Any extra was for her college fund."

"Do you think Nadine had an issue because Molly wasn't her biological child?" Fina asked.

Evan drained his glass and refilled it. "No. I think she would have been the same with any kids we had together. She thought supporting the church *was* supporting the family—that our spiritual growth and salvation were being ensured that way."

He held the bottle out to Fina.

"No, thanks. I'm good. How long had you two been married?"

"A year and a half. We were together for a year before that."

"Did Nadine buy the house before you married?"

"Yeah, before we met. I didn't move in until we got married. She didn't want to live in sin."

"I know this is painful to discuss, but were you and Nadine planning to divorce?"

He looked down at his glass. When Evan raised his eyes, there were tears in them. "My hope was that we'd figure things out. That this would just be a bump in the road."

"Was that a hope that Nadine shared?" Fina asked.

Evan slowly raised his shoulders as if the shrug required almost more effort than he could muster. "I don't know."

In the other room, animals were breaking into song. It provided an incongruous sound track to their serious conversation.

"So will you and Molly move back there now?"

"That's the plan. It's a great neighborhood with tons of kids."

"I met your neighbor Ronnie McCaffrey the other day," Fina said, leaving out the particulars of their introduction.

"Ronnie is great. So is his wife, Mary. You couldn't ask for a better neighborhood for kids. There's always someone for Molly to play with, and they do all kinds of holiday celebrations. Halloween was insane. I've never seen anything like it before."

"Your daughter must miss it."

"We both do."

Fina took a sip. "Does Molly know that Nadine is dead?"

"I told her, but I don't think she really gets it."

Fina nodded.

"I loved my wife, but if I could have predicted this church disaster, I would have thought long and hard about marrying her. It's not fair to Molly to bring someone into her life, only to have her disappear."

"But you couldn't have predicted the future," Fina said. "You couldn't have known how committed to the church Nadine would become."

He shook his head. "But we had a plan. We got married. We were going to have a baby, a sibling for Molly."

"You know what they say about plans." Fina tipped back her glass and the last drip trickled into her mouth.

"I guess."

"Can you think of anyone who wanted to hurt Nadine?"

"No. The only source of conflict in her life was CRC."

In theory, people assumed that murder victims were society's outliers, living scandalous lives fraught with danger. But Fina knew that the usual motivations for murder—love and money—played a role in everyone's lives. Many of the victims she'd encountered had the most benign profiles on paper, but that didn't make them immune to the dark forces in other people.

Evan grasped the stem of his glass tightly. "I don't like the church, and murder seems a stretch, even for them, but everyone else she knows is even less likely to be involved."

"Maybe," Fina said, "but everyone needs to be looked at: family, colleagues, neighbors. They all have to be considered."

He shook his head. "Occam's razor. The most obvious explanation is usually the correct explanation. You should focus on the church."

"Occam's razor assumes access to all the information, that you're seeing the whole picture. I need to look at all the possibilities before I decide which explanation is, in fact, the most obvious," Fina said.

"It's a waste of time."

"Such is investigative work. You don't know what you'll find until you find it." Fina stood and carried her glass over to the sink. "Who else do you think I should talk to about Nadine?"

Evan poured more wine into his glass.

"You're not driving tonight, right?" Fina asked with a smile.

"No. We're staying in, and I would never put my daughter in jeopardy."

"Just asking."

"You should talk to Nadine's parents," he said, "and her cousin, Christa Jackson."

Fina got the contact info she needed and gave Evan her card. "Thanks for taking the time to speak with me," she said, offering her hand.

"Anything to get those creeps their due."

Fina took the stairs down to the lobby, Evan's comments turning over in her head. He had said the only source of conflict in Nadine's life was the church, but that was a conflict between the two of them. Following that statement to its natural conclusion, Evan had a strong motive for murdering his wife.

ELEVEN

Fina kicked off the day with an Internet search of Christa Jackson, which was a dead end. Christa was mentioned on the website for the New England Learning Disabilities Coalition, and a picture of her eldest daughter at a gymnastics meet appeared on a YMCA website. Her husband, Paul Jackson, worked at Fidelity and showed up in some industry newsletters and in a marketing brochure for Bentley's part-time MBA program. They looked like normal people, which was always a disappointment in Fina's book.

Before heading to their home, Fina decided to stop at the office to tie up some loose ends on other cases. She took the elevator down to her parking spot in the garage and kept an eye out. The break-in alone was enough to make her vigilant, but she'd encountered trouble in the garage before and was especially cautious when coming and going.

The tableau that generally greeted her—the fire extinguisher just peeking over the roof of her car, the bumper of her neighbor's Jaguar, the light hitting her trunk just so—seemed off. As she got closer, she knew why. The car was sitting three inches lower than usual, the tires sliced open, exposing the dark rubber within.

Fina circled the car to find that all four tires had been slashed. "Goddamnit!"

She took pictures with her phone and went back upstairs. Pacing the living room, Fina scrolled through her contacts and found the number she needed.

"Hey," a male voice answered.

"Dante?"

"Who wants to know?"

"You can drop the tough pimp act. It's Fina Ludlow."

"Oh, hell no. I do not need your crazy-ass shit today." Dante Trimonti was a young pimp, an up-and-coming "man about town" with whom Fina had dealt in the past. He was sleazy, but not stupid. He was building his empire, and Fina thought he'd be a power player one day. Her job was all about relationships and information; you needed the former to get the latter, and you couldn't be choosy about your colleagues.

"I'm well, thanks for asking," she said. "Actually, I have a legitimate question. Do you still have the car repair front?"

"It's not a front, Fina. We actually do repair cars."

"Just because you *actually* repair cars doesn't mean it's not a front. Do I have to teach you everything?"

"You're calling me to get your car repaired?"

"Yes."

He chuckled. "Your bad driving finally catch up with you?"

"No," Fina said. "My car was vandalized, and that's also why I'm calling you. I thought you might be able to get some info on who did it, 'cause it definitely wasn't random."

"I didn't touch your car!"

She sunk into the couch. "For fuck's sake, Dante! Be quiet and listen! Somebody slashed my tires in my supposedly secure parking garage. I need four new tires, and I'd also like to know who did it. I thought, given your contacts, you might provide one-stop shopping."

There was a long pause on the other end of the line. "What's in it for me?"

"I'll pay you for the repairs, though I expect a fair price, and I'll owe you one. You'll also get to spend time with me. Don't pretend that doesn't hold some appeal."

"Hmmm. I haven't really gone the cougar route yet."

"Yeah, that's never going to happen, but you keep dreaming. So can you deal with this?"

"I'll send a couple of guys over to get the car, but if we have to order the tires, it'll take longer."

"Fine."

"I'll ask around to see if anyone is talking about the job, but that will probably take a few days."

"I don't have a few days. My condo has already been trashed, and I'm guessing that I'm next on the list."

"Don't you have that gun you once pulled on me? You'll be fine."

Fina gave him her address and stopped off at the concierge desk on her way out. She let Stanley know that a tow truck was on its way and she suspected that her car had been tampered with, but left out the details. There'd been no report of an intruder nor other reports of vandalism. Stanley offered to review the surveillance tapes from the garage, but Fina knew what he'd probably find: a person in dark clothes and a baseball cap ripping her tires to shreds. If she weren't concerned about drawing attention to herself, she'd raise a stink about the building's lax security.

But since Fina was part of the problem, she kept her mouth shut.

Fina walked through the hallways at Ludlow and Associates, exchanging the occasional nod or hello with a passing employee. Scotty and Matthew were well-liked at the firm, and this goodwill tended to rub off on her. Carl was feared, and this also rubbed off, at least with those people who didn't know her well. In her personal life, Fina preferred being liked to being feared, but professionally, being feared was better. Fear tended to deliver more cooperation and fewer acts of violence.

Shari wasn't keeping watch, so Fina strode into Carl's office and found him sitting behind his desk. Fina took a seat on the couch rather than standing or sitting before him like a truant called to the principal's office.

Her father finished a call and rotated his chair toward her. "Did you get my message?"

"Yes."

"So? What the hell happened the other night? Where did you and Haley disappear to?"

"She didn't want to have dinner with the man who molested her. Do you blame her?"

Carl was silent and stony-faced.

"It sounds awful, doesn't it, when you just state the facts?"

Her father adjusted the knot of his tie. "What's the latest with the church?"

"Nadine Quaynor was poisoned with antifreeze."

His brow arched. "Antifreeze?"

"It's becoming quite popular," Fina said.

"Was it someone from the church?"

"Dad, I started investigating her death on Tuesday. I don't know yet who killed her."

"Better get on it."

"That's very helpful, Dad. Regardless of the circumstances of Nadine's death, I doubt we'll convince Chloe to hold on to her property."

"We'll see," Carl said, rising from his chair.

Fina didn't know if this meant Carl had info she didn't or if his enormous ego prevented him from contemplating an adverse outcome.

"One more thing," she said. "I need to borrow a fleet car."

He stopped at the door. "The last time you borrowed a fleet car, you blew it up."

She tipped her head back and stared at the ceiling. "I did not blow up the car. Someone else did that. May I borrow a car or not? Yes or no? I need a car in order to work."

He waved her away. "Fine. Take a car, but nothing brand new."

In the Ludlow and Associates section of the parking garage, Fina asked the fleet manager for car keys. She was tempted to borrow the top-end Lexus SUV that went for about $100K, but knew that it was too showy for her purposes. Instead, she chose a silver Toyota Avalon and left the Prudential Tower in her rearview mirror.

Fina exited Route 9 in Brookline and found a place to pull over a few streets from Rand's house. A quick call to Ludlow and Associates confirmed that her brother was in a deposition, which gave her plenty of time to do her thing.

She pulled into the driveway of his colonial Tudor and scanned the facade. Nowadays, lots of homeowners trained surveillance cameras on their property in an effort to deter burglars. She didn't see any obvious ones, but kept her head down as she approached the front door. Fina didn't want to advertise her identity if she were being recorded, but she didn't make any attempt to conceal her visit, either. If she snuck around, neighbors were more likely to call the cops. If she acted like she belonged, she did.

Anyone with an eagle-eye view would have noticed that she was maneuvering a lock pick in a bid to open the front door, but Fina positioned her body and held her bag so that a Nosy Nelly would assume that she was having trouble with the lock, not that she was breaking in.

After a couple of minutes and a few drops of perspiration, Fina was in and made a beeline for the alarm panel tucked discreetly behind the sweeping staircase. This was the tricky part. She only got a few chances to disarm it and wasn't surprised when her second attempt—her brother's birth date, as opposed to his daughter's—did the trick. He was such a narcissist.

Months before, when Melanie had disappeared and subsequently died, Fina and Milloy had done a thorough search of the house. Rand had spent little time there since, and Fina was less interested in his recent activities than those of his past. She bypassed the main living areas, including the kitchen, dining room, and bedrooms, and climbed the stairs to the third floor.

The top of the house consisted of a finished family room with a large storage room at one end. Fina stood on the threshold of that room and took stock. One side was tidy and organized, but the disorder of the other side suggested that the task of organizing the room had been abandoned mid-project.

Wire shelving units held boxes and boxes of Christmas decorations, reminding Fina that her sister-in-law had treated holiday decorating as an Olympic sport. Another area was filled with boxes marked with Haley's name and a year. Fina popped a lid off of one and scanned the contents, which included report cards, certificates for participating in soccer and gymnastics, and art projects. Fina made a mental note to steal the boxes away to Scotty and Patty's one of these days; Rand had already ruined enough of Haley's childhood without being in charge of her memorabilia.

The messy side of the room was a jumble of boxes, a few pieces of furniture, and rolling garment racks that were zipped closed, their exact contents a mystery. Fina eyed the mess and tried to imagine a TV show or movie that accurately depicted the scut work of the PI life. Columbo never spent hours rooting around in attics. Jessica Fletcher never enflamed her sciatica by shifting boxes to and fro. And yet, a good portion of Fina's professional life—and those of her law enforcement counterparts—was spent riffling through dusty belongings and yellowing paperwork. Oh, the glamour.

An hour later, she was back in her car with a box labeled "Rand—college" safely stowed in the trunk. Inside, she'd found letters, term papers, and photographs, at least one of which included Lindsay Kaufman Shaunnesy. A couple of the other coeds were also fresh-faced blondes, and Fina thought they were her best bet. She knew that her brother had a type—one that included his fresh-faced, blond wife and daughter—and her gut told her that she needed to follow the blondes to get the story.

Nadine's cousin, Christa Jackson, lived in a small Cape Cod–style house in Framingham. Fina hadn't called ahead, believing that surprise visits were generally the most fruitful. She was glad to see only a Honda minivan in the driveway. The single car suggested that if Christa were home, she wasn't playing host to a group of Nadine's grieving relatives.

Bright red paint coated the front door, and there was a soccer net in the yard. Fina rang the bell and a moment later, a woman opened the door. She was wearing snug jeans and a boxy sweater. Her hair was pulled back in a loose ponytail, and heavily mascaraed lashes framed her dark eyes.

"Yes?" the woman said.

"Hi. Are you Christa Jackson?"

"Yes."

"I'm Fina Ludlow. I'm a private investigator. Evan Quaynor gave me your contact information."

"Right. He left me a message about you."

"I'm very sorry about Nadine's death," Fina said. "I wondered if you could spare a few minutes to speak with me."

Christa leaned on the door. "I've already spoken with the police."

"I know, and I realize this seems redundant, but I would really appreciate just a few minutes."

She considered the request and then stepped back. "I don't have much time, and I'm not sure what I can tell you."

"It won't take long. I promise."

Fina followed her into a dining room with a farm-style table, covered with papers and file folders. There was a half-empty mug of coffee with lipstick stains in the middle of the mess. A smaller desk at the side of the room held a computer and a large pair of headphones.

"Am I interrupting your work?" Fina asked.

Christa sat down on a spindle-back dining chair, and Fina claimed the one across from her.

"That's work," Christa said, pointing to the tidier desk. "This is just life." She swept her hand over the table.

"Got it," Fina said. "What kind of work do you do?"

"Medical transcriptionist. I specialize in ophthalmology so if you have any questions related to cataracts or corneal transplants, I'm your woman."

"I'll keep that in mind."

Christa squirmed in the wooden chair. "So you're investigating Nadine's death?"

"I was initially hired to conduct due diligence on Covenant Rising regarding a large donation. As you can imagine, my client has grown skittish given the circumstances of your cousin's death. She's asked me to follow up on the work being done by the police."

"Your client wants to know who killed Nadine?"

"More like she's interested in anything connected to the church."

Christa took hold of a curl in her ponytail and tugged on it. "You think you can figure it out better than the police?"

Fina smiled. "It's been known to happen, but at the very least, I want to give my client a comprehensive picture of the church."

"Wait." Christa's eyes narrowed. "You think someone in the church killed Nadine?"

"I don't know." Fina felt her ire rising. Why did people have to ask so many questions? "That's why I'm speaking to everyone who knew Nadine. It would be foolish to make assumptions at this point."

Christa gazed at a large framed photo on the wall. It showed three young girls in a deep pile of leaves. They had long, dark hair and wide smiles.

"Did Nadine have any enemies?" Fina asked.

"I can't think of anyone who'd want to kill her, not that she was the easiest person in the world."

"Meaning?"

"She liked things to be a certain way."

"So she was particular?"

"She had strong opinions about most things."

"And she let you know what those opinions were?"

Christa smirked, but didn't respond.

"I'm guessing you were on the receiving end of that," Fina ventured.

"I got pregnant when I was nineteen. Nadine didn't approve."

"Because of premarital sex? I'm assuming it was premarital."

"It was, and she didn't approve of that, but she also didn't like that I was careless. That whole 'to err is human' thing never held much sway with her."

Fina nodded. "Sounds kind of annoying. I don't think I'd do well with someone like that."

Christa straightened up in her seat. "Don't get me wrong, she was great in many ways."

"Did you see each other often?"

"Some, but as we got older, we got busier with work and our families."

"What do you think of Evan?" Fina asked.

Christa shook her head. "I think she was a fool to break up with him. He's a good guy and a good father."

Fina heard the edge in Christa's voice and wondered if that was about Nadine's choices or her own.

"I talked with him last night," Fina said. "He had a lot of negative things to say about CRC."

"We both thought she was in too deep."

"What is it specifically that you don't like about the church?"

"They think men are superior, and they want all your money. Why would I pay someone to treat me like crap?"

Fina shrugged. "Beats me."

Christa glanced at her watch and took a deep breath.

"I'll let you get back to work," Fina said, eyeing the piles on the table.

"If it were work, at least I'd get paid for it," Christa said, leading her to the door.

"Volunteer work?"

"No. My daughter has learning disabilities and dealing with her school is a full-time job. You can't imagine the forms I have to fill out and the meetings that are involved. It's ridiculous. All so they'll teach her how to read."

"Sorry I interrupted."

"It's fine." She took a step, herding Fina out.

"Thanks. If you think of anything, let me know," Fina said, handing Christa her card.

Fina knew that information had to be viewed through the lens of the person providing it. You could never take a character evaluation at face value; the trick was ferreting out the bias or the agenda of the interviewee.

More often than not, though, people painted a rosier picture of the deceased than was warranted. That hadn't been the case in this conversation, and Fina had to wonder why.

Fina contemplated her options on the Natick Mall directory. She'd been instructed to provide her own lunch for her meeting with Lucas

Chellew, and though the choices were varied, they all promised to raise her cholesterol. She settled on a specialty French fry place and took her bag of greasy fries and a diet soda into the Misses' department at Macy's. A sales associate directed her through a set of swinging doors into a windowless office off a long hallway.

Lucas Chellew sat behind his desk, studying his computer screen. Fina knocked on the door to get his attention.

"Mr. Chellew? I'm Fina Ludlow. We spoke on the phone."

"Of course, Miss Ludlow. Come on in."

"Please call me Fina."

"And you should call me Lucas. Let me just grab my lunch," he said, coming from behind his desk and ducking out of the room.

Fina took the only available chair, a stiff-backed one with a nubby seat, and studied the room. It looked like a cross between an office and a storeroom. Shelves were filled with boxes overflowing with clothing in plastic bags, and hanging racks were packed tightly with dresses. A pile of overstuffed binders threatened to topple off a credenza, and the bulletin board behind the desk was a flurry of notices. A stack of sales circulars occupied one corner of his desk.

"I apologize it's such a mess in here," Lucas said. He was carrying a brown paper bag and a large water bottle.

"No need to apologize. You've got a lot to keep track of."

"I do, and just when I clean things out, I get a whole new load of stuff to deal with." Once seated, he pulled out three plastic bags. One held a sandwich, another baby carrots, and the third, pretzel sticks.

Fina reached into her greasy bag for the cardboard container of French fries drizzled with ranch dressing. Lucas looked forlornly at her lunch.

"I'm sorry," she apologized. "It looks like you're following a healthy eating plan."

"Healthy and boring." Lucas bit into his sandwich, a curled edge of lettuce peeking out between the bread and turkey.

"You're welcome to some fries." Fina held the bag toward him. "Although I feel a little badly tempting you, especially in light of Pastor Greg's sermon on Sunday."

Lucas bit into a carrot with a loud crunch. Fina didn't like raw carrots. She didn't think there should be any overlap between her diet and that of a horse.

"It's okay. Just another test. Life is full of them."

"Ain't that the truth," she said, savoring a crispy fry. "How'd you get into retail?"

"Right out of college, I got a job working for a consumer goods manufacturer in Baltimore. I was transferred up here after a few years, and when we were acquired, I got this job with Macy's. My wife and daughters like the employee discount."

"How old are your kids?"

"Twelve and fourteen. They're thick as thieves, and the discount is the only thing that makes me useful in their eyes. You got any sisters?"

Fina shook her head. "Just brothers."

"Your father's lucky. Teenage girls are the worst."

Fina smiled. "My brothers' teenage behavior would suggest otherwise." She really wished people would move on from the idea that all boys were one way and all girls were another. All of her brothers had penises, but Rand couldn't be more different from the other two.

"I realize this is a difficult time for you, given your fellow congregant's death." Fina knew no such thing, but decided to throw it against the wall to see if it would stick.

"It's a tragedy. My heart is broken." Lucas bowed his head in what appeared to be a show of reverence.

"I'm sure it is," Fina said.

"Is that what you wanted to speak to me about?" Lucas asked, digging into the bag for some pretzel sticks.

"I wanted to speak with you about Chloe Renard."

"Chloe's a great gal." He took a long drink from his water bottle, the kind you refill throughout the day. "Did you say you're a lawyer?"

"I work for a lawyer. I'm just performing some due diligence on the proposed real estate deal between the church and Chloe Renard."

Lucas frowned. "Proposed? I thought it was pretty much a done deal."

"There are some details that still have to be worked out. Deals are never really done until the final paperwork is signed, right?"

"I suppose."

"So you're on the church leadership committee?" Fina asked. She chewed on a ranch-drenched fry, not sure if she liked the flavor combination. She'd have to eat more before rendering a verdict.

"Yes. It's one of my many responsibilities," he said, taking a bite of sandwich.

Fina nodded. "Chloe said you're very involved at CRC."

"The church is very important to me and my family. It's an extension of my family, really."

"Does the leadership committee make decisions about the church's finances or just serve in an advisory capacity?"

Lucas shifted in his seat. "I don't mean to be rude, Fina, but the church isn't required to disclose its financial dealings to anyone, including the government."

"Absolutely, but I don't work for the government." She took a long drink to buy a little time. "I'm sorry. I must have misunderstood. I was under the impression that Covenant Rising was happy to share any information that would keep the bequest on track."

"Well, of course." He looked around the room. It was hard to be helpful and contrarian at the same moment. "I'm wondering if the person you should be speaking to is Pastor Greg, not me."

Fina wiped her fingers on a napkin. "I am speaking with him, but Chloe also suggested I speak with you."

"I wish I could help you, but you understand that I can't talk about financial details with just anyone."

What a bunch of bull honky, but Fina chose to eat a French fry rather than voice this thought. "Of course. I understand."

She wondered why Lucas had agreed to meet with her in the first place, but his reasoning soon became apparent. As they finished their lunch, he spent the next ten minutes sharing the good word and proselytizing.

Poor Lucas.

If he'd had even a hint of the hard case sitting across from him, he wouldn't have wasted his breath.

TWELVE

Covenant Rising was a beehive of activity when Fina arrived. There was a noisy group of preschoolers engaged in some activity with a parachute in a room off the lobby, and the band was rehearsing in the parish hall.

Fina found her way to the administrative offices at the back of the building, where Betty, Pastor Greg's assistant, was fishing a crumpled piece of paper from the innards of the copy machine. The door to what Fina assumed was Pastor Greg's office was closed.

"I'm here to see Pastor Greg," Fina said. "I'm Fina Ludlow."

Betty slammed a compartment closed on the machine and returned to her desk, where she consulted her computer screen. "Do you have an appointment?"

"No. I was hoping to catch him in."

"Well," she said, sighing. "He's quite busy this afternoon."

"I know," Fina said, and dipped her head. "I just really needed to speak with him."

Betty consulted the screen again.

"Forget it," Fina said, turning away. "It's fine."

"No, no," Betty said, her charitable Christian spirit kicking in. "I don't want to leave you hanging. Give me a minute to see what I can do."

The secretary rapped on the door. She was summoned and ducked into the room, closing the door behind her.

"He doesn't have much time," she said, emerging a minute later.

"It won't take long," Fina said. "Thank you." She tried to look grateful and desperate, neither of which came easily.

Pastor Greg's office looked comfortable, but slightly run-down and untidy, like the space of someone who had better things to do than organize and clean. Fina closed the door behind her.

"What can I do for you, young lady?" Greg asked from behind his desk.

That was rich considering he was, at most, ten years older than Fina.

She raised an eyebrow in response and took a seat in a worn chair facing his desk.

"Betty said you needed some counsel," he added.

"That's a fair statement," Fina admitted. "I wondered if you were aware of the newest information regarding Nadine Quaynor's death."

Greg hung his head for a moment. "I'm aware that there was an evil force at work, yes."

"Well, certainly an evil person," Fina said.

"Where there is an evil person, there is an evil force, Fina. Satan works through us."

She felt a twinge of irritation. "If you say so. Do you have any idea who might be doing Satan's dirty work?"

Greg looked surprised. "Why would I know?"

"Because Nadine spent a lot of time at the church, and her social circle consisted mostly of fellow congregants. She wasn't killed by a stranger."

"The police know who killed her?"

"No, but with the exception of tainted Tylenol capsules in Chicago, people aren't poisoned by strangers."

Greg squinted as if she had gone out of focus. "I don't like what you're suggesting."

"Of course you don't. Who wants to believe that the devil is at work in his community?"

"What does this have to do with Chloe Renard?"

"You're a savvy man, Pastor Greg. You had to know that the suspicious death of one of your congregants would lead to questions and give some members of the community pause."

He smiled. "Chloe Renard's mother is not a member of our community."

Fina stood and rested her hands on the back of the chair. "You know what's interesting? Watching how people and communities react when the chips are down. Closing ranks may seem like a good strategy, but it usually backfires."

"Did you learn that from your family?" Greg asked, bitterness slipping through the facade.

"I sure did. I'm speaking from years of experience. Let me know if you decide you want to talk." She opened the door. "Thank you for speaking with me, Pastor. I feel so much better," she said for Betty's benefit.

Fina arrived at Frank and Peg's to find them in the living room. Peg was typing on a laptop, and Frank was reading. Fina tried to imagine her parents in the same room, coexisting in companionable silence. Nope, couldn't picture it.

"Is this a bad time?" she asked, wondering what she'd do if they ever said yes.

"Of course not, sweetie," Peg said. "How are you?"

"I'm okay."

"There are snacks in the kitchen if you're hungry," Frank said, which earned him the hairy eyeball from Peg.

"Are you on pantry patrol?" Fina asked, smiling.

"I had some of my coworkers over the other night, and they were kind enough to bring some treats, which he is not supposed to eat," Peg said. She was a middle school nurse, a job that gave Fina the willies. Was there anything worse than dealing with teenagers and puke? Give her a dangerous felon any day.

"Thanks, but I'm not hungry. This may seem like an odd question," she said, taking a seat on the couch, "but do you have any antifreeze?"

"You having car troubles?" Frank asked.

"Yes, now that you mention it, but that isn't why I'm asking."

He looked out the front window. "What happened to your car?"

"If you must know, my car was vandalized so I'm borrowing a fleet car."

"Where was it vandalized?"

Fina avoided his gaze. "In my garage."

"Your secure garage?"

"The very one."

Frank shook his head.

"Please, Frank. No lectures. I promise I'm on top of it."

Peg watched the two of them, but didn't speak.

"Any idea who's responsible?" he asked.

"I'm working on it."

"So why do you need antifreeze?"

"I don't, I just wondered how typical it is that people have it in their homes these days."

"You shouldn't have it anywhere there are children and pets," Peg said. "It can be lethal."

"It killed the victim of the case I'm working on."

"The thirty-two-year-old?" Frank asked.

Fina nodded.

"People need it for their cars," he said, "and they use it to winterize second homes, to make sure that the pipes don't freeze. I'm sure I've got some in the garage."

"I was just curious."

"Is this Cristian's case, too?"

"Yes, but it was my case first. I was investigating the church where the victim worships, and I found her body."

"I'm sure Cristian finds that to be a very compelling argument for your involvement." Frank grinned.

"Okay, of course it's his case, being a cop and all, but we've worked on the same cases before."

"How does he feel about his girlfriend working on the same case?" Peg asked.

"We're not using that word yet. We're not even exclusive, as far as I can tell."

"You sure he knows that?" Frank asked.

"Can we please talk about something more pleasant? Like an autopsy?"

Frank chuckled. "Oh, sweetie. Your life is very complicated."

"I know, and I am not happy about that."

"Is it too much to ask you to stay safe?" he wondered.

"It's not too much to ask, but I'm not in charge of the universe, Frank. I'll do what I can."

"That's not the least bit reassuring."

"Stop worrying," Fina said. "It's bad for your heart."

"When do I get to meet this mystery woman?" Fina sat on Matthew's office couch, nursing a diet soda.

Matthew was sitting next to her, his feet propped on the coffee table. Her brother looked like he didn't have a care in the world, though she knew that wasn't the case. With the exception of Elaine—who made her feelings everyone's business—the Ludlows were well trained in hiding their emotions. It was one of the reasons they made good lawyers and, in Fina's case, a good investigator. Their poker faces were exemplary.

"Sydney. You'll meet Sydney soon."

"Have you introduced her to anyone else in the family?" Historically, the Ludlow children waited as long as possible before introducing prospective mates to the rest of the clan. They could be an intimidating bunch, and one wanted to be sure the relationship had legs before subjecting it to the rest of the family.

"Scotty and Patty."

"And?"

"It went well."

"Glad to hear it. Has he filled you in on my plan?" Fina asked.

"Your investigation of our brother?"

"The very one."

"It sounds a little nuts to me."

Fina shrugged.

"What have you got so far?" he asked.

"I spoke with the woman he 'allegedly' attacked in college. It was not pretty."

"You think he did it?"

"Yes. I know he molested Haley, and that's worse than raping a peer as far as I'm concerned. Date rape seems like a gateway offense compared to molestation."

"Did this woman give you more to go on?"

"She gave me another name, but that woman lives in New Zealand, and it's not really a conversation you want to have over the phone. I'm holding off contacting her for the time being."

Matthew closed his eyes and leaned his head against the couch. "This sucks."

"I agree."

"So what's next if you're not pursuing the New Zealand angle?"

"I found some of Rand's college photos, and I'm trying to identify the women in the pictures. They might have a story to tell."

"Where did you find the photos?"

"In his house."

Matthew peered at her. "When were you at his house?"

"I don't think you really want the details."

"Promise me you'll be careful," he said, shaking his head.

"I'm always careful."

"I seem to recall the two of us being chased by a drug dealer not so long ago when you were 'being careful.'"

Fina punched him lightly on the arm and rose from the couch. "*Chased* is a bit of an exaggeration."

"Fina," Matthew said, prompting her to pause at the door. "You don't think it was an isolated case?"

"What?"

"Rand's college acquaintance."

She shook her head. "Not a chance."

"'Leo, you need to eat two more beans." Cristian gave his son a stare that was usually reserved for hardened criminals. Fina had joined the Menendez duo for dinner, and it was proving to be a tortured affair.

"No," the boy said evenly.

Cristian sighed.

Fina stuck a fork into a green bean and put it in her mouth. "That's so good," she said, washing it down with a swig of beer.

"See?" Cristian said. "Fina likes them."

"Ina." The boy pushed his plate in her direction. "Eat mine."

Cristian sighed.

"He's very generous," Fina noted, mussing his hair.

"Okay, buddy, but no sweets if you don't eat your beans."

Cristian rose and started clearing the dishes from the table. When his back was turned, Matteo crammed the two beans into his mouth and chewed laboriously.

"That wasn't so bad, right?" Fina asked.

"Beans are yucky!" he said, sliding off his chair and running into the living room.

"I finished all my beans," Fina said, rising and leaning against the counter as Cristian rinsed the dishes. "What kind of sweets do I get?"

Cristian grinned. "What do you have in mind?"

"Actual sweets," Fina clarified. "That wasn't a double entendre."

He reached into a cabinet and took out a bag of Oreos. "This is all I've got."

"It'll do." She grabbed one and twisted apart the two layers of cookie. "I interviewed Evan Quaynor last night."

"Yeah? What'd you think?"

"That church certainly did a number on his marriage."

"That church seems to be very polarizing."

"That's why I don't go to church," Fina said. "It's so divisive."

"Uh-huh. I assume you've spoken with Christa Jackson?"

"Yes."

"What's your take on her?" Cristian asked.

Fina cocked an eyebrow. "Now you want to share information?"

"I'm interested in your expert opinion."

"Well, she was surprisingly frank about Nadine's less than appealing qualities."

"According to Nadine's mother," Cristian said, "the cousins had a falling-out."

"Christa didn't mention that. Has anyone else confirmed it?"

"I'm working on it."

"And what was the falling-out over?" she asked.

"Don't know that, either."

"Let me guess: You're telling me so that I find out and report back to you," Fina said.

"I'm just trying to be cooperative."

"Sure you are."

"Teo, come get your cookies!" Cristian put two cookies and a glass of milk on the table. "After this, it's time for your bath."

The boy sat with his legs wrapped around the chair legs, his head nodding to some secret rhythm. He dunked a cookie into his milk, pulling it out only when it was limp and soaked.

"I should get going," Fina said, leaning over and giving Matteo a kiss. "Bye, buddy. See you soon."

"Bye, Ina," he said, his open mouth a mishmash of black cookie and white filling.

"You don't want to stay awhile?" Cristian asked.

"I've got work to do, but thank you for dinner."

He followed her to the door, where they shared a long kiss.

"Talk to you soon," Cristian said as Fina started down the hallway.

Her recent interactions with Cristian had been stilted and awkward. The lines they'd worked so hard to draw over the past ten years were starting to bleed, and Fina didn't know where she stood—as his date or as his colleague.

She also didn't know how she felt about his domestic situation. She loved Matteo, but a more serious relationship with Cristian also included a more serious role in the little boy's life.

Aunt Fina was one thing, but Stepmom Fina? That was a whole other kettle of fish.

The weekend brought little progress in the investigation, which Fina found frustrating, but she supposed a forced respite wasn't a completely bad thing. It had taken some time and some phone calls, but she'd discovered that former CRC member Kyle Roady hadn't moved away like Chloe thought. He was living in Medford and working at H. M. Brody's, a rug and upholstery repair company in Brighton. Unfortunately, he wouldn't be in until Monday, so Fina filled her time with family events.

Her nephews played in enough soccer games to rival the qualifying rounds of the World Cup, and Fina provided her assistance while Scotty and Haley baked snickerdoodles, her brother's specialty. Her assistance entailed licking various bowls and beaters and testing for doneness, but everybody contributes in their own way.

Fina considered attending CRC on Sunday, but quickly came to her senses. She doubted she would glean any new information by sitting through a service, and it would certainly irritate her. The Lord designated Sunday as a day of rest, and there was nothing restful about listening to Pastor Greg pontificate.

Instead, she met up with Risa at the high school pool.

"You really do spend all your time at sporting events," commented Fina when she took a seat next to her friend in the concrete bleachers overlooking the pool. A swim meet was about to get under way, and the pool deck was buzzing with activity. Tween swimmers were outfitted in snug suits and various whistles blew through the space.

"A lot of parents do."

"I don't think Elaine did."

Risa arched one perfectly shaped eyebrow. Her ash-brown hair was cut stylishly short and diamond studs winked from her earlobes. "You sure about that?"

"I don't remember her on the sidelines of my field hockey or lacrosse games."

Risa opened her large purse and dug around for a minute.

"Please tell me you have snacks," Fina said. "I didn't fuel up for this event."

"Watching a swim meet?" She handed a small Tupperware container to Fina. "Yeah, you're going to burn a lot of calories sitting on your butt."

"Yum," Fina exclaimed, examining the contents.

"Those are peanut butter brownies, and those are grasshopper." She handed her a napkin. Risa was a gourmet cook and baker extraordinaire, and Fina was a frequent beneficiary of her wares.

"So what makes you so sure my mom attended our events?" Fina asked, licking chocolate ganache from a finger.

"I don't know if she was around for your stuff, but Melanie always made it sound like she was very involved with Rand's activities."

"Well, that doesn't surprise me. As far as she's concerned, he's the Second Coming."

Risa considered that for a moment. "He kind of was, when you think about it."

A whistle cut through the noise on the pool deck, and groups of kids lined up at the end of the lanes. Fina watched a few shake out their legs and windmill their arms before ascending the starting blocks. Crouched down, poised over the water, they resembled bugs with their shiny cap-covered heads and goggled eyes.

"What do you mean?" Fina asked, before taking another bite.

"Do you guys ever talk about Josie?" Risa asked, her question punctuated by the starter pistol.

"No. It's an off-limits topic." Josie's brief life and shocking death cast a pall over the Ludlow family history, but it was a forbidden topic.

Risa pulled off a corner of peanut butter brownie and put it in her mouth. She chewed slowly. "I'm not surprised, but it's too bad. Hearing about that time might give you some insight into your parents."

"You have insight into my parents?"

"I know what Melanie heard, either from your mom or from Rand."

"And what was that?" Fina inhaled the sharp tang of the chlorine-scented water.

"The sense I got was that your mother went into a deep depression after Josie died and Rand's birth helped get her out of it. That's what I meant when I said 'Second Coming.' Rand brought your mom back from the edge."

"Uh-huh." Fina savored the sweet and salty tang of peanut butter.

"If Rand gave her a reason to keep going, it's no wonder he can do no wrong in her eyes."

"Say I agree with that, just for argument's sake," Fina said. "How do you explain her treatment of me?"

Risa's gaze drifted down to the pool, and she watched the swimmers' progress. She was silent.

"Aha!" Fina said. "You can't explain it."

"As a parent—"

"Here we go."

"Just listen," Risa insisted, patting Fina's hand. "As a parent, there comes a moment when you have to accept the child you have, not the one you wanted or the one you expected."

Fina loosened another brownie from the container.

"If you're able to do this, life is much better. If you're not, and I'm not suggesting it's easy, then life can be a struggle."

"So I'm not the child my mother wanted? She wanted my sister and ended up with me?"

Risa gave her a pitying smile.

"Just to clarify," Fina said, swallowing a bite, "is this supposed to make me feel better?"

"Does understanding your mother's behavior make you feel worse?" Risa asked.

"I don't know. Maybe? You're saying that my mother wanted Josie and will never be happy without her. That I'm a poor substitute."

Risa cringed. "It sounds awful when you put it like that."

"How would you put it?"

"I guess I'm saying that you're always unhappy with your mother, and wouldn't it be better if you at least understood why she is the way she is?"

"And accept who she is. Isn't that the part you're leaving out?"

"For your own well-being, yes, you might want to consider accepting that."

"You sound like you've given this a lot of thought."

"Not your situation, but remember, Fina, I was adopted. I've had many occasions to contemplate why mothers behave the way they do."

"And you have kids."

"And I have kids and am reminded daily of my shortcomings and inadequacies in the parenting department."

"Sounds fantastic. Sign me up."

Risa grinned.

"Okay. So what would you do," Fina proposed, "if one of your kids joined a religious organization of which you didn't approve."

"As an adult?"

A swimmer slapped the surface of the water in triumph. Fina couldn't believe the race was already over.

"Yeah. Say Jordan decided to become a Pentecostal and give them all his money?"

"I haven't ever considered that possibility, but thanks for adding to my list of parental worries."

Fina smiled. "Off the top of your head, what would you do?"

"I would try to convince him otherwise, but once he's an adult, it's up to him."

"And there's the rub."

Risa shook the Tupperware container in Fina's direction.

"No, thanks," Fina said. "They were delicious, but I'm good."

"I think Jordan's race is next," Risa said, tucking the brownies back into her bag. She waved to get her son's attention, and he responded with a quick gesture before turning his attention back to his coach.

"Haley stopped by the other day. Actually, she's been spending a lot of time at my house."

"Really? Any particular reason? I mean, in addition to your amazing food?"

"No. I love having her over, but I can't help but think she should be spending more time at her own house."

"She's having a tough time. Rand is back."

Risa cocked her head. "I would have thought she would welcome his return."

Fina contemplated, not for the first time, sharing Rand's dirty little secret with Risa. But when the starter pistol rang out, and Risa rose to cheer on her son, Fina decided it wasn't the moment.

"Teenagers," Fina said over the crowd's cheers. "They're a mystery."

THIRTEEN

On Monday morning, Fina pulled into the parking area of Kyle Roady's workplace, H. M. Brody's Carpet and Upholstery. There was a door marked OFFICE and two large garage doors, one of which was open. Fina started across the parking lot and passed a man with a large rolled carpet on his shoulder in conversation with a woman in yoga pants and a shiny, fitted parka.

Fina stepped through the open garage door and was struck by the noise echoing through the vast space. Workers were on their hands and knees on the open second story, performing some kind of rug repair. In the far corner, there was an enormous machine tended by three guys wearing headphones and safety glasses. A nearby area filled with carpet sample books and remnants acted as a showroom of sorts.

Fina entered the office area on the other side of a bank of windows. A man sat behind a desk, and two other desks were empty. He rose and came to the counter.

"Can I help you?"

"Wow. It is noisy and cold out there."

"Sure is."

"I'm looking for Kyle Roady. Do you know where I might find him?"

Fina knew that she had already found him—thank you, Facebook—but was curious to see if he would fess up.

"Who are you?" A small vein on his eyelid twitched.

"My name is Fina Ludlow, and I'm a private investigator." She handed him her ID. "I have some questions about Covenant Rising Church."

He returned the ID. "Sorry. He's not here right now, but I'll tell him you stopped by."

Fina folded her hands on the counter. "Kyle, I'm not working for the church. I'm investigating the church and have some specific questions about the leadership committee. I promise I'm not going to get you in trouble or make your life difficult."

His shoulders sagged. He reached down and pulled a release so a portion of the counter could be tipped up. "Come on back."

She followed him to his desk and took a seat. "I've been hired to look into the church before a member makes a large donation. It's just standard due diligence. My understanding is that you're no longer a member. Do you keep in touch with any of the members?"

He shook his head. "No." He was wearing a long-sleeved knit cotton shirt with a collar, dark-wash jeans, and a braided leather belt.

Fina decided to hold off on mentioning Nadine.

"Which member is making the donation?" he asked.

"Chloe Renard."

Kyle smiled weakly. "I always liked Chloe."

"Why does Chloe think you moved away?" Fina asked.

He shrugged. "I guess she just assumed that when I stopped going to church."

"Why did you stop going?"

He picked up a pen and twirled it between his fingers. Fina waited while he gathered his thoughts.

"I had a crisis of faith."

Fina examined him. "What does that mean exactly?"

Kyle took a deep breath. "It means that everything I thought I knew or believed, I began to doubt. The things I took for granted no longer made sense."

Fina nodded. "That is a crisis."

"Are you religious?" he asked.

"No, but I understand what you're talking about." Her mind moved to Haley. "I've questioned what I thought I knew, and I've tried to make peace with some ugly truths."

Kyle nodded. "It's awful, isn't it?"

"It can be," she admitted. "I know this is a very personal subject, and I don't want to pry," Fina said, as a preemptive disclaimer. "Can I ask if it was the theology that caused the crisis, or your fellow members?"

"It was both. I was drawn to CRC because it was so welcoming, and they do lots of projects in the community. I liked being of service, and I liked that someone just told me where to show up to make a positive contribution. It felt like a no-brainer."

"But?"

"But then I felt like certain groups were being marginalized. I don't support homosexuality, but I don't think people should be excluded."

Fina didn't support homosexuality any more than she supported heterosexuality. She didn't see how other people's sex lives were any of her business. And really, who wanted to contemplate other people's sex lives? Either get busy with your own or find a hobby.

"Did you voice your concerns?" she asked.

"Initially, but after a while, I just kept quiet."

"There were no like minds?"

"No one would admit that. If you had a differing opinion, you were seen as being disloyal, not truly committed to the church."

"Was that stated explicitly?"

"Eventually, but at first, it just got really uncomfortable. People gave me the cold shoulder, and I wasn't included the way I had been before. My opinions were dismissed or ignored by the other members of the leadership committee."

"Did the committee have any real oversight?"

"Of the accounts we were privy to," he said.

"The committee wasn't privy to all the accounts?"

Kyle glanced out toward the factory floor. "I don't know anything for sure. I'm just saying that the math didn't always make sense."

"What did the other committee members make of that?"

He looked at his shoes. "I don't know."

"You may not have heard, but one of your former committee members recently passed away." Fina wasn't usually a fan of employing euphemisms for death, but Kyle seemed like he could use a gentler approach.

He looked genuinely surprised. "Who?"

"Nadine Quaynor."

"Nadine died?"

Fina nodded.

"What happened?"

"She was found in her home. The cause of death is unclear."

Kyle was quiet.

"I heard that Nadine didn't get along with some of the other committee members," Fina said, taking a leap.

He nodded. "She certainly didn't get along with Lucas."

"Right. That's what I've heard," Fina lied. "Did Nadine and Lucas have a falling-out? Or just a general dislike for each other?"

"They were never really friends. They were two strong personalities who wanted to be in charge." He thought for a moment. "It did seem to get worse a couple of months ago."

"Any idea why?"

Kyle shook his head. "Nope." He glanced at the clock in the corner of his computer screen. "I should get back to work."

"Of course. Thanks for talking with me."

Fina ducked under the opening in the counter and started for the door.

"If you see Chloe, would you tell her I said hello?" Kyle asked.

"Of course. Give me a call if you think of anything else."

"Sure."

Fina needed Lucas to shed some light on his relationship with Nadine, but she knew it would take an act of God to make him tell her anything.

Hopefully, God wasn't too busy doing other things—like curing cancer or helping wide receivers score touchdowns—to come through for her.

Nadine's house looked no different than it had on Fina's previous visit, but knowing that the owner was never coming back gave it an eerie vibe. Fina parked out front and headed toward Ronnie McCaffrey's house next door. It was similar to Nadine's except it was white and a small addition had been attached to the side. There was a Saint Patrick's Day flag hanging beside the front door, and a smaller American flag was planted in a flower bed by the steps. The midsize pickup in the driveway had a sticker featuring the familiar logo of the International Association of Fire Fighters affixed to the back window.

Fina rang the bell and waited. She rang again, but started back in the direction of her car when there was no answer.

"Did you need something?" Ronnie came down the driveway, wiping his hands on a dirty cloth. He'd swapped his Patriots sweatshirt for a Red Sox one. He stopped and studied her. "Your name is on the tip of my tongue, but you're going to have to remind me."

"Fina Ludlow." She walked over and shook his hand.

"Right. The PI."

"Right." She handed him her card. "Do you have a few minutes?"

He studied the card, then slipped it into his pants pocket. "If you don't mind coming out to the garage. I'm finishing something up."

"Happy to."

He led her around the back of the house to the separate garage. Unlike Nadine's, it had room for two cars. One bay was empty, and the other was occupied by a workbench. There were garden tools and hoses off to the side, and beside the bench, a child's bicycle was tipped on its end.

"I'm fixing my grandson's bike. He'll want to ride it the first decent day we get." Ronnie reached over and turned on a space heater. The bars started to glow after a few seconds.

"I'm always afraid those things are going to spontaneously combust," Fina said.

Ronnie looked at her. "Few things spontaneously combust, sweetheart. People leave them on unattended or too close to drapes or bedding. You'll notice I didn't leave it on when I came out to talk to you."

"Right. You would know. You said the other night you're retired."

He nodded. "Retired battalion chief, but I was with the department for forty-two years."

"That's impressive."

Fina looked at the tools on the bench. She wondered what it would have been like to be raised by someone who knew how to build and fix things. Her meager competency in that area was acquired from Frank, who believed that everyone—men and women—should know how to change a tire, swap in a new AC filter, and tell the difference between a Phillips head and a regular screwdriver. Carl believed you could hire someone to do those things, but there was something to be said for a minimum level of know-how and self-reliance. Fina was going to make sure that she passed her knowledge on to Haley and her nephews.

He shrugged. "Never wanted to be anything but a firefighter." This didn't surprise Fina; it was never just a job to cops and firefighters.

Ronnie fiddled with the bike chain. "So you still working your case even though Nadine's gone?"

"I'm trying to tie up some loose ends in my investigation."

"What exactly are you investigating? You didn't say the other night."

"My client wants background on the Covenant Rising Church. I had hoped to get that from Nadine, but obviously, that didn't happen."

Ronnie made a noise that was somewhere between a grunt and a harrumph. "Well, I don't know anything about the church."

"My client wants to ensure that Nadine's death doesn't have an impact on the church, so I'm just doing some follow-up." Fina knew she was talking in circles, but she didn't want to reveal any more than she had to. She was trying to avoid having Ronnie or anyone else she spoke with tailor their answers to satisfy what they believed was her agenda.

Ronnie reached onto the tool bench and grabbed a wrench. He set to work tightening a bolt. "All I know about the church is that she was very devoted, and it caused nothing but trouble between Nadine and Evan."

"Right. I've spoken with him. He seems like a nice guy."

"He's a great guy, got a sweet daughter, too."

"Did you have much interaction with Nadine?"

"A fair amount."

She waited for more, but Ronnie was silent. Fina looked out the window and saw a large backyard with a lawn, a play structure, and a sandbox. "How many grandchildren do you have?" Even her own mother, the Wicked Witch of the East, liked to talk about her grandchildren.

"Five. Ages twelve through two. How about you?" He looked at her. "Any kids?"

"Not yet," Fina said, guessing that a lack of interest in procreation was not a policy that Ronnie would embrace.

"You're still young," he assured her.

Oh, goody.

"Are your grandkids local?" she asked.

"All of them are within six blocks, and I've also got a whole crew of honorary grandkids in the neighborhood. We do a block party in August, and a Fourth of July parade, caroling at Christmas."

"That sounds like fun."

"People seem to enjoy it," Ronnie said, righting the bike. "That's how it was when I was growing up; people were good neighbors, and they looked out for one another."

"It sounds like a different era."

"Some things really were better in the good old days," Ronnie said.

"I don't want to take any more of your time," Fina said. "Thanks for the info."

Out front a few kids had set up hockey goals and were engrossed in a street hockey game. The ball went astray, and one of the boys came over to her.

"Is Chief home?" he asked. His face was bright red, his bangs damp and sticking to his skin.

"In the garage," Fina said, nodding in the direction of the backyard.

She watched them resume their game as she pulled on her seat belt.

The Ludlow children had grown up in a variety of large houses where the neighbors hid from one another, courtesy of gated driveways and enormous shrubs. At least she had her brothers, but it might have been nice to have some choice in playmates and activities.

Ronnie McCaffrey's street was a whole different world.

Fina found a sandwich shop a few streets from Ronnie's house and grabbed some lunch. She took a call from an associate at the firm who needed clarity on an investigation she did and then killed some time surfing the Web before making the trek to Dedham. She didn't want to go home and stew about the break-in, the vandalism to her car, or her family situation, so she decided to pay Lucas another visit instead.

The Chellew house was a ranch, with a small addition off the back that led to a deck. Beds of hostas flanked the front door, but there was nothing else to indicate any real pride or effort had been put into the property. The driveway was empty, but the light coming through the bay window suggested to Fina that a stop was worth her while.

She parked in front and scanned the area before leaving her car. This was what people who lived in safe neighborhoods and countries took for granted: not having to constantly be aware of their surroundings and evaluate potential threats and risks. Watching your back was an exhausting business.

The front door was opened by a girl who looked to be about fourteen. She had long, straight brown hair and hot-pink braces.

"Hi, I'm Fina. Is your dad home?"

"No, but he should be home soon."

"What about your mom? I'm here on church business."

"She isn't here, either." The girl glanced behind her toward another room. A boy band was playing at top volume, mewling pledges of forever love.

"Shit!" There was a yelp from inside the house. "Oh my God, Courtney! Get in here!"

The girl at the door took off, with Fina close behind. Courtney stopped short at the kitchen door when she saw the flames coming off the stove top. The girl who'd screamed was standing back from the fire, a look of horror on her face.

"Do you have a lid?" Fina barked, stepping between the girls and the pot of fire.

Courtney pushed the younger girl aside and threw open a cabinet door. She dropped to her knees and shoved some pans aside before passing a lid to Fina.

Fina tried to place it on the pan, but the size wasn't quite right. Flames licked the edges of the lid and continued to climb toward the oven hood.

"A fire extinguisher?" she hollered. "And call 911!"

"Get the phone, Darcy!" Courtney yelled as she ran out of the room and returned with the red cylinder.

Fina grabbed it from the girl and pulled the pin. She aimed the nozzle at the base of the pan and depressed the lever, releasing a stream of white foam. In less than thirty seconds, the flames had disappeared. The only sound in the kitchen was heavy breathing and the drip of the melting foam.

"Should I still call 911?" Darcy asked after a moment, phone in hand.

"No," Fina said, approaching the stove top. "It's out."

"Oh my God!" Courtney yelled at her sister. "What did you do?"

Darcy burst into tears and made protestations in between sobs and gulps.

"It's okay. Everybody's okay," Fina said, steering the two girls to the kitchen table. "Just take a deep breath, you guys."

Courtney's cheeks were flushed, and she looked like she was struggling to contain her own tears. "We're going to be in so much trouble. Dad's going to kill us."

"Your dad is going to be glad you're both okay," Fina said. "This kind of stuff"—she gestured toward the stove—"can be fixed. What were you making?"

They exchanged a glance. "Fondue," Courtney said.

Fina nodded slowly. "Huh. I didn't realize people still ate fondue."

"We're studying Switzerland in history class, and our mom pulled out Grandma's fondue set."

"Mom and Dad said to wait before we used it," Darcy spat at her sister. She'd regained enough equilibrium to start assigning blame.

"Shut up!"

"We should call one of your parents and have them come home," Fina said.

Courtney glanced at the clock on the microwave. "Mom should be here by now."

"Well, I think it's still too hot to clean things up."

"Who are you?" Darcy asked, just realizing that Fina was an unfamiliar face.

"I'm Fina Ludlow, and I came to talk to your parents about some church stuff."

The girl nodded and wiped at her face with her sleeve.

Fina perked up. "What kind of fondue?"

"Meat and then chocolate."

Her eyes widened. "There's chocolate? Why didn't you say so?" Fina asked. "Don't you know that when there's a fire, you automatically get to break out the chocolate?"

The girls grinned. Darcy fetched a huge Hershey's bar from a cabinet and placed it in front of Fina, who unwrapped it and broke off generous portions for all three of them.

They were sitting at the table, munching on the squares, when they heard a door open and someone come into the house.

"Girls!" a woman's voice called out. "Where are you?" She came into the room and lifted her nose in the air. "It smells like a fire!"

"That's because there was a fire," Darcy said, rolling her eyes. Oh, this one was sassy.

The woman surveyed the kitchen with an open mouth.

"I'm Fina Ludlow." She stood and extended her hand. "I stopped by to ask you and Lucas some questions, but when I got here, there was a situation."

"Fina put out the fire, Mom," Courtney offered.

"Oh my God, thank you." She hugged Fina and then leaned over both girls to do the same. "I'm Heather Chellew." She looked at the chunks of chocolate on the table.

"I insisted on breaking open the chocolate." Fina sat back down. "It was a traumatic experience, and we needed a pick-me-up."

"Of course. Did the fire department come?"

"I was going to call them, but she put it out," Darcy said.

"I think you'll need to file a claim with your homeowner's insurance," Fina said. "There's some damage." She pointed at the blackened cabinet above the hood.

Heather sighed and shook her head. She had short brown hair and an average build that dropped from her shoulders straight down to her hips. Her boxy shape didn't bode well for her daughters' future physiques.

"We're really sorry, Mom," Courtney said, hanging her head.

"Uh-huh. Your father is not going to be pleased."

"Do we have to tell him?" Darcy wondered.

"Dummy!" her sister exclaimed. "You don't think he'll notice?"

"Courtney! Don't talk to your sister that way. I want you to go to your rooms and finish your homework."

Darcy started to speak.

"If you've already finished your homework, then read a book or clean up your room. No screen time. We'll discuss your punishment when your father gets home."

"We were just trying to help," Courtney insisted.

Heather raised an eyebrow, which seemed to signal to both girls that she meant business. "We will discuss it later."

They grabbed their chocolate and left the room.

Heather contemplated the chocolate, but decided against it. She went over to the sink and eyed the damage before filling a glass with water. "Can I get you some?" she asked Fina.

"No, I'm good," Fina said, aware that there might be a ticking clock on Heather's goodwill.

"What did you want to ask Lucas about?" Heather refilled her glass and came back to the table.

"Covenant Rising."

"Are you a member? I don't remember seeing you there."

"No, although I recently was a guest of Chloe Renard's and heard Pastor Greg preach."

"He is so wonderful." Heather swooned. "Did you just love it?"

Fina smiled. "It was like nothing I've ever seen before. I'm working with the police on the Nadine Quaynor case, and I wanted to speak with Lucas about the leadership committee."

Heather fidgeted in her seat. "What does the leadership committee have to do with it?"

"Nadine and Lucas were both on the committee, and I wanted to ask him some questions."

Realization dawned on Heather's face. "You don't think her death has something to do with the church, do you?"

"No, but I need to get as much information as possible." Fina hoped that Heather was too distracted by the kitchen fire to contemplate Fina's motives too closely.

"I just can't believe that Nadine is gone," she said. "Our hearts are broken."

Fina noticed that her words echoed those of her husband. "Chloe is very distressed. Did you know Nadine well?"

"Lucas knew her better than I did."

"I've heard that she had very strong opinions."

Heather nodded.

"I've served on committees before," Fina offered, "and it's hard when one member likes to be in charge." The only committee on which Fina had ever served was in her freshman dorm. She was appointed to the house residence committee in an effort to get her involved in community living, which backfired spectacularly. She didn't have the will to feign interest in the cereal selection in the dining hall or the fire alarm testing schedule and was swiftly counseled out of the group. Everyone was relieved by the change in membership.

"I don't mean to speak ill of the dead," Heather said, leaning closer to Fina, "but Nadine was difficult."

"In what way?"

"Had to be her way or the highway. She never wanted to hear anyone else's ideas and she couldn't let things go."

Fina nibbled on a square of chocolate. "What kinds of things?"

"I don't know the specifics, but Lucas would always complain that she was like a dog with a bone."

Fina thought that was a good quality in a financial expert, but only, she supposed, if you really wanted people to know where the money was going.

"That must have been annoying," she said.

"Very. I told him he should speak with Pastor Greg about removing her from the committee."

"Did he? Speak with Pastor Greg?"

"I think so. Of course, Lucas only did it for the good of the church. Nadine was creating problems where there weren't any."

"What exactly was she doing that was so disruptive?" Fina asked.

Heather reached over and broke off a square of chocolate, her resolve finally crumbling. "I don't know all the details, but she was involving herself in Pastor Greg and Gabby's business." She bit into the candy and chewed. "And there was also something about the church finances, but I don't know anything about money stuff."

Fina wondered if she was the kind of woman who didn't know anything about money stuff in her own home. Sure, older women were raised to leave the finances to their husbands, but Fina could never believe how many younger women didn't know the first thing about their family's assets. You didn't need a penis to keep tabs on your bank balance.

"You've been very helpful," Fina said.

"Please. You're the one who stopped my kids from burning down the house."

"They would have called 911 eventually."

Heather followed Fina to the front door. "Maybe, but would there be any house left? I'll let Lucas know you stopped by."

"You don't need to bug him with my questions. I don't want to distract him from the home fires, so to speak. I'll give him a call."

"Believe me, he'll welcome a distraction. Did you drive your father crazy when you were a teenager?"

"Actually, I think I still do," Fina admitted. "But we still spend lots of time together. It doesn't seem to have an adverse effect on our relationship." Or maybe the adverse effect was their relationship. It was so hard to tease out the dysfunctional chicken from the dysfunctional egg.

"Don't tell Lucas that. He's convinced it's a stage."

"I'm sure it is. Take care."

Heather stood on the step as Fina unlocked her car and climbed in.

She'd extinguished a fire, eaten some chocolate, and gotten some intel.

Definitely one for the win column.

FOURTEEN

Pastor Greg sat back in his chair and watched Gabby and their older daughter, Faith, clear the plates from the table. Charity slid off her chair under the table and reappeared at his feet. She climbed onto his lap to snuggle.

"You're getting so big!" he said.

"I'm three," the child proclaimed.

Gabby came back into the room and stacked silverware on a plate. She reached across the table, the size of which served as a reminder to Greg that they needed to be fruitful and multiply. His plan was to have kids every two years, but that wasn't panning out.

"I know. You're not a baby anymore," he said. "Who's going to be our baby?" He tickled the girl's neck, and she erupted in giggles. He trained his gaze on Gabby.

"Go play so I can talk to Mommy," Greg said, releasing the little girl from his lap. She scooted out of the room, and Gabby put the stack of dishes back down.

She stared at him. "Don't start, Greg. I'm tired."

"That's why I want you to see Dr. Reilly. Maybe your being tired has something to do with it."

"I had a physical a few months ago, and the doctor said I was fine."

"But you're not fine. If you were, we wouldn't be having this conversation."

Gabby crossed her arms and glared at him. "Maybe it's you? Or maybe it's God's plan? Maybe he only wants us to have two children."

Greg smiled and shook his head. "I do not believe that is God's plan. Two daughters and no sons? No, ma'am."

"Don't think you know better than the Lord, Greg. That'll get you into trouble." She took the plates to the kitchen.

Greg considered following her, but decided to hold off. Dealing with Gabby required patience and finesse. She was stubborn, and things went better if she believed she was calling the shots.

Instead, he retreated to his study where he could look at scripture with one eye and the TV with the other. When they'd purchased the house, Gabby had hired a designer who'd outfitted the room with reproductions of religious paintings and leather-bound books that had never been read. The velvet couch had thick rolled arms, and a fake Tiffany lamp threw off dappled, colored light. Decorating the room had cost a fortune, but Greg had to admit he loved the finished product. He thought it looked elegant and scholarly, like a place where deep thinking occurred.

Gabby always told the girls that he was busy working after dinner, and sometimes he actually was, but more often, he surfed the Net or watched the Discovery Channel. It wasn't something he would admit to his parishioners; he wanted them to believe his mind was only concerned with lofty ideas, not souped-up motorcycles or illegal moonshiners in Appalachia.

The doorbell rang, and Greg heard the girls run to answer it. They were at the age when a ringing phone or a knock at the door was exciting and promising, not the signal of someone needing something. He switched off the TV and picked up a pen. The girls' voices carried from the hallway, and a moment later, Lucas Chellew stood on the threshold of the study.

"Pastor Greg, I got your message that you wanted to see me."

"Come in, Lucas. I hope it wasn't any trouble to stop by."

"Not at all, but I don't want to interrupt you if you're in the middle of something."

Greg smiled and moved to the couch. "Just working on my sermon, but that can wait. Nothing's more important than my congregants."

Gabby poked her head into the room. "Would you like something to drink, Lucas? I've got coffee and tea, and we've got some of those cream cheese brownies that you like."

Lucas exhaled loudly. "I'm feeling sorely tested by the offer. I do love those brownies, but I've been trying to watch my diet."

"Why don't you bring us some, Gab," Greg said. "It's okay to indulge once in a while," he said to Lucas with a smile. "We're only human."

Sitting down at the opposite end of the couch, Lucas adjusted himself on the cushions. Greg watched him. The pastor had learned that people paid more attention when he was still and deliberate with his motions. Fidgeting brought to mind small children who had little self-control.

"Was there something in particular you wanted to discuss, Pastor?" Lucas asked.

Gabby arrived with a tray bearing two cups of coffee and a plate of brownies.

"Thank you, sweetheart," Greg said, sending her on her way. "I just wanted to touch base with you about Nadine's death. How are you doing?"

Lucas stirred a spoonful of sugar into his coffee. He broke off half a brownie and took a bite from the half that had the thicker layer of cream cheese on top. It was rare to have Pastor Greg's undivided attention, and he was making the most of it.

"Like everyone else, I was shocked by her death. I still don't believe it."

Greg nodded. He sipped his black coffee and leaned toward Lucas. "It's hard to process a sudden death, to make sense of the Lord's plan."

"I feel so badly for her family. Even when your children are grown, they're still your babies."

Greg nodded. "Losing a child is a terrible burden, no matter the child's age."

"Has the funeral been planned?"

"Gabby and I visited with her family on Thursday. They're opting for a private funeral and burial."

"The funeral won't be at CRC?" Lucas asked.

"We'll have a memorial for her," Greg reassured him. Nadine's family had been vehemently opposed to CRC playing any role in their daughter's services or burial, but Lucas didn't need to know that. "The medical examiner's office has only just released the body so they haven't made any plans yet."

Lucas paused with his brownie midway to his mouth. "Why did the medical examiner have her?"

"Her death has been ruled suspicious. Didn't you know that?" Greg asked when Lucas stiffened.

"But she was sick."

"Maybe, but she was also poisoned, according to the detectives."

"My Lord in heaven," Lucas murmured.

Greg nodded.

"What does this mean for the church?" Lucas asked.

"We need to pull together. We need to support one another, like we always do."

"Of course."

"We also need to protect what we've worked so hard to build," Greg said, his voice even. He bit into a brownie.

"Do you think this will hurt the church?" Lucas asked.

Greg shrugged. "I don't know, but I'm concerned. We don't want to be associated with a scandal."

"But it's got nothing to do with us!"

"*We* know that, Lucas, but other people might assume the worst. We have no choice but to tolerate the police and their intrusions." Greg shook his head and remained silent.

"But what about that private investigator?" Lucas asked. "She came to see me at work."

"I'll admit, she worries me."

Lucas chewed the remainder of his brownie. He washed it down with some coffee before speaking. "She has no right to interfere with the holy work that we do."

"I agree."

"There must be something we can do."

"We can pray on it," Greg said, and grasped the other man's hand. "Why don't we do that right now?"

Lucas nodded enthusiastically and bowed his head.

"Heavenly Father," Greg intoned, "please give us the strength and guidance to manage our current predicament. Help us protect your work from those who threaten it and build on what we've created in your name. Enable us to spread your love and the good word to those who have not yet seen the light. Amen." He gave Lucas's hand a squeeze. "Is there anything I can do for you? How are Heather and the girls?"

"Driving me crazy, Pastor, but what's new?"

"Just keep guiding them and leading the family. It's your job, even if they don't like it."

"I know. I just wish it weren't such a trial."

Greg stood. "How about I have Gabby wrap up the rest of those brownies? Take them home for the family?"

"Goodness, no." Lucas got up and patted his stomach. "I've already had too much. I'm going to keep praying about Nadine, Pastor Greg."

"I'm glad to hear it. I hope we both get some peace and clarity."

Greg saw him out and returned to the study.

He regretted eating the brownie, but he knew that indulging might reap benefits, depending upon what Lucas Chellew took from their conversation.

Greg would add an extra mile to his workout and pray for a favorable outcome.

The next day, Fina tracked down Evan at Nadine's house in Dorchester. Even though the couple and Molly had been living there as a family since they wed eighteen months earlier, the house remained in Nadine's name only. It was unusual for just the woman of a couple to have ownership, and Fina thought the status of the family domicile warranted some further investigation.

She rang the bell and spied Evan through the window. He was unpacking books from a box and arranging them on shelves in the living room.

"Is this a bad time?" Fina asked when he opened the door.

"It's fine, but I need to keep working. I'm trying to finish some stuff up while Molly isn't here. It's hard to get much done with her underfoot."

"I understand." Fina came in and walked over to the bookcase on the opposite side of the room. Her eye landed on a shelf of cookbooks. "Are you the cook in the family or was that Nadine?"

"I am, although you wouldn't know it given my five-year-old's meal of choice."

"Chicken nuggets?"

"Yup. I try to introduce her to other things, but it's always a battle." He dusted off a shelf with a rag. "Is there any news?"

"Not yet. Have the police been in touch?"

"Just to say they have nothing to say."

"That's not unusual." Fina skipped her fingertip across the spines. "It must be nice to be back home."

Evan shoved a stack of books onto a shelf. "Except that my wife isn't here."

"Of course. I meant that it must be comforting to be back in a familiar place with a supportive community. For you and Molly."

"Absolutely."

"One less thing to worry about."

Evan turned and looked at her. "What's that supposed to mean?"

"Just what I said. It's one less thing to worry about in a time of upheaval."

"This is my house, too, you know."

"Of course. I didn't mean anything by it."

"You're acting like there's something strange about moving back home with my daughter."

"Not at all. I just know that technically, the house belonged to Nadine. I assume you inherit it."

"You think I killed my wife for the house?"

"It's been known to happen."

"You can go now."

"Did you kill Nadine?"

He gaped at her. "Of course not."

"Then it shouldn't bother you if I ask questions to find out who did. The cops must be asking you tough questions. The spouse is always the number one suspect."

"They are asking me tough questions, which is why I don't need them from you, too. I know they have to ask, but it doesn't make it any easier answering them."

"I understand that. I'm not trying to add to your grief. I'm just trying to get to the bottom of this."

He balked. "Don't pretend this is altruistic on your part."

"It's not altruistic. I'm being paid to do a job, but I also have serious concerns about the church and the degree to which they use and manipulate their members. If there's some nefarious stuff going on, don't you want me to expose it?"

He wiped his hands on the thighs of his pants. "Of course."

"So can you tell me about Nadine being sick?"

"You can ask the police. I've discussed it with them."

"Evan."

"That's just part of your job, right?"

Fina had obviously overstayed her welcome. She walked to the door. "I'm sorry I upset you. I'll be in touch."

She replayed the conversation in her head, wondering if she could have come at it differently, thereby getting different results. Irritating Evan hadn't been her goal, but she didn't think it could have been helped. Murder was a nasty topic, and the usual conversational protocol just didn't apply.

If Evan thought his marriage was over, it wasn't out of the realm of possibility that he would try to secure a future for himself and Molly, starting with a great place to live.

People had killed for less.

Rather than alert Lucas Chellew ahead of time, Fina showed up at Macy's unannounced, armed with donuts from Dunkin' Donuts. A saleswoman said he was in a meeting, so Fina spent twenty minutes circulating through the Misses' department. She liked nice clothes, but wasn't a fan of shopping and tended to purchase things on an as-needed basis. Patty sometimes gave her hand-me-downs, and more recently, Fina had started shopping online with surprising success. The ability to try on a host of options in the privacy of one's own home was definitely one of the greatest benefits of the Internet as far as she was concerned.

She was eyeing the scandalously short options in the Juniors' department when Lucas called to her from across the floor.

Once they were seated in his office, she offered him a donut. There was a moment of hesitation, but then he reached into the bag and pulled out a jelly-filled.

"I owe you my thanks," he said, licking a drop of jelly from his finger.

"For what?"

"For saving my children from a disaster. If you hadn't been there, they would have burned down the house."

"You're welcome, but I'm sure they would have called 911. Everything would have been fine."

Lucas shook his head. "I don't know. They don't always make very good choices, obviously."

"It's hard to resist the siren song of fondue."

"Well, they won't make that mistake again."

Fina didn't know if this meant that the fondue pot had been retired or the girls had been banned from the kitchen, but at the moment she really didn't care. She needed to capitalize on Lucas's current goodwill.

"I was hoping you could clear something up for me," Fina said. She was enjoying a glazed donut and took a moment to wipe some of the sugary coating off her hand. "I understand that you requested that Nadine Quaynor be removed from the church's leadership committee. Why was that?"

Lucas sighed and put his donut down on what looked to be an old ad circular. "Fina, I've told you. I'm not at liberty to discuss church business with you."

She smiled. "Of course you are, Lucas. There are no laws forbidding it."

"I'm not talking about the law; I'm talking about my responsibilities to the church."

"I would think that your responsibility to the church—to God, even—would be to help expose whoever killed Nadine."

"But what does that have to do with the leadership committee?"

"It may not have anything to do with it, but do you want to be the reason that Nadine's killer goes free?" She was laying it on a bit thick, but what did she have to lose?

"I don't know anything so I couldn't possibly have any effect on the investigation."

Fina took another bite and chewed slowly. She finished the donut, crumpled her napkin into a ball, and put it in the empty bag. "I'm surprised you're protecting Nadine."

Lucas looked confused. "What do you mean?"

"My understanding was that Nadine was asked to leave the committee because she was interfering with church finances and wanted to intercede in Pastor Greg's marriage in an inappropriate way. If that were the case, I don't know why you wouldn't want to discuss it. It makes me think that something else was going on." Fina leaned over and dropped the bag into a trash can. "Sorry to interrupt your workday," she said, rising from her seat.

"Wait a second, now, wait a second," Lucas said, like any good car salesman when the customer had one foot out the door. "You don't need to rush off."

"I understand, Lucas. You are extremely loyal, and you need to protect the living. I'm sure I can get what I need from someone else."

"Sit back down so we can resolve this."

Fina took her seat and waited.

"I don't want to speak ill of the dead," he started.

"Of course not," Fina said, although in her experience, people were eager to speak ill of the dead, and why not? Being dead didn't make you a better person.

"I don't want this situation to disrupt the wonderful work that Covenant Rising does in the community."

"Of course not."

He took a deep breath. "Nadine wasn't a good fit for the leadership committee. This was a feeling shared by a number of the members, and ultimately, Pastor Greg agreed."

"And she wasn't a good fit because?"

Lucas wiped his hands on his napkin and tossed it, along with the jelly-stained circular, into the trash. "The only thing we want is to spread the word of Jesus."

Fina nodded. Where this was going, she did not know.

He leaned his forearms on the desk. "Nadine was a troublemaker. She questioned the leadership of the church unnecessarily."

"Uh-huh." From what Fina had seen, there wasn't any such thing as "necessary questioning" of Pastor Greg or the church's doctrine. "Is dissent frowned upon?"

Lucas shook his head. "Of course not, but we value faith and trust."

"What does that mean?"

"It means that everything will be as it should be," he said impatiently.

He really was like a car salesman. He talked a lot, but didn't say much. If Fina wasn't careful, she'd be putting twenty-five hundred dollars down on a new minivan by the time she left the room.

"I assume things went more smoothly once Nadine left the committee?"

Lucas nodded. "They did. There was some healing that had to take place, and we're better for it."

Fina doubted that Nadine would have agreed with that statement, but she wasn't going to debate life after death with Lucas. If the failure to believe was a deal breaker, any debate with him was a losing proposition.

"Do the other congregants know that Nadine was kicked off the committee?"

He winced. "It wasn't like that. Pastor Greg didn't make an announcement, if that's what you're asking."

Fina stood once more and extended her hand. "Thank you for taking the time to speak with me, Lucas. I really appreciate it."

"Glad I could be helpful."

"Please give my best to Heather and the girls. I hope their future cooking endeavors are a little less exciting."

"We're all praying for that."

Fina walked out to the parking lot and started up the loaner. During the early days of any case, the list of possible suspects and scenarios often expanded before contracting, and this case was no different.

If Lucas and Greg had been so threatened by Nadine's questions, who knew how far they'd go to silence her?

Fina was sitting in traffic when a call came in from Dante Trimonti. He needed to see her ASAP. He was at the Crystal nightclub near Fenway, where he conducted his prostitution business. Fina didn't love being summoned, but Dante communicated a sense of urgency that she couldn't ignore.

The club wasn't open when she got there, so Fina went around to the service entrance and announced herself to the muscular young man overseeing a delivery of kegs at the back door.

"I'm here to see Dante," she said. "Fina Ludlow."

His eyes descended her body and climbed back up again.

"He called me in to audition for the 'soccer mom' opening," Fina said.

The bouncer smirked. "I'll be back."

She waited thirty seconds, then ducked inside the club.

Crystal was unassuming from the front, but it filled an entire lot—

from the street all the way back to the Pike. The walls were black and the ceilings low. Empty of sweaty young revelers, the space looked especially dirty and desolate, smelling of beer and unwashed socks. There was a young man in the DJ booth, but no music, and behind the bar that stretched across one side of the room, men dressed in black were unpacking boxes of booze.

Fina went upstairs to the VIP section and found the bouncer in conversation with Dante, who sat in a large, circular booth. Dante nodded when he caught sight of her, and the bouncer sneered.

"I told you to wait outside," he said.

"No, you didn't." She looked at Dante. "Is he supposed to be security? He left the back door wide open."

"Joey! What did I tell you about that?" he asked the bouncer. "Don't be a bonehead!"

"I told her to stay," Joey insisted.

"No, you didn't, but even if you had, I'm not a dog." Fina plopped down in the booth. "Could I please have a diet soda with a lime?"

"I'm not a goddamn waiter."

"Get her the drink and get me a beer," Dante said. "Then go down and check that door."

They watched Joey place the order at the VIP bar and throw a nasty look in Fina's direction before descending the stairs.

"Why are you so testy?" Dante asked.

Fina took a deep breath and dismissed the various retorts that came to mind. "I'm my usual cheerful self. What was so important I had to come to the land of hoes and he-men?"

He grinned. "I don't take that as an insult, you know."

Dante was handsome, but it was hard to get past his slicked-back hair and tight T-shirt. In his early twenties, he was in great shape, but had an air of spending too much time on his appearance. Vanity wasn't attractive in men or women.

"What's the story with my car?" Fina asked.

"Your tires are special order. It's going to take a few more days."

The bartender came to the table with a bottle of Dos Equis and a tall glass of soda with a lime wedge tucked over the lip. Fina squeezed the lime and dropped it into the glass.

"You could have told me that over the phone; what's so important?" she asked.

Dante took a swig of his beer and wiped his mouth with the back of his hand.

"Don't be so bitchy," he said. "I'm doing you a favor."

"What favor is that?"

"Passing on information."

"Okay. I appreciate it."

Dante stretched his arms across the back of the booth. "You're going to owe me."

"Fine, but there are some things I won't do."

He grinned. "That wasn't what I had in mind, but I'd consider it."

"That makes one of us. Come on, Dante. Cut to the chase."

"I haven't found the guy who slashed your tires, but you'd better watch your back."

"Because?"

"Someone has ordered a beatdown on you."

Fina put her glass on the table. "A beatdown? There's a contract to beat me up?"

"That's what I heard."

"And from whom did you hear this?"

He shook his head. "I can't give you any one name. It's just chatter."

"Since when do you work for the NSA?"

The corner of his mouth arched up in a smirk.

Fina sat back and sighed. The escalation wasn't surprising, just annoying. "So has anyone accepted this contract?" she asked.

"Last I heard, there were no takers. People don't want to mess with you. You have a reputation for being a crazy bitch."

Fina shrugged. "If the shoe fits."

"Yeah, but eventually, someone is going to sign up for the job. It's good money." He took a drink.

"What's the going rate for beating me up these days?"

"Five large."

Fina's mouth dropped open. "That's it? That's insulting."

"People kill for less than that, Fina. You should be flattered."

"Yet, somehow, I'm not."

"You need to watch your back."

"I need more info. You've got to give me a name."

"I don't have one to give you."

"Dante, I can't stop it if I can't track down the order."

"Uh-huh, and what happens to me when it gets out that I sent you on a fishing expedition?"

"I'll be discreet."

He screwed his face up in disbelief. "Right."

"At least tell me someone else who can confirm it. Who else was privy to this chatter?"

He considered the question for a moment. "Try Glen Sullivan. He might have heard something." Glen Sullivan was a low-level con who specialized in small-time scams and fraud.

"Thank you." Fina used the straw to push the lime to the bottom of the glass. "This is very inconvenient."

Dante shook his head and broke into a big smile. "You are a crazy bitch."

"What makes you say that?"

"Most people would be scared knowing they've got a target on their back; you're just annoyed."

She held up her hands. "You expect me to curl up in a ball and cry?"

"So what are you going to do?" Dante asked.

"Like you said: Watch my back." Fina pushed herself out of the booth and put her bag over her shoulder. "I do appreciate the heads-up, Dante. I owe you."

"I look forward to collecting."

"Don't get your hopes up, tiger."

Fina left through the front door so she wouldn't have to see Joey again and revisit his poor performance evaluation. She zipped open her bag and gripped her gun in her hand. Her weapon didn't do her any good if she couldn't access it or, worse, if someone else grabbed it from her bag in a struggle. Maybe it was time to dig her hip holster out of her closet.

Making fashion decisions was so tedious.

FIFTEEN

"Pastor, do you want the worksheets on the altar or in each pew?"

"It doesn't matter, Betty!" Greg sparked at his secretary.

She dipped her head down like a dog that had been kicked, which only irritated Greg more. He liked being in charge, but occasionally, it got tiresome.

Greg took a deep breath and placed a hand on Betty's shoulder. "Forgive me, Betty. I'm sorry I snapped at you. The events of the past week have made me weary."

"You don't need to apologize, Pastor. I can't imagine the responsibility you have to bear during this difficult time."

"I just keep reminding myself that everything is part of God's plan. Even the suffering and the trials."

Betty nodded and grasped the pile of worksheets to her chest.

"Why don't you put some in every pew," Greg suggested.

She smiled and left to attend to her assigned task. He watched her start down the aisle and wondered at her satisfaction with having a designated job. The world really was full of people who just wanted to be told what to do.

Greg turned from his spot in the doorway so he could scan the lobby. There were small clusters of members chatting and laughing, and on the other side of the glass doors, some kids kicked around a soccer ball. He was surprised to see Gabby and Lucas standing in the open coat closet, deep in conversation. Lucas was leaning over Greg's wife, like a tree that climbs higher than a neighboring shrub. His face was pulled taut, somewhere between a frown and a grimace. Gabby's lips were set in a straight line, and when she opened them to speak, she pointed her finger at Lucas for emphasis.

What were they discussing? Greg knew that Gabby rubbed some congregants the wrong way, but it was mostly just the young wives who felt threatened. Despite having two babies in quick succession, Gabby had maintained her figure and could pass for a college coed. Most people looked up to Gabby, but sometimes, feelings veered into envy.

Lucas looked over and noticed Greg watching them. Lucas raised his hand in a meek wave. Gabby gestured as if to recapture his attention. They shared thirty more seconds of conversation, and then broke apart. Lucas moved over to join some other members, and Gabby drifted over to Greg.

"Everything okay?" he asked, looping an arm around her trim waist.

"Of course."

"It looked like you and Lucas were having a tense discussion."

"You know Lucas. He wants everything just so. He really should 'let go, let God' a little bit more."

"Some people struggle with their faith more than others."

"Hmm."

"Did you make that appointment with Dr. Reilly?" Greg asked.

Gabby took a step back and removed his hand from her waist. "I told you not to bug me about that."

"And I told you that we need to figure out what's wrong."

"Nothing's wrong. Now who's struggling with his faith?"

"We need to set an example for our followers, Gab. This isn't about you and me."

"Right." She crossed her arms.

"How can we expect them to follow our path if they don't see its blessings?" he asked.

"Fine. I'll make the appointment."

Greg pulled her into a tight hug. "I knew you would do the right thing."

Across the room Lucas was watching them. Greg smiled and waved his hand.

If things went his way, they might have an Easter miracle to share with the congregation.

She hadn't even been beaten up yet, but Fina was already feeling beaten down. She lay on the couch, the bottoms of her feet pressed against Milloy's thigh. They were watching a TV show about the weird foods found in China, and Fina was glad she'd already eaten.

"Do you want to be my bodyguard?" she asked Milloy.

"Is that code for something or a real question?"

"It's a real question. There's a contract out to beat me up, and I'm toying with the idea of taking additional precautions."

"That doesn't sound like you."

"I know. You're the only person I can think of who I would want to fill the position."

"Does Cristian know about this?"

"Not yet."

"You know I'd do it if I could, but I'm booked solid right now."

"I assumed as much, but I thought I'd ask."

"You should call Dennis."

"Maybe tomorrow. Nothing's going to happen to me here."

"You sure about that? Your condo was trashed, and your tires were slashed—in this building."

"True, but I had the locks changed, and I'm armed."

"I'll stay over."

The offer held appeal. Milloy was easy; she could take him up on it and not agonize over what it meant. His offer wasn't loaded with emotional baggage, but accepting it might complicate her life. If Cristian found out that Milloy was protecting her, he'd be bullshit.

"It's tempting, but I'm good."

When he left a couple of hours later, Fina threw the dead bolt after him and sat down in front of the box of Rand's belongings. She pulled out a couple of snapshots that looked as though they were taken at parties—group shots of young people grinning and holding plastic cups. Fina took pictures of the photos and e-mailed them to Lindsay. Maybe one of the faces would ring a bell.

With her gun on her bedside table, Fina climbed into bed and burrowed under the covers.

The next morning, Fina contemplated her options regarding her personal safety and concluded they were limited. She needed to figure out who was after her, and the best way to do that was unencumbered, so she held off calling Dennis. She'd give herself the day to make some headway, and she'd carry her gun and stay on guard. It wasn't necessarily the prudent thing to do, but Fina was willing to take the risk if it meant she wouldn't have to hire a babysitter.

Lindsay had answered her e-mail with the names of two of the girls in the party pictures, which she'd get to after the first order of business, which was a visit to the holy rollers.

Outside the Gatchell abode, Fina sat for a few moments with the engine idling, studying the house. It was immense and hugged the edges of the modest-sized lot. There was a small yard separated from the street by a tall white fence. The front door was framed by pillars, and a faux balcony crowned the door. Fina never understood fake balconies, but they seemed to be a popular feature in expensive new builds.

She noticed the three-car garage, which seemed superfluous in a household with two drivers unless you had a thing for fancy cars. Last she checked, pastors weren't supposed to have a thing for fancy cars. The yard was in the sad New England stage called early spring. The grass looked anemic, and the bulbs hadn't yet pierced the soil. Leftover sand littered the path, evidence of the winter's heavy snowfall.

Fina rang the bell and listened as a thunder of organ music was unleashed in the house. It was followed by the sound of running feet and the bubbling voices of small children. The door swung wide open and revealed two little girls with expectant grins.

"Hi," Fina said.

"Hi," the older of the two responded. The younger stared at Fina. There was a smear of something across her cheek—possibly jelly—and she was wearing a long-sleeved shirt and tights. The tights were like sausage casings, and the pattern on her Pull-Up was visible through the knit. Fina couldn't remember if the girls were Chastity and Charity or Mercy and Faith.

"Is your mom or dad home?" Fina asked.

"Mom!" the older girl yelled. "There's a lady!"

Fina waited on the doorstep while the girls raced across the huge foyer and started up the curved staircase. The bannisters were polished to a sheen, and an Oriental runner was draped over the risers. They were nearing the top when Gabby Gatchell came through the formal living room into the entryway.

"Yes?" she asked. She was wearing tight jeans and an oversized sweater that dropped off one shoulder. Her dark blond hair was pulled back in a ponytail at the crown of her head.

"We met about a week and a half ago," Fina said, wondering if

Gabby's lack of recognition was real or feigned. "My name is Fina Ludlow, and Chloe Renard introduced us after the church service."

Gabby's face perked up with a smile. "I remember! You're helping her with the land donation."

"Right."

The girls were descending using the opposite rail. Fina imagined the opulent stairs were an endless source of entertainment.

"Please, come in." Gabby stood back and ushered Fina inside. "What can I do for you?"

"Actually, I had a few questions for Pastor Greg."

Gabby frowned and consulted a slim watch on her wrist. "He's not available, but should be in about ten minutes. Would you like to wait? I have tea and coffee."

Fina wasn't sure why she was getting such a warm welcome. Either Greg hadn't shared their most recent conversation with Gabby or perhaps Gabby was savvy and didn't see the benefit in shutting out Fina.

"Coffee would be lovely."

Gabby led the way through a series of rooms with shiny wood floors and crown molding. There were fringed antimacassars, scrolled dining chairs, and an inlaid buffet. Everything looked expensive and put-together, but more like a hired designer's vision than that of an engaged homeowner. Some people decorated their homes because they had a passion for a certain time period or design aesthetic. Others just liked the look of certain things, but Fina was willing to bet that Gabby had given an expert a large check and accepted the deliveries. There was nothing wrong with that approach, but it suggested the homeowner was concerned with making a very specific impression on visitors that revealed little about herself.

Gabby directed Fina to a round glass table in the informal dining area next to the kitchen. The ceiling rose two stories, and a balcony overlooked the space. A second staircase—less ostentatious than the first—connected the two floors.

The girls appeared in the room a moment later, with various toys in tow. The eldest had a Tupperware container filled with Polly Pocket dolls and accessories, and the younger grasped a doll under each elbow, effectively putting the infants in headlocks. One was a baby dressed as a bunny, and the other was a flower, complete with a petal halo around her face. They dropped to the floor by the table and began to play.

"You said coffee, right?" Gabby asked.

"Yes, please." Fina looked around the room. "Your home is beautiful."

"Thanks." Gabby busied herself firing up the fancy coffee machine. "Did you enjoy the service at the church?"

"It was great," Fina said. "Unlike any other service I've attended."

"Were you raised in a church?"

"Congregationalist." Fina always thought of it as Protestant light, but that was probably just her family's approach.

Gabby put a mug of coffee down in front of Fina. "And have you accepted Jesus Christ as your savior?"

"Wow," Fina commented, reaching for the sugar and cream. "That's a big question this early in the day."

Gabby was silent. There was a challenge in the inquiry and in her gaze.

"I'm undecided on Jesus Christ," Fina offered after a moment.

"Are you married?"

"No," Fina replied, wondering what that had to do with anything.

"There are lots of available men at Covenant Rising. Decent, God-fearing men."

Fina sipped her coffee. "I'll keep that in mind."

"I'm sure God has a plan for you, but you need to buy a ticket if you want to win the lottery."

"Indeed."

Gabby's phone dinged on the counter. She retrieved it, glanced at the screen, and set it down next to her coffee.

"So did you know Nadine Quaynor well?" Fina asked.

"I pride myself on knowing all of our members," Gabby said. "I can't tell you how heartbroken I am about her passing."

"It is awful." Nadine had certainly left a string of broken CRC hearts in her wake, which was odd, considering that no one seemed to like her.

"But she's at home with the Lord now, which is comforting."

"Uh-huh."

"She was a wonderful member of our community." Gabby looked at her younger daughter, who was stripping the flower costume off her doll. "Charity, leave that on. Dolly's going to get cold."

"I've heard that Nadine wasn't universally loved," Fina commented.

Gabby frowned. "Who told you that?" Her phone dinged again, and she looked at the screen. A smile crept across her face.

"You should take that," Fina said.

"No, it's fine." She put the phone facedown on the table. "Who told you that people didn't like Nadine?"

Fina screwed up her face in concentration. "I don't remember. I talk to so many people."

"Well, that just isn't true."

"Maybe I misunderstood."

"Well, if it isn't my favorite private investigator," Pastor Greg said from the top of the staircase.

Fina looked up at him, knowing that he enjoyed looking down on her. "That must be a pretty small pool of candidates, Pastor Greg," she said.

Charity dropped her doll to the floor and scurried up the stairs to her father. He lifted her up, and she wrapped her arms around him like a koala around a tree.

Gabby's phone dinged again. She turned it faceup and glanced at the screen.

Greg came down the stairs and took a seat at the table. He settled his daughter into his lap.

"Can I get some of that coffee?" He smiled at Gabby.

"Of course, sweetheart. Do you need a refill?" she asked Fina, rising from the table.

"No, thanks."

"So what did you misunderstand?" Greg was wearing jeans and a long-sleeved crew neck T-shirt. His hair was wet, and Fina guessed his pressing business had been a shower.

"Sorry?"

Before he could clarify his question, Gabby's phone dinged yet again. Greg reached for the device, but Gabby hightailed it over from the kitchen and snatched it from his grasp.

"It's just Donna having a crisis," Gabby insisted. "She'd be embarrassed if you knew about it."

Greg looked at her with a tepid smile. "No need to be embarrassed."

"You know how she is." Gabby fiddled with a button on the phone and slipped it into her pocket. Greg watched as she retrieved his coffee from the kitchen counter, and Fina watched Greg. Spouses shouldn't be privy to each other's e-mails or phone calls, but in her experience, hypersensitivity to this tenet was also a red flag.

"You said you misunderstood something," Greg continued. "I heard you say that when I was coming downstairs."

Fina wondered what else he had heard and how long he'd been lurking in the upstairs hallway.

"About Nadine," Gabby interjected. "Fina was under the impression that people didn't like Nadine."

Charity hopped off her father's lap onto the floor, where she shoved a bottle into the doll's puckered mouth.

"Who told you that?" Greg asked.

"I wondered the same thing," Gabby said.

Fina shrugged. "I'd have to go back and check my notes, but Gabby was reassuring me that wasn't the case."

"Not at all," Greg said. "Nadine was a beloved member of our community."

"Right. So why was she removed from the leadership committee?"

The couple exchanged a quick glance.

"Fina." Greg reached out and took her hand. She struggled not to pull it from his grasp.

"Pastor Greg."

He shook his head and smiled. It was the same affectation she had witnessed during his sermon. It was a bid to communicate warmth and regret, but condescension was the prevailing feeling that Fina got.

"We can't discuss sensitive church information with you, but please know that we loved Nadine."

Fina reclaimed her hand. "But somebody didn't." She sighed. "I'm just disappointed."

"Why?" Greg asked, gazing into her eyes.

"Because the church isn't cooperating with the investigation."

"We are cooperating. We've spoken with the police."

"But the police and I are working together," Fina said, knowing Pitney would throw a fit over that characterization. "Your unwillingness to be candid with me is only drawing out the process."

"Why don't we pray together?" he asked.

"Oh God, really?" Fina couldn't help but exclaim.

"You have something against prayer?"

"Of course not. I meant that I didn't want him to think I was asking too much. I don't want to be too needy."

"There's no such thing as too needy when it comes to our savior," Greg assured her.

Clearly, given that the man never missed an opportunity to request divine intervention.

"Faith, Charity, join us."

The girls stood and joined a circle of hands with Fina, Greg, and Gabby. Fina hadn't done this much hand-holding since preschool.

"Dear Lord, please grant us the patience to surrender to your wisdom and your plan. Please give Sister Fina the support she needs as she navigates these troubled waters and tries to make peace with your sacrifice. Amen."

Why was it all about her?

"I appreciate the coffee," Fina said, bringing her mug to the sink.

Greg and Gabby followed her to the front door, where they stood, their arms around each other's waists. "I know you'll find what you need," Greg said, as Fina made her way down the path.

She stopped and turned toward the couple. "I have complete faith that I'll find out who killed Nadine, Pastor Greg, and that that person will face judgment in this life."

Pulling away from the curb, she watched them in the doorway.

She knew it was ungodly, but she really didn't like those two.

SIXTEEN

With an inkling of dread, Fina drove to the BPD. She locked her gun in the trunk of her car and hoped that whoever was after her didn't have the balls to attack her on the steps of the police station.

The clerk at the front desk took her name, and ten minutes later, a uniformed officer brought her upstairs to an interview room in the Major Crimes department. She sat in a plastic chair affixed to the floor and tried not to touch too many surfaces. Fina could only imagine the unwashed bodies that had graced the room.

Another ten minutes of waiting gave her time to text Haley and Milloy and play a game of solitaire. Her stomach was starting to growl when Pitney and Cristian came into the room and took chairs across from her.

"Why do we always have to meet in here?" Fina asked.

"Because the billiards room is occupied," Pitney replied. "What can we do for you, Fina?"

"I'm here to report a potential crime."

Cristian looked perplexed, and Pitney opened her hands in a "lay it on me" gesture. The lieutenant was true to style in a bright red top and plum-colored pants. Her curly hair provided a cushion for the lavender beaded earrings dangling from her lobes.

"Apparently," Fina continued, "there's some kind of contract out to have me beaten up."

"What are you talking about?" Cristian asked, leaning toward her.

"You know, a contract. Someone wants to hire a thug to beat me up. Put me in the hospital, I presume."

"Not kill you?" Pitney asked.

"No," Fina said, smiling.

"This isn't funny," Cristian remarked.

Fina leaned back against the unforgiving chair. "It's a little funny." She looked at the two cops. "How many people can say that someone is willing to pay to hurt them? It's like an anti–bucket list item."

"Well, at least you see the silver lining," Pitney commented.

"Don't encourage her," Cristian said, glaring at his boss.

"Give us the details."

"First, my condo was trashed."

"When?" Cristian demanded.

"Week ago Monday. After we had dinner."

"Why didn't you say something?"

"You two need to save the domestic drama for home," Pitney said. "Seriously. I'm not interested."

"And then my tires were slashed in my garage."

"Any idea who's behind it?" Pitney asked while Cristian glowered next to her.

"There were some nuts who sent me hate mail when Liz Barone died," Fina said, referring to her previous case, "but none of the letters raised a red flag. I looked at older cases, but came up empty."

"Is anyone else working on this?"

"I'm going to call Dennis Kozlowski since he did the security assessments for me on the Barone case. Also, I've been told that Glen Sullivan might have some information."

"Maybe Buckley and his guys have heard something," Pitney said to Cristian, referring to the anti-crime squad. "You don't have any idea who might be behind this?" she asked Fina.

Fina shook her head. "I really don't. If I did, I'd be on it."

"I know. Are you carrying?"

"Yes. Not at the moment, obviously."

"Have you considered hiring some protection?" Pitney asked.

"I'd rather not."

"Fina—" Cristian protested.

"You and I both know, Cristian, that having a shadow interferes with my job. I don't like having anyone breathing down my neck."

"Don't be stupid, Fina," Pitney said. "That someone could save your life."

Fina massaged her forehead with her fingertips. "I'll think about it."

"You hired a bodyguard for Haley when she was threatened," Cristian said.

"Haley is a teenager who isn't armed—thank God. Are you really comparing the two situations?"

"Wow," Pitney said, "you guys get more irritating with each passing moment."

Fina and Cristian were silent.

"I think you should hire someone," Pitney said, "but short of that, stay alert."

"I will. I'm very interested in not getting the shit beaten out of me."

"Good to hear." Pitney stood up. "I'll talk to some people, and Menendez will update you."

She left the room, pulling the door closed behind her.

"I think you should stay with me until this blows over," Cristian said.

"Not going to happen. I appreciate the offer, but it's not a good idea."

"You'll be safer with me."

"You have a child, Cristian."

"He isn't with me all the time."

Fina shook her head. "Doesn't matter. I don't want this anywhere near him, and if you were thinking clearly, you wouldn't either."

"I don't like this."

"I don't either, but I promise you, I'll be careful. Please don't make me regret telling you."

"What do you want me to do, Fina? Not give a shit?"

"Of course not." She felt badly and decided to throw him a bone. "Did you know that Nadine Quaynor was kicked off the leadership committee at Covenant Rising Church?"

"Who told you that?"

"Everyone is so interested in my sources," Fina mused.

"Who's everyone?"

"The point is that everything wasn't smooth sailing at the church."

"Not surprising, but what are you thinking? Getting kicked off gave *Nadine* a motive to kill someone, not the other way around."

"True, but what if kicking her off the committee wasn't enough? What if she had to be dealt with in a more permanent way?"

"We'll look into it."

They stood, and Cristian put his hand on the doorknob. Fina leaned her palm against the door to stop him.

"I promise you that I will talk to Dennis Kozlowski about a protection detail, and I will be extremely careful."

He looked at her. "Okay."

"Okay." She leaned in and kissed him.

Back at the car, Fina unlocked her gun from the trunk and nestled it back into the holster.

If she let some creep beat her up, Cristian would kill her.

Fina knew that she was safer in a controlled environment as opposed to the open road, so she made a beeline for the Ludlow and Associates office.

Matthew wasn't available, so she went to Scotty's office, where she found him sitting on his couch, reviewing some papers.

"Hey. Do you have a minute?"

He glanced at his watch. "Sure."

"Do you have any of those vouchers from Cheerful Cleaners?"

"You interrupted me to talk about housecleaning?"

"I need it for a case—a bribe of sorts. It says something about our modern society, doesn't it, that offers of housecleaning garner all kinds of information in return?" Matthew had won a generous settlement for a housekeeping company from a cleaning supply conglomerate. In addition to his cut, he was showered with housekeeping vouchers that Fina found most helpful.

"I thought Matthew had those."

"He does, but I can't find him or his assistant."

"You're a private eye. You'll figure it out."

She sat down next to him. "Just FYI, someone's after me, and I'm thinking about hiring a bodyguard."

Scotty began clicking his ballpoint pen.

"Don't freak out," Fina said. "It's all good."

"Is anyone else in the family at risk?"

"No. Just me, and it's not to kill me, just beat me up."

Scotty grasped his hands together as if in prayer. "Well, then. I feel much better."

"I told the cops," she said, punching him gently on the arm. "I'm totally on top of it."

Scotty gave her a pained smile.

"So I heard you met Matthew's girlfriend," she said.

"Yes. She's lovely."

"Maybe Patty could counsel her on how to deal with Mom. She's an expert, after all."

"You don't know for sure how Mom's going to be with Sydney."

"I don't? I'm pretty sure I know how she's going to react to a single mother."

"A Jewish single mother."

"Good God."

"I've got to get back to work," Scotty said, tapping his chest. "This conversation is giving me angina."

Fina gave him a kiss on the cheek and rose.

"How's the Rand thing going?" he asked.

"It's going."

Scotty looked at her, but was quiet.

"I'm assuming you don't want a detailed update," Fina said.

"I'd rather not, but I don't want all of this to be on your shoulders."

"I'll let you know when I'm further along."

Rand came into the room at that moment.

"Speak of the devil," Fina said.

Her eldest brother glared at her, then turned his attention to Scotty. "We need to talk about the Mikiyato case."

"Sure."

Fina left and looped back around to Matthew's office, where his assistant, Sue, was happy to dole out some Cheerful Cleaning vouchers. Matthew was in court, his ETA unknown, so she decided to head home and regroup.

Back at the condo, Fina made a fluffernutter with a tall glass of milk, which she ate in front of the TV, watching a *Law & Order* rerun. It was one with Detective Ed Green, played by Jesse L. Martin. For one hour, she felt pure contentment: a fluffernutter, a case she didn't have to solve, a handsome cop. What more could she ask for?

The doorbell was an unwelcome interruption, particularly when Fina peeked through the peephole and saw Stanley on the other side.

"Hi, Stanley," Fina said, tucking her gun into the back of her pants. She'd shed the holster before lunch.

"I've got a package for you, Ms. Ludlow," he said, handing Fina a box from a clothing retailer, which she placed on the floor next to the door. "And this just arrived." "This" was an unmarked brown envelope. There was no postage or return address, just her name.

"Really? Who dropped it off?"

"A gentleman asked Mrs. Bennigan to bring it in." Mrs. Bennigan was a sweet old lady who would cheerfully carry a ticking bomb onto a plane. She was very trusting.

"I'm assuming you didn't get him on the surveillance tape?"

"Afraid not."

"All righty. Thanks, Stanley." Fina pinched the envelope between her fingertips and pushed the door closed with her foot.

She dropped the envelope onto the dining room table and looked at it. She didn't think it would explode since it was flat, and it didn't have any odor. Fina knew she should call Cristian, but that required time and patience she didn't have.

Instead, she donned a pair of latex gloves and her sunglasses, thinking some protection was better than none.

Inside the envelope was a single sheet of white paper with cutout letters in the style of a ransom note.

It read: "Go away or you'll be sorry."

"Oh, for fuck's sake," Fina groaned.

She left the note on the table and dropped down onto the couch.

Was it too early to call it a day?

Fina allowed herself half an hour of self-pity, then decided that break-ins, vandalism, threats of bodily harm, and poison pen letters were no reason to have a bad day. You couldn't be a good private investigator and a wuss at the same time.

Since action was the antidote to self-pity, she decided to pay Evan a visit, but not without some trepidation. Fina was willing to take risks with her own life, but she didn't want an innocent bystander—or God forbid, a child—to get caught in the crossfire. She'd just have to be vigilant—and stay away from windows.

When Evan answered the door, she made her case before he could speak.

"I know things got tense during our last conversation," Fina said. "I've brought a peace offering." She handed him an envelope with the cleaning vouchers. "They're vouchers for housecleaning to lighten your load."

He pulled out the slips of paper and examined them.

"I'm very single-minded when I'm on a case," Fina continued. "I know that can come off as insensitivity, and I'm sorry. Can we have a do-over?"

Evan flicked the vouchers across his open palm while contemplating her offer. "Sure."

"Thank you. I appreciate it. Do you have a few minutes to talk?"

He opened the door wider, and Fina came into the house.

"I'm in the middle of a situation," he said, leading her to the kitchen. There was a plate on the counter with remnants of an English muffin, and a couple of banker's boxes were stacked on the table next to a small pile of papers.

"What's the problem?" she asked, looking around.

"The disposal." He pointed at the sink, which was filled with grungy-looking gray water. Reaching into the mini cesspool, Evan twisted something, and a horrible grinding noise kicked in. Fina winced. Another twist stopped the noise. Shredded carrot and chunks of unidentifiable food floated on the scummy liquid.

"Can I help?" Fina asked.

He sighed. "If you think you can. It's jammed up. Apparently, you can't put carrot shavings down the disposal."

"Got it," Fina said. She took off her coat and rolled up her sleeves before plunging her hand into the murky mess. She tried to start the disposal, to no avail.

"Do you have a plunger?" Fina pulled her hand out and ran the water for a moment to rinse it clean.

Evan gave her a hand towel. "I thought you were supposed to use a broom."

"If something is jammed in the disposal itself, but I think you've got a blockage in the pipe."

"There's one upstairs. I'll get it," he said, leaving the room.

Fina tossed the towel onto the counter and moved over to the table. She listened for Evan's footsteps overhead and quickly thumbed through the stack of papers. A familiar logo jumped out at her, and Fina pulled out a Boston Police Department evidence inventory work-sheet for closer inspection. Grabbing her phone from her bag, she took photos of the two-page document and returned it to the pile. Noises carried from overhead, and she pulled the top off one of the banker's boxes and scanned the folders. She'd made little progress when she heard Evan coming back downstairs.

"Sorry. I couldn't find it at first." He handed the plunger to Fina.

She placed it over the sink drain and wiggled it in an effort to get a good seal. She started plunging, which threw up waves of dirty water. The sink and disposal made a series of noises, and she dodged what looked like pieces of soggy potato before a loud belch issued from the pipes and the fetid water was sucked down.

"That's great!" Evan said as they peered at the detritus left in the sink. "Thank you so much."

Fina ran her hands under the water. "I thought you were some kind of engineer. This isn't your bailiwick?"

He looked sheepish. "I'm a project manager on the administrative side. My mechanical knowledge is limited."

She dried her hands. "Ronnie wasn't around to help?" Fina had noticed his empty driveway when she'd pulled up.

"Nope. He would have been my first call."

"Looks like you're still unpacking," she said, nodding toward the boxes on the table.

"Ah, no. Those are Nadine's. The cops were looking at those."

"Find anything useful?"

"I don't think so. They didn't take them away."

"Do you mind if I have a look?"

He hesitated. "I guess not, but there's nothing in them. It's stuff like subscription information and travel receipts."

"That's okay. It will help me get to know Nadine a little bit better."

"Suit yourself." He glanced at his watch. "I've got to pick up Molly."

They carried the boxes out to Fina's car, and she stashed them in the trunk. "I'm still not having any luck connecting with Nadine's parents. Any suggestions?"

"I know they've spoken with the police, but they're devastated. They're keeping to themselves."

"Okay. I'll keep trying, and I'll let you know if I find anything useful in this stuff," she said, gesturing toward the trunk.

"I can't imagine you will."

Evan drove off, and she sat in her car and brought up the photos she'd snapped. It was a pain looking at them on her phone, but Fina zoomed in and eyed the evidence inventory. Halfway down the second page was an entry that made her sit up and take notice.

The cops had seized a one-gallon jug of antifreeze from Nadine and Evan's basement.

It didn't mean that Evan had killed Nadine, but it sure didn't suggest he hadn't.

Fina called Carl's office from the car, but he'd already left for the day. Her parents' house was one of her least favorite destinations, but it couldn't be avoided. Someone needed to foot the bill for her increased security, and it wasn't going to be Fina.

She made the drive to Newton, amazed by how quickly the city was left behind when she entered their neighborhood, which was dominated by enormous lots and houses to match. Carl and Elaine's was a stone and shingle abomination that could have housed a family of Mormons. The sheer size of the place enabled them to steer clear of each other. Perhaps that was the secret to their long marriage.

Fina parked in front of one of the four garage doors and turned off the car. She sat and tried to find her happy place in advance of seeing Elaine, but it was useless. Just the thought of her mother brought on a wave of irritability.

She went to the side of the house, always preferring the more modest kitchen entrance to the grand foyer with its ten-foot double doors.

The kitchen was spotless and empty, and Fina couldn't resist a peek in the refrigerator to see if there were any good snacks. Her mother was a big fan of telling other people how to eat, while following a less than stellar diet herself. On the counter, Fina spotted a Tupperware container that held chocolate chip cookies, definitely baked by the domestic help. She poured herself a glass of milk and snagged a cookie. It was delicious: a touch of crisp on the outside, but chewy in the middle, a perfect counterpoint to the cold milk.

"I wasn't expecting you," her mother said, appearing in the kitchen door. She was dressed to go out in black pants and a shiny, tailored leather jacket, her purse slung over her arm.

"I need to talk with Dad."

Elaine watched her eat. "That was very rude of you to skip out on dinner the other night and to take Haley with you."

Her mother operated in a world where huge misdeeds were ignored, but slights were cataloged for safekeeping and referenced again and again. Fina was thankful for the hunk of cookie in her mouth. It provided a time delay her brain would not have.

"Sorry," Fina said, with no attempt at sincerity.

"And you owe me an apology," Elaine said.

"I just gave you an apology," Fina said once she'd swallowed.

"I mean for that outburst about your brother."

"Right. I owe you an apology." Her voice dripped with sarcasm.

Elaine shook her head. "What did we do to you that was so terrible, Josefina?"

"I don't think we should have this conversation, Mom." She broke off more cookie and bit into it.

"Really, I'd like you to explain it to me. Your father and I took good care of you. You've never wanted for anything."

Fina stared at her. "Is that all that you think parenting is? Providing nice stuff?"

"Of course not, but you've had more than most people have."

Fina placed her glass in the sink and folded her arms across her chest to still her hands. "Do you even like your kids, Mom?" The bounty on her head was making Fina feel reckless.

"What a silly question!"

"Well, humor me and answer it."

"Of course I like my children," Elaine said, in a tone of voice that bore no relationship to the statement itself.

"Because I've always thought that you didn't like me." Fina's legs felt loose, as if a tremor had moved the earth beneath her. Saying it out loud felt seismic.

"You're being ridiculous."

"Right."

They looked at each other for a moment. Elaine ran her hand through her hair and tugged on her jacket. "I'm late. Your father is in his study."

Fina stood still until she heard the door to the garage slam. She moved over to the window and watched her mother back out in her pricey sedan and take off down the driveway. Patty and Risa were always encouraging Fina to make an effort with Elaine, to see her mother's point of view, but it was like banging her head against a brick wall. Eventually, self-preservation kicked in. Unfortunately, it hadn't kicked in soon enough to avoid this particular conversation.

Fina walked the length of the house to Carl's home office. The room had high, coffered ceilings and a view of the pond and woods outside. Her father was seated behind his glass desk, a laptop open in front of him.

"Did you see your mother on her way out?" he asked Fina.

"Yes. It was a delightful encounter, as always."

Carl shook his head.

"I need to hire some protection," Fina said before he could build up a head of steam.

"For whom?"

"For me." She walked over to the window and gazed out at the pond.

"Why?"

"Someone has put out a contract on me. Not to kill me, just to put me in the hospital."

"And it's because of your case?"

"It's because of *a* case. I don't know which one yet, but in the meantime, I need some protection."

Carl sat back in his chair. "Fine, but if it turns out to be unrelated to the firm, you owe me."

She turned to him. "What else would it be related to, Dad?"

"I don't know what you do in your spare time."

Fina stared at him. "Jesus. Nothing that requires a bodyguard."

"I said you could do it. You laid up in the hospital isn't good for anyone."

"Right. Thanks." She started for the door.

"Have you met Matthew's new girlfriend?" Carl asked, looking up at her.

"Not yet, but he's told me about her."

Carl's gaze returned to the laptop screen.

"Have you?" Fina asked.

"No."

"You know she's a single mom, right? She has a young daughter."

Her father glared at her. "I know."

"Good. Just want to make sure that everyone's on high alert. Maybe I should hire some protection for the kid at the next family dinner."

Carl shook his head and sighed. "Occasionally, Josefina, you should quash your urge to speak."

"Believe me, Dad. There's so much that goes unsaid."

Fina headed home, anxious to put as much distance as possible between her parents and herself. She was tired, and the conversations with her parents had lodged a knot of tension in her neck. Fina knew that pursuing the case against Rand was the only thing that would bring real relief.

She plugged the two names provided by Lindsay Shaunnesy into a search engine and scanned the list of links thrown back at her. Jotting down the most promising contact information, she turned on the TV and found a show about houses on deserted islands. Fina was desperate to be distracted from the thoughts in her head, and the idea of being marooned in the middle of nowhere held great appeal. Images of crystal clear waters and golden sand finally lulled her into a deep sleep.

SEVENTEEN

The next morning Fina decided not to tell Cristian about the anonymous note, but she knew that the time had come to contact Dennis Kozlowski. After eating a Pop-Tart and taking a long, hot shower, she left him a message explaining her predicament.

Midmorning, she holstered her gun and got in the car for the drive to Framingham. She hoped to find Christa Jackson at home, and ideally, in a loquacious mood.

For a moment, Christa contemplated Fina's appearance at her door, but then invited her in and led her to the kitchen. "I have to get this done," she said, gesturing to a cupcake pan and a bowl of batter.

"Don't let me stop you."

"I'm Tamara's room mother, and I swear these kids are always having celebrations."

"Does it have to be homemade?" Fina asked, taking a seat at the kitchen table.

"No, but I don't feel right bringing something store-bought. Did your mom bake when you were growing up?"

"Ha! No, we had a housekeeper, and she did the baking. My mother knows the kitchen exists, but it's as mysterious to her as CIA headquarters are to the rest of us."

"Must have been nice having help."

"It was nice for her."

Christa poured the batter into the foil-lined cups of the muffin tin. She dropped the bowl into the sink and ran water into it. Fina felt her heart break a tiny bit; all that leftover batter going to waste.

"Did you know that Nadine was kicked off the leadership committee at church?" Fina asked.

"I knew that she didn't get along with one of the committee members." Christa leaned down and slid the pan into the oven.

"Do you know who that was?"

Christa pulled on a curl as she thought. "Marcus?"

Fina shook her head. "I haven't met any Marcus. Could it be Lucas?"

"Yeah, that's it."

"What problem did she have with him?"

"I don't know any details, but she didn't think he did a good job."

"Really? I've met the guy, and he seems to take his church involvement very seriously."

"But he always kowtowed to the pastor. He didn't want to rock the boat, but Nadine had no problem with that if she thought it was part of her job. If she was given a job to do, she'd do it to a T."

Fina nodded.

"Here's an example: When we were in high school, they set up some ad hoc student committee about class schedules. The principal said he wanted us to poll our peers, and do research, and then make a recommendation." Christa took a seat across from Fina. "The thing was, the principal didn't really care what we thought. He was just acting like our opinion mattered. He reviewed the recommendation and did what he was always planning to do."

"Did the rest of the student committee know the score?"

"Yes, so we didn't put a lot of work into it, knowing it was a joke, but not Nadine. She took it really seriously and then was pissed when the recommendation had absolutely no bearing on the outcome."

"You think something similar happened at the church?"

"I don't know, but sometimes she took things too literally. My aunt likes to ask our opinions about stuff, but doesn't really want to hear them. Nadine never seemed to learn that she was just supposed to nod her head and agree."

"Speaking of your aunt, I heard that you and Nadine had a falling-out."

Christa rolled her eyes. "Since when is gossip fact?"

"You know the cops are going to ask other people. You may as well just come clean. It'll look less suspicious."

"I don't care about looking suspicious; I don't like people in my personal business."

"I understand, but that's the first rule of a murder investigation: There's no such thing as personal business."

Christa got up and went over to the oven, where she clicked on the light and peered in at the cupcakes.

"In my experience," Fina offered, "people usually fight about love or money."

"You don't think life is a little more complicated than that?"

"There are different permutations, but the gist is usually the same."

Christa leaned her butt against the counter and stretched out her arms. Fina thought the pose was an attempt to appear calm, but it looked forced and awkward.

"Not that it's any of your business," Christa said, "but I asked her for a loan, and she couldn't give it to me."

"Couldn't or wouldn't?" Fina asked.

"There's no difference."

"Sure there is."

"I don't know which it was, but it didn't happen. End of story."

"But it caused tension between the two of you," Fina pressed.

"For a little while, and then we went back to life as usual."

"What was the money for?"

Christa stared at her. "That really isn't your business."

"Good enough," Fina said, and was silent. She didn't think Christa would be able to tolerate the conversational vacuum, and she was right.

"We were going through a rough spot, but we managed. Like I said, end of story."

"Got it." Fina looked at her.

"What?" Christa put her hands on her hips. "You and your family never disagree?"

"We disagree all the time."

"Right, but you're still family, and you still love one another."

That was open to debate.

"So when Nadine died, everything was okay between the two of you?" Fina asked.

"Yes."

"All right then. Thanks for answering my questions."

They walked to the door.

"Hope the cupcakes are a big hit," Fina said. She spent a moment fiddling with her zipper, but was really scanning the street, making sure no one was lying in wait.

"They always are," Christa replied.

Safely locked in her car, Fina had to wonder: If the rift between Nadine and Christa was so run-of-the-mill, why was she so reluctant to discuss it?

Fina skirted the bucolic campus of Wellesley College and pulled into the driveway of a Dutch Colonial house. Painted a dark grape color, the home had the look of benign neglect: chipped paint on the shutters, slightly overgrown hedges, and a jumble of furniture on the screened-in porch.

No one answered the doorbell, but the Nosy Nelly one house over was happy to direct Fina to a dental practice where she could find Sally Cramer, one of the women whom Lindsay Shaunnesy had identified in Rand's college picture.

Fina parked one street away from the main drag in the Vil—the name used by the locals for the downtown shopping area. She wandered by high-end clothing boutiques, a pharmacy, and a couple of sporting goods stores before finding the address she was looking for in a nondescript two-story brick building.

A bell rang out when she crossed the threshold of the second-floor dental practice and asked to see Sally Cramer.

"I don't have an appointment, but it's important. I was hoping I would catch her on her lunch break."

"Take a seat." The receptionist's hair was piled on top of her head like a messy bird's nest. Her eyelids were heavy with metallic shadow. Like going to the dentist wasn't scary enough.

Fina shared the waiting room with a couple of women and three kids amusing themselves with books and puzzles. She picked up a *Highlights* magazine and flipped to the Hidden Pictures page. The ice-fishing penguin was posing a real challenge when the receptionist summoned her to the desk.

"Go through the door to the break room, the second room on the right."

"Thanks."

The hallway was decorated with framed pictures of cartoon characters, and the faint smell of bubble gum lingered in the air. Fina winced at the sound of a whirring drill emanating from one of the exam rooms. The child in the dental chair was dwarfed by the equipment around him, his eyes trained on a screen suspended from the ceiling.

"Hi. Are you Sally?" Fina asked the woman at the table in the break room, a brown bag lunch laid out before her.

"Yup." She didn't extend a hand or motion for Fina to sit.

"Do you mind if I?" Fina gestured toward a chair across from her. "My name is Fina, and I wanted to ask you a few questions about your college experience."

Sally's shoulders relaxed and she nodded to the seat.

"Wait. Did you think I was a process server?" Fina asked.

"I'm getting divorced. Anytime a stranger wants to see me, I brace myself." Her dishwater-blond hair was spilling out of her ponytail, and dark circles ringed her eyes.

"Sorry about that. I should have been more specific with the receptionist. I'm not here about your divorce, but it is a personal matter."

Sally picked up a sandwich half and took a bite. Fina watched as a blob of tuna salad dropped onto her teddy bear scrubs. She dabbed at it with a napkin.

"I spoke with one of your college friends the other day, Lindsay Kaufman Shaunnesy."

Sally shook her head. "We're not friends."

"No, I realize that you're not friends now. I'm investigating something that happened when you were in college." Fina watched her take another bite and chew slowly. "This information isn't going to be made public. I'm just doing a background check on a man named Rand Ludlow."

Sally put down the sandwich and picked up a can of Coke. She took a long drink before looking at Fina again. "Never heard of him."

"Really? I thought you knew each other in college."

The hygienist shook her head slowly. "Nope. Never heard the name before."

Fina took a moment before continuing. More likely than not, Sally was a victim, and Fina didn't want to be a bully and victimize her again. But she really wanted to get the dirt on Rand.

"Like I said," Fina soldiered on, "I'm not trying to put you on the spot, although I realize that I am. I'm just trying to get some information about what he was like in college."

Sally shoved the remaining half of her sandwich back into a plastic baggie and sealed it before putting it in the brown paper sack. Standing up, she drained the soda and pitched the can into the recycling bin. "I don't know who you're talking about, and I have to get back to work."

"If you change your mind, you can call me at this number." She scribbled her phone number on a paper napkin and offered it to Sally, not wanting to reveal her last name.

"How can I change my mind about knowing someone?" Sally asked, and left the room. Fina heard a door close nearby and made her way out of the office.

She had little doubt that Sally knew Rand and had probably been one of his victims; no one had such a strong reaction to a stranger. But her reaction wouldn't be enough to convince Carl. Fina needed proof positive to make her case, and Sally Cramer would be no help in that department.

Fina pulled to a stop in front of the Newton Centre T stop to wait for her protection detail. Dennis had left a message directing her to the station, but she was ten minutes early, which gave her time to think about the case. Rolling down her window and breathing in the brisk spring air, Fina contemplated her lack of progress. She was finding things out and uncovering secrets, but she still couldn't connect the dots. She wasn't convinced that Nadine's death was related to the church, nor was she convinced that it wasn't. And she wasn't convinced that Covenant Rising was aboveboard, but until she could prove otherwise, her suspicions didn't amount to much.

The warm sun had a soporific effect, and Fina fought the urge to close her eyes and catnap. It would really be embarrassing if she were attacked in broad daylight while napping, waiting for her bodyguard.

She sat up straighter as a train pulled into the station and disgorged its passengers. Fina watched the people stream from the station and evaluated the possibilities. Two women were gabbing, carrying pricey purses. Some teenage boys toted skateboards and made a beeline for a stairway and its metal railings. A Buddhist monk had his head raised toward the sky, sunglasses and a jacket the only addition to his saffron-colored robe. A few car lengths down, a man with exemplary posture scanned the street, his gaze never settling on any one thing for long.

We have a winner, Fina thought, lightly tapping the horn. He came over to the car, and she rolled down the window.

"Chad?" she asked.

"Yes, ma'am." Oh, Lord. He had to be ex-military or ex–law enforcement.

"Hop in."

"I'd prefer to drive."

"Oh, Chad." Fina smiled at him. "That's not happening."

He got in the car and extended his hand. "Chad Switzer."

"Fina Ludlow. Nice to meet you."

"You really should let me drive."

"Did Dennis give you the scoop?" Fina asked, ignoring his request and pulling into traffic.

"He did."

"So I'm sure he told you that I'm very stubborn and am only hiring someone under duress."

"I just want to do my job, ma'am, and keep you safe."

"Then you need to stop calling me ma'am."

He nodded. "I'd like to do a risk assessment of your home and review your schedule."

"Fine, but my schedule is pretty free-form."

"Well, that can work to your advantage."

At a traffic light, Fina considered making small talk, but Chad didn't seem like the chatty type, which implied he was good at his job.

The fact that he looked more like a Secret Service agent than a bouncer suggested he made his living doing executive protection, a specialty that required brains, not just brawn.

Fina's phone rang, and she pressed the hands-free button.

"This is Fina, and you're on speaker," she stated.

"Fina, it's Risa. Can you stop by?"

"Sure, is something wrong?"

"Not exactly. Haley's over here, and Patty wants her home."

"All righty." Fina made a U-turn that prompted Chad to raise an eyebrow.

"She seems fine, but she's not in any hurry to get going."

"Okay. I'm on my way." Fina hung up and looked at her companion. "We have to make a detour."

"Okay."

Risa and her family lived in a large gingerbread Victorian in Newton with an expansive front porch. The intricate paint scheme was green, white, and deep red and made the house feel like it was plucked from a fairy tale. There was a large addition off the back that had been seamlessly joined to the original structure.

Risa answered the door and invited Fina in with a quizzical look at Chad.

"This is Chad," Fina said. "He's working with me for a couple of days."

"Nice to meet you, Chad." Risa shook his hand and looked bemused.

She and Fina went to the kitchen with Chad trailing behind them.

"Does Cristian know about your new colleague?" Risa asked in a quiet voice.

"Cristian insisted on it. There's a bit of a situation, and Chad has been brought on board to be an extra set of eyes."

Risa nodded.

The crash and bang of a video game filled the family room portion of the open-plan kitchen. Risa's two sons were ensconced on the sofa, Xbox controllers in hand.

"Boys, turn that down. Say hi to Fina . . . and Chad."

The boys called out halfhearted hellos, their eyes never straying from the screen.

"Can I get you two something to drink?" Risa asked.

"No, thank you, ma'am," Chad replied.

Risa looked askance at Fina, who rolled her eyes.

"Where's Haley?" Fina asked.

"In the den upstairs."

"Can you stay here a minute?" Fina asked Chad.

"I really should come with you."

"It's safe," Fina assured him. "I'll be right back."

She pulled Risa out of the kitchen and back to the foyer. "So she's becoming your third kid?"

"Kind of. She's always welcome, but Patty called and wants her home, and she's dragging her feet."

"What's she doing up there?"

"I told her she had to do her homework and then she could watch TV."

The sounds from the other room carried into the hallway, and Fina thought she heard Chad speaking.

"Did she say that something happened at home?" Fina asked.

"No, and Patty and I have talked about it. There isn't actually anything wrong, but I'm concerned that she's more interested in spending time here than at her own house." They exchanged a look. "Her new house."

"I'm glad you called me. She's been running hot and cold. Scotty and I talked about it, but we didn't come up with any brilliant plans."

"Is it something about Rand being back?" Risa mused. "I would have thought that would make her happy, but maybe he reminds her too much of her mom."

"Maybe."

Once again, Fina felt the urge to share Rand's secrets with Risa, but it had been drilled into her that family secrets were never to be revealed to an outsider. Unfortunately, the worse the secret was, the more Fina yearned to share it with a trusted friend. This wasn't the moment to unburden herself, not with Chad in tow, but maybe the time was coming to let the skeletons out of the closet.

"Haley!" Fina yelled up the stairway. "Come down here. I need to take you home."

A moment later, Haley's blond head popped up over the railing.

"Why?" she asked.

"Because you live there," Fina said. "Get your stuff."

Haley disappeared, and Fina and Risa returned to the kitchen.

Chad was standing behind the sofa, watching the boys play Call of Duty or some similar shoot-'em-up game.

"Mom! Chad totally helped my score," Jacob said. "He gave me some awesome pointers on my shooting."

"That's fantastic," Risa said, giving Fina a smile and the hairy eyeball.

"He was in the military," Jordan offered.

"Yes, ma'am, he was," Fina said. Chad looked at her with slight amusement. "We need to go."

He got up and offered his hand to Risa. "Nice to meet you."

"Next time you can show us how to use the missiles," Jacob suggested.

In the front hallway, Haley was standing with her book bag hanging loosely from one hand.

"Haley, Chad. Chad, Haley," Fina said by way of introductions.

Haley looked befuddled when he extended his hand. There was something curiously delightful about an ex-marine and a moody teenager being forced to interact. It was like a buddy movie gone wrong.

They said good-bye to Risa, and Fina tossed the keys to Chad. She climbed into the backseat next to Haley and gave directions.

"This is weird," Haley said. "Why are you sitting next to me?"

"So I can see your shining face during the drive."

Haley pointed at Chad behind the cover of the front seat and mouthed a question: *Who is he?*

"Long story. I'll tell you later. What's going on with you?"

Haley shrugged. "Nothing."

"We should hang out," Fina said, letting the non-answer slide for the moment.

"Will he be joining us?" Haley asked under her breath.

"Do you want him to?"

Haley snorted, as only pigs and teenagers can.

They pulled up to the house, and Haley moved to open the door, but Fina stopped her.

"Chad," Fina said. "Do you mind giving us a minute?"

The bodyguard climbed out, and Fina turned to look at Haley. "You didn't answer my question: What's going on with you? Why are you spending so much time at Risa's?"

"She doesn't mind," Haley insisted.

"You're right, she doesn't, but we're both worried about you."

"You don't need to be."

Fina shrugged. "Can't help it."

Haley studied Chad, who was leaning against the driver's-side window, gazing into the distance. "Don't know what to tell you."

"I know that having your father around is bad," Fina ventured. "It upsets *me*, and I have less reason to be angry with him than you do."

Haley watched two squirrels battle for a moment before scurrying up a tree. "Apparently you can do whatever you want in this family," she said, her voice dripping with sarcasm.

"Especially if you're a boy," Fina added. "It's good to be a Ludlow male, but I am trying to change that. I promise you, Haley, I'm doing everything I can to make your father go away."

They sat in silence. Fina was opening her mouth when her niece blurted out a question. "Do Gammy and Pap think I made it all up?" It came out strangled, as if the question had to fight its way into existence.

Fina shook her head. "Pap doesn't think you made it up. He just has a funny way of showing he believes you." She reached out and took hold of Haley's hand. "I honestly don't know what Gammy thinks. You may not have noticed, but we don't get along very well."

"Really?" Haley asked, wiping a tear from her cheek. "I never noticed."

The front door opened, and Patty waved from the threshold. Fina waved back.

"I should go," her niece said, reaching once again for the door.

"I love you, Haley. We're going to figure this out."

"Love you, too."

She gave her niece a hug and watched the front door close behind her. Fina climbed into the front passenger seat as Chad took his place behind the wheel.

"That was my niece," she told him.

He nodded.

"Families are so complicated, Chad."

He nodded.

At least Dennis had sent her the strong, silent type.

EIGHTEEN

Pastor Greg had felt irritable since yesterday's visit from Fina. One of his strengths was his ability to read people and figure out how to influence them. It wasn't that hard to do if you were willing to make the effort. Most people just wanted attention. They wanted someone to hear what they had to say. Looking at another person, looking into their eyes and tuning out the rest of the world—if even for a few brief moments—was enough to win over most folks. Coupled with their desire for divine intervention and eternal life, Greg rarely met a person he couldn't bring around to his way of thinking.

But that wasn't the case with Fina Ludlow. She was headstrong and focused and not the least bit concerned with the state of her soul. She was impervious to worries about the afterlife, and she didn't seem to care if Greg liked her. Maybe this was because she was an attractive woman or from a rich family or maybe it was just the way the good Lord had made her. Greg found it frustrating.

Tonight was Prayer Group night, when members who wanted extra enrichment broke into smaller groups and studied scripture. The groups were delineated by age and/or gender and led by a member of the leadership committee. Greg floated among the groups, providing counsel and support. It was a good way for him to have face time with the congregants without getting too involved with anyone in particular.

He was late to the gathering, having been delayed by a phone call in his office, and when he arrived in the parish hall, the groups were huddled in clusters, deep in conversation. He scanned the room, and wandered over to the forty-plus men's group that Lucas was leading. Greg listened to the conversation, offered a few lines of scripture and some pats on the back, and moved on to the next clump of congregants.

He visited two more groups before arriving at the young adults, which included eighteen- to thirty-year-olds. Greg had created this age bracket because he felt the younger members needed particular attention and a sense of identity. Having close friends at the church established accountability among them and helped keep them on the straight and narrow.

There were ten young adults gathered in a circle tonight, seven men and three women, and Greg was surprised to see that Gabby was leading the group. He pulled up a chair, and she smiled at him. A young man named Casey, sitting on Gabby's right, was reading a passage. Greg listened with the others and studied his wife. She was leaning toward Casey, their heads practically touching. The edges of her mouth were raised in a slight smile, and her thickly mascaraed lashes blinked slowly, like an animated doe. She was wearing jeans and a sweater that clung to her breasts.

When the reading was complete, Gabby looked at Greg.

"Pastor, could you share some of your wisdom on the subject of suffering?"

Greg took a deep breath. "'Now if we are children, then we are heirs—heirs of God and co-heirs with Christ, if indeed we share in his sufferings in order that we may also share in his glory.' Romans 8:17." Greg gazed at each member. "Sometimes you have to make hard choices, and those choices are painful, but your suffering is holy and sacred. Don't ever think that it is without purpose."

"This is a good time to take a break," Gabby said.

The young people stood and drifted over to a table of refreshments. Gabby got up and stretched back, pulling the fabric of her sweater even tighter across her chest.

"Gabby," Greg said in a warning tone, staring at her.

She stood up straight and dropped her arms to her side. "Relax, Greg. You've seen it before."

He stood next to her. "I don't think that outfit is appropriate."

She looked down at herself as if she needed a reminder as to what she was wearing. "Why not? Prayer Group is supposed to be more casual. I thought we wanted to encourage members to come and not feel they have to dress up."

"I'm not talking about the level of informality. I'm talking about how tight it is."

Gabby folded her arms across her body in what looked like a show of defiance. Her mouth was set, and she fixed her gaze beyond Greg.

"Don't be like that," he said. "You need to model modesty. You know that."

"Fine. Is it all right if I get a snack now?" she asked, her voice laced with sarcasm.

"Not yet. Why are you leading this group? I thought Sue was in charge of the young adults."

"She is, but she had a commitment tonight. I offered to fill in for her."

Laughter emanated from the refreshment table, where a few of the members were engaged in animated conversation.

"Next time, I'll fill in for her," Greg said.

"That's not necessary, honey. I know you've got better things to do with your time."

"I can't think of anything better than nurturing the youngest members of our congregation." He put an arm around her, pulling her into a tight embrace.

. . .

Chad spent fifteen minutes evaluating Fina's apartment, which was twelve minutes more than necessary.

She was sitting at the table checking e-mail when he emerged from her bedroom.

"All clear," he declared.

"Great."

"I don't see any points of entry or exit other than the front door."

"It's a high-rise, Chad. I could have told you that."

He walked over to the front door. "These locks look good."

"I had them installed after the break-in. I feel very safe here."

"I'm glad to hear it."

"You should go home. I'm not planning on going out again to-night." That said, if she needed to go out, she wouldn't hesitate, beyond checking that her gun was loaded.

"If your plans change, just call me. I can get here in half an hour."

"They won't. I'm going to do a little work and hit the hay."

"What's the schedule for tomorrow?" he asked.

"I have no idea."

"What time do you want me here?"

"I have no idea."

He frowned.

"I'm not trying to be difficult," she said. "I honestly don't know. Why don't I give you a call when I get up?"

"Okay." He looked around the room as if he was searching for something, but he wasn't sure what.

Fina got up and walked to the front door. "I'll see you tomorrow. Thanks."

"Sure. Have a good night."

She grabbed some leftover Vietnamese food and a diet soda from the fridge. A show on law enforcement in the Yukon kept her company while she ate and gave her a dose of perspective; at least she didn't have to worry about bears and avalanches. After a long, hot shower, Fina called it a day and snuggled up for a good night's sleep with her gun.

Prayer Group wound down, and only a handful of congregants remained in the parish hall. Gabby was off to one side speaking with some young women when Greg spotted Lucas at the picked-over refreshments.

"Great leadership tonight, Lucas," he told the man, patting him on the back. Lucas was selecting a cookie, but he retracted his hand into his pocket like a turtle into its shell.

"Thank you, Pastor. I'm glad you could join us."

"Spending time with our members really is a divine gift. Is Heather here tonight?"

Lucas shook his head. "We've been having some challenges at home, and we thought it best she stay with the girls."

Greg softened his features in a look of concern. "Nothing serious, I hope."

"No, no. Nothing to worry about."

Gabby threw back her head and laughed on the other side of the room.

Greg took a cup from a stack and filled it with coffee. "I noticed you and Gabby having what looked like a serious conversation the other day," he said, avoiding Lucas's gaze as he doctored the beverage.

"Really? I don't remember."

"Yes, on Tuesday."

"I'm sure it was some church business."

"Of course. I just wanted to make sure there wasn't anything I needed to know about—church business, I mean."

"Not that I know of, Pastor."

"That's good to hear. I tell you," Greg said, gesturing toward his wife with the cup, "when she gets going, it's hard to get her to stop yapping."

"Heather's the same way," Lucas said.

"Gabby, darling," Greg hollered playfully, "we need to get going."

She hugged the women good-bye and came over to Greg.

"Here I am," she said.

"We'll see you later, Lucas," Greg said, squeezing his shoulder.

"Good night, Pastor. Gabby."

The Gatchells left the room, and Lucas surveyed the table. The pastor's coffee was barely touched on the white paper tablecloth. Lucas plucked two cookies from the plate and left the rest of the mess behind.

Fina got up at six thirty the next morning and pulled on some work-out clothes. Her rapid metabolism had always been a safeguard against unwanted weight gain, even with her questionable diet. But as she aged, and as she faced threats to her well-being, Fina had started to value being in good fighting form. That wasn't just a turn of phrase for her—it was a necessity.

She climbed the stair mill for twenty minutes, then did some strength training before heading upstairs. Ceci Renard called asking if Fina could meet her for breakfast at the Taj. Breakfast at a luxury hotel was one definition of heaven on earth in Fina's book, so they arranged to meet at 9:30 a.m. She called Chad and gave him the scoop and spent the time before his arrival reviewing Nadine Quaynor's files.

She sorted through the fragments of an average life: old rental car agreements, reading lists, brochures from her health insurance plan, product warranties, and the like. The minutes from both the Covenant Rising leadership committee and the neighborhood association made for more interesting reading, and it didn't take long for a central theme to emerge: Nadine Quaynor was a pain in the ass. In the leadership committee, she asked countless questions and seemed to disagree with just about every committee member at one time or another. It wasn't that her questions weren't valid, just that her relentless pursuit of information was tiresome. If it was this irritating on the page, Fina could only imagine what it was like in person.

The neighborhood association meeting notes had a similar tone, minus the interruptions of scripture and prayer. The agenda items fell into two broad categories: upkeep/improvements and social events. Nadine had an opinion on most matters and seemed to play devil's advocate even if she abandoned the position before much discussion had taken place. It was as if she couldn't help herself. Her neighbors must have found her maddening, but perhaps Ronnie McCaffrey could shed some light on that.

Chad arrived, and they drove to the Taj with Fina in the driver's seat. They found a meter on Newbury Street, and Fina spotted Ceci as soon as they stepped into the elegant café.

"I don't like that table," Chad said, as they made their way to a round table in the bow window.

Fina exhaled out her nose. "No one can beat me up through glass. Shoot me, maybe, but not beat me."

"It's not good to be on display like that."

"I'm fine with it. Good morning, Ceci," she said as they reached the table.

"Good morning, Fina." She looked at Chad expectantly.

"This is my colleague Chad, and he's going to be sitting over there." Fina pointed to a table across the room that gave him a good line of sight.

"You're welcome to join us," Ceci said to him.

"He's good," Fina said, giving him a gentle nudge in the direction of his table. "Order whatever you want. It's on me."

She and Ceci took seats on the thick brocaded chairs and perused the menu. Ceci ordered black coffee, but Fina declined, opting for OJ instead. She had the whole rest of the day to drink unwanted beverages.

"Are you training him?" Ceci asked, looking toward Chad, who had settled at the table and was scanning the room.

"No. He's my security detail."

"A bodyguard?"

"Essentially. It's actually kind of silly, but there's been a threat, and I'm trying to take it seriously."

"Is it because of Chloe's case?"

"I'm not sure," Fina said. "But it's nothing for you to worry about. Contrary to appearances, I can take care of myself."

They placed their orders, and Fina sipped her orange juice.

"I got a call from my financial adviser," Ceci said. "Chloe has been after him to provide paperwork for the bequest. Do you have anything that can be used to interrupt the process?"

Fina shook her head. "I wish I did, but I don't have anything conclusive to share at this point."

"You have no idea who killed Nadine?"

"There are a few suspects, but nothing definitive. I can tell you that there was certainly more unrest and conflict at the church than I was initially led to believe."

"What kind of conflict?"

Fina shook her head. "I'm still figuring that out, but it may have something to do with finances. There also seem to be some significant personality clashes."

A plate of smoked salmon was placed in front of Ceci, and Fina's taste buds smarted with the arrival of her challah French toast.

They took a couple of bites before Ceci spoke. "I had dinner with Chloe the other night."

"And? How is she?"

"She's upset about Nadine, and I thought maybe she had reconsidered the bequest since she didn't mention it. Obviously, that's not the case."

"I'm sorry. I know that's very distressing."

Ceci smoothed the napkin in her lap. "It is. I'm so worried for her, but I also feel angry. That doesn't seem right, does it?"

"She's not doing what you want her to do, and you think she's making a poor choice. No wonder you're angry."

"I have to fight the urge to shake her or yell at her to snap out of it. It was so much easier when she was younger and I could make her do things."

"Nothing would please Pastor Greg more than you and Chloe falling out," Fina said. "Keep that in mind when you feel that urge. These types of organizations strive to put a wedge between their members and the members' support systems."

"I suppose." Ceci used a tiny fork to scoop capers onto a toast point, as Fina cut through her thick slice of syrup-drenched French toast. If being dainty were the goal, this would qualify as an epic fail.

"I'm confident that if there is dirt on Covenant Rising, I will find it," she said. "I can't promise that it will change Chloe's mind, but it's all we can do."

Ceci nodded and accepted a coffee refill from the waiter.

"Your bodyguard looks unhappy," she commented.

"I am not a good client," Fina admitted. "I don't like having someone hanging around."

"I suppose temporary inconvenience is better than permanent injury."

Fina paused her fork midway to her mouth. "When you put it that way, it sounds so reasonable."

When they parted, Fina promised she'd be in touch. She wanted to ditch Chad, but tried to keep Ceci's comment in mind. She wasn't put off by the idea of a physical fight, but she'd had a cast on her wrist over the summer and not being able to bathe herself was a nightmare. She conjured up the image of sponge baths and greasy hair and reluctantly unlocked the passenger door for her companion.

As they made their way to Nadine's neighborhood, Fina kept coming back to Ceci's remark about making Chloe do things when she was younger. Unlike Ceci, Carl still controlled his children using a variety of tactics, including thinly veiled bribes and threats. He held things over his children's heads to force them to behave, and Fina had tried to turn the tables when she threatened to expose Rand's misdeeds. She wasn't proud of it, but she was desperate. Rand was also desperate, and she had to wonder: Was he holding something over their father?

Evan wasn't home, so Fina couldn't return the boxes of files, and Ronnie wasn't around, either. His wife, Mary, suggested she swing by the local firehouse, where he was wont to hang out.

"You need to stay in the car for this one," Fina told Chad.

He shook his head. "What's the point of having me if I'm not providing protection?"

"No one is going to attack me in a fire station, and if they do, I'll have EMTs right there to provide care."

"You have an excuse for everything."

"I prefer to think of them as reasons, not excuses."

The station was a two-story structure fronted with three enormous garage doors and a flagpole flying the Stars and Stripes and a POW/MIA flag. Fina stepped inside and nearly collided with a firefighter.

"Is Ronnie McCaffrey around?" Fina asked.

He pointed down the hallway. "He's in the lounge."

She followed the sounds of laughter and TV and arrived at a space that looked like a tired living room. There were two big couches on

which three firefighters were lounging, watching ESPN. A table anchored the other side of the room. Two firefighters sat at it with Ronnie McCaffrey, the only person other than Fina who was wearing
civilian clothing.

Conversation quieted when she entered the room, and Ronnie
looked up at her.

"I'm really sorry to interrupt, Ronnie. Do you have a minute?"

"Ronnie, what are you up to?!" one of the guys hooted. "Wait until
Mary hears."

"Mary sent me," Fina said with a wide smile.

There were a couple of whistles and comments, and Ronnie
grinned and pushed back from the table. "All right, that's enough. I
can't help it if the rest of you are losers," he said.

He gestured for Fina to follow him down the hallway and into the
garage where the trucks were parked. He steered her to a ragtag group
of office chairs off to the side.

"What can I do for you?" he asked once they were seated.

"Just a couple of quick questions. Sorry to interrupt your visit."

"It's okay. Any news on Nadine?"

"There are some leads, but nothing concrete. I see that Evan and
Molly are back in the house."

"Yup. I think it's good for them, being back in the neighborhood."

"Definitely. Molly must have missed her friends."

He shook his head. "I know everybody breaks up these days, but
it's terrible for a kid to have to live in two places."

"How long have you and your wife been together?" Fina asked.

"Forty-one years."

"Wow. That's impressive."

He looked at her. "It's worth it."

"Well, I'm sure it's a relief to Evan that he and Molly are back for
good."

Ronnie shrugged, but didn't respond.

"Evan gave me the minutes from the neighborhood association meetings," Fina said. "I think it might be the greatest neighborhood in the whole city."

He smiled. "I think so."

"How long have you lived there?"

"Forty years. These days, young people talk about starter homes, but I don't see the point of moving around. What? So you can buy new furniture?"

"I guess. My parents like to move around a lot. They always want something fancier or bigger."

"That's what I'm talking about. It's an empty nest before you know it; why get more space?"

"I bet people think twice about moving out of your neighborhood," she said.

He nodded. "It's definitely one of the best in the city."

"In the meeting minutes," Fina said, shifting her weight in the broken-down chair, "it seemed like Nadine was kind of a pain."

Ronnie folded his arms across his chest. "She could be opinionated."

"That must have been frustrating."

"We always worked through it."

"I saw that she was unhappy about the sky lanterns that you lit for New Year's. She worried about them being a fire hazard or creating litter?"

"Fire's scary to a lot of people," Ronnie said.

"And she complained about the food options at the holiday party?"

"It all worked out."

"I guess some people are just killjoys," Fina noted.

He pushed himself out of the chair. "Was there anything else?"

"Nope. That's it."

He walked Fina to the door and pulled it closed behind her.

Most people, given the chance, spilled a little dirt. Ronnie's equanimity suggested that either he was an extremely nice man or a very tight-lipped one.

"Can you turn that down?" Christa snapped. Her husband, Paul, looked at her and reached out to silence the car radio.

"Try to relax. You're going to stress her out," he said, glancing at McKenna in the backseat.

Christa turned in the seat and looked at her daughter. "She doesn't seem stressed to me." The girl was watching the scenery go by, humming a tune.

They pulled into a visitor's parking space and followed the signs to the admissions office.

"Remember to look people in the eye and shake their hands," Christa told McKenna.

"I know, Mom. You already told me that."

A long staircase led to a green quadrangle bordered by gray stone buildings. Christa took a deep breath and admired the scene. It looked like a university, the kind of place where the leaders of tomorrow would debate lofty ideas and craft groundbreaking theories. She reached for Paul's hand, and they walked to the main entrance.

During McKenna's interview, Christa and Paul were left to wait in an anteroom. Paul flipped through copies of the alumnae magazine, but Christa couldn't keep still. She paced the small space and glanced at her phone, as if it might provide an update on the activities in the office next door.

"I'm worried that you're getting your hopes up," Paul said after watching her do another circuit of the room. He tossed the magazine he was scanning onto the side table.

"Of course my hopes are up. Aren't yours?"

"You know what I mean. I want McKenna to get in and be able to go here, but if she doesn't, it's okay."

"Well, of course you think it's okay. You've only got one job; I've got three between work, the girls, and managing McKenna's education."

He sighed. "Let's not do this now."

"I'm not saying that you don't work hard, Paul. I know you do. And I know that night school is incredibly demanding, but at least you get a moment to yourself."

"We talked about this. I can take a semester off."

"No. Let's just get it done. The sooner you finish, the sooner I'll get some relief."

"If this doesn't happen"—he gestured to the room—"we're going to have to figure out a way to manage."

"I know." She looked out the window at the green space. It was the break between classes, and students were making their way across the grass. They were laughing and bumping into one another. They looked so carefree.

What was that like? Christa wondered.

NINETEEN

Fina knocked on Frank and Peg's front door, Chad right behind her on the front steps. She could feel his breath on her neck.

Frank opened the door and greeted her with a look of surprise.

"Since when do you wait to be invited in?"

"Since I have a guest with me."

"Please come in," Frank said, and stepped back. He raised an eyebrow to Fina.

"This is Chad, and this is Frank," she told the men. "Could I speak with you privately?" Fina asked Frank.

"Do you want me to clear the house?" Chad asked.

Frank chortled, and Fina pulled him down the hall to the master bedroom. It was a small space with a three-piece furniture suite and a headboard shaped like a scallop shell.

"I'm going crazy," she confessed.

"Is this a date?" A grin curled the edges of his mouth.

"Hilarious. He's my security detail."

"What happened?"

"Apparently, there's a contract to give me a beatdown."

Frank's eyes widened. "Well, that's not good."

"No kidding, but I'm beginning to think that I'd rather be beaten up than have a shadow for another minute."

"What possessed you to hire him? It's very unlike you."

Fina sat down on the end of the bed. "I don't know. It seemed like I should."

"Since when do you do what you should?"

"Since this feels different. Someone is going to a lot of trouble to make my life difficult. It feels more organized than my past troubles."

"Sure, but when that guy jumped you in the supermarket parking lot, that seemed organized." Frank took a seat next to her.

Fina shrugged.

"And when he ran you off the Pike, and you flipped your car, a fair amount of planning went into that."

She massaged her temples. "Where's this going exactly?"

"Peg would kill me for saying this, but I'm not convinced this is so different from all the other times."

"True."

He looked at her. "So what's really going on?"

Fina considered his question. "It's Cristian," Fina admitted. "I feel like I'm supposed to do things differently because of our current status."

"Which is?"

"Dating? Involved? More than what it used to be."

"So if you weren't dating, you wouldn't have hired your friend out there?" He gestured toward the living room.

"I doubt it. He's complicating things, not making them easier."

"Are you talking about Cristian or Chad?"

Fina was silent.

"I don't want anything bad to happen to you," Frank said, "but you need to do what you need to do."

She digested his words. "Thanks. You're the best."

"Don't tell Peg about this conversation," Frank cautioned as he followed her down the hall.

"It's our secret."

"Chad," Fina said as he stood up from the couch, "you're fired."

One and a half days. Not even thirty-six hours. That was Fina's limit
for having a bodyguard. She'd always known that she was independent and liked to work by herself, but her brief experience with Chad
made her realize just how deep her free spirit ran. Maybe in another
life she was an Aboriginal male on a perpetual walkabout.

Back at home, reveling in her freedom, she answered a call from
Matthew while lying on the couch.

"Hey."

"Hey. There's going to be a family thing at the club, and I need you
there."

"What kind of family thing?"

"Just dinner."

"When?" she asked.

"Tomorrow night," Matthew said. "It was just going to be me, Sydney, Rachel, and Mom and Dad, but I'm having second thoughts."

"As you should."

"Can you come?"

"Will Rand be there?" She closed her eyes as if to ward off his
response.

"I assume Mom invited him."

"For you, I'll be there. I'm dying to meet the woman who's going to
make an honest man out of you."

"Don't get ahead of yourself."

"Before you hang up, I have a question."

"Okay."

"What do you think is the worst thing that Dad's ever done?"

Matthew was silent for a moment. "What kind of question is that?"

"It's an odd one, I'll give you that, but I'm curious."

"I have no idea. That's not something I want to contemplate, and I don't think you should, either."

"Why not?" Fina struggled into a sitting position, the conversation demanding her full attention.

"Because that kind of speculation can't lead anywhere good."

"Please, you make your career on speculation."

"I've got to go. Let's not continue this bizarre conversation later."

"Sorry, I didn't realize it would be such an upsetting topic."

"Good-bye, Fina."

Matthew and Scotty were ruthless lawyers, but when it came to family, they had blind spots. Fina wished she suffered from the same affliction, but she was never good at putting things out of her mind.

It was a trait that made her good at her job and bad at keeping the home fires burning.

Fina made the trip the next morning to CRC eager to learn more about the leadership committee meetings. Unfortunately, neither Greg nor Gabby were there, according to Betty, so Fina returned to the parking lot, ruing the wasted trip.

Music emanating from a car one row away caught her attention, and she glanced toward it. Fina could see two passengers in the front seat and decided to take a closer look. This wasn't high school, after all; who would be hanging out in the parking lot blasting music?

Fina slowly approached the Ford Fiesta and laid eyes on Gabby Gatchell and a young man. They were facing each other, laughing and smiling. Fina crouched down behind a nearby car and watched. Gabby reached over and touched the man's shoulder and flipped her hair.

Fina couldn't imagine that Pastor Greg would approve of the scene, and she surreptitiously snapped some photos with her phone. She waited, hoping she'd be rewarded with a make-out session, but nothing materialized. Five minutes after she arrived on the scene, the passenger-side door opened, flooding the parking lot with a cheesy love song.

Fina waddled around the car on her haunches so as not to reveal her presence. Gabby's laughter bubbled through the air, and she exchanged words with the driver, but Fina couldn't make them out. A moment later, the door slammed, and Gabby sauntered back to the front door of the church. Fina scooted out and snapped a picture of the young man's license plate before he roared out of the parking lot.

'Cause nothing says cool like hanging with the pastor's wife in your Ford Fiesta hatchback.

Fina offered to buy Cristian lunch, but he'd already eaten. He was interested in an ice cream cone—one of his few vices—so they planned to meet at Mirabelle's, an ice cream parlor near Mass Ave. First, she called her contact at the Registry of Motor Vehicles and left a message asking for a callback. She wanted an ID on Gabby's youthful friend, but it wasn't a favor she wanted to commit to voice mail. The request for the plate information wasn't legal, but Fina couldn't worry about that. She'd never get anything done if she got caught up in legalities and ethics. Canoodling wasn't illegal, but if Gabby was misbehaving, it might help convince Chloe that the Gatchells weren't holier-than-thou after all.

After claiming a parking spot a few streets away from Mirabelle's, she fell into step behind a group of Goth kids. Fina firmly believed that teenagers should be free to express themselves during those difficult years, but she just didn't get the Goth thing. Were they trying to look dead? Like vampires? Were they purposefully blunting the edges of their genders? And didn't they get hot under all those layers of heavy black clothing and pancake makeup?

Cristian was waiting for her inside Mirabelle's, contemplating the chalkboard menu mounted overhead.

"You're studying it as if you might actually order something different," Fina said, resting her chin on his shoulder.

"I just wanted to see if anything new caught my eye."

Fina looked at the options. "Oooh. Black sesame. That sounds like something you'd enjoy."

He shook his head and stepped up to the counter, motioning for her to order. Fina got two scoops of salted caramel with jimmies, and Cristian opted for his usual pistachio.

"Where's your protection?" he asked, pulling napkins from a dispenser.

"That's part of why I wanted to see you."

"Do you mind walking?" he asked. "I need some air."

Armed with their cones and napkins, they walked in the direction of Commonwealth Ave and the grassy strip that bisected it. They focused on their ice cream until they arrived at the Boston Women's Memorial and took a seat on a bench with minimal bird droppings.

"So you don't have a bodyguard because . . ." Cristian prompted.

"I tried, Cristian, I really did, but I couldn't do it."

"You don't have to do anything. Just let someone follow you around."

"That's what I couldn't do. It was irritating, and it slowed me down." Fina watched him. He was licking his cone with more concentration than the task required. "Is there something you want to say?"

"I'm not going to argue with you about this, Fina."

"Okay." She wiped some salted caramel drizzle off her hand. Fina found his unwillingness to comment unsettling. She was used to Carl, who never held back when he disapproved. "I'm just asking you to trust me on this."

He gazed at the statues of the three women in front of them.

Fina decided it wasn't the moment to tell him about the poison pen letter she'd received. "Have you guys found anything?" Fina asked. "Related to the contract?"

"Pitney's got some feelers out, but nothing so far."

"What do you make of Gabby Gatchell?" Fina asked, changing topics.

Cristian wasn't thrown by the shift, good cop that he was. "She and her husband seem well-suited to each other. Why? What do you think?"

"I agree. They both strike me as opportunists who use religion for their own gains." She licked a jimmy from her hand.

"Anything else you want to tell me about your investigation?" Cristian asked.

Fina thought about the crime scene inventory she'd seen, her conversation with Ronnie, and Gabby's young friend. For all she knew, he was aware of all of it, but if not, she wasn't ready to share just yet.

"Nope. I'm just plugging along."

"You free tonight?" he asked.

"Unfortunately, no. I've got a family thing."

"I thought you just had a family thing."

"I did, but Matthew needs some backup. He's introducing his new girlfriend to Elaine and Carl."

"What's the problem? Is she Latina or something?" He grinned.

Fina looked at Cristian. "She's a Jewish single mother, and she has a young daughter."

He exhaled deeply. "That's not good."

"No, it's not." They sat quietly for a moment. "Maybe my wannabe attacker will show up at dinner tonight and I could redirect his energy."

"It's the Ludlows; you never know what might happen."

"A girl can dream!"

Cristian leaned over and kissed her.

"I don't want anything to happen to you," he said.

"Finally, something we can agree on."

They pitched their sticky napkins in the trash, and Fina scanned the area.

She was glad to be rid of Chad, but didn't like having to assume his workload.

Fina called Evan and offered to drop off the boxes containing Nadine's belongings. Since he agreed, Fina assumed the cleaning coupons and her disposal assistance had softened his attitude to her.

At the house, Fina hauled the boxes onto the porch and rang the bell. A girl with long, curly black hair who looked to be around twelve opened the door.

"Is Evan around?" Fina asked. "I'm Fina. I'm dropping off some boxes I borrowed."

"One second. Uncle Evan!" she hollered. "Fina's here."

She opened the door wider, and Fina brought the boxes into the entryway. Through the kitchen door, Fina spotted three girls playing a board game at the table.

"Is Christa your mom?" she asked the girl who lingered next to her.

"Yup." She nodded. "I'm McKenna."

"Nice to meet you, McKenna. I recognized you from the photo in your dining room. Those are your sisters?"

"Nicole and Tamara." She walked into the living room and took a seat on the couch. "And that's Molly."

"I know Molly."

Evan came into the room. "You've met McKenna?"

"Yes, she has very good manners and introduced herself."

He grabbed the two boxes, one stacked on top of the other, and headed for the stairs.

"Do you want help with those?" Fina asked.

"No, I'm good." He nodded at the load in his arms. "I found some more stuff like this. Did you want to take a look?"

"That would be great, if you don't mind."

"Give me a minute."

Fina sat down across from McKenna. She was settling on a question to ask, but McKenna beat her to it.

"Did you know Aunt Nadine?" the girl asked.

"No, I didn't. I wish I had."

Her face sagged.

"It's hard when someone dies unexpectedly," Fina offered. "Someone in my family died not so long ago, and I'm sad when I think about it."

McKenna nodded. "We've been looking at scrapbooks at home. Mommy's got lots of pictures from when they were young."

"It's nice to remember happy times." Christ, she was turning into a human greeting card.

"And there are some of Nadine and Daddy."

The statement gave Fina pause. "At family gatherings?"

"And at the prom."

Fina felt something shift inside her—that blip in her nervous system that told her to pay attention.

"Your dad and Nadine went to the prom together?"

"It was an under-the-sea theme. The decorations were pretty lame."

"Do you guys decorate for dances these days?" Fina asked, not wanting to spook the girl. "Do you even have dances?"

"We've had one. I thought it was stupid."

"So did Nadine and your dad dress up for their dance?"

"He had a hideous blue suit, and he got her a blue carnation corsage to match. My mom says it was the ugliest thing ever."

"Who'd your mom go with?"

McKenna shrugged. "I don't know his name, but he was kind of a dweeb."

"Did your dad and Nadine date for a while?"

A dispute broke out in the kitchen related to Lollipop Woods and Gumdrop Mountain. McKenna pushed herself off the couch and went in to referee, just as Evan came down the stairs with two new boxes.

"It's the same kind of stuff as the others," he said, "but give it a shot."

"Thanks, Evan. I appreciate it." The voices had settled down in the kitchen. "It's nice of you to have Christa's girls over."

"They're the closest thing to siblings that Molly has, and Christa needed a break."

"Do you have a minute to answer a couple of questions?" Fina asked.

His shoulders sagged, but he joined her on the couch.

She wanted to question him about this newest twist in the family history, but needed to digest it first. "What can you tell me about Nadine being ill?" Fina asked instead.

"She was sick on and off for a couple of months." He placed his feet on the coffee table. "She went to the doctor, but they couldn't find anything obvious."

"Did she miss work or other commitments because of it?"

"Sometimes. She'd get sick to her stomach, which limited her activities. Other times she was dizzy or just out of it."

Giggles floated in from the kitchen. "Was there any pattern to her being sick?" Fina asked. "Certain days of the week or time of day?"

"That's what the cops asked." He frowned. "I know I'm a suspect."

"The spouse is always a suspect. Don't take it personally."

"Kind of hard not to."

"They wouldn't be doing their jobs if they didn't investigate you, too. So was there an obvious pattern?"

"Not that I could tell. I tried to piece together a timeline, and I gave it to the cops."

Fina started to rise from the couch. "Do you mind sharing it with me?"

"I guess not. The sooner someone solves this case, the sooner I'll be cleared of any involvement. I'll e-mail it to you."

He followed her out to her car and helped her load the boxes into the trunk.

"I'll let you know if I find anything," Fina said, climbing into her car.

As was usually the case, Nadine's familial relationships were more complicated than Fina had been led to believe. Nadine, Christa, and Paul made an interesting triangle indeed.

The Whittaker Club was in Chestnut Hill, and if Carl tried to become a member today with his booming personal injury practice, he'd probably be rejected. Luckily for the Ludlows, he'd joined decades earlier when he was an up-and-coming attorney without television ads or sensational cases.

Fina often felt out of place at the club. Not because of the family business, but because the net worth of the members was so immense, and there was a caste system between the members and staff that was straight out of *Gone with the Wind*. That didn't stop her from having lunch at the pool during the summer and attending compulsory family gatherings, but she felt like a canary in a coal mine; she knew her discomfort was an indicator of an intact sense of justice.

Walking through the front door, Fina was greeted by the manager, an obsequious man with a foreign accent who always made her skin crawl. She followed him to the bar.

The room was all dark wood and leather, and two large TVs were mounted on the wall, one tuned to ESPN, the other to CNBC. Rand was leaning against the bar talking to Carl. The others were sitting around a table. Matthew saw Fina and beckoned her over.

Greetings were exchanged, and Scotty pulled a chair over for her. "Sydney, this is my sister, Fina."

Fina shook hands with the woman. She had long brown hair and was exceedingly pretty. She was wearing black pants and a fitted jacket and perched on her knee was her pint-sized twin.

"Is this Rachel?" Fina asked.

"Yes," Sydney said, smoothing the child's hair. The girl buried her head into her mother's chest. "She's shy."

"That's understandable. There are a lot of new faces."

Patty engaged Sydney in conversation, and Fina watched her mother's reaction. Sydney's arrival could go one of two ways: Elaine could contend that no one—including Sydney—was good enough for her son; or she could embrace her as the daughter she never had. Fina found both options galling.

Fina got up to fetch more drinks, and Carl intercepted her before she got to the bar. He made a show of looking over her shoulder.

"Where's your bodyguard?"

"I gave him the night off."

"I like saving money, but that seems like a bad idea."

"It'll be fine," she said. "I'm carrying." She pulled back her jacket to show her father her gun.

"Christ. Don't let your mother see."

Fina planted herself at the opposite end of the bar from Rand and ordered another round. She pretended to pay close attention to the stock market report, but he wasn't dissuaded and sidled over to her.

"You going to give me the silent treatment? Is that the plan?"

"I'm just doing what I was told—to steer clear of you."

Rand turned and leaned his back against the bar so that he had a clear view of Matthew and the others.

"She's beautiful, don't you think?" he asked.

It took Fina every ounce of effort not to smash his teeth in with her fist.

"I'm talking about Sydney, of course." He rattled the ice cubes in his glass. "Did you think I was talking about the little girl?"

"Could you bring those over when they're ready?" Fina asked the bartender, and returned to the group.

The conversation gave her time to take some deep breaths and reclaim her equilibrium, but when she looked up, Matthew was studying her.

"Why do you two look so serious?" Elaine asked.

"It's nothing, Mom," he said, and Fina nodded in agreement.

She looked at Sydney and Rachel, and her stomach turned.

TWENTY

This time, Fina let herself into 56 Wellspring Street without waiting for permission. Frank was in his recliner, his nightly bowl of vanilla ice cream on the side table next to him.

"I'm glad to see you're still in one piece."

"I am. Where's Peg?"

"There was some puberty thing at the middle school. She should be home soon."

"That sounds horrible."

"Somebody's got to teach them that stuff."

"Well, at least it's not me. That's something, I suppose."

"Does that mean things have gotten worse?" Frank asked.

"I'm making progress on the case, but the family situation is not good."

"Anything I can do?"

"Not about that, unfortunately."

"Let me know if you change your mind," he said, scooping up a spoonful of ice cream.

"Do you have any interest in a job?" Fina asked.

"Depends on the job."

"There's a woman I suspect is up to no good, and if she is, I'd like photographic evidence of it."

"A domestic?"

"It's part of the church case. I think the pastor's wife is getting to know a congregant in the biblical sense."

"If you need 24/7 coverage, I can't do that."

"Nah. I was thinking just start with a few hours and see if anything materializes. She's pretty sloppy."

"What do you know about the suspected boyfriend?"

"Nothing at the moment, but I should have his info on Monday. Tuesday at the latest."

"Why aren't you doing the surveillance yourself?"

"My plate is full, and Carl is footing the bill. Hiring you is a win-win."

"Let me check with the boss lady, but it sounds like an entertaining diversion."

"I can't imagine the boss lady will object," Fina said, smiling. "There's nothing dangerous about it. You can relive the good old days."

"The good old days of leg cramps and peeing in a cup?"

"The very ones."

"Why don't you stay here tonight? I don't like the idea of you heading home at this hour." Frank and Peg had a finished basement with a couple of guest rooms, one of which was Fina's de facto bedroom. She stayed there on occasion when she needed a change of scenery or wanted to feel like home wasn't just a high-rise condo borrowed from a dead grandmother.

"I don't want to put you and Peg in danger."

Frank looked offended. "You think I can't hold my own?"

"Of course you can, but you shouldn't have to."

"Wait until Peg gets home. You can decide then."

Fina contemplated fixing herself a bowl of ice cream, but she'd already maxed out with the salted caramel. Instead, she got a diet soda from the fridge, snuggled into the corner of the couch, and watched the headlines with Frank.

She felt safe, something that even Chad couldn't deliver.

Fina woke from a deep and dreamless night in Frank and Peg's basement guest room to the reality that she wasn't making much progress on Rand's case. Her conversation with Sally Cramer had gotten her nowhere and though she had another lead to chase down from Rand's college pics, it wasn't much to go on. She was starting to feel desperate and knew that she would have to shake more trees in an effort to flush out her brother's victims.

After eating breakfast and helping Frank with his honey-do list, Fina made a plan to meet Risa at the Chestnut Hill Reservoir for her friend's daily constitutional. Fina swapped the low boots she was wearing for a pair of sneakers she kept in her trunk and pulled her hair into a ponytail.

Risa was waiting at the water's edge, wearing fancy workout gear and marching in place.

"This must be important if you didn't want to discuss it over dinner," Risa commented as they started around the loop.

"It's not really a family-friendly conversation."

Risa eyed her. "That doesn't sound good." She began walking at a brisk pace.

"First of all, thank you for taking good care of Haley. I know you didn't sign up for an extra kid, but we appreciate your involvement in her life."

"Of course. I love Haley, and I loved Melanie. I'll do whatever I can to be supportive."

"I need to tell you something, but it's incredibly sensitive and needs to stay between us."

"What's going on, Fina?"

"Ugh. I hate this."

"Just spit it out."

"Rand has done some stuff, and I'm trying to get dirt on him."

"What kind of stuff?"

A young woman was running toward them, her face contorted in discomfort. If running were really a good idea, people doing it wouldn't look like they were being tortured.

"He hired prostitutes, and he molested Haley."

Risa froze in place and gaped at Fina. "What?"

"He paid for sex, and he sexually abused Haley."

"Wait." She grabbed Fina's arm. "What are you talking about? And why are you telling me this here, now?"

"Easy, killer," Fina said, peeling Risa's fingers from her arm. "There's no good time or place to spill these beans, Risa. I'm telling you now because he's back in town, and I want him to leave for good. I think his presence is the reason Haley is going off the rails."

"Does the family know about this?"

"The adults and Haley, obviously."

"And your parents have welcomed him back?" Risa wrapped her arms around herself as if to ward off the chill of the disturbing news.

"Yes. I got him to leave town for a while, but now he's back."

"How can they allow that?"

"Well, according to you, Rand was my mother's miracle baby, and he can do no wrong. As for my father, I don't understand why he's willing to turn a blind eye. I think there's something going on between my dad and Rand."

"What do you mean?"

"I don't know, but there has to be a reason why Carl is siding with him. More than just being loyal to his son."

"Well, whatever's going on, you have to do something about Rand."

"Yes, thanks. I'm working on it."

Risa starting walking again, and Fina fell into step next to her.

"What about Scotty and Matthew?" Risa asked. "Where do they stand on this?"

"They want to deal with Rand as much as I do."

"And the police? Have you told Cristian?"

"Yes. He knows about it, but for Haley's sake, we haven't gone the criminal charges route."

"What does that leave?"

"I'm trying to build a case against him that my father won't be able to ignore."

"Meaning?"

"Rand has always gotten into trouble. I'm gathering info about his crimes, which I will present to my father. Either he'll have to deal with it or I'll find someone who will."

"I don't understand how I can be useful."

"I tracked down a woman who Rand raped in college, and spoke with another victim, but she denies even knowing him. I have another name to pursue, but I'm starting to feel a little desperate. Is there anything you can think of? Anything that Melanie ever told you that might help?"

"Like what?" Risa's color dulled. "Did Melanie know what he was doing to Haley?"

"I don't know."

"She couldn't have," Risa insisted. "She would never have let that happen."

Fina suspected that her sister-in-law knew, but without proof, it wasn't a conversation worth having.

"Do you know if Rand was ever involved with someone else?" Fina asked. "Or were there any weird relationships you can think of?"

"I just can't believe any of this. Not that I don't believe you, I just mean that I can't process it."

"I understand. It's a lot to wrap your brain around. Instead of thinking about what Melanie did or didn't tell you, can you think of any stuff that seemed off?"

Risa stopped and grabbed Fina's arm again. "Do you know the DeMarcos' daughter?"

"No, I don't think so."

"Kelsey DeMarco. She used to babysit a lot for Haley, would even go on trips with them."

"That's vaguely familiar."

"Well, it seemed like everything was great, and then one day, she stopped babysitting for them."

Fina's stomach muscles began to tighten. "When was this?"

"When Haley was around six or so."

"How old was Kelsey at the time?"

"Sixteen or thereabouts." Risa turned around and started walking back in the direction from which they had come. "Oh no, Fina. Really?"

"What does she look like?"

"Kelsey? I haven't seen her in years, but she was a very pretty girl. Petite with long blond hair. I think she was a cheerleader in high school."

Fina was silent. They passed a couple of teenage boys loitering on a set of stairs, doing tricks on their skateboards with varying degrees of success.

"Can you get me contact info for Kelsey DeMarco?"

"I've got her mom's number, but I don't know where Kelsey is these days."

"Could you call her mom? Make an excuse if you need to? I really need to talk to her."

Risa nodded. "You have to be careful, Fina. If people catch wind of this, the rumor mill is going to go into overdrive."

"I know. I'm walking a very fine line, but it's a risk I have to take. We can't sit back and watch him wreak havoc." Fina dodged a pile of dog poop, silently cursing the owner. "I'm sorry I had to tell you, Risa, but given that Haley is spending so much time at your house, I thought you should know."

"You were right to tell me. I just feel sick to my stomach is all."

They arrived at Risa's car, and Fina leaned against the hood. "Sorry about ruining your walk. We could have kept going."

Risa made a gesture of dismissal. "Forget the walk."

"As soon as you get me Kelsey's info, I'll try to track her down."

"Okay." Risa pulled her into a tight hug. "I'm so sorry. Your family has been through so much misery."

Fina inhaled the scent of Risa's perfume before pulling away. "Keep in touch."

Fina returned to her car and watched her friend drive away.

Risa was right. Her family had been through a lot of misery, but they were architects of that misery. With the exception of Haley, none of them was innocent.

Early Monday morning, Fina accepted a plain brown envelope from Stanley with a sigh.

"Any idea who dropped this one off? Don't tell me Mrs. Bennigan was being helpful again."

Stanley shook his head. "I think it was Mr. Samworth this time."

"Great. So nothing on the security camera?"

"Afraid not. If something dangerous is going on, Ms. Ludlow, I'm going to have to mention it to building management."

"I'm taking care of it, Stanley. No need to worry anyone else."

He shifted from one foot to the other. "You just hear about people sending anthrax through the mail, that sort of thing."

"There's no possibility of that happening," Fina said. She had no basis for that statement, but anthrax and most other deadly biogens weren't available at the corner store. The ransom-note quality of the letters suggested her correspondent was an amateur, and until she had proof suggesting otherwise, she would assume that he or she was an irritating crank.

Fina ripped open the letter and examined the missive. It was similar to the last one, suggesting that Fina mind her own business or else. She tossed the letter on the dining room table, stripped off her clothes on the way to the bathroom, and placed her gun on the vanity next to the shower. If Chad were here, she could shower without the weapon, confident that nobody would bust in while she shaved her legs, causing her to slice her femoral artery. Instead, she kept an ear cocked, just in case someone breached her heavy-duty dead bolt.

Maybe firing Chad had been unwise. What was going to slow her down more: having a shadow or having to watch her back every moment? Ditching him had seemed like a good move on Friday, but now she was second-guessing herself, exactly what her letter writer wanted. That realization pissed her off and hardened her resolve. She'd have to make some concessions given the threats—leg stubble and more time spent looking over her shoulder—but she wasn't going to turn her life upside down for some schmuck with a glue stick or some coward who couldn't even do his own dirty work.

Dressed and resolute, Fina decided to dig into the latest papers she'd gotten from Evan. This was the tedious work that was the bread and butter of any investigation, but it wasn't sexy. Sorting through the dross of Nadine's life might be a colossal waste of time, but Fina wouldn't know that until she did it.

The minutiae of life—anyone's life—were generally boring, but at least Fina felt like she was learning something from the church and neighborhood-related items. Covenant Rising did perform a lot of community service, and with a careful read, Fina could sense the underlying tension between Lucas and Nadine.

The neighborhood association minutes gave her a clear picture of the denizens of the block and the hot topics. Mrs. Anderson wanted a new stop sign installed, and Gil Kressig thought the Fourth of July celebration should start an hour earlier. Jane Covalsky was annoyed that Girl Scouts from the other side of town were selling their wares in her daughter's territory. Mr. Sheffel's cockatoo was still missing, and Ronnie McCaffrey wanted to build a swimming pool. It was an active neighborhood with an engaged population.

After sorting through one box, Fina stretched her aching back and reached for her computer. If money was at the heart of the case, she needed to up the ante. She typed in Covenant Rising's Web address and watched it load. The church's website was user-friendly, and parting you from your money was a painless process. Donations could be made to the general operating fund or steered to the Frontier Fund, which supported an orphanage in Africa. Food, medicine, and education were provided to needy children in Angola, and more importantly, at least according to the site, the hope and comfort that only God's word could provide. Fina didn't believe that reading a Bible passage was as restorative as antidiarrheal medicine or mosquito netting to guard against malaria, but what did she know?

Two thousand dollars seemed like a good number; big enough to warrant some attention, but not so big as to seem suspicious. Fina donated five hundred dollars to the general fund and the rest to the Frontier Fund and printed out a receipt of the transaction.

Next, she called Christa Jackson.

"Christa, it's Fina Ludlow." Fina walked into the kitchen.

"Hi."

"Do you have a minute?"

"That's about all I have."

"I wanted to arrange a time to talk more about Nadine." Fina stared into the cabinet, her eye moving between a box of Wheat Thins and the box of Hostess cupcakes. Feeling virtuous, she grabbed the crackers.

"I have no time today."

"I don't doubt it, but we really need to talk."

"I'm totally booked, Fina."

"Anything I can tag along for?" If Christa was going to the ob-gyn, Fina was out, but she didn't mind pushing the grocery cart if it got her some time with an interviewee.

There was a long pause on the line. Fina brought the crackers back to the couch and took a seat.

"I suppose you can talk to me while I get my nails done," Christa said. "It's the only thing I do for myself all week. I refuse to cancel."

"Understood. I'd be happy to meet you there. Just give me the details."

"It's Morning Glory salon in Framingham. Call them and let them know you want to be at the station next to me."

"I don't need a manicure," Fina insisted, examining her nails. She wasn't opposed to beauty rituals, but she rarely had the time or patience for them, nor were they practical. Picking locks and maintaining one's manicure tended to be antithetical.

"If you're going to be sitting there, they should be making some money."

"Okay, and you're comfortable discussing Nadine at the salon?"

"Yes. I've been going to Han for years. I completely trust her."

Christa gave her the number for the salon, and they agreed to meet right after lunch.

Fina thought about calling Elaine and announcing she was getting her nails done, but thought better of it. There was no point in getting her mother's hopes up that she was adopting a new standard of personal maintenance.

Morning Glory Nail Salon was in a strip mall and looked like every other nail salon Fina had ever visited, not that she'd been to many.

There was a tall reception desk behind which sat a young Vietnamese man. Half of the manicure and pedicure stations were occupied with clients. The Vietnamese aestheticians wore masks, bent over the customers' hands and feet. The scene reminded Fina why she wasn't a fan of pedicures; there was something vaguely biblical about having someone wash your feet that did not sit well with her. It was a little too Jesus and Mary Magdalene for her comfort.

On a credenza behind the desk, there was a small collection of bonsai trees and a framed painting of Niagara Falls featuring fiber optics that animated the water.

Fina saw Christa beckoning to her from the back of the salon. She took a seat at the station next to her manned by an older woman.

"This is Han and her sister Thien," Christa said, indicating her manicurist and the older woman.

"Pick your polish," Thien said.

The wall behind her featured acrylic shelves lined with bottles of colorful polish. Fina pulled down a dark plum shade and tipped the bottle to read the name, Odessa Destiny. She liked the idea of going bold, but knew that it would chip within a day and end up looking cheap. She swapped it for Honeymoon Sweet, a boring pale pink.

"I've been coming here for over ten years," Christa said, blowing an errant curl away from her nose.

"I can't remember the last time I had my nails done," Fina commented.

"I know it's an indulgence," Christa said, "but it keeps me sane." She closed her eyes.

"Sorry to crash it."

Thien grasped Fina's hand and started to trim and file her nails. Her motions were swift and assured.

"You wanted to talk more about Nadine?" Christa asked.

"I wanted to talk about Nadine and Paul."

There was a flutter of movement under Christa's eyelids before she opened them. "What do you mean?"

"I understand that they dated at one point," Fina said.

"Who told you that?"

"I'm an investigator, Christa. I find stuff out."

"They dated, but that's ancient history," she said as Han dunked one of her hands in a shallow dish of soapy water.

"When?"

"What does this have to do with Nadine's death?"

"I'm not sure, but unless you know who killed her, the police and I need to keep asking questions."

"Obviously, I don't know who killed her."

"Okay, so when did your husband and your cousin date?"

She glared at Fina. "The end of high school, beginning of college."

"Was it serious?"

"It was an on-and-off thing."

Thien began pushing Fina's cuticles back with a wooden imple-ment. "Why didn't you tell me this when we first spoke?"

"Why would I?" Christa asked. "Like I said, it's ancient history."

Fina didn't buy it. If it was so unimportant, why avoid mentioning it? "So why did they break up?"

Christa shrugged. "They just did."

"And how soon after that did you and Paul start dating?"

"It wasn't long."

Fina studied Thien's fingers as she tended to Fina's. Her nails were short and ragged with flecks of coral polish. They were a disaster, and Fina couldn't tell if they were an occupational hazard or the result of inadequate grooming. Either way, they were poor advertising.

"Was Nadine upset that you and Paul got together?"

"I don't think she was thrilled," Christa said, "but we were young. Everybody moved on."

"It must have been a little hard," Fina suggested. "I saw pictures of Paul at your house. He's a handsome guy, has a good job, is getting his MBA."

"Except for the handsome part, none of that was true when we were nineteen-year-olds."

"Okay, so let's just stick with the handsome part. It must have hurt Nadine to have her ex take up with her cousin."

"Believe me, she felt quite superior when I got knocked up."

Thien had moved on to the buffing and soaking stage of the process. Fina felt uncomfortable with both of her hands occupied and out of her control.

"Got it. So it was never awkward? Having your husband's ex at family gatherings?"

"She was my cousin before she was his girlfriend. And no, it wasn't awkward."

Fina wondered if despite her disapproval, Nadine wasn't actually jealous of her cousin. Yes, their start was inauspicious, but from the outside, Christa and Paul had built an enviable life for themselves. Nadine had only recently established her family, which was already on the brink of breaking apart.

"Do you think Nadine and Evan wanted to have more kids, I mean, before the whole church debacle?" Fina asked.

"I assume so."

Thien suddenly barked at the young man behind the reception desk, and Fina shifted her hand slightly. The manicurist gave her a withering look.

"Well, it's great you guys were able to put aside your shared history and stay close," Fina said. "Not everyone would be able to do that."

"It really wasn't a big deal," Christa said, moving one hand in front of a small fan. Her nails were a deep berry color.

"People have family feuds over less."

Thien applied the polish, three quick strokes up each nail.

"Even if we wanted to, that wouldn't have been tolerated. Her mom and my dad have always been close."

"Speaking of your aunt, I haven't been able to reach her." Fina swapped hands, narrowly missing crashing her hand into the fan. That would be typical, ruining the manicure without even moving from the chair.

"I'm not surprised. They talked about leaving town for a bit. They're devastated. There's nothing they can tell you, anyway."

Fina would have preferred to be the judge of that, but that was one of the disadvantages of being a private eye. Unlike the cops, you couldn't force people to talk to you.

Han and Thien finished polishing and then reached into Christa's and Fina's bags to retrieve money and car keys. Fina followed Christa to a sitting area in the front window where small UV dryers were lined up. They gingerly slipped their hands under the blue lights.

"How long do we have to sit here?" Fina asked.

"About ten minutes."

Fina looked annoyed.

"Have a couple of kids," Christa suggested. "Then you'll be cursing the invention of these speedy dryers."

"I'll take your word for it."

Christa closed her eyes, and Fina watched the blue UV light glowing over her fingertips.

She still wasn't convinced that the teenage love triangle between Paul, Nadine, and Christa was as amicable as she'd been led to believe.

Unfortunately, the only definitive thing she was leaving with was polished nails.

TWENTY-ONE

Fina tracked Glen Sullivan down at a car wash in Jamaica Plain. She parked in a side lot near the line of vehicles waiting to roll onto the automated track. After the harsh winter, cars were caked with dirt and sediment, badly in need of a wash. They entered the building gray and matte and emerged bright and shiny.

A team of Hispanic men wielding damp rags clustered around a dripping SUV at the exit. They rubbed at it as if polishing an apple, with each man taking charge of one portion of the car. Fina asked for Glen and was rewarded with a nod toward the building.

Customers sat in a waiting room outfitted with plastic chairs, dog-eared magazines, and a TV blaring a cable news channel. Interested parties could watch the transformation from a windowed hallway that ran alongside the car wash itself. Fina started down an enclosed parallel passageway to empty offices, a small kitchen, and restrooms. One of the last doors led to an office that had a window onto the observation walkway and the slow parade of cars.

"Glen?" Fina poked her head into the room. A young man sat behind the desk, fiddling with his phone.

"Yes." He looked up at her. Although she assumed he was in his mid-twenties given his connection to Dante, he'd retained a layer of baby fat in his face and around his middle that made him look younger. He had a large, square head topped with red hair and wide-set eyes. His pale skin called to mind a newborn mouse.

"Dante Trimonti sent me."

He put down his phone and crossed his arms. The pose read more nervous than powerful. "I'm not working with Dante anymore."

"My name's Fina Ludlow."

His eyes darted to the side, indicating a hint of recognition.

"May I?" She gestured to the chair across from him.

He shrugged. His desk was a standard metal model with a couple of overflowing wire in-boxes on top. An enormous Slurpee sat in front of him. It was a lurid purple color and dripped with condensation.

"I'm a friend of Dante's, and I'm looking for some information. Someone put a contract out on me." Fina smiled sweetly. "I'd like to know who."

Glen shook his head.

"Not to kill me," Fina clarified.

"I don't know anything about stuff like that." Behind him, an explosion of blue and pink suds rained down on a car. "Look, I've got a good job here, and I don't want to screw it up."

"I'm not looking to jam you up," Fina assured him. "Just relax."

Glen reached for the Slurpee and took a pull from the drink. Fina got a cold headache just watching.

"Do you know anything about it? Fina Ludlow is a pretty unique name. It's kind of hard to forget."

He put the drink down and shoved his hands into his pockets. "I heard about it," he finally admitted, "but I don't know anything."

"Tell me what you heard."

"I just heard that the job was making the rounds, and someone picked it up."

"Someone took the job, you mean?"

He nodded.

"Who took the job? I promise this won't blow back on you." Fina had no business making that promise, but she was getting desperate and had to put her own needs before Glen's. It wasn't fair, but it was the world she lived in.

Glen rotated his chair slightly so he had a better view of the cars rolling by. "I don't know. Like I said, I don't want to be involved in any of that stuff."

Fina considered his reluctance for a moment. "What's changed?" she asked. "Why are you turning over a new leaf?"

He looked at her. "My girlfriend and me, we're having a kid."

"Congratulations. When is she due?"

"Four months." The hint of a smile snuck onto his face. "We're having a boy."

"That's great. I applaud your efforts to get on the right track."

Glen shook his head. "It's not easy. We're trying to find a place to live, and we want to get married." He fiddled with the lid of his Slurpee. "And I've got some legal stuff to deal with."

"What kind of legal stuff?"

"Bad checks. That sort of thing."

"Do you have an attorney?"

"My cousin's friend is helping out."

Fina reached into her bag and pulled out one of Matthew's cards. "If you give me the name of the guy, I'll hook you up with excellent representation, free of charge." She held the card out like a small carrot.

His hand hesitated midair.

"You and I both know that innocent people don't go free, Glen," Fina continued. "It's the people with good lawyers who go free."

Glen took the card. "The guy's name is Jimmy Smith. That's all I know."

"Seriously? Jimmy Smith? You might as well tell me to look for John Doe."

He held his hands up in defense. "It's what I heard. Don't shoot the messenger."

Fina sighed. "Is he white? Young? Does he have a nickname that you know of?"

"I know he's white and in his twenties. That's it."

"You're sure he's the one who took the job? If he doesn't turn out to be the guy, our deal is off."

He nodded. "He took the job."

Fina considered the information for a moment. It wasn't much to go on, but it was more than she had when she walked in. "When you call the office," she said, nodding at the card, "tell them that you're a referral from Fina Ludlow."

"Okay." He tucked the card into his pocket.

"Thank you, Glen. Good luck with your new life."

She was at the door when he spoke. "Why does someone want to beat you up? What did you do?"

Fina smiled. "Nothing. Everything. Who knows?"

On the way to her car, she left a message for Matthew giving him a heads-up on his new client. He wouldn't be thrilled with the worthless business, but sometimes you had to use what you had to get what you needed.

Evan agreed to meet Fina during his lunch break. His office was near a fancy organic supermarket with lots of prepared foods, and she grabbed a container of spicy tuna rolls from the sushi section and met him at a table in the café area. He was tucking into what looked like chicken tikka with a side of naan.

"I don't suppose I can get a real diet soda in this place," she said, craning her neck toward a refrigerated case.

"Good luck."

Fina slipped out of her seat and filled two cups from a watercooler. She gave one to Evan before sitting down.

"How is it being back at work?" Fina asked.

He chewed slowly, then had a drink of water. "Work's fine. My brain can't make sense of the home part."

"That Nadine isn't there?"

"That I'm there without her. I hadn't been living at home for a couple of months, and I always hoped I'd be back, but she was supposed to be there, too."

"How's Molly?"

"She's been acting out a little. I don't know if it's because of Nadine or she's just going through a phase."

Fina placed a small piece of ginger in her mouth. "Why didn't you tell me that Paul and Nadine used to date?"

"I forgot," he said, tearing off a piece of naan.

"You forgot that your wife used to date her cousin's husband? A cousin you see often?"

He rested his elbows on the table and looked at her. "I've had other things on my mind, Fina."

"Right. Well, maybe now you could enlighten me."

"Nadine and Paul dated some in high school and at the beginning of college."

"And where did Christa fit into this?"

"Nadine and Paul broke up for a little while, and that's when Christa got pregnant."

"Wait." Fina put down her water. "Were Nadine and Paul broken up for good when he hooked up with Christa?"

Evan focused his attention on his plate and a corner of naan. He swiped it around the dish, soaking up sauce.

"Nadine and Paul broke up. Paul and Christa were together for a little bit, and then Nadine and Paul got back together."

"And then Christa learned she was pregnant?" Fina dipped a piece of roll into the soy sauce and put it in her mouth. She liked the taste of the fish roe on top, but knew she'd be digging tiny orange orbs out of her teeth for the rest of the day.

"Basically."

"So when Christa got pregnant, Paul was in some ways more Nadine's boyfriend than her own."

He shook his head. "Nadine and Paul weren't together when Christa got pregnant."

"But they got back together shortly afterwards, which would suggest that their relationship still had some life in it."

"I suppose."

Fina's gaze drifted to the bulk foods self-service area. A woman in yoga pants was filling a bag with some kind of nut or grain that probably cleansed her system. Fina never understood that concept; wasn't it her body's job to clean itself out? What was it there for otherwise?

"I'm not suggesting that Paul and Christa did anything wrong," she said, "but that must have been painful for Nadine."

"I guess," Evan replied.

"So what happened when Christa discovered she was pregnant?"

"Paul broke up with Nadine."

"And married Christa?"

He nodded. "Right before McKenna was born. Neither wanted to have the baby out of wedlock."

"So in six months' time, Nadine went from being Paul's girlfriend to being first cousins, once removed, to Paul's child?"

"I guess. I don't know how all that works."

Fina swallowed her irritation. "My point is: They became related in a very different way than Nadine probably anticipated."

"Right," Evan conceded.

Fina ate another roll. The seaweed was chewy, but provided a nice contrast to the soft rice and tender fish. People assumed Fina didn't like food that was good for her, but they were wrong. It's just that her main criterion for food was ease in preparation, and in one's own home, ripping into a Hostess cupcake was easier than rolling up some sushi.

"Nadine must have been pissed," Fina said.

"I wasn't around then, but I think she was upset."

"I spoke with Christa about this, and she downplayed the whole thing."

"Of course she downplayed it. She ended up with her cousin's boyfriend." Evan dropped his napkin onto his plate and pushed it away. "Everything worked out for the best, though."

"True. You and Nadine wouldn't have gotten together if she'd been with Paul."

"Exactly."

"Did Nadine have a serious boyfriend before you two got together?"

He shrugged. "She dated some people, but nothing serious."

Fina ran her fingertip along the ruffle of fake grass in her sushi container. "So she had a lot of time to watch Christa's happy family grow."

Evan threw up his hands in exasperation. "She wasn't jealous of Christa. Why does any of this matter? Nadine is the one who ended up dead."

"But if her relationships were more complicated than they appeared at first glance, they could have something to do with her death."

"So now you think Christa killed her?" He piled his trash on an empty tray another patron had left behind.

"I didn't say that, but it wasn't one big happy family like I'd been led to believe. I have to ask these questions, Evan."

"So you say."

Fina didn't want to cause him additional grief, but if that was the price of solving his wife's murder, so be it.

"What about the antifreeze in your house?" she asked.

Evan's features seemed to stretch tight across his face. "How do you even know about that?"

Fina looked at him. "Really? That's the important part of that question?"

"What can I tell you? We had antifreeze in our house. So do a lot of people."

It was a weak response, but short of confessing to killing his wife, it was the best explanation she would get.

"Thanks for talking to me," Fina said.

Evan's face was slack, and when he stood, she noticed that his jacket was hanging loosely on his frame.

In every case, layered relationships and complicated histories were revealed with time, and Fina knew it was part of the process, the slow unfolding of the truth. But just once, she wished someone would tell her the truth the first time she interviewed them.

Fina screwed up her courage after lunch and headed for the police station. Only when she was coming through the front door and took a deep breath did she realize how tightly coiled her body was, being in a constant state of alert. Watching over her shoulder and bracing for an attack were draining, and being surrounded by armed police officers let her put down the burden for a bit.

She needed to update Cristian, but there was a small part of her that hoped he was out. Fina wanted credit for trying to be in touch, but didn't actually want to be in touch. Unfortunately, fate was not on her side, and she was escorted by a uniformed officer to the department gym in the building's basement.

Most large police precincts have their own workout facilities in the hope that the employees will make an effort to stay in shape. Fina had encountered some cops who fit the donut-eating, overweight stereotype, but most of the cops she knew were in good shape and could easily beat the average citizen in a footrace.

There were half a dozen cops in the windowless gym. Loud classic rock rang out from the speakers, and a TV in the corner was tuned to a soap opera with the sound muted. Two guys were running on treadmills. Another pair were doing bench presses, and a woman worked her triceps on a cable machine. Cristian was in a corner manipulating a heavy bag of sand over his head. If the cops in the gym were a representation of the force, the city was in good hands.

Fina waited until Cristian was between sets, then navigated through the equipment to his spot. He was wearing gray gym shorts and a sweat-soaked BPD T-shirt.

"Hey," he said.

"Hi. I don't want to interrupt. I can catch you later if you'd prefer."

"It's fine. I'm done. I just need to stretch."

She followed him to some mats and took a seat with her back against the wall. Cristian dropped down into a lunge to stretch his legs.

"What's up?" he asked.

"I just wanted to bring you up to speed." Her eyes strayed to his ass, the muscles of which strained against his shorts.

"I would appreciate the decency of your making eye contact when you speak to me, ma'am," he said, grinning.

"I can't help it, Detective."

"Uh-huh. You were going to bring me up to speed?"

Fina crossed her legs at the ankles. "I don't suppose you have an opinion about Evan and the antifreeze you found at the Quaynor residence?"

Cristian switched legs. "A: How do you know about the antifreeze, and B: 'bringing me up to speed' means you tell me things, not the other way around."

She shook her head. "I always get that wrong."

"No shit. How'd you find out about the antifreeze?"

"I investigated."

Cristian frowned.

"Don't worry. I didn't do anything illegal." Last time she checked, being nosy wasn't illegal. "Back to your opinion."

"No comment." He took a seat and reached for his toes.

"Does that mean you also have no comment about the romantic relationship Nadine had in her twenties?"

"I don't have time for guessing games, Fina."

She hesitated. Telling Cristian about Nadine and Paul didn't gain her anything in the moment, but it might generate some goodwill that would come in handy when she told him about the anonymous letters.

"Nadine Quaynor and Paul Jackson dated when they were younger, and Christa got pregnant in the middle of the whole thing."

Cristian grinned. "He knocked up his girlfriend's cousin?"

"Technically, Nadine and Paul had broken up, but then they got back together. Apparently, Paul had been with Christa during their break."

"That must have pissed off Nadine."

"I assume so, but they're all being rather circumspect about the whole thing."

"Even though Nadine had the biggest reason to be angry, and she's the one who ended up dead?"

"Exactly what I thought. I understand if they're embarrassed; it's not something to crow about, but acknowledging it doesn't make any of them look guiltier."

"Who told you about it?" Cristian mopped his face with a towel and scooted next to her against the wall.

"Their daughter McKenna. She was looking through photo albums and found pictures of Nadine and Paul at the prom. Obviously, it's not a family secret, but I imagine she might have some questions about the timing when she gets older."

"I would think."

Fina playfully punched his thigh. "How 'bout that? I just brought you up to speed!"

"Well done."

"Any news from your guys regarding my contract?"

Cristian shook his head. "I'll check in with Buckley, but I haven't heard anything. You?"

"I got the lead of a lifetime: Jimmy Smith."

He burst out laughing. "Good luck with that."

"I appreciate the encouragement. Could you run him through the system for me? I don't think Pitney would mind."

"Let me clear it with her. She's very persnickety when it comes to you."

"Lucky me."

"Are you missing your bodyguard?"

"Nah. I really am a lone wolf."

The statement hung between them, Fina realizing it was ripe for interpretation.

"It may have been that guy in particular," Cristian said. "You could try someone else."

"He was good at his job. I just didn't like having him around." On the TV, a bleached blonde was crying, and a man stood behind her, peering over her shoulder. His face was crimped with emotion. Did anyone actually have conversations that way in real life? "Did I mention that I got a couple of anonymous letters?"

Cristian stared at her. "No. You didn't 'mention' that you got a couple of anonymous letters. I'm guessing they were of the threatening nature."

"They weren't fan mail, that is true." Fina reached into her bag and pulled out the two letters.

"Way to preserve evidence," he commented, taking them from her.

"'Cause you have the resources to run a DNA profile on the saliva? I'm sure that's at the top of the department's to-do list."

Cristian studied them for a moment. "Any ideas?" he asked, handing them back to her.

"Not really, but I find it hard to believe that the same person is putting out a contract on me and sending me these arts and crafts projects."

"*Or* that's what he or she wants you to believe."

"Yes, that's always a possibility." Fina tucked them back into her bag. "I'm just sharing them with you in the spirit of full disclosure."

"Full disclosure means you share things in a timely fashion."

"Can't you just be happy that I shared at all?" Fina pleaded.

"Under-promise and over-deliver? Is that your approach?" He pushed himself up and offered his hand to her.

"Exactly."

Cristian escorted her upstairs to the lobby. "I'll see you later," he said stiffly, keeping his distance.

It made sense to keep their evolving relationship under wraps for the time being, but if it was going to become a thing, people would have to know—people like cops. Fina wondered if Cristian had really considered the implications of that news flash.

"Always a pleasure, Detective," Fina called out after him.

On the way home, Fina ducked into an office supply store and purchased a large desk blotter calendar that featured a page per month. At home, she taped the calendar pages for the previous three months onto the living room wall. She pulled up the e-mail from Evan and plotted the dates he had provided of Nadine's illness. Without any context, the information wasn't particularly helpful, so she sent him an e-mail asking for a copy of Nadine's schedule.

Next, Fina turned to the issue of Jimmy Smith. A search in an online paid database netted dozens of James Smiths in the Boston area. She was able to whittle the list down to thirty-seven by looking for white guys in their twenties, but the field was still too large. Rather than traipse around the eastern part of the state, she'd put out some feelers with her contacts and see if that netted any results.

Fina typed in the address for the Covenant Rising website and checked out the event schedule for the week. In a few hours there was an informational meeting about the church's Frontier Fund. Fina picked up the phone and dialed Chloe's number.

"Chloe? It's Fina Ludlow. Do you have a moment?"

"Sure. How are you?"

"Good, and you?"

"I'm fine."

"I wondered if you knew much about the church's Frontier Fund."

"I haven't been involved in it. Why?"

"There's an informational meeting tonight at the church, and I thought I might go and learn more about it."

"Because you're interested in supporting it?" Chloe asked doubtfully.

"Because you keep telling me about the church's good works. Do you want to join me?"

Chloe consulted her calendar, and they agreed to meet at Covenant Rising. The listing promised snacks, which Fina knew was the key to a good turnout at any event.

"I'll see you there," she said before hanging up.

Her RMV contact had called while Fina was on the line. She called her back and made the request for information on Gabby's parking lot friend.

Fina knew it would cost her, but nothing came free in her line of work.

TWENTY-TWO

A couple of hours later, Fina slipped into a seat next to Chloe in the Covenant Rising parish hall. There were about two dozen people sprinkled amid the pews. A screen had been deployed from the ceiling, and soft conversations buzzed around the room.

"Where are the promised snacks?" Fina asked quietly.

"Over there." Chloe gestured to the side of the room.

"Can I get you some?"

"If there's crudité, I'll have some of that."

Fina touched her arm.

"What is it?" Chloe asked.

"I'm just checking that you're real. I've heard there are people who choose to eat crudité, I've just never met any in the flesh."

Chloe smiled. "We exist. We aren't like unicorns and leprechauns."

Fina squeezed by and walked over to assess the options. She made two small plates. One was heavy on crudité, dip, cheese, and crackers. The other was dominated by the sweet offerings, including a lemon bar, two Hershey's kisses, and a peanut butter cookie. She balanced the plates and two cups of water in her hands and returned to her seat.

They were chatting and nibbling when Pastor Greg stopped by their pew. "I'm surprised to see you here, Fina."

"I keep hearing about your good works, so I made a sizable contribution on the website."

Chloe looked pleased. "I didn't think you were serious."

"As a heart attack, Pastor Greg."

He looked at her, but reined in his response, presumably in deference to Chloe's presence. "Chloe, how are you?"

"I'm well. And you, Pastor?"

"Very well. Thank you."

"Is Gabby here?" Fina asked.

"Yes. I think she's catching up with some members. If you'll excuse me."

A few moments later, Gabby appeared and joined Greg at the front. Fina did a quick scan of the room and caught sight of Gabby's young friend, the owner of the Ford Fiesta. He was seated a couple of rows behind them, off to the side.

Greg and Gabby led a prayer and then a film came to life on the large screen. It seemed to Fina to be a long-form version of those commercials that run on late-night TV, the ones that try to guilt you into donating a dollar a day to change the life of a disadvantaged child in some godforsaken country on the other side of the globe. She knew that these children existed, and that their needs were real, but she couldn't draw a clear line from the Frontier Fund to an improved standard of living. Proselytizing and conversion seemed to be at the heart of the campaign, and those weren't things you could eat.

The other thing that bothered Fina about the pitch was the absence of Covenant Rising members on the ground in Africa. There were plenty of white missionaries in the film, but Fina couldn't be sure that any of them actually worked for the church. Did that mean there was an intermediary, another organization that did the fieldwork, and if so, how much of the fund went to supporting their operation?

The lights went up twenty minutes later, and Fina noticed that some of the viewers were dabbing at their eyes and sniffling. Pastor Greg opened the floor to questions and what followed was a flurry of praise and admiration for him and Gabby. One woman asked about the medical care provided for the children, but it wasn't exactly a hardball question. Fina knew that she had to tread lightly. She didn't want to offend Chloe or alienate her, but she had some legitimate questions that she'd ask of any charity, not just Covenant Rising.

"Pastor Greg," Fina said after he'd steadfastly ignored her raised hand. "Could I ask a question?"

He adopted a grimace masquerading as a smile. "Of course."

"Have you and Gabby visited the orphanage to see your good works firsthand?"

"We'd like nothing more, but we haven't had the opportunity as of yet."

"Have any of the Covenant Rising members made the trip?"

"No, but it is on the agenda." He scanned the room. "Any other questions? Well, then," he said, aborting any attempts at further discussion, "thanks so much for coming. There are donation envelopes on the table, or you can do it online."

He strode up the aisle, leaving Gabby to chat with some congregants.

"I didn't realize the scope of their work," Chloe commented. Fina murmured appropriate responses and trained her eye on Gabby. She was exchanging surreptitious glances with the young man. The parish hall started emptying out, and Gabby greeted a few other members before arriving at their pew.

"Thanks, Gabby," Chloe said. "That was really informative."

"You're so welcome, Chloe. Fina." She nodded in greeting.

"You must be anxious to visit the orphanage," Fina said, "since you're such a dedicated mom."

"I do love the little ones," she said, smiling beatifically.

"Well, it won't be like home," Fina continued. "I don't think they have the same creature comforts we do, like running water. I'm sure you don't even notice it after a couple of days."

Gabby's smile dimmed.

"That part of western Africa doesn't have a strong infrastructure," Chloe commented.

"Whatever the good Lord wants us to do, we'll do," Gabby said.

"I think you have to use a latrine in the middle of the night," Fina said.

"There's a lot of wildlife," Chloe piped up innocently. "When we were on safari in that area, you needed an armed guide to escort you at night to ward off a big-game attack."

"That must have been scary," Fina said, thrilled that Chloe's worldliness was coming in handy.

"I'm sure Pastor Greg will take all of those things into consideration and determine what's best for the church," Gabby said, looking beyond them. "It was good to see you both."

"I have a little trouble picturing Gabby in the wild," Fina admitted to Chloe as they walked through the parking lot.

Chloe's eyes widened. "I don't think she's looking forward to making that trip."

"Nope."

The thing about Africa was that it was very far away. You could do all kinds of wonderful projects there. Or not.

And who would be the wiser?

Fina left Dante a message asking if he ever crossed paths with a Jimmy Smith, and she also inquired when her car might be fixed. She was growing tired of the loaner.

Since the family dinner at the club, Fina hadn't been able to ignore the increasing dread she felt about Matthew's new girlfriend and her young daughter. She didn't think she was being paranoid, worrying about the child's well-being, but reinforcements were required if she was going to make a case against Rand, and she wanted to hash out a strategy with Scotty.

She kept an eye out as she made the drive, and Fina didn't see anything out of the ordinary. Lights blazed in Scotty and Patty's house, but the driveway was empty. Either the cars were in the garage or the family was out, with little regard for their electric bill and the earth's dwindling natural resources. Fina rang the bell, but there was no answer. She couldn't easily peek into the house at the front, so she decided to walk around back and see if the drapes were open in the great room.

Fina followed the path to the backyard. It was edged with large arborvitae, which provided a natural screen from the neighbors. The patio furniture was safely packed away, and the outdoor kitchen with its high-end grill was still wearing its winter coat. A taut cover stretched across the pool.

A loud crack, like a branch being snapped in two, startled her. She sensed movement out of the corner of her eye and reached for her gun, but it was too late. A man knocked her down, her head striking the cold, wet grass and narrowly avoiding the stone pool-deck. She fought to free her hand and keep the gun in her holster; she didn't want to struggle for the weapon with her assailant on top of her. Either she needed a clear shot or no shot at all. She'd rather take her chances in an old-fashioned fight than get shot with her own gun.

His first punch landed on the side of her eye, and Fina grunted. He reared up slightly in preparation to strike her again. She kicked him in the groin, and he momentarily loosened his grip on her. Fina scuttled out from under him, but he grabbed her leg and punched her in the stomach. She staggered back, but stayed upright as he got to his feet.

There was a brief moment, a second before he reached his full height, and Fina knew it was her only chance. She tightened her abs and curled forward, smashing the hard bone at the crest of her head against the man's nose. He cried out in pain, and blood poured from his nostrils. Stepping backward, he tripped and landed on the pool cover. Fina pulled back her leg and kicked him in the ribs. She reached into her jacket, but was distracted by a light turning on in the kitchen, her attention briefly pulled in the other direction. Her assailant crawled to the edge of the pool on all fours and through the trees into the dark. Gun in hand, Fina watched him disappear into the shadows.

She hobbled over to the grill area and leaned against the counter. Teddy was visible in the window of the great room. She took some deep breaths and briefly contemplated walking over and knocking on the window, but was worried she'd scare the shit out of her young nephew. Instead, she returned to her car.

Her dread had been replaced with actual pain, not a fair trade in her estimation.

"You should have called Cristian," Milloy scolded her. He applied a bag of frozen peas to her head, and she winced.

"Oww." They were sitting on her couch.

"Do you think you broke a rib?" he asked, gently running his hand over her midriff, which was already discolored.

"I think he was going for my kidney."

"You need to get checked out."

"Maybe tomorrow," she said, avoiding his disapproving gaze. "If I go to the ER now, there are going to be all kinds of questions."

"And what's wrong with that?"

"I need to think about it before I involve the cops."

"What's the downside to involving the cops?"

Fina adjusted the peas. "Cristian would find out, and I'd have to make a statement and say that it happened at Scotty's house, which would then involve him. It would get out of my control very quickly."

"It's already out of your control."

"Is there anything to eat? I could really use some comfort food."

Milloy got up from the couch and retreated to the kitchen.

"Thanks for coming over," she called after him.

"You're welcome."

He returned a moment later with two spoons and a pint of Ben & Jerry's Cake Batter ice cream. Fina lifted her legs, and he sat down and pulled them onto his lap. He handed her a spoon laden with ice cream.

"Maybe you should rethink that bodyguard," Milloy suggested.

"Maybe. Kind of like closing the barn door after the horse is out."

"Unless he's planning to do it again. Or worse."

"I realize he may not be done. He was supposed to beat me up, and frankly, in my defense, this doesn't really qualify."

He peered at her. "I guess it's all relative."

"Indeed."

"Cristian is going to figure it out when he sees you with a shiner."

Fina held out her spoon, and he passed the pint to her. "I'll burn that bridge when I cross it."

"Ahh. Something to look forward to."

Fina handed the ice cream back to him and closed her eyes.

She'd assumed that encountering her assailant would be the end of her troubles, but it might just be the beginning.

Fina awoke to a painful reality. Rolling over was a mistake. So was stretching her limbs and sitting up. Basically, moving was a bad idea.

She did some simple stretches under a hot shower and tried to get the blood pumping. Her torso was sporting a deep purple bruise the size of a salad plate. Examining herself in the mirror, she was pleased that the blow to her face had glanced off her eye. Most of the damage was around her temple, which was less noticeable than a standard black eye would be, though still obvious.

Milloy had taken off early for an appointment, but he'd left her a note suggesting she eat a couple of the hard-boiled eggs he'd made for her and some toast and fruit. She peeled the eggs and slathered them with salt and butter, but toast and fruit seemed unnecessary; she didn't want to shock her system. Fina was craving a diet soda, which she took into the living room, where she checked her messages.

Shirley, her contact at the Registry, had called as had Risa. She'd contacted Kelsey DeMarco's mother and gotten her daughter's contact info, including her place of employment. Fina tapped out a text to Risa praising her stellar investigative chops and then dialed Shirley's number. As she navigated her way through the Registry phone tree, she watched a tanker making its way across the harbor.

"Hello."

"Shirley, it's Fina Ludlow returning your call."

"Right. Let me find the info."

Fina heard papers shuffling on the other end of the line. It wasn't legal for Shirley to provide the information, but most organizations and companies had people who were willing to disclose private information for the right price. Fina wasn't proud that she was a part of this black market economy, but her job would be much harder if she opted out of it.

"Have I mentioned how much my grandson wants to go to Fenway on opening day?" Shirley said.

"You've mistaken me for a miracle worker. That's beyond even my powers." She compensated people like Shirley with hard-to-get sports and theater tickets.

A loud sigh emanated down the phone line. "I don't know, Fina. I'm not sure I can keep helping you."

"Then don't, Shirley." Fina was in no mood to be strong-armed, having been literally strong-armed the night before. "I'm sure I can find someone who's happy to be in a luxury box during the Sox–Yankees game. Take care."

"Well, wait a second. I didn't say we couldn't work together."

"Glad to hear it."

"The car is registered to Casey Andros. DOB is June 12, 1992, and the address is 139 Macomber Place in Wayland."

"Thanks. Talk to you later." Fina hung up.

Everybody was a negotiator these days. Quid pro quo was one thing, but Shirley was just being greedy. It would be a pain to replace her, but Fina would if necessary.

She toyed with the idea of visiting Frank, but Fina didn't have the energy to deal with a lecture. She lay down on the couch and called instead.

"How's it going, sweetie?" Frank asked when he answered.

"Fine. How's the surveillance?"

"As boring as I remember."

"Anything interesting?"

"Not really. I've got a lot of pictures of the subject with various people, but nothing that screams out 'tomfoolery' at this point."

"This might help," Fina said, reeling off Casey Andros's address.

"You want me to switch over to him?"

"Yeah. I'm interested in the two of them together, but it will be interesting to see what he's up to the rest of the time."

"Your wish is my command. Any news on your would-be attacker?"

Fina took a deep breath, but didn't speak.

"Fina? Is there something you'd like to tell me?"

"There's something I'd like to *not* tell you."

"What happened?" She could hear anxiety in his voice.

"We had an altercation last night, but I'm fine. No need to worry."

"Are you hurt?"

"He got in a couple of hits, but I did better."

"Did you see a doctor?"

"No, but Milloy helped me out."

"No offense to Milloy, but he isn't a doctor."

"I know. I'll probably see someone later today."

"Why Milloy and not Cristian?" Frank asked.

"The Cristian thing is very complicated."

"Why's that?"

"Can we talk about this later? I really should get some work done."

"We'll talk about it later then."

"Great. Let me know what happens with Casey Andros."

"Will do, and be careful. If you really humiliated that guy, he might come back for another round just to soothe his pride."

"I know. I'll be careful."

Fina hung up and dropped the phone on the coffee table.

She'd be careful, but was that enough? As long as she left the house on her own, she wouldn't be completely safe. The smart move would be to rehire Chad, but she felt irritated just contemplating it.

But dying because she was stubborn would be really stupid.

"What do you want?" Dante asked when he returned her call.

"Is my car ready yet?"

"Yeah. You can come get it."

"How about you bring it to me?" Dante's shop was in Revere, and Fina didn't want to make the trip.

"What do you think this is, a chauffeur service?"

"I'm sure you have some business in the city. Just meet me, and I'll drive you wherever you need to go." There was a fumbling sound on the other end. "Dante?"

"Yeah, okay. Where do you want to meet?"

"I have to drop the loaner at Ludlow and Associates, so I can meet you in Back Bay."

"I'll pick you up outside the Pru on Boylston. Let's say three hours."

"Fine. See you then."

What did it say about her, she wondered, when the idea of meeting with her neighborhood pimp filled her with hopeful anticipation?

Fina returned the loaner car to the fleet manager and headed up to Scotty's office. He waved her in and did an appropriate double take when she got close enough for him to register the damage on her face.

"Seriously?" he asked. He came around the desk and examined her face. Fina humored him for a moment, but then grabbed a diet soda from the bar and dug a few Advil out of her bag.

"Not a big deal," she said, stifling a groan as she dropped down onto his couch.

"What happened?"

"Don't act surprised. I told you someone was after me."

"I thought you were going to hire a bodyguard."

"I did, but it didn't work out."

He sat down next to her. "Why not?"

"What difference does it make? It didn't work out, and things . . . happened."

"Where else are you hurt?"

Fina lifted the hem of her shirt and showed him the kaleidoscope bruise that was creeping across her midriff.

"Jesus." He reared back. "That looks terrible."

"Thanks. It feels great."

"Where did this happen?"

Fina took a sip of soda. If she told Scotty that it had happened in his backyard, he'd have apoplexy. "That's not important. I'm interviewing a witness in a little while for Operation Stop Pedophile."

"That's great. Nothing like coming up with a code name for taking down our brother."

"All great military offenses have catchy names. It helps rally the troops."

"Good luck and be careful."

"I don't think a twenty-six-year-old female witness poses a real threat."

"I was thinking more of Rand."

"I'm always careful when it comes to him."

She left without asking Scotty about Carl's potential misdeeds, as she had Matthew. Scotty may be an attack dog in court, but she knew his soft heart wasn't up for the discussion.

TWENTY-THREE

With time to kill before Dante's arrival, Fina walked the few blocks to Newbury Street and Newbury Comics. Even if Kelsey DeMarco wasn't working, it gave her the opportunity to stretch her legs and get some blood pumping. She'd learned over the years that movement hastened one's recovery after a fight, even though curling up on the couch was a more appealing option.

Stepping into the store was like stepping back into her early teens, when she and her brothers frequented this outpost of cool. The store used to be the go-to spot for vinyl records, comic books, and music paraphernalia, but it had changed with the times and offered even more clothing and offbeat housewares than it had back in the day.

Some kind of noise was blasting from the speakers—an amalgamation of drums and screeching guitars that promised a migraine from extended exposure. A handful of shoppers were flipping through the stacks of records slotted into the display stands. A teenager was manning the register while a second balanced precariously on a ladder as he stapled posters to the wall.

"Hi," Fina said to the boy behind the counter. His shaggy black hair hung over his eyes, and his chin was camouflaged with a swirling-patterned tattoo that crept from his neck to his lower lip. The lobes of his ears held gauges that had stretched the skin wide to accommodate large holes. Fina tried to avert her gaze from the self-mutilation. "I'm looking for Kelsey. Is she working today?"

"Kelsey!"

Fina turned toward the back of the store where he directed his hollering.

A moment later, a young woman emerged from between a beaded curtain, the decoration swaying in her wake.

"Yeah?" she asked.

"This lady wants to talk to you." He gestured at Fina.

"What's up?" Kelsey asked, and did an assessment of Fina's attire. They were separated in age by less than ten years, but the difference between the two women was pronounced. Kelsey was whippet thin, her scrawny arms a map of veins and tattoos emerging from her black T-shirt. She wore black leggings and combat boots, and her nose and one eyebrow were adorned with silver hoops. The long blond hair from her babysitting days had been replaced by jet-black dreadlocks. Fina looked like a Republican soccer mom in comparison.

"You're Kelsey DeMarco?" Fina asked.

"Uh-huh. Who are you?"

"Is there someplace we could talk privately?"

"I was doing stock in the back room. We can talk there."

Fina followed her back through the beaded curtain, mesmerized by the tattooed serpent that seemed to undulate on Kelsey's neck when she walked. They headed down a short hallway to arrive at a window-less room stacked with boxes, a few of which were open and spilling their contents.

"My name's Fina." She cleared off a stool and took a seat. "I'm friends with Risa Paquette."

"Mrs. Paquette? I haven't heard that name in a long time."

"You used to babysit for her kids, right?"

"A little bit. I don't babysit anymore if that's why you're here." She pulled a heap of sweatshirts from a box and marked something down on a sheaf of papers.

"It's not. I'm a private investigator, and I'm doing a background check on a man named Rand Ludlow."

Kelsey's pen slipped, and she made a blue line across the middle of the form.

"I've heard some things about him, some negative things, and I'm just trying to confirm that what I've heard is true."

"Why are you doing a background check on him?" she asked, avoiding Fina's gaze.

"My client has a business relationship with him, but is worried that he's a liability."

Kelsey didn't speak. Instead, she grabbed a box cutter and thrust it into the seam of a box. It made a screeching sound as she pulled it through the packing tape.

"Whatever you tell me will be kept in confidence," Fina said.

"Wasn't he arrested for killing his wife?" Kelsey asked.

"He was, but he didn't kill her. I've heard that he mistreats women in other ways."

The young woman glared at her. "Why should I talk to you? I've never met you before."

"I know I'm asking a lot, but Risa wondered if something had happened when you used to babysit for Haley Ludlow. Risa is a good person and wouldn't send me here if she didn't think it was important."

"She seemed okay, but I didn't really know her."

"Okay. How about we trust each other?" Fina asked.

Kelsey smirked. "Like what? You want to fall back into my arms and see if I drop you?"

Fina chuckled. "God no, but what if I tell you a secret, and then you'll know something about me. Something that I don't want to become public knowledge."

Kelsey shrugged.

"Rand Ludlow is my brother, and I'm not checking up on him for a business client. I'm trying to get dirt on him so he'll be punished."

"He's your brother?" She put down the box cutter and hugged herself as if a chill had blown into the room.

"Yes, and I know that he sexually assaults women. You don't need to worry that I won't believe you. I know what he's capable of."

"Well, that would make you the first person to believe me."

"Who else did you tell?"

"My mother."

Fina sighed. "She didn't believe you?"

"No. She thought I was making it up to get attention. Who makes up that kind of shit? Who wants that kind of attention?"

"Very few people."

"Exactly. Sure, I had lied about other things, like missing my curfew and smoking pot, but I was a teenager. Lying about a neighborhood dad raping you is a whole other thing."

Fina felt a familiar knot assert itself in her stomach. "Did it happen more than once?"

"Yes. He didn't start with raping me, of course. He worked his way up, and it took me a while to figure out what the hell was going on."

"So you told your mother, and she did nothing?"

"Yep. I finally just stopped babysitting for them and started spending as much time as I could away from my house. I couldn't stand to be in the same room as her."

"I'm so sorry."

Kelsey reclaimed the box cutter and tore through another seam.

"Do you know if he assaulted anyone else?" Fina asked.

"Other babysitters you mean? Probably, but I never heard about it. It's not something that you advertise."

"Of course not."

"So what are you going to do? Is that asshole actually going to get punished?"

"That's my goal, but I don't know what's going to happen. Right now I'm just trying to put the pieces together." Fina stood and pulled out her business card. "If you think of anything else or if I can be helpful in any way, let me know."

Kelsey studied the card. "So much got fucked up because of him."

"I know."

"I've fantasized about blackmailing him. Making him pay."

"Why haven't you?"

"Because people like that always win."

Fina started toward the door.

"I always felt badly about leaving Haley and not saying good-bye," Kelsey said. "I liked taking care of her."

Fina nodded and left the stockroom.

She'd assumed that building a case against Rand would make her happy, but with each new woman—each new story—all she felt was growing despair.

Dante pulled up to the curb too fast for Fina's taste and slammed on the brakes. She went around to the driver's side, and he stepped out, grinning.

"Wicked funny," Fina said. "Did you drive like that all the way from Revere?"

"Maybe." He pointed at her face. "Woo-hoo! What happened to you?"

"Just get in." She adjusted the mirrors and seat. "Put on your seat belt," she instructed Dante.

"I don't like seat belts."

"And I don't like people's brains on my dashboard."

Dante reached back for the belt and nodded at a slip of paper in the cup holder. "The bill. I expect prompt payment."

Fina glanced at it before pulling into traffic. "Eleven hundred bucks for tires?"

"That's with a discount on the labor, so stop your bitching."

"Where am I taking you?"

"Chinatown."

She started down Boylston, struggling to put Kelsey out of her mind. "So you never told me if you know a guy named Jimmy Smith."

"You're kidding, right?"

"Dante, I left you a message about it. Glen Sullivan said that Jimmy Smith was the one who was gunning for me."

"I don't know him."

"Well, could you put out some feelers and find him?"

Dante rubbed his chin with his hand as if stroking a nonexistent beard. His posture in the passenger seat was the epitome of man-spreading—legs wide as if to accommodate an oversized package.

"This situation is getting old." Fina tapped her horn at the driver in front of her, who seemed to think that a yellow light meant slow down, not speed up.

Dante sighed. "I'll make some calls."

They pulled up to a light, and Fina looked at him. Dante's attention was trained on a pretty woman on the sidewalk.

"Now? Could you make the calls now?" she asked impatiently.

"No, I can't make them now. I need privacy. Jesus, I don't work for you."

"Privacy? What is this? Pimp-hooker confidentiality?"

"Do you want me to do this for you or not?" he asked, his voice rising.

Fina took a deep breath. "Yes, please. Sorry." She placed a hand on his arm. "I'm sore and stressed. Not a great combination."

"Maybe you need to do a better job with your work/life balance."

His head was turned away from her, but Fina could see the hint of a smile.

"I'll get right on that."

Chinatown was clogged, its narrow streets no match for the car and pedestrian traffic. Dante directed her through the maze of dim sum places and fabric stores until they reached a nondescript two-story building with a Chinese pharmacy on the first floor. Fina bent down to get a better look.

"I can only imagine what you're doing here."

"Don't worry your pretty little head," Dante said. "So, do you think the guy who came after you is done?"

"You tell me. How do these things work? Did I actually have to be hospitalized for the contract to be fulfilled?"

"Beats the hell out of me, but I wouldn't let down your guard if I were you." He climbed out.

"You're going to get me some info, right?" she asked. "I need to find Jimmy Smith ASAP."

"I don't know the guy, Ludlow! I'll do what I can, but no promises."

"Get to it."

"Damn, you're impatient."

"I've been called worse," Fina said before he slammed the door closed.

Her impatience was a function of wiring and environment, and it had served her well.

Growing up, if she'd waited to be given what she needed by Carl and Elaine, she would have been waiting her whole life.

Fina was missing some of the neighborhood association minutes—assuming the group met every month—so she decided to stop by Evan's house to see if she could fill in the gaps. The driveway was empty, and her knock on the door went unanswered. Walking back to her car, Fina realized that Ronnie McCaffrey might be able to help.

A woman answered the doorbell wearing a sweatsuit covered by an apron. It said THIS GRANDMA BELONGS TO, with a depiction of five kids, their names by their likenesses.

"I'm Fina Ludlow. I think we spoke on the phone. Is Ronnie home?"

"Did we? I don't recall, but don't take it personally. Things go in one ear and out the other these days." She stepped back, her expression briefly registering Fina's face. "I'm Mary. Ronnie's wife."

"Nice to meet you in person." Fina followed her into the house.

It was a traditional center hall Colonial with a dining room to one side of the stairs and a den to the other. The dining room looked like a place that was only used during holidays and family functions. A couple of Lladró figurines were on the mantel beneath a large family portrait.

"Ronnie!" Mary hollered up the stairs. "You have a visitor!" Mary directed her to the den. "You can wait for him in there."

Fina took a seat on a nubby plaid couch, and Mary went to the kitchen at the back of the house.

The low coffee table in front of Fina was oval shaped, its surface unmarred. A nearby set of coasters was probably the reason. The *Herald* was on the table next to a stack of flyers announcing the Ronald McCaffrey Junior Annual Go-Kart Derby. Fina grabbed one and studied it. The event was slated for May at the local high school.

Seeing the name reminded Fina of a news story she'd stumbled on during her Internet search of Ronnie. A piece in the *Herald* detailed the death seventeen years earlier of Ronald McCaffrey Jr. He had been killed by a drunk driver on his way home from the movies. Two other eighteen-year-olds were in the car with Ronnie. One was killed instantly, and the other suffered serious injuries. The tragedy had all the elements of titillation and was featured heavily in the *Herald*: a good working-class family, a father who was a public servant, a young man cut down in his prime, a villain, and plenty of people to blame, including a criminal justice system that had failed spectacularly. It would have made for a great soap opera if only it weren't true. The drunk driver had previously been arrested eight times for DUI and was sentenced to seven years in jail—hardly a fair punishment for killing two people.

She heard footfalls overhead, and a minute later, Ronnie came into the room wearing dark blue pants, a Boston Fire Department sweatshirt, and slippers.

"What can I do for you, Tina?" he asked, settling into a recliner across from her. He didn't react to her appearance, which was refreshing.

"Fina. It's Fina," she corrected him. "Sorry for dropping by like this. I stopped by to see Evan, but he isn't home."

"I think Molly has a class. Dance or something like that."

"I thought you might be able to help me. I've been reviewing Nadine's papers, and I'm missing some of the neighborhood association minutes. I assumed you'd have copies."

Ronnie clasped his hands across his stomach. "What do you need with the minutes? They're not exactly exciting reading."

"I'm trying to learn as much about Nadine as I can." Fina shrugged. "It's just due diligence."

Ronnie pushed himself out of the chair and walked to a drop-front desk in the corner. Donning a pair of glasses, he reached into a slotted compartment and pulled out some papers.

"Which ones do you need?" he asked Fina, returning to his recliner.

"I'm not sure. Do you mind if I take them all? I can run out and make copies. I'll have the originals back to you within an hour."

He shrugged. "Sure."

Fina reached over and took the papers.

"Any news on who's responsible for Nadine's death?" Ronnie asked.

"Still under investigation."

"Antifreeze," he said, shaking his head.

"Lethal stuff," Fina said, wondering how Ronnie knew about the antifreeze.

"I have contacts in the department," he said as if reading her mind. "That's how I heard about the COD."

"Lots of people have it around the house, but I don't think they realize how dangerous it is."

"No need to have it at home," Ronnie commented. "Go to the auto supply store and buy what you need, then get rid of it."

"How do you get rid of it?" Fina asked.

"The city has hazardous waste disposal sites. You don't want that stuff in the water table."

"So, you don't keep any around?"

He looked at her. "Not with all the kids and pets in this neighborhood."

Fina rested her finger on the go-kart flyer. "How many years have you been doing this?" she asked.

"Seventeen."

"Do you have to live in the neighborhood to participate?"

"Nope. Everyone's welcome."

Fina scanned the notice again. "Maybe I'll bring my nephews. They'd love it. And it's for a good cause." She pointed at the MADD logo at the bottom of the page.

"All the proceeds go to getting drunks off the roadways."

"You must have seen a lot of accidents when you were working."

Ronnie looked away. "I did."

Fina followed his gaze to a framed picture on a side table. It was of a young man in a baseball uniform, a younger Ronnie standing next to him, beaming with pride.

"It's great you do it every year," she said. "It's a nice way to keep your son's memory alive."

"You can just drop those minutes in the mailbox," Ronnie said, rising from his seat. Obviously, he didn't want to discuss Ronnie Jr. or anything else with her.

"Thanks. I really appreciate it." Fina shook his hand, and he closed the door behind her.

One nice thing about her conversations with Ronnie McCaffrey? Unlike everyone else these days, he didn't seem the least bit concerned about the state of her body or soul.

Fina found a Staples store near Ronnie's and made copies of the minutes she hadn't yet read. She slipped them back into his mailbox, as instructed, and called Lucas's number. It went straight to voice mail so she dialed the Chellew house, and Heather Chellew was kind enough to direct Fina to Darcy's softball game. Heather was still grateful for Fina's firefighting abilities and was happy to part with the information.

On the way to the Dedham middle school, Fina stopped at a McDonald's drive-thru and ordered large fries, a large diet soda, and an apple pie. It was a starchy, carb-heavy meal, but seemed appropriate given that she was heading to a sporting event.

Fina found a parking space overlooking the softball field and watched the action while eating. For someone without any children, she spent a remarkable amount of time at kids' games. Between her own niece and nephews and the interviews she conducted on sidelines, she was a regular booster.

She made a quick call to Hal, her financial wizard, and left a message asking to see him. On the way to the field, she stuffed her trash into the bag and deposited it in a barrel. She tucked her drink between her elbow and side and searched the sidelines for Lucas. He was sitting in the first row of the bleachers, at a slight remove from the other parents.

Fina took a seat next to him, and he turned to say hello before realizing who it was. His smile was short-lived.

"Hi, Lucas. Heather told me I'd find you here."

He stared at her. "What happened to you?"

"Minor accident. I'm fine. Which number is Darcy?" Fina asked.

"Eleven," he said grudgingly. "She's on third base."

Fina narrowed her gaze across the field and tried to look interested. "Does she like playing?"

"Loves it. She's a great little athlete."

They were quiet as they watched the next batter. The sound of the bat connecting with the ball rang across the field.

"I went to a presentation about the Frontier Fund last night," Fina said after a moment.

"It's an amazing program."

"That's what I thought. I've donated two thousand dollars to the church."

Lucas looked at her. "Really?"

"You seem surprised," Fina said, applauding a good play by Darcy's team.

"I am. I didn't think you were much of a believer."

"You and Chloe and Pastor Greg keep urging me to keep an open mind. And who wouldn't want to help orphans in Africa?" She sipped her drink.

"It really is God's work."

"Have you been? To Africa?"

Lucas shook his head. "I haven't had the privilege. One of these days, I'd love to."

"So who's in charge of the programs in Africa? I assume there's someone from the church over there?"

Lucas watched as Darcy caught a hit to left field. "Good job,

Darcy!" he hollered between cupped hands. "We don't have a member there; it is Africa, after all. We have a local organization that we work with. They handle things on that end."

"What organization is that?"

"I don't know the information off the top of my head," Lucas said. "I'd have to look it up."

"Could you? That would be great. Thanks, Lucas," she said, knowing the information was unlikely to materialize.

Fina took a few more sips of her drink and tossed the cup into a nearby garbage can. "I've been reading the minutes from the leadership committee meetings. Interesting stuff."

Lucas frowned. "Those are confidential, only to be read by committee members."

"Ehh, not really," Fina said. "They aren't legally binding documents, so really, anyone can read them."

"Where did you get them?"

"From a trusted source. But why the concern? Is there something you don't want nonmembers to know about?"

"Go, Darcy!" Lucas yelled.

"Go, Darcy!" Fina parroted.

"I'd rather not discuss church business at my daughter's game," Lucas said, offering Fina a pained smile.

"Of course. I'll let you get back to your cheerleading. I'm really excited about the Frontier Fund."

"We're all just instruments of God," Lucas said.

Fina returned to her car.

She wasn't sure where the Frontier Fund inquiries would lead her, but she was pretty sure it wasn't Africa.

TWENTY-FOUR

Christa sat at the table with the kids while they finished their dinner. Paul had class tonight, and Evan had a late meeting, so she'd offered to feed Molly. The girls were engaged in an animated conversation about a Disney movie they had all seen countless times, yet it still warranted endless discussion.

Molly pushed back her chair and climbed onto Christa's lap. The two older girls didn't miss a beat, but Tamara eyed Molly. Her youngest liked being the baby, and Christa wondered if she felt threatened by the younger girl. She didn't want Tamara to feel insecure, but Molly needed all the love she could get. Even before Nadine died, the child had gravitated toward Christa rather than Nadine. The natural instincts that kicked in with other people—the slow swaying motion when holding a baby, the unconscious rubbing of a small child's back—seemed absent in Nadine. Maybe that would have changed if she'd had a child of her own, but Christa doubted it; some people just weren't wired that way.

Christa leaned down and inhaled the scent of Molly's hair. It smelled like her girls' hair. Evan must have started using the watermelon shampoo she recommended. He was a good father. He didn't always know what he was doing, but he would learn.

The front door opened, and Molly bolted from the room. Christa could hear her greet her father as Tamara claimed the free space on Christa's lap.

"Hey, girls," he said when he came into the room with Molly in his arms.

"Hi, Uncle Evan!" Nicole crowed and the others followed suit. The room filled with the chatter of the reports of their days.

"Did you eat?" Christa asked. "There's some baked ziti and salad."

"Sounds great. They had some cheese and crackers, but nothing substantial."

"I'll fix you a plate." Christa shooed Tamara away.

"I can get it myself," Evan insisted.

"No need. Girls, why don't you go into the family room? You can play for a little while before reading and bedtime."

"When do we get dessert?" McKenna asked.

"In a little while. Uncle Evan and I need to talk before you have dessert."

Evan released Molly to the floor, and she followed the others out of the room. He took a seat at the table, and Christa doled out the pasta and placed it in the microwave.

"You want a beer?"

"Yes, thanks."

The microwave dinged, and she put the food and beer in front of him. She topped off her wineglass and took a seat.

"Was Molly okay?" he asked.

"No problems. She's a good kid."

"Thanks for helping out."

"Of course. We're family. I'm happy to help."

Evan dug into the ziti with enthusiasm.

"When's the last time you ate?" Christa asked, grinning.

"Lunch, but your cooking is so good. It brings out the glutton in me."

"I'll take that as a compliment."

"So you wanted to talk about something?" he asked, wiping his mouth with his napkin.

Christa rotated her wedding ring on her finger. "It's kind of awkward."

He nodded at her, encouraging her to speak. "Like you said, we're family."

Christa picked at something on the table that was invisible to the naked eye. "Did Nadine mention anything to you about the loan for McKenna's school?"

Evan narrowed his eyes in thought. "Doesn't ring a bell. Why would she need a loan for school? Doesn't she go to the public school with the other girls?"

"She does now, but she's applied to the Graymoore School. Their program is geared toward kids who have learning disabilities."

"I've heard of it. That's great."

"Well, she hasn't been accepted yet, but we're hopeful." Christa glanced toward the doorway to ensure the girls weren't lurking. "Nadine and I discussed the possibility of a loan if McKenna was accepted."

Evan looked surprised. "Wow. I'm impressed."

Christa cradled her wineglass between her hands. "What do you mean?"

"She agreed to give money to you instead of the church? How'd you manage that?"

"Well, it's for educational purposes. It's not like I asked for it so we could take a cruise." She had a large swallow of wine.

"Even still. It actually makes me happy, the idea that she wasn't completely blinded by those people."

Christa smiled weakly. "Not completely."

"I'd love to help out. Let me know when you hear from the school, and we'll figure out the details."

"Thank you so much, Evan, and I swear, it's just a loan. Paul thinks he's in line for a promotion, which would mean more money. We'll pay you back, even if it takes forever."

Evan speared a piece of ziti. "Like I said, we'll figure it out."

Molly rushed in at that moment, eager to tell her father about an incident at school.

Christa sat quietly and waited.

She waited for the wash of guilt, for the nagging regrets, but they didn't come.

The path to the money had been circuitous, but she would get the loan, and she didn't feel the least bit sorry for that.

Fina didn't have the energy or the will to keep traipsing around the city, so she went home and curled up under Nanny's afghan on the couch. She snoozed, but it wasn't satisfying. Fina felt hyperaware of the routine sounds in the condo and struggled to find a comfortable position. After forty-five minutes of skimming the top layer of sleep, she got up and chugged a glass of water. Milloy was always extolling the benefits of water, but she usually opted for diet soda. Given her compromised state, she needed all the help she could get.

A knock on the door interrupted her second glass. She picked up her gun and walked quietly to the door to peek through the peephole. Hal was standing on the other side.

"I didn't mean that you had to drop everything and come over," Fina said, letting him in.

"I had some business downtown. I thought I'd take a chance that you'd be home."

"Here I am."

Hal stepped toward her and examined her face. His mouth opened, but no sound came out. "I thought you were turning over a new leaf," he said finally.

"When did I say that?" Fina asked, motioning for him to take a seat. She went to the kitchen to fetch his usual glass of water before joining him.

"Last time we met," he said, "you were in one piece, and now look at you."

"It's just a bruise, Hal, and I don't think I promised that I would stay out of trouble."

He shook his head. "It's not right."

Fina handed him the glass. "It's an occupational hazard. Believe me, I'd rather be in the occasional fight than sit at a desk job all day or have to punch a time clock."

"There are other options," he insisted.

"Don't worry. It's not good for your health." She reached up to massage the bruised area near her eye, then thought better of drawing attention to her injury. "I need some more information about that church you looked into before."

"Sure. What do you need?"

"I made a donation to Covenant Rising and earmarked most of the money for their Frontier Fund," Fina said. "It's their fund for orphans in Africa."

Hal nodded. "Okay."

"Since I designated the money for that purpose, they can't use it for anything else, right?"

"Not legally. What were the other options for directing the money?"

"Just the operating fund and the Frontier Fund."

"If you indicated you wanted it used for the Frontier Fund, that's what it's supposed to be used for." He took a sip of water and placed the glass on a makeshift side table Fina had fashioned out of packing boxes.

"So is there any way to actually follow the money?"

"Generally speaking, that's what annual reports are for."

"Right, but how can I be sure that my money was used where I wanted it to be used?" Fina asked.

"Well, you can't. Not for certain, and not unless the church has opened their books to an independent firm for review."

"So I'm just supposed to trust that my money is being used properly?"

"Yes, because generally, people don't give money to organizations they don't trust."

Fina nodded. "Right." She could feel a sneeze coming on and braced herself. "Achoo!" She doubled over in pain. "Oww!"

Hal's brow crinkled with worry.

"Damn. That hurt." She took a sip of water and then adjusted the pillows behind her back, searching for a more comfortable position. "So here's the other thing that's niggling at me: No one from the church has been to this orphanage, but they claim that there's an organization in Africa doing the work on their behalf."

"And you don't believe them?"

"I just don't understand why it's such a mystery. I've asked one of the members to provide me with the name of that organization, but I'm not holding my breath."

Hal took out his phone and began tapping at the keys. "You want me to try and locate this mystery organization?"

"Yes. I think it makes sense to follow the money, or lack thereof, rather than just trying to poke around the orphanage. These people are champion excuse makers; I'm not going to get any traction unless I can confront them with concrete information."

"Where in Africa specifically?"

"Angola."

Hal made a few notes on his phone before draining his water.

"Do you have contacts in Africa?" Fina asked. "I guess I should have started with that, but I have such faith in your abilities I just assumed you would."

"I've got contacts. The information may be pricey, though."

"Whatever you need to do," Fina said. "Carl's footing the bill. If I get the name of the local organization, I'll send it to you, but get started in the meantime."

"Understood."

Once Hal had left, Fina changed into sweats and foraged in the kitchen. She poured herself a glass of milk and made half a fluffernutter.

Cristian called when she was mid-bite.

"You're eating? I thought we might grab dinner."

"Sorry. I've had a long day, and I just want to take a hot shower and call it a night."

"What happened? To make your day so long, I mean?"

Fina knew without a doubt that she should tell Cristian about the previous night's attack, but she just couldn't do it. She couldn't muster up the energy it would take to reassure him and deflect his criticism. She was all tapped out.

"Just this case. I'm at that stage where I feel like some pieces are coming together, but it's still out of reach."

"I know that feeling."

"Did Pitney give the go-ahead on the Jimmy Smith background check?"

"Yeah, but I haven't done it yet. I'm drowning in paperwork."

"Was your day okay?" Fina asked, feeling like a horrible person.

"It was fine. Matteo drew you a picture at preschool."

"That's so sweet," Fina said, shriveling inside, convinced that her heart was two sizes too small.

"It's very sweet, and it drives his mom nuts, so that's a bonus from my perspective."

"She can't be threatened by me, of all people."

"You know mothers when it comes to their sons; they don't want anyone else competing for their affection."

"So true."

"You sound tired," Cristian said. "I'll let you go."

"Sorry about the rain check. Thanks for calling."

"Don't worry. I'll redeem it soon."

Fina finished her sandwich and zoned out, watching TV for a couple of hours.

In the bathroom mirror, she examined her face, not pleased with what she saw. The swelling was subsiding, but the bruises were darkening. She brushed her teeth and took a Tylenol PM.

A quick check of the door reassured her that the condo was secure, so she climbed into bed, her Glock within arm's reach.

It was becoming a habit she was eager to break.

Fina met Frank at Dunkin' Donuts the next morning. She felt worse than the day before, which wasn't surprising, but it was annoying nonetheless.

"You're getting quite the bruise," he commented, gesturing toward her face.

"You should see my abdomen," Fina said. She started to untuck her shirt.

"I'll take your word for it," Frank said, averting his gaze.

"I wasn't going to take my shirt off."

"Even still, I haven't had enough coffee yet to assess your injuries."

"Has the surveillance made you want to ditch retirement and get back in the game?" Fina asked. She pulled off a piece of glazed donut and put it in her mouth. She knew people ordered all sorts of things at Dunkin' Donuts, like bagels and breakfast sandwiches, but she didn't understand why. It was like ordering chicken at Legal Sea Foods.

"Not in the least. Not that I haven't enjoyed the change of pace, but my full-time detecting days are over." Frank bit into his cruller. "This is what I've got so far." He handed her a small stack of papers, each page featuring six photos. Gabby Gatchell was in all of them.

"Anything jump out at you?" Fina asked, flipping through them.

"Well, your young man has yet to make an appearance. I assume you want me to stay on him?"

"Yes, please."

"But I did find this interesting." Frank tapped the bottom sheet, and Fina passed it back to him. "These few here."

He pointed at a row of photos, and she took a closer look.

"That is interesting," she murmured.

"Who is he?" Frank asked.

"That's Gabby Gatchell, obviously, and that guy is Lucas Chellew. He's a member of the church. Kind of the pastor's right-hand man."

"The pastor who's married to Gabby?"

"The very one." Fina traced her finger over one of the photos. It showed Gabby and Lucas standing in front of her car. Her hands were on her hips in a pose of defiance, and Lucas was leaning toward her, his face frozen in a pained expression.

"I don't suppose you heard the conversation?" Fina asked.

Frank sipped his coffee. "No. I couldn't get close enough, but it was not a happy one, I can tell you that."

"The few times I've seen the two of them together, I haven't gotten a sense of any animosity, but I don't really know them."

"You don't have to know them to see there's something going on here," he said, tapping the photo. "Their bodies are speaking the universal language of conflict."

"This is great, Frank." Fina slipped the photos into her bag.

"You have any idea what it's about?"

"No, but when has that ever stopped me?"

He smiled. "Never, as far as I can recall."

"It's not proof of anything, but it's something. It's ammunition."

"It warms my heart to see you so thrilled by surveillance photos."

"I'm a simple girl with simple needs. Let me know what happens," Fina said, rising from the molded orange booth. "I think the plot is going to thicken."

She got in the car and pointed it toward Framingham. She loved starting the day with a purpose.

Fina asked around at the church and found Gabby in the Sunday school classroom. She watched her from the doorway before making her presence known. The pastor's wife was perched on a low bookcase under the window, glued to her phone. The corners of her mouth were curled up in a sly smile.

Fina made some noise outside the door and watched the other woman spring to life. She put down the phone and knelt before the bookcase as if entranced by the collection of Little Golden Books.

"Hi, Gabby," Fina said.

"Hi." She tidied the thin volumes, then rose and began straightening the tiny plastic chairs. "Greg isn't here right now. He's at a meeting off-site."

"Actually, I'm here to see you."

"Mmm-hmm."

Fina wandered over to the other side of the room and examined the artwork pinned to the wall. There were about twenty copies of the same worksheet depicting Jesus carrying the cross. The pages had been colored twenty different ways, obviously by young hands. Few stayed within the lines, and most were scribbled with a wide array of colors. Jesus had a flowing purple mane in one, green hands grasping the cross in another.

"You wanted something?" Gabby asked.

"I just wanted to hear what you had to say about your conflict with Lucas."

Gabby straightened up. "What are you talking about?"

"I thought you'd like a chance to comment on it," Fina said. This was a technique that reporters employed. They pretended to know more than they did and suggested it was your chance to set the record straight. Of course, Fina didn't have a media outlet with which she was sharing the story, but the hint of exposure was oftentimes enough to get people to talk.

"Which Lucas are we discussing?" Gabby dipped her hands into a bin of LEGOs. She grabbed a small handful and picked through them.

Fina grinned. "How many Lucases does Covenant Rising have? I think you know that I'm talking about Lucas Chellew."

"Well, we get along great," Gabby said. "Guess you're mistaken."

"I don't think so." Fina moved down the line of drawings, studying them as if she were at the Museum of Fine Arts. "I wonder if Greg knows."

"You have quite an active imagination, Fina." She was dividing the blocks into color-coordinated piles. "I'm beginning to think that you're doing the work of the devil."

Fina guffawed. "Like I'm possessed?"

"You don't have to be possessed to work on his behalf. If you give in to sinful temptations or defy God, you're furthering his cause."

Fina leaned her hip against the wall and looked at Gabby. "I'm not sure how I'm defying God in this instance."

"You're making trouble for people who are doing the Lord's good work."

"That's where I always get stuck on this whole religion thing, Gabby. You guys decide what's righteous, and anyone who isn't on board is deemed sinful or subversive. Why do you get to make those determinations?"

"Because it says so in the Bible." Gabby pushed her fingernail between two blocks that were stuck together and pried them apart.

"The Bible also says you shouldn't wear mixed fibers or eat a ham sandwich. Are you telling me you've never worn Lycra? I find that hard to believe."

"I'm not going to debate the Bible with you."

Fina smiled. "Of course not."

"I'm just asking that you not bring your evil ways into this house of worship."

"So you have no comment on your conflict with Lucas?"

"That's right. I have no comment." She scooped up the LEGOs and returned them to the bin from which she had plucked them. "I'll escort you out."

Gabby brought her to the front door and waited as Fina climbed into her car.

The church was private property so Fina would have to mind her step, but that was the great thing about doing the devil's work.

You could plant a seed and then step back and watch it grow.

"Have you heard from Haley?"

Fina was sitting at a red light, still basking in the irate glow given off by Gabby Gatchell. Patty was on speaker.

"No. Why? Isn't she at school?"

"No. The school just called, and she was seen in homeroom first thing this morning and hasn't been seen since."

Fina sensed the familiar flutter in her gut that often accompanied talk of her niece. "Obviously, you've tried calling her."

"Obviously," Patty said, "but she hasn't answered."

"Did any of her friends skip out?"

"No, and none of them seem to know where she is."

"Let me pull over," Fina said, taking a quick detour into a gas station. The patient driver behind her sat on his horn and flipped her the bird in response to her last-minute change of plans.

"I'm sure she's fine, Patty."

"Uh-huh."

"Is any of her stuff missing? Any clothes? That sort of thing?" Fina asked.

"Her room looks the same as it always does."

"Have you talked to Scotty?"

"Not yet. I didn't want to worry him needlessly."

Sometimes Fina wished people felt that way about her. No one ever seemed to care about worrying her needlessly. She was number one on everyone's speed dial when things went awry.

"Let me call her. Does she have any favorite hangouts?"

"Sometimes she goes to the Chestnut Hill mall with her friends," Patty said. "Usually, they just go to one another's houses."

"Have you tried Risa?"

"I left a message for her, and I considered calling Elaine, but thought I should wait."

"Good thinking. Let's not involve her unless it's absolutely necessary."

"I don't have a good feeling about this, Fina."

"It's too early to panic. If she were a typical teenager this would just be annoying, not worrisome."

"But she's not a typical teenager." The tenor of Patty's voice was rising.

"She is, and she isn't. Just because her experience has been unusual, it doesn't mean she won't also display typical teenage behavior."

Patty sighed. "I hope you're right," she said before ending the call.

Fina dialed Haley's number and left a message imploring her to be in touch and then texted her the same. Next, she tried Risa. There was no answer. What was the point of all these devices if you could never actually reach anyone? It was maddening.

Fina wasn't that far from Risa's and decided to swing by in the hope of catching her in. As she suspected, there was no answer at the gingerbread Victorian, and she couldn't justify breaking into her friend's house to check if Haley was hiding out. Instead, she sat in her car out front and contemplated the situation.

There was no point in searching for Haley. They didn't live in a small town that could be covered with a quick driving tour. The only thing that Fina knew for sure was that Haley was playing hooky.

There was nothing to do but wait.

TWENTY-FIVE

Fina wondered if Gabby had alerted Lucas to their conversation. She called his cell and got no response, and the helpful woman at Macy's informed her that he was visiting other stores all day. His absence might be a good thing; sometimes she found that poking someone indirectly reaped better results.

Her background search of Lucas hadn't indicated whether Heather Chellew had a job, so Fina decided to swing by the house and possibly catch her in.

She was in luck. There was a minivan parked in the driveway, and Heather answered the door wearing jeans and a yellow sweater. Her face was free of makeup, and small earrings featuring cats were nestled in her lobes.

"Hi, Fina," Heather said, motioning her inside.

"Sorry to drop by unannounced. Is this a bad time?"

"Just doing chores. I could use a break."

Fina tried to picture Elaine doing chores. As far as she knew, her mother had always outsourced her chores. That said, Fina wasn't big on chores, either. She did the bare minimum to keep her life functioning smoothly.

She followed Heather to the kitchen, where the evidence of the fondue debacle was still on display; the oven hood was blackened and misshapen.

"The adjuster came out to take a look," Heather commented. "He said it could have been much worse. Do you want coffee or a soda?"

"A soda would be great," Fina said. She caught a glimpse inside the fridge and cringed. There was a stack of Coke cans on a shelf, no diet in sight.

"Do you want a glass and ice?"

"The can's fine."

Heather handed her the cold drink and pulled out the chair next to her. They popped the tops, and Fina watched as she took a long chug of the liquid.

"Ahh. I didn't realize I was so thirsty," Heather said, stopping just short of smacking her lips.

Fina braced herself for the rush of sweetness and took a sip. The soda was worse than she remembered. How could she be so betrayed by sugar, her oldest friend and most trusted companion?

"I thought maybe I'd get lucky and find Lucas at home," Fina said.

"No, but he's not at the office, either. He had an off-site meeting today. I do expect him home a little early," she said, glancing at her watch, "but not for a couple of hours."

"That's fine. I just talked to Gabby Gatchell and wanted to get his opinion on something."

"Are you making any progress on the case?" Heather's hand grasped the can of soda, and Fina looked at her nails. They were short and bare.

"I am. I'm feeling very confident."

Fina rarely told anyone the truth about the status of a case. Instead, she tailored an answer to elicit the most fruitful response from the person asking the question. At this stage in the investigation, when she knew people were up to no good, she liked to turn up the heat and make people as nervous as possible.

"You can't believe that anyone related to the church had anything to do with Nadine's death," Heather protested.

"When it comes to murder, no one is above suspicion, even the pastor's wife."

"You think Gabby hurt Nadine?" she asked with wide-eyed concern, but Fina could sense an undercurrent of excitement. Some people lived for drama.

Fina matched her wide eyes and lifted her shoulders in mystification. "This is such a complicated situation," she said.

Heather took a drink, her eyes wandering off to the side.

"What?" Fina asked.

"Nothing."

"You look like you have something to say."

"I just . . . Gabby is a mystery sometimes."

"I'm having trouble figuring her out," Fina admitted with as much "aw shucks" as she could muster.

"Sometimes she's sweet and warm, and other times she seems kind of cold and distracted."

"I wonder why that is," Fina mused.

"It can't be easy, being the pastor's wife," Heather said, backpedaling.

"Of course not."

"You're held up to such scrutiny, and everyone always wants your time and attention."

Fina nodded and sipped.

"But she and Greg do a wonderful job." Heather tipped her head back and took a long drink.

Fina sensed that the slight crack in the facade had closed. Heather's sense of loyalty had kicked in, and she wouldn't be speaking out of turn no matter how Fina approached the subject. It was time to change tack.

"I asked her this morning about her conflict with Lucas," Fina said, tapping her nail on the side of the Coke.

Heather squinted her eyes in puzzlement. "Her conflict with Lucas?"

"Well, you must be aware of the tension between the two of them."

"Where'd you hear that there's tension between the two of them?"

"I can't remember. I'd have to look back through my notes."

Heather shook her head. "Gabby and Lucas are the two most important people in the church after Pastor Greg," she insisted, suggesting that their roles bred cooperation and respect. Fina thought it was just as likely that their positions relative to Greg made them natural rivals.

"Right, which is why it was worrisome that they might be at odds."

"They're not at odds." Heather rose from the table and brought her soda over to the counter. Fina knew she'd worn out her welcome.

"I attended a great presentation the other day about the Frontier Fund." She stood, grasping her can. "Chloe Renard went with me, and I made a donation."

Her hostess brightened at the mention of a donation. "That's wonderful. They do such amazing work."

"Have you visited the orphanage?"

"No, we haven't had the chance, but we'd love to. I would love to take the girls and give them some perspective on life. They're convinced they've got it bad."

"Unfortunately," Fina said, "you probably wouldn't have to go very far to find examples of people who are worse off. There are plenty of shelters downtown full of the disenfranchised."

Heather didn't respond, and Fina supposed the feasibility of the suggestion was the problem. Africa was across the ocean, unlikely to be visited and therefore confronted, but Boston was just a few miles away. If the Chellews saw the situation in their own backyard they'd be forced to face some tough realities, and few people really wanted to do that.

"Thanks for the soda," Fina said. "And I'll contact Lucas and apologize if I've stirred anything up with Gabby. That wasn't my intent."

"It's fine."

"That's what happens when you talk to lots of different people; you hear all kinds of crazy things."

Fina returned to her car and waved to Heather as she drove away.

She didn't get what she came for, but maybe Heather would share the conversation with Lucas and set something else in motion.

Haley hadn't been in touch, so Fina dialed Matthew's number. She opted not to leave a message and called his office line instead. His assistant, Sue, said that he was playing squash downtown at the Boston Athletic Society. Unsure if she'd have to return to the western suburbs, Fina didn't relish driving back into the city, but she always had to go where the day took her and that rarely followed a logical pattern.

The Ludlow men had been members of the BAS for years. Carl occasionally worked out there and enjoyed power breakfasts in the club café; Rand used to attend regularly; Scotty never set foot in the place; and Matthew played squash there a couple of times a week. The squash games provided exercise, but more importantly, they were networking opportunities that didn't require an entire Saturday, like golf.

Fina showed her ID at the desk and took the stairs down to the lower level where the courts were housed. She waited for a point to be played before crossing by a glassed-in court and locating Matthew a couple of courts down. While Fina watched from a viewing area, Matthew and his opponent squeaked and sweated their way across the polished floor.

Ten minutes later, the men emerged, toweling off and swigging water.

Introductions were made, and Matthew's opponent headed toward the locker room. Her brother dropped down next to her on a bench and slung the towel over his shoulder.

"How goes it?" he asked. "What happened to your face?"

"There was a skirmish."

"Is this related to the threats you've been getting?"

"I'm not sure. I've got some anonymous letters and the contract out on me. It's hard to keep up."

He took her chin in his hand and angled her face to better examine it. "Sorry, sis."

"I'm fine. I didn't come here for sympathy, although it is appreciated. Have you heard from Haley by any chance?"

"I haven't checked my phone during the last hour, but not before that, no." He inclined his chin. "Why?"

"She's playing hooky, and Patty is concerned."

"I'm sure she'll turn up."

Fina nodded. "I liked Sydney and Rachel," she said as two men in pristine white workout gear entered the court.

"They thought you were great."

The men started warming up, hitting the ball to each other with a laconic ease that gave no indication of the fiercely competitive game that would most likely follow.

"The stuff I've been gathering on Rand? It just keeps getting worse," she said, staring straight ahead.

Matthew followed the small, hard ball with his gaze.

"Even if Dad keeps him away from Haley," Fina continued, "I'm not sure how we'll keep all the other women and girls in the world safe."

"So what do you have in mind?"

"Can pedophiles go to some kind of rehab? Can they be repro-grammed?"

Matthew leaned back, as if to get a better view of her. "You think Dad is going to send Rand to rehab?"

"A girl can dream. He can't be left to do as he pleases."

"That's why there's a sex offender registry, to try and keep track of these people."

"But you're only on the registry if you're convicted of a crime," Fina noted.

He shook his head. "That would be a disaster of epic proportions."

She took a deep breath. "I'm convinced Rand has dirt on Dad."

"I thought we weren't going to talk about this."

"We don't have that luxury. Think about it, Matthew. Dad is hell-bent on protecting Rand, regardless of the horrible things he does, and don't tell me"—Fina held up her hand to silence him—"that it's just parental affection."

"I can't speak to parental affection, but does anybody ever know how far they would go for their kids until they're tested?"

"For something really awful? I'm not talking illegal, because we know that isn't compelling in our family, but what about immoral and reprehensible? Do you think Scotty would let his grown kids abuse women? I don't believe that. I don't want to believe that."

"So what do you think he's got on him?" Matthew asked.

"I don't know. That's why I asked you about it the other day. I don't want to have to investigate both Dad and Rand, and short of a significant crime, I can't imagine what he did that would buy his compliance."

"It would have to be big," Matthew agreed. "This is such a cluster-fuck."

"I'd rather believe that Dad is supporting Rand out of self-preservation, as opposed to condoning his behavior."

"But that means the fallout could be worse than we imagined."

"Possibly."

They sat in silence, neither knowing where to go next.

She rose from the bench. "If you hear from Haley, tell her to call Patty."

Matthew nodded.

Fina was almost to the door when he called out to her. "Thanks for being such a badass."

A grin crept onto her face. "You're welcome."

It was so nice to be appreciated.

Fina tried Haley's line again.

"I was just about to call you," her niece said when she answered after five rings.

"Where are you? Aunt Patty is freaking out."

"I'm fine. I'm getting some food with my friends."

"Where were you earlier when you were supposed to be in school?"

There was no response.

"Haley?"

"We were hanging out. It's not a big deal."

"Where are you? I'm coming to get you."

"Don't. I'm fine."

"I'm still coming to get you. Location, please?"

She sighed loudly, and Fina could imagine the attendant eye-rolling. "I'm at Ruddy's," she said, naming a diner that was popular with teens and senior citizens.

"Call Patty and tell her I'm on my way."

"Aunt Fina."

"Nope. Don't want to hear it." Fina hung up.

She spent the half hour it took to get to West Newton stewing, alternating between being angry with Haley and worrying about her.

On the walk from her car to the diner, Fina tried to do some deep breathing and calm down.

"Do you want some fries?" Haley asked when Fina took a seat across from her. "They're sweet potato."

"Think you can bribe me?" she asked, reaching across the table and pinching some fries between her fingers.

"I thought it was worth a try. What happened to your face?"

"It's fine, just a little mishap." Fina gestured to Haley's drink. "Is that diet?"

She nodded and pushed it in her aunt's direction. Fina took a long sip and then leaned back in the booth.

"You cannot do this shit," Fina said.

Haley avoided her gaze.

"Seriously. It's not fair to Aunt Patty."

"It's not a big deal. Everybody ditches once in a while."

Fina bit her tongue. Patty was right: Haley wasn't everybody, but the more they pointed that out, the greater the odds of her past becoming her future. Fina didn't want her to feel like damaged goods, but she also couldn't pretend that Haley hadn't sustained damage. She didn't know what to do.

"Okay," she conceded a moment later.

Haley looked befuddled. "Okay, what?"

"Okay, you're right. Everybody ditches once in a while."

Haley looked askance at the other patrons. "What just happened? Did some kind of exorcism take place before my very eyes?"

Fina sighed. "I have no idea how to be most helpful to you, Haley. I'm just making it up as I go."

"Obviously."

"Hey! Give me a little credit."

Haley reached across the table and patted Fina's hand. It was something you might do to reassure an elderly relative who had misplaced her teeth. "You're a good aunt, and you're a great Ludlow."

"Which is not saying much," Fina pointed out, "but I'll take what I can get. Did you call Aunt Patty like I asked?"

"Yes. I told her you would bring me home."

"Good."

"Do you think we have time for a frappe?"

Fina dropped her head into her hands. "Haley, have I taught you nothing? There's always time for a frappe."

Fina dropped Haley off and jumped on Route 9 toward Framingham. In Christa Jackson's front yard, her daughters were running around kicking a soccer ball. A man who Fina assumed was Paul sat on the front steps, calling out encouragement. Fina climbed out of her car and waved at the girls. They waved back as she approached, and Paul fixed on her with a curious smile.

"Hey," she said. "Is Christa home? I'm Fina Ludlow. I'm a private investigator working on Nadine's case."

"Paul Jackson." He stood and offered his hand. "Christa's not here. Was she expecting you?"

With blue eyes and perfectly symmetrical features, Paul Jackson was easy on the eyes. He looked to be just over six feet, and his height was nicely balanced against his broad shoulders and muscular build.

"No, but I was in the general vicinity and hoped to catch her in," Fina said. "Any idea when she'll be back?"

He shook his head and sat back down on the steps. "Not sure. She's at her mom's. I think she was going to help her aunt and uncle—Nadine's folks—sort through some stuff."

"Ah," Fina replied. They both seemed to agree on a moment of silence in which to honor the idea of Nadine's grieving parents.

"You're welcome to hang out, but I can't promise when she'll get back." He shifted his position on the step, and Fina joined him.

"Thanks," she said. "You're working on your MBA, right?"

"Yeah. At night, at Bentley."

"And working full-time?"

Paul nodded.

"That sounds exhausting."

"It's a grind, but it's worth it."

Fina had heard that about so many things: parenthood, graduate school, marriage. She'd yet to be convinced.

The youngest girl, Tamara, had abandoned the soccer game and was plucking leaves from a tree and twirling them between her fingers.

"I imagine having an MBA will be an asset. My brother has three kids—four, actually, but that's a long story," Fina said. "They aren't cheap."

"No, and if they don't outgrow something, they ruin it." He nodded toward Nicole, who was sliding into the muddy ground, her knees coated in black ooze.

"It looks like she's having fun at least," Fina commented.

They sat in silence and watched the girls.

"I'm sure the police have talked to you, but I wondered if you had any idea who might have wanted to hurt Nadine." She felt Paul stiffen next to her.

"No idea. The whole thing is just insane."

"Yup," she agreed. "Christa told me that you dated Nadine before you dated her."

Paul eyed her. "I'm surprised she talked about that with you."

"I found out about it on my own, and I think she figured she might as well be forthcoming."

"I don't like focusing on the past." The soccer ball bounced over to them. Paul palmed it in his large hand and tossed it back to his daughters.

"I understand that, but a lot can be gleaned from the past."

Paul laced his fingers together and rested his elbows on his knees. "I'm not going to pretend that it wasn't a tricky situation, but we all got through it. Christa and I were meant to be together, and Nadine knew that. She was okay with it."

"Eventually."

"It actually didn't take that long for everyone to settle into a good relationship."

Fina wanted to ask Paul about Christa and Nadine's money disagreement, but there was something that made her hesitate. She hadn't felt the same trepidation when revealing Lucas and Gabby's conflict to Heather, so why was she balking now? Was it because she inherently didn't trust Lucas? Or maybe because, in her experience, sometimes women were at risk of bodily harm when their secrets were revealed? Whatever the reason, she decided to hold back for the time being.

"Girls, time to go in," Paul announced. Tamara and Nicole came bounding across the yard, but McKenna lingered behind, dribbling the ball.

"She wants to play soccer next year," Paul explained. "She's been practicing a lot."

"That's great," Fina commented, trying to sound enthusiastic. Her feelings about soccer were complicated as a result of her recent case involving soccer and traumatic brain injuries.

"McKenna! Let's go!"

The girl trotted over and brushed her hair away from her sweaty face.

"Hi," she said to Fina.

"Hey, McKenna. How's it going?"

"Good. Dad, did you see? My dribbling's getting better."

"I know, kiddo. You're going to be ready to go in the fall."

"You won't play until then?" Fina asked.

"I'm going to play at my new school," the girl volunteered.

"You *might* be playing there," Paul gently corrected, "or you might play in the town league."

"What's your new school called?" Fina asked.

"The Graymoore School. I'm thirsty," she said, climbing past them and banging open the front door.

"Graymoore's a great school," Fina noted.

"We don't know yet if she's been accepted," Paul said sheepishly. "We don't want her to get her hopes up, but she's having trouble tempering her enthusiasm."

"Well, I hope it works out. Can you tell Christa that I stopped by?"

"Sure. Take care."

In the car on the way home, Fina contemplated McKenna's acceptance to the Graymoore School. It was a highly regarded private school that specialized in students with learning disabilities. If your kid faced academic challenges and you lived in the Boston area, Graymoore was the place to go to ensure the best possible education. But it wasn't just the best education, it was also one of the most expensive. Maybe the Jacksons qualified for financial aid, but full rides were increasingly hard to come by. Just where were Christa and Paul finding the money for tuition?

Fina put the issue aside and called Dante on speaker as she sped east on the Pike.

"Any word on Jimmy Smith?" she asked him in lieu of a greeting.

"I'm working on it. Why don't you work on it? Isn't finding people your job?"

"I am working on it, too, Dante. Call me as soon as you have something."

The phone rang a moment after she disconnected the call. It was Hal, requesting a breakfast meeting. They worked out the details, and Fina hung up knowing she'd sleep better with visions of pancakes dancing in her head.

TWENTY-SIX

For the first time since the attack, Fina woke up feeling better, not worse. Showering wasn't such a chore, and she opted for two Advil instead of the four she'd been taking.

"Did I keep you waiting?" she asked Hal, sliding into the booth across from him.

"Nope. I got here early and was just finishing a call."

They perused the menu, and Hal accepted the offer of coffee.

"So you've got something?" Fina asked after they placed their orders.

"Well, I've got nothing, but I think that's something."

Fina nodded. Sometimes the absence of information told you as much as its presence.

She ordered hot chocolate, and Hal pulled out his laptop and fired it up. He started to give her an in-depth account of his investigation into CRC's activities in Africa. Fina listened, struggling to keep her mouth shut and be patient. She knew that describing his work process gave Hal great pleasure, and he was such a good guy, she didn't want to deprive him of the opportunity. That said, listening to long-winded descriptions made her yearn for a cyanide pill for herself or a cattle prod for him.

"So it was the third guy in Luanda who put me in touch with the head missionary, Brother Ted."

"And Brother Ted didn't have any information about Covenant Rising?"

"*No one* has information about Covenant Rising." A waitress brought over two plates, one holding Hal's omelet, the other weighted down with Fina's pancakes.

"And you checked out all the orphanages and programs related to kids?"

"Yup. If that church is supporting an orphanage, it's not in Angola."

"Well, if it's not in Angola, it doesn't exist." Fina chewed on a pillowy bite of syrup-soaked pancake. "But we can't be the first people to wonder about this. Wouldn't the government figure it out?"

"Ours or theirs?"

"Either. Both."

"Not necessarily. Angola has a reputation for serious corruption, and our system can be gamed."

"Great. So if my fifteen hundred dollars isn't buying mosquito nets in Africa, what is it being used for?"

"Maybe it's going toward a Mercedes-Benz E-Class sedan or a week in the Caribbean," he said, grinning.

"Lovely. How does one go about proving all of this?"

Hal shook his head, chewing a mouthful of roasted potatoes. "It's not going to be easy. Obviously, you'd need to follow proper channels to get information that could be used in court."

"Different channels than the ones you used, I'm guessing."

He nodded. "Some of them."

Fina nibbled on a piece of bacon. "But I don't actually have to prove anything. I can just report my suspicions to the proper authorities or put a bee in a reporter's bonnet."

"Either approach would probably cause trouble for the church. That reminds me." He pulled a file folder out of his computer bag and handed it to her. Inside, Fina found screenshots from the Covenant Rising website, specifically from the section describing the Frontier Fund. At the bottom of the file were screenshots from a different website, but some of the photographs were the same.

"What's this?" Fina asked, indicating the second site.

"It's the website for a Christian community organization in Nigeria."

Fina laid the pages side by side. In both, a young black boy was crouched down on the dirt with a wide smile.

She looked at him, grinning. "This is stock photography."

Hal nodded. "Maybe the church indicates that somewhere on the site, but if so, I couldn't find it."

"When I looked at the Web pages for the Frontier Fund, I assumed the photos were of children they were actually helping."

"That's exactly what you're supposed to assume."

"But this could be a child actor in LA," Fina said, pointing at the identical photos.

"Or he could be a real kid in Africa, but he sure does get around."

Fina savored a sip of hot chocolate. "What a delightful start to my day. Thank you, Hal."

"Happy to be of service," he said, and they clinked mugs.

Life wasn't great for the real African orphans who weren't getting any money, but it sure was looking up for Fina.

Fina got in the car with a renewed sense of purpose. She still didn't know who had killed Nadine, but she was making headway on Pastor Greg and his nefarious money management that had brought her to the church in the first place. Finding Nadine's killer was still a priority, but if she could uncover enough to make Chloe rethink her donation, that would also be a victory.

Pastor Greg was in the parish hall, searching for something on the pulpit, when Fina found him.

"I've got good news," Fina called from the back of the room.

Pastor Greg smiled. "Is that right?" He grasped the lectern with both hands.

"I've been thinking a lot about the Frontier Fund, and I'd like to make another donation."

"Really? I'm surprised. You still don't seem ready to embrace the Lord and be reborn."

"I thought lost souls were your specialty, Pastor." Fina walked down the aisle and took a seat in the front pew.

He smiled that annoying, knowing smile. "The good Lord does like to challenge me."

"Can I sponsor a specific child?" Fina asked.

"Some organizations do that, but that hasn't been our approach."

"There's a child I saw on the website." Fina pulled her tablet from her bag and scrolled through some pages. "This one." She held it up for Greg to see. It was one of the stock photos that Hal had pointed out to her. "I feel a deep connection with this boy. I don't know why."

"It's not about a particular child, Fina. It's about providing help where it's needed most."

"But what if the pull I'm feeling toward this child is actually God working through me? What if it's some kind of sign?"

"Then you need to have faith that God will lead you." He straightened up as he warmed to the topic. "You have to believe that God knows best. You cannot substitute your judgment for his own."

She watched him, not sure what was more striking; his manipulation of her every word or his unwillingness to step down from the pulpit and concede the physical advantage in the conversation.

She shook her head. "I don't know. I just feel very strongly about this child."

Greg leaned forward on the lectern. "How large a donation do you have in mind?"

"Certainly more than the first."

The silver lining of dealing with bullshitters was that they couldn't call bullshit on you. If Pastor Greg called her bluff, he'd be betraying his own lack of faith. He couldn't question her motives without calling his own into question.

"Why don't I talk to our people on the ground in Africa and see what I can do? It's not the usual procedure, but I'm moved by your commitment to helping this child."

Fina rose, tucking her tablet into her bag. "Thank you. I'm really excited by the prospect."

"Can I ask you a question, Fina?"

"Sure."

"Have you considered having children of your own?"

Fina dipped her head down. "It just hasn't happened." She tried to tap into a well of sadness, as if someone told her she could never eat chocolate again.

"Well, maybe your interest in this child is the Holy Spirit telling you something."

"Telling me what, exactly?"

"That you were created to be a mother. That your work on this earth hasn't even begun."

Oh, Christ. Really? There was a divine to-do list in addition to her earthly one?

"You think?"

"Maybe it's the Holy Spirit telling you it's time to reproduce, to do his most holy work."

"Maybe," Fina said, seriously doubting the Holy Spirit had any interest in her uterus. She was quiet for a moment, as if his suggestion were worthy of her consideration. "You'll be in touch?"

"I promise." He smiled beatifically.

Fina made a beeline for the door before those delicious pancakes made a return visit.

"I need to see you," Cristian told her.

She was on the Pike, heading toward the city. Fina glanced in the rearview mirror and assessed the damage on her face. It was obvious that she'd been in some kind of altercation, but she looked better than she had a couple of days ago.

"Okay. We can meet somewhere."

"How about you come to the station. Pitney wants to talk to you, too."

"I was hoping your need to see me was purely social."

"*My* need is, but you might as well kill two birds with one stone."

"Okay." She wasn't looking forward to seeing Pitney, but her presence might mitigate Cristian's annoyance with Fina.

"Meet us at the Starbucks near the precinct."

Half an hour later, Fina parked and scanned the landscape before getting out of her car. Being so close to a police station where cops were milling around, it seemed unlikely that anyone would make a move on her.

Pitney and Cristian were at a table in the corner when she arrived. Fina purchased a bottled water and joined them. Cristian stared at her face, and Pitney stared at Cristian.

"Looks like your would-be attacker became your actual attacker," Pitney commented.

Cristian continued to stare at Fina, his jaw set.

"Yes," Fina said, taking a seat.

There was an uncomfortable moment of silence.

"That's all you have to say?" Cristian asked.

"I'm fine. That's what matters, right? Let's discuss it later."

"Yes, let's," Pitney said.

"What did you want to talk to me about?" Fina asked.

"I got a complaint about you." The lieutenant crossed her arms, which prompted the shiny fabric of her orange shirt to stretch across her chest.

"A new complaint?"

Pitney shook her head. "The fact that you have to even ask that indicates a problem."

Fina put up her hands in an "oh, well" gesture.

"Yes, a new complaint," Pitney continued.

"It's the pastor from the church," Cristian said. Clearly, he wasn't in the mood for banter.

"Greg Gatchell?" Fina's eyes widened.

"Yes."

"When did he make this complaint?"

Pitney consulted her notebook. "On Tuesday."

"I just came from there, and he didn't have any complaints."

"Great." Pitney tapped out a staccato rhythm on the table with her nail. "I can expect a call from him before the day's out."

"We had a perfectly pleasant conversation. Well, except for the fact that my childbearing abilities came up." Cristian looked bewildered. "But that's a different story."

"I don't want to know," Pitney said.

Fina played with the cap of her bottle. "When he filed the complaint, did he mention that he'd accepted my money?"

"What money?" Cristian asked.

"I made a donation to the church, and he was pleased as punch about that. If he finds me so onerous, I think he should give back my money. Did he file a formal complaint?"

"No," Pitney said, "and I would obviously suggest he return your money before doing so."

"There's no way he'll do that, not as long as he thinks he might get more."

"Do you think he killed Nadine?" Pitney asked.

"I'm not sure, but both he and his wife aren't as admirable as they'd lead you to believe. Any news on Jimmy Smith?"

Cristian reached into the breast pocket of his jacket and pulled out a folded sheaf of papers. He tossed them in Fina's direction. "There are twenty-one men in the greater Boston area named James Smith who have a criminal record."

"Dammit." Fina unfolded the papers and skimmed them. "It's going to take forever to find the right guy."

Cristian's phone rang, and he stepped away from the table to answer it.

"I knew you two were a bad idea," Pitney said in a low voice, nodding toward him.

"We're figuring it out as we go, but it's none of your concern."

"Yes, it is. I spend more time with him than you do. It's not good for me if he's in a pissy mood or distracted."

Fina leaned forward, resting her elbows on the table. "If he's in a pissy mood or distracted on the job, that's his problem. He can pull his shit together. I'm not going to take responsibility for his job performance."

Cristian returned to the table. "We've got to go," he said to Pitney, gesturing toward the door.

"Try not to cause too much trouble, Fina," Pitney said. "I have plenty of work without having to corral you."

Fina ignored her and reached out and grabbed Cristian's hand. "Can I see you tonight?"

He looked away, then returned his gaze to her bruises. "I'll call you when I have time."

A few hours later, Fina had a message inviting her to dinner at Frank and Peg's. Dinner at their house was an early affair, which always brought to mind shuffleboard and canasta in Miami Beach. She knew she'd be hungry again by eight p.m., but it was a small price to pay for a home-cooked meal and companionship.

Peg was in the kitchen when Fina got there, and Frank beckoned her to the small table, which wasn't yet set for dinner.

"I've got more pictures for you," he told Fina.

"Ooh, goody." She sat down next to him and paged through the photos.

"That little scamp," Fina said, examining a zoomed-in shot of Gabby and Casey in a lip-lock. "Was this in his car?"

"Yes. It gets better."

The photos progressed until one showed Gabby straddling the young man in the back of the car.

"I've never understood the appeal of car sex," Fina commented, turning the next picture this way and that, trying to match up body parts with their owner.

"The cars used to be much bigger," Peg said from the stove, where she was stirring a pot of chili.

"Remember that Buick Roadmaster?" Frank asked.

"Very roomy," Peg said, grinning.

"You two enjoy this, don't you?" Fina asked.

"You make it so easy, sweetie." He patted her hand.

"So she's having an affair with a younger man who is also a member of her husband's church," Fina mused. "Very complicated."

"She's definitely breaking some commandments," Frank said.

"Where'd you take this photo?" She pointed at the most explicit one.

"In the parking lot of an office park in Natick. Did you get anything from yesterday's photos?" he asked. "The ones showing Gabby and the other guy?"

"I asked Gabby why she and Lucas were so worked up. She said I was imagining it. Then I brought it up with his wife."

"How'd that go over?"

"Eh. It didn't net any bombshells."

"Do you think this has something to do with it?" Frank gestured to the picture of Gabby and Casey.

"It's certainly a possibility, but who knows? Nothing would surprise me at this point."

"Enough shop talk," Peg said. "Can you set the table, honey?"

Frank put the photos in a neat stack, and Fina rose to do as she was asked.

She wasn't big on following directions, but when they came from Peg, she toed the line.

Fina wanted to talk to Gabby, but she couldn't handle another conversation with Greg about her uterus. She sat in her car a few doors down from the Gatchell house and considered her options. The risk of keeping an eye out in a nice neighborhood was that eventually someone might call the cops to complain. Fina was beginning to think that she'd overstayed her welcome when one of the Gatchell's garage doors opened, and a Lexus SUV backed out. Gabby was driving. Fina gave her a head start, then pulled out to follow.

The Lexus wound through the leafy neighborhood and merged onto Route 9 West after a couple of minutes. It wasn't hard to hang back and keep Gabby in her sights, given the traffic. Fina wondered if she was headed to the church, but nixed the idea when the pastor's wife took the exit for the Natick Mall and then parked in the garage closest to Nordstrom. Fina grabbed a space the next row over and followed her into the store.

Gabby meandered through the makeup and perfume department, spraying samples on her wrist and testing out eye shadow colors before riding the escalator up two floors to the intimate apparel department. She watched Gabby lay a few items over her arm while perusing the racks. Fina busied herself with a display of shapewear, which seemed a misnomer since its whole point was to "correct" one's natural shape.

Gabby was holding up a black lace bodysuit for inspection—the embellished lace barely covering the naughty bits—when Fina wandered over.

"Hey, Gabby."

She started. "Are you following me?"

Fina made a face as if the question were ludicrous. "To the lingerie department? Actually, I'm in the market for some new bras, although," she said, peering at the bodysuit, "that's another option."

Gabby hung it back on the rack with excessive force. "If you had a husband, I'm sure he'd be happy to buy it for you."

"Someday," Fina said wistfully. She took a step closer to Gabby and lowered her voice. "But seriously, is that for Pastor Greg or your boyfriend?"

Color flooded Gabby's cheeks, and she jammed the remaining hangers onto a rack and started to leave.

"I guess that's my answer," Fina said.

Her smug tone was enough to halt Gabby's progress.

Gabby took a few steps and closed the distance between them. "You don't know what you're talking about."

"I know exactly what I'm talking about. I've seen photos of you with Casey. He barely looks old enough to drink, but maybe that's part of the appeal."

Her cheeks were changing from flushed to ashen. "What photos?"

"The ones that show you having sex in the backseat of his car, which looked pretty uncomfortable."

There was a small seating area a few yards away to which Gabby retreated. She sat down on the upholstered settee and seemed to be gathering her thoughts.

"What do you want?" she asked after a moment.

"Depends on what you have to give," Fina said, joining her on the couch.

"You're blackmailing me?"

"No, I don't want your money."

"Then why are you here? So you can threaten me?"

"I'm the least of your problems. You don't think Greg or another member is going to figure this out? Or that Casey won't brag about it?"

"He promised he wouldn't tell anyone."

"Right, because twentysomething guys are known for their discretion."

"If you don't want money, why are you here?"

"Does Lucas know about the affair? Is that why you two are at odds?"

Confusion darted across Gabby's face, but it was gone as quickly as it appeared. "You're so full of shit."

Fina's eyes widened. "Yikes. That's not very Christian."

"You know why Lucas is annoyed? He's worried I'll tell everyone that he borrowed antifreeze from the shop at the church."

Fina leaned her head against the back of the couch. She knew she should be glad for a potential lead, but instead she just felt drained. For all she knew, Gabby was orchestrating an elaborate scheme of misdirection.

"Who told you that antifreeze was part of the case?" Fina asked.

"The cops."

"And did you share your suspicions about Lucas with them?"

"No."

"So why are you telling me?"

"Because I'd like you to keep your mouth shut about other things."

"How do I know you're not making it up?"

"I'm not. Ask Greg. Lucas borrowed the antifreeze a couple of months ago and brought it back right after Nadine died."

"Why would Lucas want to kill Nadine?"

"You'd have to ask him, but those two never got along."

"And how do you know that Lucas borrowed the antifreeze?"

"I was there when he told Greg he was going to borrow it, and then I saw him bring it back."

Fina shook her head. "You should have told the police."

Gabby scoffed. "I'm not going to help in their witch hunt. You and the cops want to smear us at any cost."

"Not true, but if you are doing something illegal, then you better believe that we want to nail your ass to the wall. It's just a matter of who gets there first, me or the cops."

Gabby stood and ran a hand through her glossy blond hair. "Tattling on me will backfire."

"How do you figure?"

"Because we forgive in the church, but we don't like it when outsiders get in our business."

"I'll keep that in mind," Fina said. "Hey, do you happen to know a guy named Jimmy Smith? Young, white guy with a criminal record." She thought it was unlikely, but there was no harm in asking.

"No," Gabby said, looking genuinely puzzled.

Fina watched as she threaded her way through the racks and disappeared down the escalator.

She always knew it was time to wrap up a case when she felt the urge to strangle the suspects.

Back home, Fina took a shower and pulled on jeans and a T-shirt. Even though it was the end of the day, she put on a little makeup and ran a brush through her hair. Cristian was going to stop by and she didn't want to look like a sad sack in sweats recovering from a beatdown. She briefly considered tidying up the living room, but there was only so much gilding of the lily she was willing to do.

Before settling into the couch, Fina put in a call to Emma Kirwan, her computer expert. Emma was a hacker, but the most uptight, conservative lawbreaker that Fina had ever encountered. If you met Emma on the street, you'd assume she was a Girl Scout leader on the way to story time at the library.

"Emma, it's Fina."

"I know. That whole caller ID thing."

Fina could sense her rolling her eyes on the other end of the line. "I have a job for you."

"Yes?"

"Do you have much experience with facial recognition software?"

"Yes. What's the job?"

Fina spelled out the assignment and braced herself for the disclosure of Emma's exorbitant fee. It always took her breath away, but Emma was the embodiment of the free market she so loved; what she supplied, Fina demanded.

Her work done for the moment, Fina curled on her side to watch a show counting down the world's best cakes. Fina rooted around for her phone when it rang.

"Yes?"

"It's Dante. So I didn't find your Jimmy Smith, but I found a guy who knows him."

"Okay. That's something, I guess."

"Hey! Have you done any better?"

"No, I haven't," she admitted. "Who's the guy?"

"His name is Travis Whalen."

"Okay. Where do I find him?"

"He's going to call you and set up a meeting."

"Dante," Fina groaned, making no attempt to hide her frustration. "You can't give me his address or his number?"

"It doesn't work that way."

Fina sighed. "Why would he call me? What's in it for him?"

"He's doing me a favor, so now you owe me two favors."

"Terrific."

"When he gets in touch, don't keep him waiting."

"I wouldn't dream of it."

"Yeah, right. Looking forward to cashing in those chits," he said, ending the call.

Another hour passed, and the world's best cakes rolled into the world's best pies. When Cristian finally showed up, Fina led him to the couch and got him a cold beer. She sat down next to him.

She looked him in the eye. "I'm sorry. I should have told you about the fight. I'm just trying to figure this out as we go."

He took a swig and put the can down on the coffee table. "Me, too."

"Since work is such a hot-button issue, how about we not talk about it, just for tonight?"

"That won't be easy."

"Pretend I'm not a PI," Fina said.

Cristian leaned back and grinned. "What else would you be?"

"Whatever you want me to be," she said, lifting one leg over his lap so she was straddling him.

"I can't imagine you doing any other job."

She grasped his shoulders and started kneading. "How about a flight attendant?"

He burst out laughing. "You would be the worst flight attendant ever!"

"Why do you say that?" Fina ran her fingers through his thick hair.

"You would make everyone get their own drinks, and you'd yell at people who wouldn't keep their seat belts fastened while seated."

"Well, really, how hard is it to keep your seat belt fastened? How is that worse than smashing your head against the cabin ceiling?"

"You're proving my point. How about we steer clear of the service industries?"

"Okay, then: pilot. Fighter pilot."

"That's definitely easier to imagine." He leaned forward, and his lips brushed her neck. "You'd look hot in one of those flight suits."

"I *would* look hot in one of those," she agreed, grasping his head between her hands and kissing him on the lips. Cristian put his hands on her waist and pulled her closer.

Fina felt her muscles relax and allowed herself to sink into him. In a sudden burst, he pushed them both off the couch, and Fina gripped him around the waist with her legs. He carried her into the bedroom, where he dropped her onto the bed and started to peel off his shirt.

Fina pulled off her clothes and lay back on the bed. "Fasten your seat belt, Detective."

TWENTY-SEVEN

"You actually have some food in your refrigerator," Cristian commented the next morning. He was standing at the foot of the bed, shirtless.

Fina grinned. "Maybe someone broke in." She burrowed under the covers and inhaled his scent on her pillow. "Why are you up so early?"

"That whole work thing."

"Ah, that." She rolled onto her back and stared at the ceiling. "Reality comes crashing back."

"It has a tendency to do that," he said.

"Did you know that Gabby Gatchell is having an affair?"

Cristian pulled on his shirt and sat down next to her. "We suspected as much."

"With Casey Andros, a young congregant. She *really* doesn't want Greg to find out about it."

"No surprise there."

"So much so that she told me Lucas Chellew 'borrowed' the church's antifreeze."

Cristian raised an eyebrow.

"I assume you didn't find any antifreeze at his house?" Fina asked, pushing herself to a sitting position.

"Nope."

"But you did find some at Covenant Rising?"

He nodded.

"Gabby would like me, and therefore, you, to believe that Lucas poisoned Nadine."

"Why?"

"I asked her the same thing. She just cited their bad blood."

"That's a lot of work just for bad blood."

"But remember, Lucas got her kicked off the leadership committee because she was nosing around too much."

"And getting her kicked off wasn't enough?"

"Maybe."

He rubbed her bare shoulder. "You know, it's not too late for you to join the force."

"Don't let last night cloud your judgment, Detective."

"I'm serious. Then we could work for the same side."

"We already do work for the same side. Or near the same side," she said, taking in his mien of doubt.

Cristian kissed her. "Talk to you later. Be careful."

"You, too."

Fina threw on some sweats when she heard the door close behind him and got a cinnamon roll–flavored Pop-Tart from the kitchen. She was sitting down to check her e-mail when there was a knock at the door. For a moment, she thought maybe Cristian had returned for an encore, but a peek in the peephole dashed those hopes. Stanley, her increasingly beleaguered concierge, had another unmarked plain brown envelope for her, origin unknown.

Fina's good mood made the arrival of the third anonymous note a little easier to swallow, but it didn't change the fact that she needed to figure out the identity of the letter writer before he or she decided to escalate.

Sitting at the table, Fina studied the note. She'd had an inkling over the last few days that there was something about the threats that seemed familiar, but she couldn't put her finger on it. Nothing about the materials used struck her as unique or difficult to source. A stop at the newsstand and the local CVS would provide everything needed. The notes could be from anyone who wanted her to go away, and frankly, that was a rather long list these days. She put the latest threat aside, hopeful that her brain would chew on it even if she didn't give it her full attention.

Switching her attention to her e-mail, Fina found that Evan had sent a complete list of the dates of the leadership committee meetings to fill the holes in the timeline. She carried her computer over to the wall and marked the missing meetings on the calendar.

Fina took a step back and surveyed the wall.

Wouldn't you know it? Nadine's illness coincided with not only the neighborhood association meetings, but also the leadership committee meetings.

So much for narrowing down the field.

Fina had spent more time in Macy's in the previous two weeks than she had in the previous three decades. Her forays into the store confirmed her feeling that unlike some women, she was not born to shop. Searching through racks of merchandise and trying on countless items qualified as the tenth circle of hell, and the only reason she was making a return trip was to get some answers from Lucas.

She didn't bother to announce herself to a salesperson, but instead, entered the "employees only" area and wound her way back to Lucas's office.

Fina knocked on his open door and leaned against the frame. He was on the phone, gabbing about hem lengths. When he looked up and saw Fina, he tripped over his words, and his smile dimmed.

"I need to call you back, Ann," he said before replacing the receiver. "I can't talk. I'm working," he told Fina.

"I'll be quick." She took a seat across from him. "A little birdie told me that you borrowed antifreeze from the church."

Lucas's face froze.

"That's right, Lucas. Someone is throwing you under the bus."

He kept staring at her, but didn't respond.

"You've got nothing to say about it?" Fina asked.

"Who told you that?"

"Does it really matter? It's out there now."

He cleared his throat. "'I tell you, on the day of judgment, people will give account for every careless word they speak.' Matthew 12:36."

"That may be, but I'm not holding my breath for judgment day. Nor are the police."

"You told the police?"

"No, but the cops hear stuff. People are not good at keeping secrets."

Lucas folded his hands on his messy desk and closed his eyes. Fina waited while he consulted his higher power.

"People who gossip destroy the fabric of a community," he said. "It shouldn't be tolerated."

"So you didn't borrow the antifreeze?"

"If I did it was for purely innocent reasons. I want to know who told you this. He or she should be brought up before the leadership committee."

"That's going to get a little tricky," Fina said under her breath.

Lucas leaned forward quickly, prompting a stack of circulars and folders to sail off the desk in Fina's direction. She reached down and collected them before placing them on the corner of the desk.

He narrowed his eyes. "It was Gabby, wasn't it?"

"You two don't like each other much, do you?"

"Was it her?"

"I can't give up my sources, Lucas. That would be bad for business, but I am curious about the beef between you two. Is it because you're always competing for Greg's attention?"

"Don't be absurd. We're not in competition."

"And yet, you assume she's telling tales about you."

Lucas studied his fingernails. "It was just a guess. She isn't as perfect as she would lead you to believe."

"I'm well aware of her imperfections. Is Greg aware of them, do you think?"

"Pastor Greg needs to focus his energy on leading the flock. He can't be bothered with gossip and innuendo."

"I'm just trying to figure out if that's why you might have killed Nadine—because her presence was distracting Pastor Greg from his holy work."

"You need to leave. I've got to prepare for a meeting," Lucas said, reaching for the stack of papers and tidying them needlessly.

"Always a pleasure," Fina said. "I'm not sure how I've gone through life up to this point without a daily dose of scripture."

"Your soul would benefit from some reflection and study," Lucas said harshly.

"I'll take that under advisement."

Fina left the mall and inhaled deeply. It was a relief to be free from the recycled air heavy with perfume and teenage angst.

It wasn't clear who was lying about what, but at the moment, it didn't really matter.

Fina would apply pressure, and she had no doubt that something would give.

Christa had to rewind the tape three times before she got it right: "Supranasal and superotemporal sclerotomies were performed." She'd been checking her work carefully the past few days, realizing that she was distracted, her attention wandering off as the ophthalmic terminology spooled past her ears. After one p.m., once the mail was delivered and she knew she'd have to wait until the next day, Christa could focus on the task at hand. Until then, it was a battle.

She pulled off her headphones and refilled her coffee cup in the kitchen. She was stirring in some creamer when she heard the familiar bang and whoosh of the mail coming through the slot. Jogging to the front door, Christa knelt down and gathered the pile onto her lap. She tossed the junk mail aside and was left with a handful of envelopes. One had the return address of the Graymoore School, and it was of medium thickness, which was no help in determining what lay inside. Was it a lengthy rejection? A thin offer of enrollment?

Christa knew she should wait for Paul, but she couldn't stop herself from tearing open the envelope and scanning the cover letter. The opening sentence said it all: "It gives us great pleasure . . ." She yelped in excitement and flipped through the other pages, the last of which promised a more comprehensive package in the weeks to come.

She was in.

McKenna was in, and for the first time in as long as she could remember, Christa felt unadulterated happiness. McKenna would get what she needed, and Christa would get a tiny bit of her life back. She wouldn't have to fight for her child every day like she did now. This would change everything.

At the table, Christa smoothed the letter down and read through it a second time. Then she looked at the other documents more closely, noting that the financial aid grant was as small as expected. Christa had hoped that Graymoore would magically offer more money and she wouldn't have to borrow any from Evan, but that was just a fantasy.

They needed Evan's loan. Without it, McKenna would be stuck

where she was, and Christa would never get out from under the crushing responsibilities that were her life.

Greg sat at his desk behind his computer. Betty occupied the chair across from him.

"I told him that I would have to check with you, Pastor, but you know how insistent Mr. Joyce can be."

"You did the right thing, Betty. What's next?"

"I've compiled the list for the potluck . . ."

Greg tuned out, letting his mind wander from the particulars of casseroles and baked goods to his most recent conversation with Fina. He knew she was working an angle, but if he could wring some money out of her in the meantime, what was the harm? As long as he stayed one step ahead of her, it would be okay. If she was going to make a nuisance of herself, at least the church should profit.

"Don't you think?" Betty asked, her pen poised over her notepad.

"I'm sorry, what was that?" He smiled to offset his inattention. Greg knew that Betty liked their daily check-ins; it made her feel important.

"I said that I think there should be a couple of additional sides. We're getting a bit heavy on the sweets, no pun intended." She giggled at her own joke.

"You know best, Betty. I defer to your wisdom on this particular issue." Greg didn't understand leaders who insisted on being involved in every decision affecting their organization. He didn't care about the dish distribution at the potluck, but Betty did. Allowing her to be in charge of this inconsequential detail made her feel special and valued, and it was one less thing he had to do.

"Pastor, I need to speak with you." Lucas had appeared in the doorway. He was flustered, his hair a mess and his shirt untucked.

"We're in the middle of a meeting, Lucas," Betty said.

"I know, and I'm sorry, but this is important."

"So is this," Betty insisted, gesturing with her notebook.

"Betty, you have this well under control. Let me speak with Lucas, and then you and I can finish up," Greg suggested.

"Of course, Pastor." She vacated the chair and pulled the door closed behind her.

"Have a seat."

Lucas dropped into a chair and opened his mouth to speak.

"And take a deep breath," Greg entreated.

Lucas did as he was told. Then he scooted to the edge of the chair, resting his hands on the edge of Greg's desk.

Greg inched his chair back just a touch.

"I've been praying all the way over here, Pastor, asking for direction."

"Is it Heather and the kids? Is everything all right?"

"They're fine. It's nothing like that."

"Then what has you in such a state?"

"I had a visit from Fina Ludlow this morning." He gulped, as if he were short on oxygen.

"Uh-huh."

"I feel like we're under siege from this woman, and I fear the damage she can unleash on the church."

"Slow down, Lucas. What happened exactly? Do you want some water or coffee?"

"Water would be good."

Greg buzzed out to Betty and asked her to bring in some refreshments. Lucas sat back in the chair and pulled on the hem of his shirt to get airflow through the garment.

Betty came in a minute later with two cups of water and a package of Lorna Doone cookies, the sting of being dismissed clearly affecting her inclination to be a good hostess.

Lucas sipped his water, and Greg nodded that he should open the cookies. Lucas took two from the package, but Greg plucked only one from the plastic sleeve.

"What exactly is troubling you?" he asked his congregant, after taking a small bite of shortbread.

"Not what. Who. Fina Ludlow is troubling me."

"What did she say that has you so upset?"

"Someone told her that I borrowed antifreeze from the church shop."

Greg nibbled on his cookie and took a drink of water. "That's not true?"

"It is true, but she made it sound like I kept it a secret, and that I poisoned Nadine."

Greg reached over and patted his arm. "Lucas, we all know that's absurd."

"*I* know it's absurd, but do the police know that?"

"The police will investigate and find the perpetrator. We have to let them do their job."

"But someone is spreading lies about me." He grabbed another cookie.

"You just said that it was true; you did borrow the antifreeze."

"But I didn't poison Nadine."

"Is that what this person is claiming?" Pastor Greg asked. "Or is that Fina's interpretation?"

"Does it matter?" Lucas asked. "If she reached that conclusion other people will, too."

"You can't worry about people who gossip."

Lucas eyed the box of cookies again. His hand moved toward it, but pulled back when he spied Pastor Greg's half-eaten cookie.

"It's not just people," Lucas said quietly.

"What do you mean?"

He swallowed and blinked slowly. "I think it's one person who is saying wicked things about me."

Greg cocked his head to the side.

"But I'm not sure I should tell you," Lucas continued.

"What does the Holy Spirit tell you?"

"He tells me that you should know the truth."

The pastor sat back in his seat with his hands folded in his lap. "I'm here to listen, Lucas. Whatever you need to tell me, it's okay."

"The person gossiping about me . . . well, it's Gabby."

Greg's head jutted forward like a turtle, and his eyes widened. "My Gabby? Is that what Fina told you?"

Lucas's eyes bounced from one corner of the room to another. "Not exactly."

"Meaning?"

"I guessed that it was Gabby, and she didn't disagree."

Greg shook his head and rose from his seat. "Lucas, Lucas." He walked around to the front of the desk and perched on the edge. "You're making a serious accusation against another congregant who also happens to be the female spiritual leader of this church and my wife."

Lucas curled over as if overcome with a stomachache. "I know this is serious, Pastor, but I don't know what else to do."

"You truly believe that Gabby told Fina you took the antifreeze and poisoned Nadine?"

"Gabby told her I took the antifreeze and then strongly suggested that I killed Nadine."

"Why would Gabby say something like that?"

Lucas opened his mouth and shut it without speaking. He looked like a guppy struggling for air.

"Even if Gabby would do such a thing—which I have difficulty believing—why would she want to hurt you?" Greg asked. "Unless she believes in her heart that you hurt Nadine and feels compelled to share what she knows with investigators."

"But she doesn't know anything!" Lucas exclaimed. "She's just gossiping to get me in trouble."

Greg walked back behind his desk and took a seat. "It could be argued that you're gossiping, Lucas, in an effort to get her in trouble."

"I'm doing what I think is right for Covenant Rising. I can't stand to see our community undermined by outsiders."

"Nor can I." Greg clasped his hands tightly on the desk blotter. "But I'm very troubled by this, Lucas."

"So am I! These past few weeks, it's been eating away at me. I've lost sleep wondering if I should share the burden with you."

Greg's gaze narrowed. "What do you mean the past few weeks? I thought Fina Ludlow just came to see you today."

Lucas plucked at the hem of his shirt again. "I just meant in general. I've had some concerns, and I didn't know how to handle them."

"Concerns about what, Lucas?" Greg couldn't keep the impatience out of his voice. He didn't want to hear what Lucas had to say, but ignoring a brewing crisis wasn't wise. Given Lucas's level of distress, he would probably tell Heather, who would share it with another member, and on and on. Greg needed to nip it in the bud, whatever it was. "I hate to see you suffer like this. You need to unburden yourself. Jesus loves you, no matter what."

Lucas shook his head. "I don't know, Pastor Greg."

Greg stared at him, trying to convey a mixture of compassion and expectancy.

"There's been talk that Gabby spends too much time with a certain congregant," Lucas finally said, the words spilling out in a rush.

Greg gestured for him to continue.

"It's one of the young men, Casey Andros. I don't know if it's true, but people are starting to talk."

"'A dishonest man spreads strife, and a whisperer separates close friends,' Proverbs 16:28," the pastor warned.

"I'm not spreading gossip," Lucas insisted. "I haven't told anyone else. I'm just telling you. What kind of servant of God would I be if I didn't alert you to the threats in our midst?"

"I wasn't referring to you, Lucas. I was thinking of the people who are disrespecting Gabby and discussing our marriage as if it were fodder for their gossip mills."

"Maybe I shouldn't have said anything," Lucas said, casting his eyes downward.

"You did the right thing. I rely on you. I trust you."

"So you're not upset with me?"

"Go forth and pray on all of this," Greg said, sidestepping the question. "Give it over to God." He placed his palms on his desk as if summoning some spirit or power. "Can you do that? I need to get back to work, but I need to know that you're okay."

Lucas nodded vigorously. "I am. I feel much better, Pastor."

"Good."

Lucas rose and went to the door.

"And Lucas?" Greg asked. "Please keep this between the two of us. 'For lack of wood, the fire goes out.'"

Lucas smiled. "Proverbs 26:20. Of course, Pastor Greg. I won't say a word."

Greg watched him leave.

Some days, it would be so much easier to lead the church if it didn't have any members.

Fina was sitting in a parking lot, sipping a diet soda and trying to decide what to do next. What she really wanted to do was take a nap at Frank and Peg's or Patty and Scotty's, but they'd want to know why she was so tired, and she didn't want to lie or tell the truth. The night with Cristian had been fun, but hadn't delivered much quality sleep. Not only because they were busy, but also because she wasn't used to sharing her bed with someone. Milloy stayed over sometimes, but they'd been hopping in and out of bed since college—she was used to him. She and Cristian had slept together before, but rarely did they spend the whole night together. Her parents had always had a king-sized bed, and Fina was beginning to see the wisdom: the other person was within reach or not, depending upon your mood.

A private caller lit up her phone.

"Hello," she said.

"Is Ludlow there?"

"Who's asking?"

"Travis."

"Yes, this is Fina Ludlow."

"Dante said you wanted to talk."

"Yes. Just tell me when and where."

"It's going to have to be tonight, probably around ten."

Fina adjusted her butt in the seat, a physical response to the discomfiting suggestion. "Where?"

"There's a bar downtown. I'll call you when I get there, but I won't be able to hang around. You're going to have to make it quick."

"Fine, but you have to give me a little bit of notice. I may not be in the neighborhood already."

"Whatever." He disconnected the call.

Fina stared at the phone. It's not like she was a great conversationalist or Miss Manners, but what was it with these young guys who had barely evolved beyond the Cro-Magnon stage? What were their love lives like? Did they ask women out or just drag them by the hair back to their caves?

TWENTY-EIGHT

There was a car in Evan's driveway when Fina pulled up. She assumed he was home and pulled the boxes of paperwork out of her trunk and climbed the front steps. She balanced the boxes between her hip and the house while waiting for someone to answer the door.

He appeared a moment later, wiping his hands on a dish towel.

"Hi." He took the top box from the pile.

"Hi. I was nearby so I thought I'd return these."

"Find anything useful?"

"Maybe. Do you have a few minutes to talk?"

"Sure. Let me just get Molly settled."

They stacked the boxes in the front hallway and Fina followed him into the kitchen, where Molly was sitting at the table. She was bent over a coloring book, her nose a few inches from the page.

"Hi, Molly. What are you coloring?" Fina asked.

"A kitty."

Fina craned her neck to get a better view of the picture. It was a round, puffy puppy with a smile, a breed that Fina doubted existed in real life. Molly had slashed across its fur with purple and blue lines.

"It looks good."

"We're getting a kitty," the girl informed her.

"You are?" She looked at Evan, who was rolling his eyes. "That's exciting."

"It's actually 'to be decided,'" he said. "Why don't we go into the living room?"

"So you found something in the paperwork?" he asked when they were seated on the couch.

"Not a smoking gun, by any means, but I was able to piece together the dates of Nadine's illness and some of the regular activities in her life."

"Like?"

"Well, specifically, the leadership committee meetings at the church and the neighborhood association meetings."

Evan studied her. "You think someone in one of those meetings poisoned her?"

"I don't know, but the alignment of the dates suggests that the antifreeze could have been administered at either of those gatherings."

"That can't be easy, poisoning someone in plain view."

"You'd be surprised. A slug of antifreeze in her coffee wouldn't be too tough to pull off. The other option is that someone *wants* it to look like there's a pattern with the meetings."

Evan shook his head. "We're back to that? You suspecting me?"

Fina smiled. "I never stopped suspecting you, but you're not the only person on that list."

"Who else is on it?"

"Well, I'm still having a little trouble buying the 'one big, happy family' picture, the one with Paul and Christa."

Evan tugged on the cuff of his shirt. "I don't know what more I can say to convince you."

"Then I guess you won't be the one to convince me." Fina stretched her legs in front of her. "I talked to Paul the other day. He said that McKenna might be going to the Graymoore School."

Evan's face brightened. "Yeah, she got in. She's so excited."

"That's great. That school has a terrific reputation."

"I know. I think it's going to take a huge weight off Christa's shoulders."

Fina nodded. "When I was at her house, she was under a pile of paperwork related to McKenna's current school."

"McKenna's lucky to have Christa for a mom, and I'm just glad I could help out."

Molly came into the room at that moment with her coloring book and a box of crayons. She dropped down at her father's feet between the coffee table and couch and resumed her coloring.

"You're helping out?" Fina asked, keeping her tone mild.

"Yeah. Nadine had promised her the money, so I'm just doing what she wanted."

"I'm surprised Nadine would give to a cause other than Covenant Rising."

"So am I, to be honest, but Christa says that's what she wanted."

"Well, that's wonderful for McKenna. That cat's looking great," Fina told Molly.

"My cat's going to be called Snowball."

"Is that so?" Fina asked her, giving Evan a look. He shook his head lightly.

"Uh-huh," Molly said.

Fina stood, and Evan followed her to the door. "A neighbor's cat died, and now she's obsessed with getting one."

"She sees her chance?"

"Exactly. At least cats don't need to be walked."

"This is true, although, I do see people in my neighborhood with cats in strollers."

"Seriously?"

Fina nodded. "Thanks for letting me borrow those papers."

"Sure. Let me know if you find something out."

"Will do."

She climbed into her car and sat for a moment before turning the key.

Christa had told her that she'd asked Nadine for a loan, but Nadine had turned her down. Was that the loan intended for McKenna's tuition? Had Nadine had a change of heart or was Christa pulling a fast one on Evan?

Fina was confused.

But confusion wasn't always a bad thing; it usually meant that someone wasn't telling the truth.

Greg sat behind the desk in his home office, waiting for Gabby to appear. He'd asked one of the women from the fellowship committee to take the girls to her house for dinner so that he and his wife would have a block of uninterrupted time. The Bible before him was open to Proverbs 6:16.

Gabby strode into the room and took the seat across from him. She was wearing yoga pants and an oversized sweatshirt that exposed her tanned shoulder.

"I need to pick up the girls," she said.

"I've arranged for Mrs. Teeson to drop them off."

Gabby made a face. "Since when do you arrange playdates?"

"Since I feel compelled to schedule time with my wife to discuss her behavior."

Her eyes widened, not in an expression of disbelief, but rather one of challenge. She folded her hands on her lap in a pose of pious subservience.

"I want to read a piece of scripture first." Greg took a sip of water from the glass on his desk and began. "'There are six things that the Lord hates, seven that are an abomination to him: haughty eyes, a lying tongue, and hands that shed innocent blood, a heart that devises wicked plans, feet that make haste to run to evil, a false witness who breathes out lies, and one who sows discord among brothers.' Are you familiar with that quote?"

"Of course. Proverbs 6:16."

Greg smiled at her. "I know that you love the Lord, Gabby, and I know that there is goodness in your heart, but I've heard things that worry me. I've heard that you are spreading gossip and even breaking a commandment."

"And you believe these rumors?" she asked, folding her arms across her chest and sitting back in the chair.

"I don't know what to believe."

"I'm your wife, Greg. Your partner. You're supposed to believe me over anyone else."

He closed the Bible. "I want to believe you."

"Then do." She started to rise from her chair.

"We're not done."

Gabby lowered herself back down.

"Whether or not I believe you is one issue. There's a second issue."

"What's that?"

"The accusations are coming from Lucas."

"Of course they are." Gabby sneered. "He is such a teacher's pet."

"And you're sloppy." The grin slid from Greg's face. "What were you thinking putting us in a position of vulnerability?"

Gabby's mouth was set in a line. "Maybe you should be less worried about me and more worried about him. *I'm* trying to protect the church. Lucas is just gossiping and stirring up trouble."

"That's not what he says."

"All he cares about is being your lapdog; that's his first priority. If he really cared about you and the church, he wouldn't be gossiping and troubling you with this garbage."

Greg rubbed a hand over his chin. "I'm not convinced that Lucas is the only problem."

Gabby stood up and walked to the door. Her trim legs looked like ostrich legs sticking out from her billowing top. "Remember, Greg, there's a line of people waiting to fill his spot, but I'm a little tougher to replace," she said before walking out.

Greg didn't doubt that Gabby had tattled on Lucas to Fina. He knew that her tongue could be sharp, especially when she felt threatened, but he didn't want to believe that she was violating their marriage vows.

If she was, there would be hell to pay—for all of them.

Fina couldn't sit still. She tried to lie on the couch and watch TV, but then she'd get antsy and do a lap of the condo. It was 10:23 p.m., and she still hadn't heard from Travis Whalen.

"Sit down," Milloy urged her. "You're stressing me out."

She returned to the couch and rotated her head on her neck. Her not-so-subtle play worked, and he reached over and massaged her shoulders.

"Jesus, you're tied up in knots."

"I know. I need a massage."

Milloy turned to face her. "Just tell me when you want one, and I'll put it on my calendar. It isn't complicated."

"Our schedules are complicated."

"I think we can figure it out if we put our minds to it, but you have to have the will to make it happen."

"Oh, right there," Fina said, directing him to a particularly troublesome spot. "My ability to plan ahead has been compromised recently."

"By?"

"By this case and the threats against me. I just want to get through this stuff, and then I'll regroup."

"Yeah, but there's always something."

"Sure, but I'm going to pretend that's not the case."

"Good plan." His thumb dug into her shoulder.

"Ow."

They were watching *SportsCenter* when Fina's phone rang ten minutes later.

"This is Fina."

"It's Travis. There's a packie on the corner of Mills and State. Meet me there in twenty minutes."

"I'll have a guy with me, but he's cool."

"This isn't a group event."

"And I'm not meeting some guy I don't know at the liquor store at eleven p.m. by myself. Do you think I'm a total idiot?"

"Suit yourself."

"How will I know it's you?"

"I'll be smoking." Travis ended the call.

"He really is a man of few words," Fina said, pushing herself off the couch. She retrieved her holster from the chair where she'd hung it and put it on. "Let's go."

Travis Whalen was leaning against the window of the liquor store smoking a cigarette. He was just shy of six feet with a thick build. Fina couldn't be sure if his girth was due to fat or muscle, but he looked formidable regardless.

"Travis?" she asked, taking a wild guess.

"Yeah?" He eyed her up and down. Fina put her hands on her hips, providing a peek at her gun.

"Can we go somewhere to talk?" she said. "I'm not wild about hanging around outside the packie."

Travis dropped his cigarette to the sidewalk and ground it out with his scuffed white sneaker. He left it there, which irritated her. How hard is it to pick up your litter?

Pushing himself off the wall, he started down the street. Fina and Milloy fell in step behind him.

The neighborhood was quiet at this time of night. Not many people lived there relative to Back Bay and Beacon Hill. A few restaurants
and bars were open, but much of the street-level retail was devoted
to cafés and lunch places that closed when the business day ended. It
felt eerie.

Travis turned a corner into an alley.

"Oh, this is much better," Fina said under her breath. Milloy looked
at her. "Hey, Travis? I was talking about someplace *more* public, not
less."

He stopped and turned to face her. "Do you want to see Jimmy
Smith or what?"

"Yes, please," she responded, and scowled when he turned his
back.

In the middle of the alley, a set of stairs led down to the basement
level and what looked to be a bar. An illuminated Miller Lite sign cast
a glow on the stone steps. Travis started down, turning his body sideways in order to plant his entire foot on each tier.

Fina followed and hooked her fingers over the pocket of her jeans
near her gun. Milloy brought up the rear.

The door had a small window at eye level. Travis pulled on the
knob, and it swung open to reveal a dark room that reeked of beer and
body odor.

"Don't say it," Fina warned Milloy.

"You always take me to the nicest places," he murmured, grinning.

Fina surveyed the space and couldn't figure out if it was a business
or a private club. There were tables and chairs, a jukebox, and a small
bar with pleather stools that looked like they belonged in a 1970s
basement.

She scanned the room and the dozen or so men in it. There were a
few at the bar who looked three sheets to the wind. The others were
drinking at tables, engrossed in their conversations.

"So," Fina asked. "Which one is he?"

Travis nodded toward a table at the back of the room where two guys who looked to be in their twenties were sitting.

Fina took a step in their direction. As she closed in on the table, one of them looked up and made eye contact. He had bruises under his eyes, and a piece of white tape covered the bridge of his nose. He jumped up, his chair clattering to the floor. Looking past Fina, he must have spotted Milloy, because he turned toward the back of the room and bolted through a swinging door.

"Dammit!" Fina yelled and took off after him.

He sprinted through a small, dingy kitchen and slammed open a metal door. Halfway up a set of steep stairs, Fina reached out and grabbed his pant leg, but he shook her off and sent her tumbling back into Milloy. She regained her footing, and they clambered after him.

On the street they swiveled their heads, searching. The slam of a car door drew their attention to the spot where the alley intersected with another. Fina watched as her assailant drove off. She sprinted after the car, hoping to catch the plate, but it turned the corner before she could register any of the letters or numbers.

"Fuck!" she hollered, bending over with her hands on her knees. "I'm going to kill Travis."

"Sorry I wasn't any help," Milloy said as she strode past him on her way back to the bar.

"I just wanted to talk to the guy. If I'd thought he was going to run, I would have had you cover the back."

Fina banged open the door leading to the kitchen. A young man in dishwashing whites was sitting on the counter, smoking a joint. She didn't suppose the health department made many visits.

Back in the main room, Travis was shooting the shit with the bartender, a beer in one hand.

"What the hell was that?" Fina asked.

Conversation in the bar quieted.

Travis turned toward her slowly. "What?"

"I wanted to talk to the guy."

Travis rotated back to the bar and stared at the TV on the counter. "I guess he didn't want to talk to you."

Fina plucked the beer from his hand and grabbed his wrist. She twisted his arm out and behind his back until Travis yelped in pain.

"Where can I find him?"

Milloy reached over the bar and grabbed the bartender's hand as he reached for a bat.

"Thank you," Fina told him.

"I'm going to call the cops!" one of the old drunks declared.

"Please do," she hollered back. "That would be most helpful."

Travis grunted, his face reddening.

"I will break your arm," Fina said, applying more pressure. "It will be the highlight of my week."

"He works at the print shop on Wellington," he spit out.

"When he isn't beating the shit out of people?" Fina released him, and he crumpled over, grasping his wrist. "Why didn't you just tell me that in the first place, you fuckwit?" Fina asked.

Travis shot her a venomous look. He took a step toward her and raised his fist, but Fina saw it coming. She blocked his punch and struck him on the forehead with her open palm.

"Come on, Sugar Ray," Milloy said. "Let's go." He nudged her toward the front door.

"That was a waste," Fina said when they were back on the street.

"You got the location of the guy."

"Exactly. Instead of the actual guy."

"You'll get him tomorrow."

"Minus the element of surprise."

"No offense, but I don't think this is going to drive him out of town."

"Offense taken," Fina said, reaching out and playfully squeezing his neck.

They both stayed alert for the walk home just in case Travis or Jimmy decided they still had business to attend to.

At least Fina had finally found *the* guy who attacked her, not just a guy who had information.

The only question that remained was who was footing the bill.

TWENTY-NINE

Fina awoke itching to make progress, but when she called the print shop using a burner, she learned that Jimmy Smith was off for the weekend. Instead, she got dressed and drove to Framingham.

Christa Jackson was unloading groceries from the back of her car when she pulled up.

"Let me help," Fina said, hefting a bag onto each hip.

Christa eyed her warily, but seemed to decide that it was more trouble to reject than accept the offer.

Once inside the house, they took the bags into the kitchen and placed them on the table next to the *Globe*. Christa didn't invite her to sit down, so Fina leaned against the counter and watched her unpack the bags.

"You have more questions?" Christa asked, shoving two boxes of frozen waffles into the freezer.

"I'm going to have questions until I answer the big question, which is, who killed your cousin?"

"Okay, but I have nothing new to tell you."

"I heard that congratulations are in order."

Christa grabbed a perspiring gallon of milk, her fingertips slipping slightly on the damp surface. "What are you talking about?"

"McKenna got accepted to Graymoore."

Christa frowned. "That's right. We're very proud of her."

"As you should be," Fina commented.

"That's got nothing to do with Nadine."

Fina leaned her hand on the counter, but drew back. Her palm was tender from the blow she'd given Travis Whalen. "Actually, it kind of does. Evan told me that he's providing some money for tuition, which is curious. I thought you asked Nadine for that money, and she turned you down."

Christa stopped moving, a can of baked beans in each hand. "She changed her mind."

"Really?"

"Yup." Christa placed the cans in a cabinet and slammed the door closed.

"'Cause it looks to me like you didn't get the money, then Nadine died, and then you did get the money."

"You think I killed her for tuition money?" she asked, her hands on her hips.

Fina shrugged.

"This is good news for my family. Please don't twist it into something nasty."

"So my interpretation of events isn't accurate?"

Christa pulled a carton of eggs from one of the grocery bags and flipped open the top. One had been smashed in its little cardboard nest, the yolk smeared over the other shells. Christa blew out her breath in annoyance and took the eggs to the sink. "It's an interpretation. That's all. Just because things happened in a certain order doesn't mean they're connected."

"No, but you definitely benefitted from Nadine's death."

"Except for the fact that my cousin died."

"Right, the cousin who had once planned a future with the man who became your husband."

Christa ran the water and began plucking the intact eggs out of the carton. "The cousin who married a nice guy and was going to start a family of her own."

"So you say."

"Fina, either you need to prove something or you need to leave us alone," Christa insisted, rinsing the sticky yolk off the eggs and placing them in a bowl. She wiped her hands on a dish towel.

"All righty. Will do."

Christa placed the bowl of eggs in the refrigerator and looked toward the front door, which Fina assumed was her cue to leave. She pushed herself off the counter, the newspaper catching her eye as she did.

"Is that today's paper?" Fina asked.

Christa gave her a strange look. "Yes. Why?"

"Just wondering."

Fina sat in her car, racking her brain. She closed her eyes and rested her forehead against the steering wheel, trying to will the pieces to fall into place. After a few frustrating minutes that resulted in no greater clarity, she started the car and snaked through the streets to Route 9.

With the hum of the road beneath her, finally something clicked.

Greg hadn't slept well.

He kept coming back to his conversations with Lucas and Gabby and the holy mess they had created. He supposed that their behavior was just another test from God, another indication that Greg was up to the tough job of leading a large, successful church. Trials were part of the deal. Some people might assume that trials indicated the absence of God, but he believed otherwise. The good Lord was testing Greg, making sure he was ready for bigger and better things.

Sweat trickled down Greg's back as he pushed through another set of biceps curls and overhead presses. He'd eked out the last rep when there was a knock at the door, and Gabby poked her head into the home gym.

"Lucas is here to see you," she said with a sneer on her face. She pushed the door wide open.

Lucas stepped into the room and moved to put some distance between himself and Gabby. They avoided eye contact.

Greg racked the dumbbells and sipped his water. He knew the silence was making both his wife and his congregant uncomfortable, so he drew it out a little longer as he took a swig from the water bottle.

"We're all set, Gabby. Thanks."

She gave Lucas a sour parting look and left the room, pulling the door closed behind her.

Lucas stood with his back to the mirror, which gave Greg a view of his backside. He was wearing ill-fitting khakis and a sweater over a button-down shirt. He looked like any middle-aged dad who was getting soft and flabby, his shoulders sloping with the years.

"You wanted to speak with me, Pastor Greg?"

Greg didn't invite him to sit down or suggest they move the conversation to a more comfortable setting. With Lucas shifting from one foot to the other, Greg had him just where he wanted him.

"I've been thinking a lot about our conversation yesterday."

Lucas nodded.

"I appreciate that you came to me with your concerns," Greg said. He took another gulp from his water.

"Of course, Pastor."

"And I prayed on it and reflected about what would be most healing under the circumstances."

"Uh-huh."

"God calls on each of us to do our part," Greg continued.

"Of course." His face was pinched.

"And I think you need some space to reflect on your role in the church."

Lucas blinked a few times. "I don't understand."

"I think it's best that you take some time off from the leadership committee. I don't want those responsibilities to distract you from what's really important, which is the state of your soul and your relationship with God." Greg stared at Lucas as he delivered the command masquerading as a suggestion.

"Pastor Greg, I can still attend to my duties on the committee, even if I take some time to reflect."

Greg smiled at him. "I know how committed you are to the church, Lucas. I want to see you be equally committed to your own spiritual well-being."

"But . . . I . . ." Lucas kneaded one hand with the other. "Am I being punished? *I* didn't do anything wrong."

"Of course you're not being punished. This is an opportunity, Lucas. You're an important member of the church, and I need you to be completely focused. Believe me, this was a difficult decision, but it's the right decision."

"But I don't understand. You said I did the right thing, but it feels like I'm in trouble."

Greg frowned. "Lucas, do you trust me?"

"Of course."

"Then you need to believe that a temporary leave from the committee is in your best interest and the church's best interest."

He nodded slowly. "If that's what you think is best."

"I do, and I can assure you that Gabby and I are going to pray on this, and she's going to do the work she needs to do."

Lucas's features had grown slack. He started to leave, but paused at the door. "Are you going to tell people why I'm off the committee?"

"I'm going to tell them that you have a great number of responsibilities, and it would be selfish of the church to expect so much of you." Greg went to Lucas and patted him on the back. "It's all going to work out. It's not for us to question God's plan."

"Of course not."

Greg walked him to the front door. "I don't want you to worry. This doesn't change our relationship."

"I hope not, Pastor," Lucas said, lingering on the front stoop.

"I'll see you at church," Greg said, closing the door.

He looked toward the kitchen and caught a glimpse of Gabby in the doorway, a small smile perched on her face.

"Do you have today's paper?" Fina asked the moment she stepped into Peg and Frank's living room.

"Well, hello to you, too," Frank said. He had a hammer in one hand and was studying a wall of family pictures.

"A new arrival?" Fina asked.

"Another picture of great-nephew Oliver." He held up a framed eight-by-ten of an adorable baby tenuously balanced on a stack of pillows.

"He's outgrown his angry old man phase," Fina said. "Such a cutie."

"The paper should be in the recycling bin by the door to the garage."

"Thanks."

Fina found both the *Herald* and the *Globe* on the top of the stack and brought them back to the living room.

"So what are you looking for in the paper?"

Fina flipped through the pages. "Did any circulars come today?"

"Anything that came today should be on the top."

Frank hammered a nail into the wall while she continued looking. He gingerly placed the photo on the nail and stood back to take a look.

He admired his handiwork. "Looks good, if I do say so myself."

"Ahh." Fina pulled a stack of circulars out that were nestled in the *Globe*'s business section. She pulled one out and spread it open on the coffee table.

"What'd you find?"

"Not sure."

Frank took a seat in his recliner and watched her skim the shiny pages. Fina pulled the most recent note from her bag and smoothed it down next to the circulars. She carefully ran her finger down each page of the Macy's insert.

"Those are baby clothes," Frank noted. "Is there something you want to tell me?"

Fina snorted. "Hardly." She flipped to the next page, which featured Misses swimwear. "Look." She pointed at the print. "Doesn't that look identical?"

Frank scooted forward and stretched out his hand. She passed him the note and then the circular. He studied the two items.

"See how the *S* looks the same," Fina said, "and you can just see a teeny bit of that turquoise background."

"Looks like a match to me," Frank said.

"Yippee!"

Frank patted her shoulder. "Sweetie, I don't mean to rain on your parade, but everyone in eastern Massachusetts got this circular."

Fina grinned. "But how many of them got the circular before it was delivered in the newspaper?"

"When did you get this note?"

"Yesterday. I could be wrong, but I'm guessing only someone with access to the circular prepublication could have sent me this note and the other two."

"And you know someone who fits the bill?" he asked.

"I do indeed. Not only would that clear up the mystery of who's sending the notes, it means I can breathe a little easier. There's no way that guy would ever hurt me."

"No?"

"No." Fina grinned. "In fact, I think I could make him cry if I looked at him wrong."

"I'm not sure that idea should make you so gleeful."

"Let me take my pleasures where I can get them, Frank."

"So what's next?"

Fina sat back on the couch. "Give me a moment to relish the discovery."

Frank held his hands up. "Of course. I don't want to rush the creative process."

"This must be how doctors and nurses feel when they save a patient—that sense of satisfaction."

Frank nodded. "I would definitely draw a parallel between saving someone's life and uncovering the identity of the author of your poison pen letters. Exactly the same."

"We really are two birds of a feather, Frank."

He threw back his head and laughed.

Fina wasn't sure how best to use the knowledge of Lucas's little art project, so she decided to do nothing for the moment. As long as Lucas didn't know the jig was up, Fina had the upper hand. She'd developed enough self-control over the years to hold back until she could leverage information to her advantage.

Her stomach was growling, so Fina stopped at her favorite sub shop in Newton and ordered a cheesesteak with mushrooms and onions. She took her sandwich over to one of the molded plastic booths and took a seat. The cheese was dripping out of one end of the roll. Fina took a bite and licked salty grease off her finger.

She wiped her hands on a napkin before scrolling through her e-mail. The phone rang a moment later, Carl's name illuminating the screen.

"Yes, Father?"

"I saw Ceci last night. Where are you on the case?"

"I'm on the cusp. Where did you see Ceci?"

"At a benefit. Your mother dragged me to it."

"Got it. I was planning to give Ceci a call, but I've been too busy solving this thing."

"You just said you were on the cusp. Which is it?"

Fina held the phone away from her ear for a moment. "I'm on the cusp of solving it," she replied once she'd taken the pause to control her irritation.

"What about Chloe's donation?"

"I'll have a fair amount of ammunition against making it, but there's no telling what she'll do."

"Your job was to make her withdraw the land deal."

"No," Fina said, popping a mushroom into her mouth. "My job was to try to dig up some dirt, which I'm doing. If she's hell-bent on supporting the church, nothing anyone says will make a difference."

"Figure something out, Fina."

"It's at the top of my list."

She hung up and took a few bites, washing them down with her soda.

Fina was a woman of principle, and one of her principles was to never let anyone ruin a good meal. Her father tested her sorely in this department, but she took another bite, committed to enjoying her sub despite his heartburn-inducing demands.

Fina spent most of Sunday lolling around in her sweats and was refreshed and ready to go when her alarm sounded on Monday morning. She was itching to get her hands on Jimmy Smith, and walked to the print shop with a spring in her step. She wanted to channel her inner Gene Kelly, by swinging on the lampposts and pirouetting on the pavement, but that would look crazy.

The store was on the first floor of a mid-rise stone building, next door to a smoothie place. First, Fina walked by the front of the store and glanced in without stopping. There were two men inside, one of whom was Jimmy Smith, the other of whom looked barely out of his teens. Fina turned the corner at the end of the block and walked into the alley behind the building. All of the metal doors were closed and judging from the depth of the shop and the building, she surmised that the shop didn't open directly onto the alley. This was good news; it suggested that Jimmy wouldn't be able to make a quick getaway from the rear of the building like he had the other night.

Returning to the street, Fina touched her gun for reassurance before pushing open the door. Her arrival was heralded by the tinkling of a bell. Fina flipped the OPEN sign to CLOSED and approached the counter where the younger man was typing something into the computer. Jimmy, hunched over a copier, had his back to her.

"Can I help you?" the young man asked without raising his eyes. His hair was long and lank, bringing to mind a hippie, and he wore a faded T-shirt that might have done double duty as his sleepwear. When did dressing for outside and inside become the same thing?

Fina put her hand on her hip and watched his gaze travel to her waist. He blinked rapidly and started to raise his hands.

"I don't have any business with you," Fina said. "I'm here to see Jimmy."

Jimmy's head popped up, and he turned toward his visitor. The quick jerk of his head toward the back of the store indicated his urge to run.

"If you even think about making me run after you again, you will regret it."

"Do what she wants, man," the younger man pleaded.

"I'm not going to hurt you," Fina reassured him, "but Jimmy and I have business."

"What do you want?" Jimmy asked her, folding his arms over his chest. The bruises under his eyes had faded, and his nose was tape-free.

"I want to know who hired you to beat me up."

The hippie's eyes enlarged to saucers.

"I can't be giving up my sources."

"Oh, please. You didn't finish the job, and I found you. Let's just agree that you suck at this."

Jimmy sneered. "I couldn't tell you even if I wanted to. He didn't tell me his name."

"C'mon. You're not that dumb," Fina said. "You must have seen the guy. How'd he pay you?"

"He gave me cash when we met up."

"Where did you meet up?"

He jerked his head toward the street. "In the alley behind the BAS, that fancy gym."

Fina looked at him. "The gym?"

"That snobby place down the street."

A wave of something—nausea, anxiety, dread—pulsed through her body. Fina placed a hand on the counter to steady herself. "What did he look like?"

Jimmy screwed up his face in annoyance. "I don't know. I wasn't dating the guy."

"Try to remember," Fina said slowly. The hippie stood as still as a statue, only his eyes moving back and forth, following their conversation.

"About six feet, dark hair, but kind of going gray. He was in good shape."

She pulled out her phone and clicked open the browser, willing her hands not to shake. She could feel the pulse in her neck throbbing.

"Tell me if you see him on this page," she said, handing Jimmy the phone.

While he looked, Fina took a deep breath in through her nose and exhaled through her mouth. She'd heard this kind of breathing was used by soldiers and cops to control their adrenaline. She did it again, but felt closer to hyperventilation than she had before.

"This is the guy," Jimmy said, giving the phone back to her.

Fina knew what she would see, but she forced herself to look at the Ludlow and Associates partners' page. She squeezed the phone in her hand.

"Thanks, Jimmy, and by the way, stay the fuck away from me."

Throwing open the door, Fina bolted out of the shop and took a few shaky steps toward the entrance of the smoothie shop. She leaned against the glass, pressing her cheek to the cold surface.

There was a small part of her that always expected the worst, but even that part couldn't possibly have predicted this turn of events.

THIRTY

Fina went home, threw on the dead bolt, and collapsed on her bed. She didn't want to think about the information she'd just discovered, but she could think of nothing else. Her own brother had paid to have her attacked. The concept was mind-boggling. But it confirmed what Fina had suspected for a long time: Rand was a monster. The bonds of family, the expectations of society, the law—none of it mattered. There was just Rand and the things he wanted. Anyone or anything that got in his way would be dealt with. Fina was just another obstacle.

The fact that he hadn't had her killed should have warmed her heart, but it didn't. All this time, she'd been looking over her shoulder, worrying about the family's safety, trying to stay one step ahead of Jimmy Smith, and it was all because of him.

Fina pushed her face into the pillow and lay there. She wanted to find him and kill him, but unlike Rand, she had a conscience, and she knew that other people would be affected by her actions.

Rolling off the bed, Fina went to the living room and got her phone. She walked to the window and watched a tanker make its way into the harbor. Living up so high with a bird's-eye view was generally a good reminder of her relative place in the world, but at that moment, it didn't have the desired effect. Her smallness made her feel impotent.

The revelation about Rand felt like a disaster, and Fina wanted desperately to talk about it with someone; but the question was, who? If she led a normal life, she would pick up the phone and dial her boyfriend. He would console her and give her advice, and she would feel that his top priority was her happiness and well-being. But Fina wasn't normal, nor was her life. Her boyfriend was a cop, and the law was always paramount in his mind. If he put Fina first, he was shirking his professional responsibilities, and if he put her second, then he wasn't being a very good boyfriend, or at least not the kind she wanted.

Cristian would want to build a case against Rand. He would want to let the law do its job, and although that was an option Fina would consider, she knew that her consideration wouldn't be enough for him. He'd want to do things by the book, and Fina didn't know if she could, not when it came to family.

She fetched a diet soda from the kitchen and dipped her hand into a bag of miniature Reese's peanut butter cups. On the couch, Fina placed her phone down and popped open the soda. She took a few gulps of the caffeine-laden liquid and then turned her attention to unwrapping the minicups. The familiar flavors of chocolate and peanut butter settled on her tongue. After accumulating a hillock of foil wrappers, Fina reached for her phone.

"I need to see you right away," she told Matthew.

"This is not a good time."

"When is a good time?"

"Uh . . . let me see." He was quiet for a moment. "Tomorrow, right before lunch."

"No, Matthew. It's an emergency. Cancel stuff."

"Fina, I can't just cancel stuff."

She was silent.

"Are you there?" he asked.

"Yes."

"So say something."

"I need to see you and Scotty. I'll meet you wherever you want, but it has to happen by the end of the day."

"What is this about?"

She was silent again.

"Your lack of ranting is freaking me out," Matthew said.

"As it should."

"Do you want me to include Dad?"

"No! Just you two."

"Fine. Let me talk to Scotty, and I'll call you back," he said, disconnecting the call.

Fina unwrapped another Reese's and popped it in her mouth. After five minutes, she was starting to get antsy for a callback, but decided to distract herself by putting away the candy and turning on the TV. There was a shark show on one of the nature channels, which seemed appropriate. A great white was tearing into a defenseless seal when the phone rang. Matthew's assistant was calling to let her know that her brothers would see her at seven p.m. at Scotty's house.

Rather than spend the next couple of hours ruminating, Fina endeavored to keep busy. She saw that Evan had sent her an e-mail with an attachment of minutes from more neighborhood association meetings. There were two sets of notes, and Fina perused them, trying not to drop flakes of chocolate or peanut butter on the screen.

The first set didn't offer much of value, just confirmed Fina's suspicion that she should never move to the suburbs and join the neighborhood association. Either the boredom would kill her or she'd be arrested for killing a neighbor who wanted to endlessly debate whether her birdbath violated neighborhood rules.

The second set started out in the same vein, but toward the bottom of the second page, an item caught her eye. There was a brief mention of Ronnie's proposed pool, including a timeline for the actual construction work.

Fina took a drink and searched her memory. The last thing she remembered about the pool was that Ronnie was seeking a property-line variance to which Nadine objected. Fina flipped through the older minutes, which confirmed that fortunes had changed markedly when it came to Ronnie McCaffrey's pool. In earlier meetings, Nadine had voiced concerns about the plans, even suggesting that she would officially oppose his application for a variance. But in the most recent notes, Ronnie discussed the pool as if it were a done deal.

Fina pulled up the website for the city's Inspectional Services Department and clicked through until she found a list of variance applications. They were designated by address and case number, and each listing specified the status of the request. Some were listed as "applications," others were "revised applications," and the third category was "decisions." Fina scrolled down, found Ronnie's address, and clicked on the "decision" listing.

She scanned the page, her eyes settling on the "GRANTED" verdict at the bottom of the page. Her phone rang before she could process what it meant. "Covenant" lit up her screen.

"Fina Ludlow," she answered.

"This is Betty, Pastor Greg's secretary. He needs to meet with you as soon as possible."

"Okay."

"Can you be here in an hour?"

"Sure. What's this about?"

"He didn't tell me the specifics, just that he has some good news."

"I could use some good news."

"Well, then. Your prayers have been answered."

Good news from the pastor. She hoped it wasn't his version of good news, like that the Lord was coming.

That didn't really qualify in her book.

.   .   .

At Covenant Rising, Fina took a gander into the parish hall and saw a familiar figure. She walked down and sat in the pew behind him.

Lucas turned to face her. His face was pale, but his eyes were a spiderweb of red.

"Wow. Rough day?" Fina asked.

"I'm in the middle of prayer if you don't mind."

"Far be it from me to get between you and your Lord, but we do have something to discuss." She got up and joined him in his pew.

He sighed. "What is it?"

"Did you really think your letters were going to dissuade me?"

Lucas didn't look at her, but she could tell by the tremor that coursed through his shoulders that she'd hit a nerve.

"I don't—"

"Seriously? Just don't. I've had a rough day, too."

They sat in silence for a moment.

"What I'm still not sure about," Fina ventured, "is who exactly you're protecting, or from what."

Lucas tugged on the hem of his shirt.

"My guess," she continued, "is that you're protecting the church. I think you're a true believer."

He looked askance at her. "Of course I'm a believer."

"But lots of people believe, Lucas, and they don't commit criminal acts to protect their faith or further their cause."

"I didn't do anything of the sort. I didn't do anything criminal."

Fina stared at him. "Of course you did. You threatened me."

"I wasn't really going to hurt you."

"I know, but you can't go around threatening people," she said, hoping that if there were a God, he wouldn't strike her down on the spot. "I think you'd do just about anything to protect Pastor Greg and the church. The question is, would you kill to protect them?"

Lucas's head swiveled toward her. "Absolutely not."

"No? Why not? Because it would violate the Ten Commandments? So does lying, and you've done plenty of that."

He grasped his hands together tightly. "I was wrong to send you those notes, but I'm already being punished for it."

Fina peered at him. "What kind of punishment? And mental angst doesn't count."

Lucas swallowed. "Pastor Greg asked me to step down from the leadership committee."

Fina raised an eyebrow. "Not because of me. I haven't told anyone that you're responsible for the letters."

"I didn't mean that I was being punished specifically for the letters. I meant that I'm being punished in general for my sins."

"Which sins are we talking about?"

"I told Pastor Greg information about another congregant, and now I'm the one paying the price," he said quietly, as if he wanted her to know, but didn't want God to hear.

Fina nodded. "Gabby."

He nodded.

"You told Pastor Greg that she was telling people you had the antifreeze."

He shifted his feet. He was wearing sturdy-looking shoes with scuffed toes. "That's part of it."

Fina could see the struggle. He wanted to speak ill of the dutiful wife, but he didn't want to get into more trouble.

"Did you also mention her affair to Pastor Greg?" she asked.

Lucas swallowed. "How do you know about that?"

"I'm a private investigator. I find stuff out. I know that you sent the letters, and I know that Gabby is getting it on with a young congregant."

Lucas sat up straighter. "I thought the pastor should know."

Fina shook her head. "Never get in the middle of a marriage, Lucas, not unless someone is paying you to be there. The messenger is always killed."

"I was trying to do the right thing."

She tilted her head side to side as if evaluating two options. "Maybe, or maybe you were just fed up with Gabby and wanted to make life difficult for her. Kind of backfired."

"What are you going to do?" he asked.

"About what?"

"The letters."

"If I find out that you killed Nadine, I'll turn the letters over to the police."

"I didn't kill her."

Fina looked at the threatening depictions of the Ten Commandments that decorated the walls. Using fear as a motivator was not foolproof. Sometimes it came back to bite you on the ass. "If that's true, then I don't think anyone else needs to see them."

"Really?"

"Really, as long as you stay out of my way and promise you won't do something like this to anyone ever again."

He nodded. "I promise."

"I mean it, Lucas. Those letters would have frightened the average person. As it is, they caused a lot of wasted time and energy."

"I won't do anything like that again. Ever."

"Good." She stood and waited for him to speak. He was silent. "This is the moment that you thank me, Lucas."

"Thank you," he said, dipping his head.

"You're welcome."

She strode up the aisle and headed to the pastor's office.

She was primed for good news.

Betty pointed toward Greg's inner office, where Fina found him sitting behind his desk. His appearance was a sharp contrast to Lucas's. Pastor Greg looked energetic, and he gave her a wide smile.

"Ahh, Fina. Thanks for coming in."

"My pleasure." She took a seat in front of his desk. "Betty said that you had some good news."

"I do." He freed a folder from the bottom of a stack and opened it. "That child you were asking about? I made some calls, and it turns out he is available for sponsorship."

Fina smiled. "Wow. That's great."

"I know you felt a special connection with him, and as it turns out, he's currently without sponsorship."

"Hard to believe. He's such a cute kid."

Greg nodded. "I know, but the Lord works in mysterious ways. He knew that this child was the key to your involvement."

To my money, Fina thought.

"Can I see the materials?" she asked, nodding toward the folder.

"Of course."

Fina looked through the papers, which included an enlarged version of the same photo of the boy from the website and a fact sheet, which gave his particulars. She doubted the biography had any truth to it, but someone had made an effort to craft a believable backstory for little Azekel.

"It says his father was killed by a land mine," Fina said, reading the bio, "and his mother died in childbirth."

"Unbelievable what some of God's children have to bear," Greg said, his smile morphing into an expression of sympathy.

"That's for sure. So I assume you need a check from me?"

"*I* don't need the check, Fina. Azekel does."

She fought the urge to smack him across the face with the folder. "Of course. I don't have my checkbook with me, but I'll take care of it the moment I get home."

"Credit cards work also."

She frowned. "I only use credit cards in emergencies."

"Of course."

"Can I keep this?" Fina held the folder in her hand.

"It's all yours."

She'd almost made her escape when he spoke again.

"I assume that you're going to share the news of your sponsorship with Chloe Renard? She'll want to move ahead with her own generous donation now that you've had a change of heart."

"Don't worry, Pastor Greg. I'm going to tell her everything."

"That's wonderful. God is good, Fina. God is good!"

"Amen."

Fina put the folder in her bag and returned to her car.

True, some things were falling apart, but others were finally coming together, which felt like a miracle.

The lights were on at Scotty's house when Fina arrived a couple of hours later. She rang the bell and found the door unlocked, which added to her irritation.

"What do you people have against locking your door?" she hollered, stepping into the front hall.

"What?" Scotty yelled from another room.

Fina found him in his office, sitting behind his desk. Matthew was on the couch, his tie peeking out from his jacket pocket.

"I said, 'What do you people have against locking your door?' You should lock your door. Anyone could just waltz in and help themselves."

"I think our neighborhood is a little safer than yours."

She dropped onto the couch next to Matthew. "Fine. Suit yourself."

"So what's the emergency?" Scotty asked.

"Are Patty and the kids here?"

"No. Ryan had a soccer game, and then she's taking them out to dinner."

"Good." Fina picked up a plastic Skylanders figure and fiddled with it. Her brothers looked at her expectantly. "You know how there was that contract to beat me up?" she finally began.

"Yes," Matthew said. "Although he didn't have much success."

"Except he did get a few punches in," Fina said, "and he did it right here in your backyard." She looked at Scotty.

"What?" He sat forward in his chair.

"I didn't tell you that part because I thought it might freak you out, the idea that someone was willing to attack me where your children live."

"It does freak me out."

"Then you better brace yourself for the next part."

Her brothers exchanged glances.

"Will we need a drink?" Matthew asked.

"It's a safe bet," Fina said.

He went to a small bar at the side of the room and picked up three glasses with one hand. With the other, he grabbed a bottle of scotch around the neck and brought everything back to the coffee table.

"What's the next part?" Scotty asked once he had a glass firmly in hand.

"I found out who ordered the contract."

"And?"

Fina threw back her head and swallowed her drink in one motion. She coughed as the liquid burned a trail down her throat into her gut.

"Rand," she squeezed out. "Rand hired the guy to put me in the hospital."

Matthew sat back and stared at the wall, and Scotty froze, his drink midway to his mouth. Fina reached for the bottle and poured herself another finger.

"Wait," Matthew said, turning to Fina. "What?"

"I said that our brother paid some lowlife to beat me up and put me in the hospital. And this lowlife followed me here," she looked at Scotty, "to your home, to do it."

The two men were silent. Matthew downed his drink, but Scotty just stared at his. Fina's eyes volleyed between them, waiting for a response.

"Really?" Fina asked when none was forthcoming. "Nothing?"

Scotty finally mustered up the will to speak. "You have proof of this?"

"The guy who did it IDed Rand." Fina took a deep breath. It felt good to share the burden.

"Jesus Christ." Scotty shook his head. "I can't believe he would hire someone to hurt you."

"No?" Fina said. "I can."

Matthew rubbed his eyes with his palms before raising his gaze. "I can, too," he said. "I don't want to admit it, but when I consider the other things he's done, it's not that farfetched."

"Does Dad know?" Scotty asked.

Fina shook her head. "I wanted to tell you guys first so we present a united front."

"Have you told Cristian?" Matthew asked.

"Not yet."

"You could have Rand arrested," he said.

"Yes. I could have him arrested," Fina replied.

Scotty was shaking his head. "You're talking about a trial, a possible conviction, and jail time, and the publicity. That's not the way to go. You've got to gather all the dirt you have and give it to Dad," he said in a rush. "Now."

Fina took a pull from her drink. "There are a couple more leads I need to chase down."

"Fina! This is serious!"

"No shit, Sherlock! I'm working as fast as I can."

"Calm down, you guys," Matthew implored. "We'll figure something out. What about the dirt on Dad?"

"What dirt on Dad?" Scotty asked, glancing between the two of them.

"I think Rand has something on Dad, but I don't know what."

"We better figure it out," Matthew said.

"I'm doing the best I can," Fina said.

"If Rand is blackmailing Dad, whatever he has on him must be bad," Scotty said.

Fina stared at him. "Yeah, that's my point."

Anger and hurt roiled her stomach, and she barely trusted herself to speak. "You guys can keep thinking about it." She pushed herself up off the couch. "I'm tired. It's exhausting trying to stay one step ahead of your evil sibling."

"Fina, sit down," Matthew urged. "We know that Rand is nuts, and we're not going to let him do anything to you."

"Uh-huh."

She walked out the front door and pulled it closed behind her.

As if on autopilot, Fina started the car and drove for a few minutes before pulling over and putting the car in park.

She sat, sniffling, tears rolling down her cheeks.

THIRTY-ONE

Fina didn't cry for long. She went home to her computer and vowed to relegate Rand to the deep recesses of her mind for the time being.

She gazed at the calendar on her wall and tried to make sense of the dates of Nadine's illness and the people who had access to her at those times. The problem was, lots of people had access. At the church, Nadine crossed paths with Lucas, Greg, and Gabby with regular frequency, and Fina had seen firsthand that coffee and snacks were the lifeblood of the Covenant Rising meeting and event circuit. Christa, Evan, and Ronnie also saw Nadine on a regular basis.

There was something niggling at her—some conversation that she couldn't recall—but Fina had solved enough cases to respect her instincts. If there was something her subconscious wanted her to know, she needed to pay attention, and in time, it would be revealed. At the moment, though, the sense of a critical piece of information being just out of reach was maddening. Fina would just have to keep at it, reviewing what she had and revisiting things she'd dismissed early on.

She changed into sweats and had settled on the couch with her laptop when there was a knock on her door. A peek through the peephole revealed Cristian on the other side. She rested her head against the door. There was no good time to have the conversation they needed to have, so she let him in.

"Hey," she said.

"Hey." He gave her a kiss, but she pulled away too soon for his taste. "You okay? You don't look great."

"I don't feel great."

Fina curled up on the sofa, and Cristian took a seat next to her.

"You got a bug or something?"

She shrugged. "Does being sick of life qualify?"

He reached out and rubbed her shoulder. "What's going on?"

"I can't tell you."

The shoulder rub stopped abruptly. "You mean you won't tell me."

"Fine. I won't tell you, because if I tell you, you'll want to take matters into your own hands and do things I don't want you to do."

"If this is related to a crime, you know that I'm obligated to do certain things."

She nodded. "I know."

He grasped her hand. "You need to trust me."

"I trust you with my life, Cristian. This has nothing to do with trust."

"So tell me why you're upset."

"Ugh! I can't!"

He shoved off the couch and started pacing. "I hate seeing you upset. All I want to do is help."

"I know you do, and I wish it were that simple, but it's not. I'm okay. I can take care of myself."

"It's not a sign of weakness allowing other people to take care of you."

"No," Fina said, "but there are always strings attached."

He stopped and looked at her. "Is that how you see our relationship? An arrangement with strings attached?"

"Cristian, every relationship has strings attached. Maybe you don't like that idea, but everything's conditional."

"You're so cynical."

"I come by it naturally. Don't fault me for my upbringing."

"This isn't about your upbringing," he insisted. He was standing in what Fina thought of as his cop stance: legs parted, knees slightly bent, hands at the ready, as if waiting to ward off any threat. "This is about the choices you make as an adult. Your choice to continue living the Carl Ludlow way."

"So everything's my fault? I'm the one who's supposed to change and turn my life upside down, but you just go on being right and perfect."

"That's not what I said."

"But it's what you mean. I'm supposed to become a better, updated version of myself to accommodate you," Fina insisted.

"It's not about accommodating me. It's about the law."

"That's convenient."

"It's true, Fina."

"You're right. You have the law on your side, and that means I'm always going to be wrong." She stared at him. "I don't see the upside for me."

His mouth hung open. "We're together. That's the upside."

"Not really. Not if it's Fina 2.0 that you actually want to be with."

"Fina, I can't violate my job and the oath I took."

"I know, and I don't hold that against you. Really, I don't, but you're asking me to be someone that I can't."

Cristian ran his hands over his face. "So where does that leave us?"

The refrigerator motor whirred to life in the kitchen, then quieted, leaving the condo silent.

"Nowhere." Fina shook her head. "It leaves us nowhere."

Cristian looked at her with a mix of sadness and bewilderment. Perhaps he hoped that Fina would surprise him and throw her luck in with love, but he should have known better. She was who she was.

He left, pulling the door closed behind him, much like she had an hour earlier at Scotty's house.

Fina rested her head against the couch and stared at the ceiling. She needed to go to bed before the day got any suckier.

Fina woke up having slept like a log, but feeling exhausted nonetheless. She was tired—of her family and this case—and she knew that more rest wouldn't make her feel better. The only thing that would help was figuring out who killed Nadine and dealing with her brother. Just the prospect was enough to send her back to bed, but she rallied, knowing that Milloy was on his way over. She'd texted him before turning off the light the night before. Cristian's claim that she wouldn't let anyone take care of her was erroneous; she just preferred her caregiving to be less complicated than it always seemed to be with him.

Milloy arrived with a big dose of chocolate for her in the form of cocoa and a chocolate croissant.

"You brought me chocolate?" she asked, peering into the bag. "You must be concerned."

"Your text last night was pitiful," he said, taking a seat at the table.

"I didn't mean to worry you."

"You didn't worry me, but I wasn't sure what shape I would find you in this morning. I thought your drug of choice was in order."

"Thank you." She pulled out the croissant and tore off a piece.

"So what's going on?" he asked.

Fina chewed for a moment, holding up her finger. She washed the bite down with some cocoa before answering. "I tracked down Jimmy Smith."

"And?"

"And Rand hired him to beat me up."

Milloy stared at her, his features slack with surprise. "Holy shit."

"Yes, thank you. That's the response I was going for."

"Jesus, Fina."

"My family is so crazy that sometimes I lose perspective, but that's crazy, right?"

"That's crazy."

"Just checking."

"What are you going to do about it?" He was sipping a watery-looking beverage that she guessed was some kind of tea brewed in the depths of the earth by indigenous people. The health benefits were probably off the charts, in inverse proportion to the flavor.

"I told Scotty and Matthew last night."

"You going to the cops?"

"Not sure."

"Did you tell Cristian?"

Fina licked chocolate off her finger. "No."

"That can't have gone over well."

"It didn't. The romance is over."

"Huh." Milloy nodded as if considering the information.

"What does that mean?"

"Nothing. I'm just taking it all in."

She sighed. "Do you have an opinion you'd like to share?"

"I always thought that was going to be a tough row to hoe."

Fina held up her greasy hands. "Why didn't you say something?"

Milloy tipped his head back and laughed.

Fina stared at him.

"Really?" he asked. "You would have welcomed my romantic advice?"

"I value everything you have to say, Milloy."

"No doubt, but that doesn't mean you want to hear it."

"Well, it's over, and I think I screwed up one of my best friendships."

"You and Cristian are not going to stop being friends. You share way too much history, and you couldn't avoid each other even if you tried."

Fina picked at a crumb. "I suppose."

Milloy glanced at his watch. "I've gotta go."

"Thanks for stopping by. You gave me a reason to get out of bed."

"You didn't need me for that. You've got work to do."

They hugged at the door, and Fina returned to her computer. There had to be something she was missing, so she opened a browser and kicked things off by putting Evan Quaynor's name into the search engine.

She studiously clicked through the first five pages of links and tried to review them with a fresh eye. After an hour, she went to the kitchen for a diet soda and to stretch her legs. The renewed search of Evan's online presence hadn't revealed anything, but it still served a purpose. Sometimes you had to look at suspects in terms of probability of guilt; ruling them completely in or out wasn't always realistic. She hadn't found anything that made Evan seem a more likely suspect, and she just had to hope that digging into the others would yield something more fruitful.

She plugged in Christa Jackson's name next and went through the same process with the same result. The search on Paul Jackson was equally unsatisfying, and Fina decided to take a closer look at Ronnie before changing gears.

Her phone rang at that moment with Emma Kirwan's name lighting up the screen.

"I wondered when I was going to hear from you," Fina said.

"You always hear from me when I have something to tell you, Fina."

"I wasn't suggesting we call each other and chitchat, but I do like the occasional progress report, even if you have no progress to report."

"Well, I have actual progress to report if you'd like to hear it." Emma's tone was withering.

"I'm all ears."

Emma gave her a rundown of her findings and sent Fina a zip file with the supporting data.

"You're very good at your job, Emma."

"I hear you're good at yours, too," she said grudgingly.

"That's why we're such a good team," Fina said.

Emma hung up without comment.

Fina was eager to act on the new info, but wanted to revisit Ronnie's online presence before she did. A deeper dive into Ronnie's links revealed more in-depth articles related to firefighting. He was quoted in a piece in *Fire & Rescue* and offered tips for safe barbecuing in the *Herald*. Fina was able to trace his advancement through the department by piecing together announcements of passed exams and promotions. Ronnie's career had been steady and without any black marks, but there was something about his promotion to battalion chief that gave Fina pause. A colleague and candidate for the same job, Mike O'Brien, had withdrawn his application due to illness. When Fina searched for him—not an easy task to find a particular Mike O'Brien in the Boston Fire Department—she discovered that he ascended to the rank of battalion chief only a year later after regaining the bloom of health. She couldn't find any information about his illness, and as far as Fina could tell, he was still in the department.

It wasn't much, but it gave her an excuse to hit the road.

Greg sat on the edge of their bed, listening to the shower in the bathroom. Gabby always took long showers. She loved soaking in the hot water and rubbing various scrubs and lotions into her skin. Stepping into the bathroom in the wake of her shower was like walking into a bakery or a flower shop, depending upon the potion of choice. When they first dated, Greg found her fondness for these products alluring—proof that he was spending time with a woman who embraced her femininity—but over the years, he'd grown irritated. The bottles cluttered the bathroom counter and shower. Sometimes after touching her he noticed that his own skin smelled like gardenias or peaches, hardly an appropriate scent for a man who was trying to have a commanding presence.

Greg listened as the minutes ticked by on the chiming wall clock out in the hallway. He could have gone into the bathroom and spoken to Gabby, but he didn't want her to retreat into the distraction of her morning routine. He wanted her full attention.

She came out of the bathroom in a silk robe, her hair piled on her head in a towel turban. "Oh! You scared me, Greg. What are you doing sitting out here?"

"I'm waiting for you."

Gabby glanced toward the hallway. "Why? I'll be downstairs soon."

"Have a seat," he said, reaching out for her hand.

She frowned, but clasped his hand and took a seat next to him. "What's wrong? Has something happened?"

Greg adjusted himself on the bed so he was facing his wife. "Is there something you want to tell me, Gabby?"

She inclined her head in a question. "Like what?"

"That's what I'm asking."

Gabby pulled her hand away and stood up. She straightened her spine to get every inch of advantage over him that she could. "I'm not in the mood for playing games."

"Nor am I."

Greg watched her stomp to the bathroom. He heard the banging of drawers opening and closing with unnecessary force. A few minutes later, Gabby emerged in a pair of yoga pants and a long top that grazed the tops of her thighs. She was winding her hair into a bun at the crown of her head.

"Gabby, 'a false witness will not go unpunished, and he who breathes out lies will perish.' Proverbs 19:9."

"I don't know what you're talking about. The girls need breakfast."

"What's this?" Greg asked, holding up a white object the size of a magic marker.

She was still, but for the rapid blinking of her eyes. Gabby smoothed her shirt along the contour of her hips.

A weak grin worked to get purchase on her face. "Why didn't you just say that's what you were talking about?"

"Why was this hidden in the trash in one of the guest bathrooms?"

"Why are you rooting through the trash, Greg?" she asked, her voice dripping with accusation.

"I don't like being lied to."

Gabby walked over to him and placed her hand on his shoulder. "I wanted to be sure before I told you. I didn't want you to get your hopes up."

He nodded slowly.

"I know how much you want another baby," she said. "I have an appointment with Dr. Reilly later this week."

"When? I'll come with you."

"That's not necessary. They're just going to do some blood work. It's too early to see anything."

He pressed the palm of his hand against her stomach. "But he'll give you a due date."

"Sure, but I can tell you what he says. You don't need to take time from your busy schedule for that."

"So when he figures out the due date, he'll be able to tell you the date of conception, right?"

Gabby took a step back and folded her hands in front of her. "Why would we care about that?"

Greg looked at her. "Gabby."

"The Lord has blessed us with a baby." She put her hands on her hips. "We have no business questioning his ways."

Greg stared at her, his mind running calculations like a chess master looking six moves ahead. Which move would give him the most leverage? Which move would draw out the game?

"You'll need to cut back on your church activities. No subbing at

Prayer Group, that sort of thing," he said finally. "I don't want you putting yourself or the baby at risk, especially since you had such trouble conceiving."

She looked poised to respond, but just nodded.

"I only want what's best for you and the child," Greg continued.

"You know Grace Sweeny?" Gabby asked. "She's my age and her baby was born early, almost six weeks before the due date."

"We'll pray that that isn't the case. We'll trust that God knows best."

Gabby held his gaze.

"Once you have confirmation from the doctor," Greg said, "we'll decide how to tell the congregation."

"They'll be so excited," she said.

Greg walked over to the wastebasket in the corner. He dropped the pregnancy test into it. "'Blessed are those who hear the word of God and obey it,' Luke 11:28."

He left the room and started down the stairs.

Every challenge presented an opportunity, and he'd sure as hell make the most of this one.

Fina's breakfast with Milloy precluded her from catching Evan at home before his workday started, but he had a commitment downtown and agreed to meet her for coffee midmorning.

She found him at a bagel place in the Quincy Market food colonnade, sitting at a table with a cup of coffee.

"Thanks for meeting me on such short notice," Fina said.

"Sure."

She sat down across from him and unzipped her coat. It was cold outside, but the sun was shining through the colonnade's windows, heating up the place.

"I need to know about the neighbor's cat," Fina said.

Evan looked at her. "What?"

"Molly said that the neighbor's cat died."

He looked puzzled. "Yeah, that's right."

"Indulge me, would you? What exactly happened to the cat?"

He shrugged. "He died. End of story."

"Was he old?"

"No."

"Sick?"

Evan shook his head. "Not that I know of."

"Where was he found?"

"Back near the fence, between our house and Ronnie's." He gestured with his coffee as if they were in his own kitchen.

"So nobody knows the cause of death?"

"It was a cat, Fina. I can't imagine the owners paid for an autopsy. It got sick and died."

"That's all I needed to know. Thanks."

"What does this have to do with Nadine?"

"I can't tell you yet, but I will as soon as I'm sure."

Evan sighed.

She knew this was the moment to tell Evan about Christa's deceit, that Christa had duped him into providing the tuition money, but she wasn't sure what would be gained by giving Christa up.

"Talk to you soon," she said, leaving him in a blissful state of ignorance.

She had more important lies to uncover.

THIRTY-TWO

Fina made some calls to try and locate Mike O'Brien, but had to wait to hear back. She hated waiting in general, but it was especially excruciating when she was so close to cracking a case. Staying busy was the best course of action so she decided to pay a visit to her wannabe spiritual adviser.

During the drive to Framingham, she mulled over the sins of Pastor Greg. She didn't have proof that would hold up in a court of law, but that wasn't her job. She just needed to point someone else, like the attorney general, in the right direction.

Walking in the front door of Covenant Rising, Fina heard the pastor before she saw him. He was exalting about the power of sacrifice—oh, the irony—to an empty parish hall. There was a slight hiccup in his delivery when Fina walked down the aisle and entered a pew. She gave him an encouraging smile and listened as he continued. Fina knew that every form of public speaking was a performance—Carl and her brothers excelled in court because they were gifted orators—but sermon as theater was discomfiting.

Greg said his final "amen" and hopped off the stage.

"What do you think?" he asked, pulling the wraparound mike from his head.

"Very powerful," Fina replied.

"Sacrifice is good for the soul."

"Indeed."

"I assume you brought the check?" He took a seat in the row in front of her and turned sideways so he could face her.

"I did. Just one quick question before I hand it over."

"Sure." His teeth looked particularly shiny, bringing to mind a wolf or a barracuda.

Fina reached into her bag and pulled out a folder with the photos of her orphan, the ones that Hal had provided to her. "I found these other pictures of Azekel online." She handed them to Greg.

He flipped through them, grinning. "He's a good-looking boy."

Fina looked at him. She waited.

"Was there something else?" he asked. "I have a meeting in a few minutes."

"Yeah, there's something else. I don't understand why his picture is on other websites. That one is for a church in California, another is for a children's hospital in Minneapolis," she said, indicating the various photos. "The one on the bottom is for a life insurance company."

He shook his head. "I think you're mistaken. Why don't we leave it with one of the tech guys? I'm guessing it's got something to do with your computer."

"Oh my God," Fina said, throwing her head back.

"Fina, there's no need to take the Lord's name in vain."

"If ever there were a time to take the Lord's name in vain, this is it. Azekel pops up so much because he's a child model whose image has been sold to a stock photo company." She smacked the stack of photos. "There's no Azekel. There's no orphanage in Angola. There's no Frontier Fund. There are just fancy cars and houses and a narcissistic egomaniac who's breaking the law."

He gave her a pained smile. "Fina, do you assume that all black children look alike? You know, that's racist."

"I assume nothing, which is why I had an expert run facial recognition software on adorable Azekel. It's what the government uses to track terrorists, and as it turns out, it's also extremely useful when it comes to compiling a child model's presence on the Internet."

"I think you need help."

"You and many others, but you're going to have bigger problems than me."

Greg leaned over the pew, his smile weakening at the corners. "Don't threaten me."

Fina leaned closer, which prompted him to pull back. "I'm not making a threat," she said. "I'm telling you that after I leave here, I'm going to One Ashburton Place in the city. Do you know what's at One Ashburton Place, Greg?"

"No, and I prefer Pastor Greg."

"Well, I prefer Your Highness but that never happens. One Ashburton Place is where the office of the Massachusetts attorney general is located, and I'm going to file a report accusing you, your lovely wife, and your church of fraud."

He let out a sharp bark that was supposed to be laughter. "That's an outrageous accusation. You know, you'll be punished for this."

"I know, that whole 'no good deed goes unpunished' thing. Believe me, I'm counting on it."

"I mean that God will punish you for trying to destroy our work. You will not succeed. We will prevail and become stronger than ever."

"Uh-huh." Fina got up and started up the aisle. She was almost to the door when Gabby walked in.

"Greg, Betty is looking for you. There's some issue with the food pantry van," she said.

The pastor strode up the aisle and put his arm around his wife, who looked up at him adoringly. "Fina was just leaving," he said.

"I was," she confirmed, giving Gabby the eye. Whatever the status of her affair, she was certainly making a show of being the dutiful wife. "You should think about who's going to take care of your children when you're both in prison."

"What?" Gabby asked, her eyes narrowing.

"Your hubby can fill you in. I just think you should get your ducks in a row."

"Don't threaten our family," she replied, planting her hands on her midriff.

Fina looked at her stomach and then at the two of them. "Oh, you've got to be kidding me."

Gabby scowled. "What's that supposed to mean?"

"You two so deserve each other." Fina shook her head and chuckled. "Maybe the prosecutor will take pity on you. There's something particularly pathetic about a pregnant inmate."

Greg's face turned beet red, and he balled up his fists.

"It hasn't been a pleasure exactly," Fina said, walking out, "but it definitely hasn't been boring."

She skedaddled to her car before Greg lost it, although that wouldn't have been the worst thing in the world.

A preacher punching a lady like herself? Priceless.

Fina didn't stop at the attorney general's office. Instead, she made a few calls and sent off an e-mail package outlining her suspicions about Covenant Rising. Despite her threats to Greg and Gabby, she knew nothing would happen overnight; there would be a long, drawn-out investigation, and if she had anything to do with it, oodles of bad publicity. There was no way Greg and Gabby would emerge unscathed.

In the car, Fina picked up the phone and dialed her father's number with a feeling of satisfaction. Most of her conversations with Carl consisted of his asking questions to which she didn't have the answers, so it was nice to be the bearer of actual news. Also, if she could dazzle him with her skills on the Renard investigation, it might make him more amenable to handling the Rand debacle once and for all.

"Any way you can schedule a meeting with Ceci and Chloe Renard for tomorrow?" she asked when he answered.

Carl grunted. "That's a little last-minute."

"It's not absolutely critical that we talk then, but I'm anxious to update them."

"So you've got what you need?" he asked. "You're going to be able to put an end to this bequest?"

"I've got dirt, Dad. If it doesn't convince Chloe, nothing will."

"Let me see what I can do."

"Have you talked to Scotty and Matthew today?" she asked. Fina wondered if they'd spilled the beans to Carl about the Rand situation, but didn't want to ask outright.

"What kind of question is that? I talk to them every day, Josefina."

"I was just wondering. They were supposed to call me."

"You know how to use the phone. Call them."

"Huh. I never would have thought of that."

"I'll have Shari call you about the meeting."

"Thank you. And by the way, I'm going to have some news for you soon relating to Rand."

"What kind of news?"

"Newsy news."

"What have you done, Fina?"

She wanted to ask him the same question. "*Moi?* Nothing. Good-bye, Father."

She'd gotten a message during the call with her father. One of her contacts said she could find Mike O'Brien at a boatyard in Charlestown. Fina fastened her seat belt and pointed her car toward the Pike.

It was only in the forties, but the sun was bright, suggesting that the approach of summer was more than just a figment of everyone's imagination. In Charlestown, she parked in a dirt lot next to a one-story white clapboard building. The docks themselves were empty except for a few lobster boats. There was a big building resembling a hangar, inside of which Fina could see a large cabin cruiser up on stilts. The rest of the space was packed with boats of all sizes, most of them shrink-wrapped for the winter.

Fina entered the single-story building and found a man and woman inside, both sitting behind battered metal desks. The smell of burnt coffee permeated the air, and the animated voices from WEEI provided background noise.

The woman looked up and peered at Fina over her reading glasses. She had wavy blond hair and the weathered skin that was the calling card of boaters of a certain age.

"Can I help you, hon?"

"I'm looking for Mike O'Brien. His wife thought I might catch him here."

"Jimmy," the woman said over her shoulder to the man behind the other desk, "where's Mike?"

The man consulted a sheaf of papers hanging from a bulletin board. "Row C, space 17."

Fina zipped her coat up against the sharp wind off the water and navigated her way to Row C. Space 17 was halfway down, occupied by a powerboat on a trailer. The boat looked to be close to thirty feet long, and a man knelt by the bow.

"Good morning," Fina said, smiling and raising her hand in a wave. "I'm looking for Mike O'Brien."

He stood and walked toward her. "You found him."

"My name's Fina Ludlow." She offered her hand.

"Nice to meet you."

"This is a nice boat," she commented.

"It's a good one. Enough room for the family, but not too big to handle. Are you a boater?" Mike O'Brien was tall and lean. His face looked as if it had been carved with a knife, his features were so pronounced. There was no extra fat on his frame.

"I grew up around boats, and my dad and brothers still have them."

"Can I help you with something?" Mike asked.

"I'm a private investigator, and I'm working on a case related to a recent murder."

Mike's eyebrows rose and then returned to their usual spot. "Is this related to the department?"

"No, it's nothing related to a fire. Actually, I wanted to speak with you about a more personal matter."

"Do you mind if we sit in my truck and warm up?" He nodded in the direction of a pickup truck at the end of the row.

"That's fine."

Fina followed him and climbed into the passenger seat. The truck was tidy, the only detritus a Dunkin' Donuts cup in the center console and a pack of Tic Tacs.

Mike started up the truck and adjusted the heat. "Do you have any ID?"

"Yup."

He examined her license. "Nobody I know has been murdered lately."

"That's good to hear," Fina said, smiling. "My line of questioning might seem odd, but I'm interested in a period of time seven years ago when you were originally up for the battalion chief job. My understanding is that you had some health problems and withdrew your name only to reapply a year later."

He shrugged. "Sounds like you know all there is to know. I was sick, so I pulled my application. I got better and threw my hat back in the ring the next year."

"But you're fine now?"

"Fit as a fiddle. Wouldn't be on the job if I weren't. What is this all about?"

For all Fina knew, Mike O'Brien was best buddies with Ronnie McCaffrey and would be on the phone to him the minute she left. She wanted to avoid that.

"My murder victim was ill on and off for a few months before she died."

He looked puzzled.

"She was nauseous, vomiting, dizzy, had chest pains—basically, felt like crap. I was wondering if you had a similar experience."

Mike eyed her. "Why would you wonder that?"

"I'd rather not say for the moment."

"You just want me to give you my personal health history?" He cocked his eyebrow.

"I know it seems presumptuous. How about this? I'll describe the circumstances of my case, and you let me know if it sounds familiar. Then we'll go from there."

Mike nodded and adjusted in his seat, as if prepping himself to really listen.

"Okay. A healthy thirty-two-year-old woman starts getting sick, but always gets better within a couple of days. She feels sick to her stomach, has fatigue, weakness, headaches. The doctor can't find anything wrong with her after running a full battery of tests. In my case, she eventually succumbs to the illness, and the autopsy reveals that she died from acute organ failure brought on by antifreeze poisoning. If she hadn't received a fatal dose, she could have made a full recovery as long as she was no longer getting poisoned."

He didn't speak for a moment. "Jesus. I thought my job could be dark."

"I've identified a common denominator between my case and your experience, Mike. I'm wondering if you were poisoned, too."

He looked out the side window and seemed to consider her words. "The doctor never did figure out what was wrong with me."

"Was there a pattern to your illness? Did the episodes coincide with any particular activity or place?"

"We thought it was the job. That was the only constant, but none of the other guys got sick, and even though it can be dangerous, we obviously try to minimize our exposure to anything hazardous."

Fina felt the pulse in her neck beat harder. It was all just conjecture, circumstantial, but that didn't mean it wasn't true.

"But there's no way to tell now, right?" Mike asked. "That stuff leaves your system pretty quickly."

"Yeah. It's long gone from your system by now, hence the reason you're alive."

"So if this is true, and you've got to admit, it sounds a little farfetched, does that mean you know who poisoned me?"

Fina grinned, feeling like a weight was being lifted from her. "You know, Mike, I think I do."

Before leaving the boatyard, Fina dialed the number for police headquarters, a small flutter in her chest. If she called his cell, she wasn't sure that Cristian would pick up the call, and she wanted to talk to him, regardless of how he felt about her at the moment.

"Menendez," he answered, when the call was transferred.

"Hey. It's Fina."

The line was quiet except for the squad room chatter in the background.

"Didn't think I'd pick up my cell?"

"Wasn't sure."

"What's up?"

"I wanted to talk to you about the Nadine Quaynor case."

"Can it wait? I'm on my way out."

"Uh, sure. How about in a couple of hours? It's important."

There was rustling in the background. Fina imagined he was struggling into his sport coat, the phone gripped between his chin and shoulder.

"Fine," he said, with no hint of enthusiasm and took down the address.

If she could offload the Quaynor case to the cops, there would only be one more problem to solve.

Fina stopped by the office in hopes of talking with Scotty and Matthew. Their discussion the night before didn't sit well with her. She hated feeling at odds with the two of them, and they needed to regroup.

Distracted by the loose ends she was tying up, Fina didn't notice her eldest brother until it was too late.

"Fina, I need a minute," he called out with a broad smile. He was standing in one of the kitchenette areas chatting with a colleague.

"Sorry. Gotta go." She took off down the hall.

Rand patted the associate on the back and trotted after her. "Wait up, sis."

Beads of sweat were emerging on her hairline. Fina stopped in the busy hallway, deciding that the more witnesses to their conversation, the better.

"What is it? I have a meeting."

Rand stood in front of her, invading her personal space. "What's going on? Scotty gave me the cold shoulder this morning."

"So? What's that got to do with me?"

"What did you say to him?" he asked quietly, as conservatively dressed attorneys bobbed and weaved around them.

"I didn't say anything. Back off, Rand."

He shook his head. "*You* need to back off and mind your own business or I'm going to . . ."

"What? What are you going to do to me?" she asked, bending her head toward his as if sharing a secret. "Beat me up? Put me in the hospital?"

He reared back and struggled to regain his composure.

"You're such an arrogant prick," she said, glaring at him. "Always convinced you're the smartest guy in the room. Your life is about to get very complicated. Now get out of my way."

"If you keep this up, there's going to be hell to pay."

"What exactly are you threatening to do?"

"Do you want to be responsible for the downfall of this family?" he asked.

"I think you've got that covered."

"You think things are bad now? Just wait. You can't even begin to imagine the things I know. If you keep this up, Dad will never forgive you."

Fina was speechless, sick that her suspicions were most likely true. She left the office, abandoning her original mission. She couldn't be in the same place as Rand for a second longer.

Evan and Molly were on the front porch when Fina pulled into their street. Fina waved and visited with them for a few minutes before heading to Ronnie McCaffrey's house. Evan didn't ask why she was visiting his neighbor, but she could read the confusion on his face. She left him to be distracted by his daughter's chatter.

Mary McCaffrey directed Fina to the backyard. In the waning light, Ronnie was pounding stakes into the newly pliant earth. The yellow streamers on the ends flapped in the breeze.

"You're still working on the case?" he asked. A mallet hung loosely in one hand.

"I'm wrapping up my part, getting ready to hand stuff over to the cops."

Ronnie didn't say anything. He walked around the perimeter of the large rectangle he'd mapped out in the yard.

"So this is for the pool, right?" Fina asked.

"That's right."

Fina dug the toe of her shoe into the loose earth. "You know, Ronnie, I've been doing this job for a while and have seen some crazy shit, but I've never seen anyone killed over a pool before."

Ronnie looked at her, confusion etched in the furrow of his brow.

"The thing I find most curious," she continued, "is that, on the one hand, you dedicated your life to helping people, to saving them, and on the other hand, you killed someone who got in your way."

Ronnie shook his head. "You seem like a nice girl, but you're way off base."

Fina followed him as he inspected the stakes. "Aren't you even a little curious as to why I think you did it?"

"Not especially."

Fina stayed a few steps behind him, cognizant of the blunt object in his hand. "Do you think if Ronnie Jr. were alive, you would have done this?"

He spun around to face her. "Don't talk about my son," he said in a flash of anger.

"I can't imagine the rage you feel. Some asshole kills your kid and essentially gets away with it. I can understand feeling like the universe owes you."

Ronnie's voice rose. "You make it sound like I live in a mansion with a driveway full of fancy cars."

"You've got a nice life, Ronnie, and on the occasions when some obstacle appeared, you neutralized it."

"I don't know what you're talking about."

"When you and Mike O'Brien were up for the same job, Mike came down with a mysterious illness and had to withdraw from the race. And then, he magically got better."

Ronnie's grip on the mallet tightened.

"And then when Nadine was poised to thwart your plans to be the world's best grandfather and neighborhood good guy, all of a sudden, she started getting ill."

"That's all coincidence."

"But you seemed pretty sure in the minutes from the association meetings that her opposition wasn't going to be a problem. You even applied for a zoning variance. Seems overconfident unless you knew Nadine wasn't going to be in the picture much longer."

"That's your proof?" He chuckled. "Neighborhood association minutes and a city permit?"

"And the cat. I assume he got into the antifreeze. Probably thought he was getting a sweet treat only to drop dead shortly thereafter."

"So now you're blaming me for the cat's death? A bird flew into our window the other day; I suppose that's my fault, too?" He smiled, but it was a cold, flat version of cheer.

"I agree it's very circumstantial, but it will be catnip to the right DA. Probably someone up-and-coming who wants to make a name for herself."

"People like you," he said, shaking his head. "You're unbelievable."

"Oh, yes. Let's talk about people like me. I always love when morally bankrupt criminals want to critique me."

"You had everything handed to you, never wanted for anything."

"That's true. I've never wanted for material things. But there are plenty of other things I've wanted for and didn't resort to murder to get them. That's the real difference between us, not our bank accounts."

Footsteps echoed on the driveway, and Fina turned to see Cristian and Pitney approaching.

"Why are they here?" Ronnie asked.

"I told you. I'm ready to turn my findings over to the cops." Fina walked away from him.

"Mr. McCaffrey," Pitney said, coming toward him. Cristian hung back. "Could you please put down the mallet? We just want to talk to you."

Ronnie stood still, shaking his head in disbelief. He tossed the heavy object a few feet away and crossed his arms over his chest.

Fina stopped next to Cristian.

"This is what you wouldn't tell me last night?" he asked.

She shook her head. "Nope. I didn't know all this last night. That was something else."

He was silent. "You know this is going to be practically impossible to prove."

"I know," Fina said, "but you have to try, right?"

"Right." He started to walk away.

"Cristian. Any way you could come over later, once you're done with this?"

He turned to face her. "What's the point, Fina? There's nothing to talk about."

"I disagree. We need to clear the air. The longer we go being weird, the harder it's going to be."

He walked back to her side and lowered his voice. "So you think we should just pretend we weren't dating? That we don't have romantic feelings for each other?"

She closed her eyes before responding, trying to find a last bit of energy. "I think we should try to figure out where we go from here. Give me a little credit, Cristian. I don't like talking about this stuff, either, but I want to fix this. I can't *not* have you in my life."

He looked at Pitney and Ronnie, who were engaged in a heated conversation. Cristian sighed. "Fine. I'll stop by later."

"Great."

Fina walked back to her car. Evan and Molly had retreated inside, and she could see them in the kitchen.

Their lives were about to begin another bumpy chapter, but it couldn't be helped.

Life was messy.

THIRTY-THREE

Fina treated herself to dinner at the bar at Legal Sea Foods. She was craving a good meal and a dose of oblivion. Watching the headlines on the TV perched over the bar was oddly relaxing and saved her from having to make small talk with the other barstool denizens. She munched on warm sourdough rolls and a platter of fried clams that she washed down with a diet soda. Sated, she drove home ready for a hot shower and some mindless TV.

Fina arrived home to find a box holding her latest clothing purchase. She left it on her coffee table before showering and putting on some cozies.

She knew she needed to follow up with Scotty and Matthew, but decided it could wait until morning. Fina didn't have the emotional reserves to deal with them, particularly since she still had a conversation with Cristian ahead of her.

In the kitchen, she grabbed another soda, a Hostess cupcake, and a knife with which to open her delivery. There was a TV show on about the world's best waterslides, which only required what little attention she had to spare. Her brain didn't need to be engaged until Cristian arrived. Reclining on the couch wasn't the healthiest way to eat dessert, but it felt good, which was all that mattered. Fina tossed the empty cupcake sleeve onto the coffee table and burrowed further into the couch.

The sound that woke her wasn't a knock but a rattling noise, as if someone were struggling to fit a key in the lock. From the depths of sleep, it took her a moment to make sense of things. Fina instinctively looked around for her gun and realized it was in the bedroom where she'd dropped the holster on the way to the shower.

She was barely across the living room when the front door burst open and a man was on top of her.

The man was her brother.

Later, Fina would remember wondering why Rand was wearing a tracksuit. It was the kind of thing he only ever wore at the athletic club, and yet, somehow, he was in her condo, pinning her to the floor, wearing a tracksuit.

He pushed her onto her back and grabbed her wrists, holding them over her head. She kneed him in the groin and managed to free one hand when his torso accordioned from the blow. Rand let out a guttural noise when she punched him in the throat and tried to crab walk out from under him.

Two thoughts crowded her brain: her gun and the knife. If you were going to engage in hand-to-hand combat, you didn't want weapons to be part of the equation. Cramped quarters and adrenaline—paired with a weapon—posed an equal threat to the good guy and the bad guy. Fina knew her best chance of beating her brother was to engage in a good old-fashioned fight.

She tried to scramble away, but he grabbed her leg and tugged her closer. Fina didn't have enough breath to both fight and scream, so they continued grappling with only the animal noises of a struggle for a sound track.

They were locked in a violent embrace with no obvious conclusion when Rand got a gleam in his eye. Fina struggled to stop him from reaching onto the coffee table, but knew it was futile. He'd seen the knife and it was in his hand now, poised at her neck.

"Stop struggling," he said through gritted teeth. Rand kneed her in the kidney. Her body seized up in pain, and she fought to control her breathing.

"It's going to be messy," she gasped. "Spurting. Everywhere."

"Shut up!" He pushed the knife harder against her neck. Fina flinched at the sharpness against her skin.

"There'll be spatter," she wheezed, "all over." She could only hope that the image would force Rand to reconsider, not plunge ahead and slice the knife across her carotid arteries.

With his free hand, he grabbed her hair and smacked her head against the floor. Intense pain shattered behind Fina's eyes, and what she could see the moment before, she couldn't anymore. She was aware of an odd sensation—heightened feeling and greater detachment all at once. The pain in her head and the sharpness of the knife were growing unbearable, but at the same time, she felt separate from her body, as if this terrible thing were happening to someone else.

There was a loud crash, and she felt the floor vibrate beneath her. There was yelling. Something had changed in the room. A heavy weight crushed her, and then nothing.

The first thing Fina noticed was the pain. Her head throbbed, and the thought of opening her eyelids was more than she could bear. But she heard noises around her—breathing, objects being moved—and her curiosity forced her to push through the pain.

She looked and saw her father pulling the door open to leave.

"Wait," Fina croaked.

"Go back to sleep," he said, turning toward her.

Fina moved to adjust her head on the pillow, but winced from the effort.

"You've got a concussion," he told her.

"Oh, great."

"It's just one. You'll be fine."

She gestured toward the plastic cup and pitcher on the table. Carl came over to her bedside. He poured some water into a plastic cup and unwrapped a straw. He held it close to her face so that Fina could sip with a minimum of effort. Her lips were chapped, but asking her father to find and apply lip balm seemed a bit much.

"Get some rest," he said. "There are people waiting to talk to you."

"Who?"

"The cops, obviously. Cristian and Lieutenant Pitney. Frank and Peg are here and so are Milloy and your brothers."

Fina's eyes widened. "Don't let him near me."

"Not Rand. He's in surgery."

Fina laid back against the pillow and tried to summon a memory of the altercation in the condo. "Did Cristian shoot him?"

Carl's head dipped down before he responded. "Yes. He says that Rand was going to cut your throat."

"He was," Fina said, glaring at her father. "I don't suppose my mother is one of those people waiting to see me."

Carl was silent.

She balled up the sheets in her hands. "He was going to kill me, and she still sides with him."

"It's not that simple, Josefina."

"Right."

"I have to go," he said. "I've scheduled a meeting with Ceci and Chloe for tomorrow afternoon."

"I can't deal with that right now, Dad."

"You'll be fine once you sleep."

"Yeah. Thanks for the vote of confidence."

If Fina could have rolled over, turning her back on her father, she would have. The ache in her head made that physical statement impossible. Instead, she closed her eyes. A moment later, she heard the whoosh of the opening door and the faint click it made when it closed behind him.

Fina pulled the blanket up to her chin and wrapped her arms around herself. She was on her own.

When Fina awoke it was morning, the room bright with sunshine. The pain in her head had lessened to a dull ache. She depressed the button on the remote to raise the bed so she could take stock.

She was sipping from the plastic cup when the door opened, and Milloy stepped into the room. He gently kissed the top of her head, and she slumped against his chest. They stayed that way for a minute.

"Your head still hurt?" he asked.

"Yes, but not as much." She pulled away from him. "Is this as much of a clusterfuck as I suspect?"

"Pretty much."

"Fuck."

"You don't need to think about it right now, though."

"Can you find my clothes?"

"You've been discharged?"

"Yes."

"By what doctor?"

"By Dr. 'I Don't Give a Shit; I'm Getting out of Here.'"

"That's great, Fina. He's known for making sound medical judgments."

"Just find my clothes."

Milloy located her belongings in a plastic bag in the closet and doled them out to her. She was pulling her hair into a ponytail when a light tap on the door got their attention.

"Can I come in?" Cristian asked, poking his head around the door.

"Sure," Fina said, climbing back onto the bed.

"Do you want something from the cafeteria or the gift shop for the ride home?" Milloy asked.

"Yes. Chocolate, soda, and lip balm."

Milloy reached into his pocket and took out a tube of expensive lip salve that featured botanical extracts from a Brazilian rain forest. He tossed it onto her lap.

"Ahh. Thank you," Fina said, unscrewing the tube.

"Can I get you anything, Cristian?" Milloy asked.

"I'm good. Thanks."

Once the door closed behind Milloy, Cristian pulled the pink vinyl recliner closer to the bed and took a seat.

"They're discharging you?" he asked.

Fina started to speak, but Cristian raised his hand to stop her. "Don't. Don't even say it."

"Say what?"

"Whatever you were going to say. Whatever lie or half-truth you were going to manufacture."

"I was going to tell you the truth. They didn't discharge me, but I've got to get out of here. I can't stand being in the same building as him."

Cristian didn't argue. "How do you feel?"

"Like someone smashed my head against a wooden floor."

He nodded.

"But not like someone slit my throat." She looked at him and didn't try to stop the tear that was hovering on her lid from rolling down her cheek. "Thanks to you."

"I'm just glad I came over. I don't know what would have happened otherwise."

"He would have killed me." Fina brushed at her cheek. "Did you hear that he's the one that put out the contract against me?"

"Yes. Why didn't you just tell me?"

"I was trying to give my other brothers the chance to do the right thing."

"Which was what, exactly?"

"That hadn't been determined yet."

"Not your smartest move," Cristian said.

"Perhaps not." Fina fiddled with the cap of the lip salve. "Thank you for saving my life. I know the last thing any cop wants to do is discharge his weapon."

He nodded. "You're right, but it was a clean use of force, and he's going to survive."

"That's too bad," Fina said. Cristian frowned. "Not for you, of course. You don't need that on your conscience—let alone the paperwork—but it's too bad for me."

"He's not going to hurt you, Fina. He's going to be charged for attempted murder."

She closed her eyes. "My family must be going nuts."

"Scotty doesn't look good. I'll give you that."

"What happened with Ronnie?" she asked, not wanting to contemplate her family situation at the moment.

"We found antifreeze hidden under the crawl space at his house."

"He told me he never kept the stuff around the house. It's pretty circumstantial," Fina admitted.

"But it's something," Cristian said.

"He didn't confess?"

He scoffed. "Hardly."

"But you guys think that he's responsible?"

Cristian nodded. "We're going to dig into the Mike O'Brien situation. That may not have been the first time Ronnie poisoned someone."

"Sounds like a lot of work," Fina said. "So glad it's you and not me."

"I think you need to take it easy for a little while," Cristian said, rising from the chair.

He was on the threshold when she called to him.

"Cristian. I think our relationship just got more complicated."

"I think you're right," he said, and disappeared.

Fina went home and slept until her alarm sounded at three p.m. She took a long, hot shower and finished the chocolate bar that Milloy had purchased at the hospital. Rather than get behind the wheel, she summoned a car from Uber and stared out the window during the drive to Cambridge. Her head still ached, but the rest of her body was suffused with a sense of calm. No one was after her. For now, anyway.

Carl was sitting in his car outside Ceci's house when she arrived, and they wordlessly climbed the stairs to the front door. Fina wasn't sure what was stopping her father from talking, but she was too angry and tired to make any unnecessary conversation.

The maid let them in and led them to the same room in which the case had started. Ceci and Chloe were seated on the couch, a fire throwing heat into the room. They got to their feet and hugged Fina and greeted Carl. Ceci motioned for Chloe and Fina to sit on the couch, and she and Carl took the wing chairs. It felt very much like there was a divide between the children and the adults, though Fina didn't think that had been Ceci's intent.

"Are you okay, sweetie?" Ceci asked Fina, her eyes squinting with concern. "You don't look good."

"I think I'm coming down with something." She'd surrendered her coat to the maid, but tugged the scarf around her neck a little tighter.

"Do you feel up to meeting?"

"I'm fine. I didn't want to postpone this conversation."

Chloe sat still next to Fina. A small part of Fina felt badly about what was coming next, but Chloe was a grown-up. She'd manage.

Ceci seemed to sense that Fina's patience was limited, so although she gestured toward a tray with tea, coffee, and cookies, she assumed a posture of intent listening.

"Yesterday," Fina began, "I forwarded a compilation of information to the Office of the Attorney General."

Ceci glanced at Chloe.

"I don't believe that Nadine Quaynor's death is related to Covenant Rising, but I do believe that Greg and Gabby Gatchell are guilty of various crimes, including fraud."

"Do you have proof?" Chloe asked.

"Enough to satisfy the attorney general? I don't know. My hope is that they'll launch a full-scale investigation and gain access to records that are beyond my reach. But I've seen enough evidence to convince me that they are getting donations under false pretenses and then using that money inappropriately and probably illegally."

No one spoke. Ceci reached out to touch her daughter's hand. Chloe didn't pull away, but she didn't grasp her mother's hand, either. She merely tolerated the touch.

"I'm really sorry about this, Chloe," Fina said. "I know the church means a great deal to you, and I'm sure there are many decent, principled people in the congregation. Perhaps those of you who are truly committed will figure out a way to weather this."

"Can you give us more specifics about the malfeasance?" Carl asked. Ceci shot him a grateful look, and Fina understood that he was asking the tough questions so Ceci didn't have to.

"There's a fund called the Frontier Fund, which is supposed to be used to support an orphanage in Angola."

"And it does," Chloe insisted.

"No, it doesn't." Fina fought to rein in her frustration. "I couldn't find any evidence that this orphanage existed. In fact, when I expressed interest in supporting a specific child, Pastor Greg promised that was possible, only for me to discover that my 'orphan' was an adorable black kid who's all over the Internet."

"But how can you know exactly what's going on in Africa?" Chloe asked.

"That's precisely Pastor Greg's thinking. No one was in a position to dispute his account of the orphanage, but I have an expert who took a closer look, and no one in Angola had ever heard of Covenant Rising."

"That's the sort of thing the AG can delve into," Carl added.

Fina nodded. "I think Greg and Gabby have been using the money to fund their lifestyle, which is quite cushy for a pastor and his wife who draws no salary."

"Are you referring to the houses and cars?" Ceci asked.

"Yes. And the trips and the luxurious standard of living they enjoy."

Chloe leaned forward on the couch. "Is that it?"

"Actually, two other things," Fina said, touching her arm. "The behavior of a couple of other people should give you pause. Lucas Chellew, Greg's right-hand man, sent me a series of threatening letters. I haven't revealed this to the cops or to the Gatchells, but I want you to know. He's not dangerous, but he's not a good guy, either."

Chloe looked like she might be ill. That was just what Fina needed—to be puked on.

"What's the second thing?" Carl asked.

"Gabby Gatchell has been having an affair with a young congregant. This has no bearing on any criminal case, but I think you should be aware of the Gatchells' hypocrisy. Greg is aware of the affair, and yet, they judge other people mercilessly and hold themselves up as models of good Christian behavior. I don't care if people sleep around, but don't judge me while you break every covenant you claim to hold sacred."

Fina didn't have the energy to fill the awkward silence that followed. Her tanks were empty.

"Under the circumstances, Chloe," Carl finally said, "I strongly suggest you put the brakes on that bequest."

Chloe looked at him, her eyes glistening. "I feel so stupid."

"Oh, Chloe," her mother said sympathetically.

"You have nothing to feel badly about," Fina assured her. "The Gatchells took advantage of a lot of people. I agree with my father, though. This isn't the moment to make a large donation to the church."

"What's going to happen to the church?" she wondered. "All of the good work they do."

"All of the good work *you* do—you and your fellow congregants," Fina insisted. "That doesn't have to stop."

Chloe nodded. "I need some air," she said, and left the room.

"I'm sorry, Ceci," Carl said, glancing toward the door. He reached out and squeezed Ceci's hand. Fina watched. A look passed between her father and Ceci that held more than lawyer-client appreciation. It held more than the looks that ever passed between Carl and Elaine.

"I'm not," Ceci said, shaking her head. "Of course, I'm sorry that Chloe's heart is broken, but she had to know the truth. These people are charlatans."

Fina stood and took a step closer to the fire. She was feeling chilled, not sure if it was the meeting or her compromised physical condition that was having that effect.

Carl and Ceci started to debate the bill, and Fina studied the photos on the mantel. There were graduation photos and a candid shot of the Renards on a sailboat. Another showed Ceci and Victor Renard dressed to the nines, presumably at a gala or charity event. Next to that was a baby photo that looked like Chloe. She wore a white dress that puffed out around her on a velvety pillow.

It was the next photo, however, that took Fina's breath away. It was another baby photo, but this time the child was propped up on a couch, smiling at the camera.

"Who is this baby?" Fina asked, interrupting Carl and Ceci's discussion.

Ceci looked askance at Carl before answering. "That's my eldest daughter, Veronique."

Fina steadied herself with a hand on the mantel.

"We should be going," her father insisted, rising to his feet.

"How old is she now?" Fina asked.

Ceci stood and kneaded her hands together. "She's thirty-eight. I'll have Iris fetch your coats." She threw a glance at Carl and left the room.

Fina studied the picture, tracing the edge of the frame with her fingertip. Veronique looked nothing like Ceci, but she looked a hell of a lot like Carl. If Fina hadn't known better, she would have sworn she was looking at a photo of her dead sister, Josie.

She glared at her father, shaking her head.

"I told you it was complicated," Carl hissed.

Fina opened her mouth to speak, but for once, words failed her. She pushed past him and made her way toward the front door, where Ceci was taking their coats from the maid. Fina grabbed her coat and threw open the front door.

"Fina, wait!" her father called after her.

She broke into a slow jog, her head pounding with each step, putting as much distance as possible between them.

A million miles wouldn't be enough.

ACKNOWLEDGMENTS

Thank you to the friends who sustain me with their good humor, wisdom, lunches out, sales pitches on my behalf, and careful readings of manuscripts: Lauri Bortscheller Nakamoto, Davenie Susi Pereira, Catalina Arboleda, Matina Madrick, and Allison Walker Chader.

In the course of writing this book, my wonderful agent, Helen Brann, passed away. I miss her wicked sense of humor and unwavering support. Thanks to Carol White at the Helen Brann Agency, who was wonderful during a difficult time and eased the transition to my new home. I am enormously grateful to now have an amazing team working on my behalf at ICM. Thank you, Esther Newberg and Kari Stuart, for championing me and Fina. Cheers to Zoe Sandler for keeping the administrative wheels turning.

I feel extraordinarily lucky to have the guidance and support of the people at Putnam. Under the leadership of Ivan Held, every department has done a fantastic job bringing Fina and the Ludlows to readers. The art department and the sales, marketing, and publicity teams do essential work, which I greatly appreciate. I'd also like to thank Christine Ball, Sally Kim, Carrie Swetonic, Alexis Welby, and Ashley Pattison McClay. Katie Grinch is a terrific publicist who works tirelessly and juggles many details to smooth the way for Fina in the book world. My editor, Chris Pepe, is the best. She makes me a better writer and is a tremendous friend. I'm honored to work with her.

Thanks to Mary Alice Kier and Anna Cottle for representing Fina so well in Hollywood. I appreciate their perseverance as we've navigated the never boring world of TV.

One of the unexpected joys of my work as a writer has been the opportunity to develop friendships with other writers. Reed Farrel Coleman and Ace Atkins have supported me and been extremely generous with their time and advice. It's amazing to find that the writers you admire are also wonderful people whom you can call friends. Whether at events or in the Twittersphere, I'm continually delighted by David Joy, Meg Gardiner, Jeffrey Siger, Barbara Zilly, Tim Hallinan, Eleanor Brown, and Hank Phillippi Ryan.

Writers Chevy Stevens and Carla Buckley are never more than a text away, thankfully. Their loyalty, cheerleading, and appreciation of a good cocktail are priceless.

I've had the honor of spending time with Detective Jim Garner and Officer Mike Virgilio of the Seattle Police Department, who have been nothing but gracious when answering my seemingly endless questions and educating me about their work. They are a credit to their profession and department, and I can't thank them enough for sharing their expertise with me. I'm so glad that Fina provided an entrée to meet them, and I blame her for any subsequent inaccuracies or misrepresentations of the Boston Police Department and its members.

I am indebted to booksellers and librarians who connect readers to my books and fight the good fight for books and literacy. The Seattle Public Library, the Seattle Mystery Bookshop, the Poisoned Pen Bookstore, Murder By The Book, and Liberty Bay Books have been supportive since day one. Thank you so much.

My family deserves a huge shout-out: Erika Thoft-Brown, Chris Thoft-Brown, Owen Thoft-Brown, Sophie Thoft-Brown, Riley Thoft-Brown, Lisa Thoft, Cole Nagel-Thoft, Arden Nagel-Thoft, Kirsten

Thoft, Ted Nadeau, Zoe Nadeau, Ella Nadeau, Escher Nadeau, and last but never least, Sharon Padia Stone.

My mom, Judith Stone Thoft, continues to be my first reader and brainstorm buddy. She helps me do the work I love, and we have lots of fun along the way.

Words fail me when it comes to my husband, Doug Berrett. There's no one else I'd rather spend each day with.

Last, thank you to the readers who have embraced Fina and the Ludlows in all their glorious dysfunction. Thank you for spreading the word about the series and cheering me on via social media. I love to hear from you; keep in touch!

Ingrid@ingridthoft.com

www.ingridthoft.com

https://www.facebook.com/IngridThoftauthor/

@ingridthoft